Lindsay Maple

HOLLY JOLLY JULY

W0006341

CANARY STREET PRESS

**CANARY
STREET
PRESS™**

Recycling programs
for this product may
not exist in your area.

ISBN-13: 978-1-335-01659-1

Holly Jolly July

Canary Street Press
22 Adelaide St. West, 41st Floor
Toronto, Ontario M5H 4E3, Canada
CanaryStPress.com

Printed in U.S.A.

To all the bisexual bookish babes who are tired of choosing between mf and ff spice.
I got you, girl.

Land Acknowledgement

This novel was written in Chilliwack, BC, where I live, work, and play. Chilliwack is the traditional, ancestral, and unceded territory of the Stó:lō Coast Salish First Nations Peoples and an intersection of five tribes: Shxwhá:y, Squiala, Skwah, Kwaw-kwaw-a-pilt, and Aitchelitz. Jimmie is a common surname from Squiala First Nation, and this name was used with permission as respectful representation to the history of Chilliwack and its First Nations Peoples.

Content Warning

- Mention of drug use and overdose, bullying, and depression
- Mention of unsupportive family with LGBTQIA+ community
- Partner infidelity on-page (not main love story)
- Includes early and frequent open-door love scenes between both a man and a woman and two women together

Chapter 1
ELLIE

*T*here is nothing better than getting an extra Christmas.

Even with the intense July sunshine bearing down upon my pale, freckled skin, the scene before me screams winter. Cheerful two-story brick buildings are strung with lights and garland, windows are frosted and white blankets are strategically placed to give the illusion of piles of snow.

I've never been to Chilliwack even though it's only a quick ninety-minute drive from Vancouver, but I'm impressed. The architecture of the new downtown core has been modelled after an old-timey village, but with all the perks of new buildings. Narrow cobblestone alleys with gas lanterns provide access to shops with quaint script signage, and the apartments above the businesses seem like the type to have exposed brick walls, apron sinks, and rooftop patios.

Yep. I could live here.

That's the dream, isn't it? To be whisked away from the big city and end up in a cute town like this. Not that Chilliwack is a town; it's a city for sure, but this adorable little city centre makes it seem otherwise.

The only thing marring its charm are the bright blue temporary fences, crowding film equipment, and the bustle of film crew finalizing the preparations to turn everything into a winter wonderland in the midst of a July heat wave.

Dopamine tingles run down my back and arms as I stare at it all from across the street while waiting for the lights to change. It's not my first time working on set, not even my first Christmas movie, but I still feel that excited flutter in my belly as if it is. This will never get old.

Finally, the lights change. I clomp forward in my winter

boots and readjust my bag on my shoulder, feeling sticky with the sweat prickling at my nape and starting a rivulet down my back. My oversized Rudolph sweater was fine in the comfort of my Subaru's air conditioning, but now not so much in the blaring sunshine; I have switties. Swoobs? Either way, I'll need to sop up the girls before trying on my costume so I don't ruin it. But I'm not going to let thirty-degree heat get in the way of my Christmas spirit, or my method acting. Did Tom Hanks back down after getting a staph infection on the set of *Cast Away*? Nope. So I can handle a little heat. If it were comfortable then it wouldn't be worth it.

Waving at the techs crowding the coffee shop where all of my scenes will be filmed, I turn down one of the adorable cobblestone alleys and make my way to a burgundy door next to a craft beer brewery. I show my ID to the security guard, walk through the door and up the flight of stairs to the door on my left with a sign that reads *Hair & Makeup*.

The room is swarming with people talking animatedly and prepping for the first day of filming tomorrow. I can't help the giant grin on my face as I step into the familiar chaos.

A flash of red hair at the far end of the room alerts me to Marlene Byrne, our producer. The older white woman is looking over the top of her glasses and pointing at her iPad with a long fingernail, while Yueyi Lei, our director, nods emphatically, her black curls bobbing up and down. Yueyi is Chinese Canadian from Richmond with years of experience in the Vancouver theatre scene, and Marlene is originally from California but moved to Canada some years ago, bringing with her a wide knowledge base from her time working on films in Hollywood.

Hollywood.

I dare to dream.

With the two of them on board I know the movie is in great hands and am excited to see the magic they can make with only two weeks of filming. It's a tight deadline, but it's not unusual for Christmas movies to be filmed so quickly. Two years ago, we did one in ten days. Yeah, it wasn't the best quality, but it still brought joy to thousands of people.

Okay, hundreds.

I wave at the pair, but they're too caught up in their conversation to notice me. Working my way around the side of the room, I keep an eye out for my station, but can't spot my name tagged on anything. Unsure of where to go, I look for a familiar face but see none, which isn't uncommon; they tend to hire a lot of locals for movies like this to keep costs down. Regardless, I say hello to everyone I pass, introducing myself as I do, since we'll be a tight-knit crew over the next two weeks.

Finally, I catch up to Marlene and Yueyi.

"Hello, Ellie." Marlene greets me with her customary forearm squeeze, long nails digging into my skin.

"Hey, team. Merry Christmas!" I gesture at my sweater and give a little shimmy, which earns a half-hearted chuckle.

"Darling, it's a heat wave," Yueyi states, giving me a pursed-lip tut.

"Don't mind me, just getting in the zone." I wink. "At least this place has air conditioning." I clap my hands and bite my bottom lip. "That script—the ending! The writers really did an amazing job with it. I mean, top-notch. Way better than last year's, and even that was really good. I didn't see the twist coming at all. It really is a—"

Marlene and Yueyi look past me, both pairs of eyes lighting up.

I twist to look behind me and nearly trip on my own two feet when I see him. *The* Oscar Fizak. Knowing he would be here did nothing to prepare me for seeing him for the first time in real life. How they got him to star in a Christmas movie, I'll never know. Maybe they have some dirt on him. Regardless, his presence is taking this whole production to new heights. With his bronze skin, high cheekbones, deep brown eyes, salt-and-pepper hair, and the type of body you only get from a no-carb diet and getting paid to work out, Oscar has all the classic good looks of old Hollywood, but with the sizzle of a good modern romance hero. He's exactly the type of guy you'd hope to meet during your stay in a small town, who'd inevitably convince you to leave the big city behind in favour of white picket fences and cups of tea on your front porch.

Now, *he* could show me the true meaning of Christmas.

Oscar greets Marlene and Yueyi, his voice smooth, low, and a little husky, like he's smoked a cigarette and followed it up with a shot of bourbon. Then he looks at me all nonchalant, his smile practised and easy. "Hey, Allie."

Oh my *god*. He almost knows my name! Allie, Ellie, close enough.

"Are you excited to film your first Christmas movie?" I manage to ask.

He gestures at my sweater. "Looks like you're excited enough for the both of us."

I can't help my blush. "Have to keep the Christmas spirit alive."

He nods.

"I'm so excited to work with you!" I clench my fists and grin so hard my face hurts. "We're going to have so much fun. I mean, we don't have a lot of scenes together, and even when we do you won't be talking to me, but just *knowing* that ending and how the story unravels, it's like we're not *together* together, but we're together, you know?"

His smile wanes and he looks away, searching for an excuse to leave.

I try a different tactic. "I haven't seen you in anything for a while. You must be excited to get back at it, and with a lead role no less."

His smile falls to nearly a frown. That was the wrong thing to say.

Before I can think of a redeeming question, all eyes turn to the front of the room. It's as if July has been captured in a bottle, shaken, and released in concentrated form.

Julia Miles. She's all long tanned legs, effortless blond waves, and teeth so white they'd glow under a UV light. Not only that, she seems to have some control over gravity, as the entire room is sucked toward her. She graces everyone with her presence in a royal way, her chin lifted and her plush lips opening to a perfectly balanced smile.

Ah. The lead.

While I wasn't sure how or why they managed to score Oscar Fizak, I know exactly why they cast Julia Miles—and it's not because of her acting experience. I'm pretty sure she's only ever been in a toothpaste commercial before this, hence the white teeth. But damn, she's got "effortless beauty" down.

"Hello everyone," she sings, the melodic lilt of her voice carrying easily through the room. If she's not careful we might be inundated with small forest creatures.

I can't help but sigh, just as enraptured by her presence as the rest of us peasants.

"Anyway, Oscar—" I start after picking my jaw up off the floor and turning back to him.

But it's too late. I've lost him. His eyes have gone glassy as he gazes upon his co-star, and I'm sure there's at least 10 percent less blood in his brain than there was five minutes ago. I guess this conversation is over.

Yueyi and Marlene's attention has also been taken over by Julia's presence, the director now moving through the crowd to help her find her station. Not that she needs the help—Julia's name is clearly visible in bold lettering.

"Marlene, sorry, but where do I . . . ?" I venture, unsure if I've simply missed my sign.

"Oh, darling, you're over there." She points with a talon.

"Great. Thank you!"

There is no sign; my station is bare. *Where is my makeup artist?* I set down my purse and settle into my chair, with nothing to do but look past my reflection to the hubbub behind me. Julia is being fawned over, her hair and makeup already underway, while Marlene grips her forearm with those talons of hers and Yueyi flips through the script. Oscar is seated next to Julia, stealing glances even though his makeup artist keeps poking at him to close his eyes. Another actress I don't have scenes with, Aimee Ladams, has joined them now, too. All three of them are lined up at their stations, smiling and laughing together while they're prepped.

There's a tinge of pain in the centre of my chest. It's small, but it's there. An unsettled feeling that—once again—I'm on the wrong side of the room. I should be over there, flirting with my co-star, going over our lines, blushing about our kissing scene, living out a pretend whirlwind romance and getting that coveted happily-ever-after. Instead, I'm here, watching from the sidelines.

Always the supporting character, never the star.

A duffel bag thunks down next to me, startling me out of my pity party. I give myself a shake and smile brightly at the person who's just approached. Their skin is white with a pinkish hue, and while their height and envious curves catch my first impression, I'm also drawn to their hair. It's shaved on one side, poofed up through the centre with wild curls, and is coloured a mix between white-blond and teal. And their makeup, my god—it's flawlessly applied with swooping eyeliner, a deep burgundy lipstick, and contouring that would garner RuPaul's approval. Aside from the hair and lipstick, their wardrobe is otherwise entirely black, from the pants ripped at the knees to the camisole hugging their enviable breasts.

"Hi, I'm Ellie! My pronouns are she/her. What's your name?"

They meet my gaze with a bored expression. "Mariah. She/her."

"Ooh, named after the Queen of Christmas herself!"

Mariah's brow pinches together, but otherwise she ignores the clever connection. "I'm your makeup artist and hair stylist."

"Nice, a two-for-one deal." I giggle at myself, but my joke doesn't earn even a twitch of a smile from my new friend.

She unzips her duffel bag and bends, rifling through it.

I fidget in my seat. "Have you ever worked on a movie set before?"

"Nope," she replies, not even looking up.

"Ooh, congratulations! First film gig, that's so exciting."

She straightens, eyeing me through the mirror while comparing my skin tone to a couple different bottles. She drops back down and continues her rummaging without replying, or even making eye contact.

"Don't worry, I'll help you with anything you need. This is my third Christmas movie, and my sixth time on set with this team, so I'm practically a veteran at all this. Have you seen our other films?"

Mariah spreads a bit of foundation on my cheek, comparing two tones, then chooses one bottle, setting it down on the desk in front of us while letting the other drop unceremoniously back into her bag. "No," she replies, a full thirty seconds after I asked the question.

"Oh, well, you're in for quite a treat. We're a blast to work with, practically a party every day." I raise my pointer fingers in the air and do a little wiggly happy dance.

Mariah meets my gaze through the mirror for half a second, her expression stony, before bending back toward her bag.

Tough crowd. Maybe she didn't sleep well last night. Maybe she's nervous about her first time working on a movie. Maybe she had to get up super early to do her fancy hair and makeup and she hasn't had her coffee yet.

Or maybe I'm stuck with the grumpiest person on set.

A chorus of laughter draws my attention through the mirror to the other side of the room. Aimee's hair and makeup people are howling at something she said. Oscar is laughing so hard he's wiping away a tear, his own makeup artist chasing his fingers away with dabs of tissue. Julia's radiant smile is already accented with rosy lipstick and her eyes pop with big fake eyelashes.

Despite my best efforts, I feel my shoulders sag a bit, my stomach souring. If only I . . .

Nope. Don't go there.

I snap my focus back to my own reflection and give myself a stern look. *Be grateful you're here. You're an actress, living your dream, working on the set of a Christmas movie, for crying out loud. It doesn't get much better than this! Five years ago, you were dreaming of being exactly where you are right now.*

Well, not *exactly.*

But close. So close I can smell it—literally. Whatever hair spray they're using over there is potent.

I take a deep breath and force a smile back on my face. "How lucky are we to be here together, hey?" Mariah doesn't reply, which doesn't surprise me. "We have an excellent script, the dynamic duo of Yueyi and Marlene, we have Oscar-friggen-Fizak, and we're here in beautiful Chilliwack of all places! It's all going to be great! Are you stoked or what?"

She gives me a flat look, eyes half-lidded. "Thrilled."

My hundred-watt smile dims to maybe a ninety as I struggle to keep the excitement alive for the both of us. Usually by now I've won over whoever it is I'm working with, we have an amiable conversation going, and we're equally pumped for the work ahead. But Mariah seems to be immune to my charms. If I'm not careful, she might suck the Christmas spirit right out of me.

This is going to be a long two weeks.

FADE IN

EXT. DOWNTOWN HEMLOCK GROVE - DAY

ANNIE, age thirty, dressed in a business suit with red blouse and black heels, steps out of a parked car. She twirls in a circle as she admires the festive décor on quaint downtown businesses. The sidewalks are covered in piles of snow, lights twinkle, and garland is draped on every sign.

Annie grabs her luggage from the trunk and walks down a cobblestone alley.

SHOPKEEPERS greet PEDESTRIANS as they walk past dressed in winter clothes while quiet instrumental Christmas music echoes through streets.

Annie takes note of a café conspicuously devoid of décor, then walks to bright red door with a wreath and presses the buzzer.

INT. APARTMENT HALLWAY - DAY

The interior hall door swings open to JENNA, age twenty-six, wearing an oversize sweater with stains on her pants and hair in a messy bun. She smiles and holds her arms out wide.

                    ANNIE
          Merry Christmas, little sister!

Annie steps into the apartment.

INT. JENNA'S APARTMENT - HALLWAY - DAY

Annie sets her bags down and hugs Jenna.

                    JENNA
        Merry Christmas!

They pull away from the hug and Annie looks to BABY
HENRY who lies on the floor.

                    ANNIE
        And Merry First Christmas, little
        Henry!

Annie kneels beside baby Henry.

                    ANNIE (CONT'D)
        Oh, my goodness, he is so cute! Is
        there anything better than a baby's
        first Christmas?

                    JENNA
        I'd say three hours of uninterrupted
        sleep and strong coffee.

Annie laughs.

                    JENNA (CONT'D)
        I'm not kidding. I'm out of coffee. I
        hate to be a pest and I know you just
        got here, but can you go grab me some
        from the café downstairs? I'm going to
        need something strong to get me
        through decorating the house today,

and hubby won't be home until late
tonight.

ANNIE

Oh, of course! That's why I came here
from Seattle, to help you with
everything baby related. Washing
dishes, changing diapers, and fetching
coffee is all included.

JENNA

You are the best sister ever. Fair
warning, though. The guy who runs the
place is a bit of a grump. Just get
the coffee and leave, okay? I get
weird vibes in there, but the coffee
is amazing.

Chapter 2
MARIAH

*T*his is going to be a *very* long two weeks.

Despite knowing my way around this city as if I'd never left it, the commute from Vancouver to the Fraser Valley can be unpredictable and I ended up getting caught in traffic, arriving fifteen minutes late—not the first impression I wanted to make. As a result, I'm neither set up nor prepared for my day ahead. Luckily today is a short day since I only have one person to get ready.

My head hurts and I wince as I straighten too quickly after grabbing several shades of blush from my bag. With the giant windows in this place it's already so bright, but compounded by the vanity lights framing the mirror it's enough to make my headache go from slight pressure to painful throb.

The noise isn't helping, either. Not just the crowd behind me, but the incessant chatter of the woman sitting in my chair. You'd think someone would take the hint and stop talking after a few minutes, but not her. What did she say her name was? I forgot it as soon as she'd said it, and there's no signage on this table to clue me in otherwise.

". . . and *last* year's Christmas movie we had this hilarious costume problem—my clothes were all too small! My shirt was so tight it nearly took the movie from G-rated to PG-13, if you know what I mean . . ."

I should have remembered to pack my earplugs.

After sanitizing my hands, I squirt some primer onto my fingertips and begin spreading it over her face, which doesn't slow her motormouth. She has good skin, evidently using a decent moisturizer, which makes my job easier. The light fawn of her skin is speckled with freckles over her nose, which has a proud bump to it, giving her a regal look. There is a small mole just below her left eye, adding a bit of character. Round eyes, light brown, innocent-looking. I'll use my bronze Deja Vu through the centre of her lids, highlight the edges with Frosting, make that goldish tone in her eyes pop. Her sandy-blond hair falls in unruly curls, which I'm not sure if they want me to accentuate or straighten. I'll have to ask Jimmie.

After priming I bend back down to find my brushes, pushing past my piles of costume makeup I probably should have left at home rather than lugging it all around with me. It's not like I'll get a chance to use it while I'm here, besides possibly entertaining my measly five hundred TikTok followers.

Finding my brush sets, I place them on the dresser in front of us and begin applying foundation. My colour match is spot-on. Without having to be prompted, she lifts her chin and lets me blend from her rounded jawline down her long neck. Afterward, I move on to the blush, highlighting and lowlighting her cheekbones.

"I've never really been out this way before. I hear there's some great hiking. It's a tight schedule, but most of my scenes are near the end, so I'll have a few days to go out and explore. Maybe I'll go see that waterfall I saved on Pinterest years ago . . ."

I don't interrupt to tell her that she's looking for Bridal Falls, and it's a twenty-minute drive east—wouldn't want to encourage her. She'd force me to talk more, which will make *her* talk more, and nobody wants that. She might even want me to give her pointers on cool stuff to do nearby or show her around. The last thing I want to do is be someone's tour guide, especially someone as obnoxious as her.

Nope. As soon as this job is over, I'm beating it back to Vancouver—where I belong.

I left Chilliwack behind six years ago and never looked back. From that first year in cosmetology, with its unbelievable highs and devastating lows, to my first job backstage at drag shows, to assisting weddings, to my freelance work with family photographers, I've slowly found a small place in the world for myself. I'm not where I want to be yet, putting my costume makeup skills to good use. Even though I'm here, working on a movie set like I've always dreamed of, I'm still doing the same boring crap I've done for work every day. And it's sucking the life out of me.

When I applied for this job I thought this would be a step up, furthering my goals, my dreams, my ambitions, but so far it seems lateral at best.

Maybe even a step back.

I mean, it's a Christmas movie for fuck's sake. It's the exact opposite of what I wanted to do with my life. Surely at some point, if I ever get my resume looked at by someone wanting to make a movie with *actual* makeup, they'll take one look at *CHRISTMAS ON THUNDERBIRD LANE*, have a hearty laugh, and throw it in the dumpster.

Well, click Delete, and move on to the next.

It seemed like a good idea at the time. And the pay is decent. But is it enough to put up with all of this?

I eye the woman blathering on in front of me.

Probably not.

"Close," I say, gesturing to her eyes.

She complies, though her lips keep moving as she prattles on. I brush on some eyeshadow, blending throughout, the colour accenting her skin just as I knew it would.

My phone rings, and I pause what I'm doing to fish it out of my bag.

Mother.

My gut twists as I remember why I'd chosen to drink too much wine last night. Feeling suddenly nauseous, I silence my phone and toss it back into my bag.

"Everything okay?" the woman asks.

"Yep. Close." I gesture at her eyes again, and she does as she's told. I apply a dark brown eyeliner to her lids, giving her a "makeup-less look" while still getting her eyes to pop for the camera.

"Good, because I was just thinking about how, two years ago, oh my god, it was the funniest thing, the reindeer they brought on set . . ."

"I gotta do your lips now, hun," I interrupt, though I have to admit, my interest has been piqued.

She sets her lips in a relaxed, half-open pout, her throat bobbing just so. She has beautiful, full, bow-shaped lips, and I know exactly what to do with them. It takes me a few moments to apply dusty rose lipstick to her. She sits still, evidently well-practised from her time working on set.

"Okay, open," I tell her, then turn her to the mirror.

She gasps so loud it makes me jump.

"Oh . . . my . . . *lanta!* Girl, you're amazing. Look at my eyes!"

I begin threading my fingers through her hair. Where is Jimmie? I still don't know what he wants me to do with this, although it would be a shame to straighten these natural curls.

The woman is still flattering me with all sorts of remarks, which I ignore, while I flag down the lead makeup artist—Simon Jimmie, who goes by his last name after his great-great-grandfather. Jimmie's russet skin is accented with bold makeup, highlighting his sharp cheekbones and dark eyes. His long black hair is tied back in a ponytail, and his plain sage button-up shirt is contrasted by a colourful beaded necklace. I'd FaceTimed him once before during the interview process, but my phone screen didn't do him justice.

Despite being a small man, Jimmie carries the aura of a person twice his size. Jimmie's worked with Samuel L. Jackson and the late Phillip Seymour Hoffman, and learning from him is the only thing that makes this job worthwhile. Hopefully he'll give me a good reference so I can further my career in the industry—and by further, I mean get me far, far away from this holly jolly hell hole. Jimmie spots me and approaches, clipboard in hand.

"Hey, Jimmie, for her hair, do you want me to—"

"No, no, no," he cuts me off. "This is all wrong."

I look back at my work. She looks stunning. "What?"

"First of all, you're late."

"I'm sorry, it won't—"

"First ones on set, last ones off. Understood?"

I nod.

"We don't need you to stay today since it's just blocking and promotional shots, but tomorrow and every day after you'll be here the full day."

"No problem," I say, even though my stomach is curdling.

"Now, for your work." Jimmie purses his hand as if he's Italian and gestures at me. "She stands out way too much. The script makes it obvious, she has to blend *in*to the background. We can't have her eyes popping like that, it's distracting."

"Oh . . . sorry?" I say, not quite sure what he expected.

"You *did* read the script, didn't you?" Though Jimmie is small, he is fierce, and I find myself shrinking under his intense gaze.

"I haven't got around to it yet, but . . ."

He sighs, pinching the bridge of his nose. "Always, always read the script." He flails his arms wide. "How are you supposed to know what to do with your actors if you don't know their place in the story?"

"Do you want me to redo it?" I venture, fiddling with the brush in my hand.

He looks at his Apple Watch then shakes his head. "We don't have time. Wipe it off a bit and you'll have to try again tomorrow. But for next time, more pale, less eye-popping, and very little on the lips, okay?"

"Uh, okay. And the hair?"

"Do it up in a bun—loose, messy, like she doesn't care about it."

"Okay." Easy enough.

Jimmie switches his attention to the woman in the chair, brightening instantly. "Ellie, good to see you again. Everyone else will be ready for blocking in the coffee shop in ten, okay?"

"Sounds great, thanks, Jimmie!" the woman, Ellie, chirps.

Jimmie stalks away and I turn back to Ellie, embarrassed and a bit frazzled after such a public reprimand. I've been on set for all of thirty minutes and already it seems my future in the industry will be shorter than the filming schedule of this movie. Hopefully I can make up for it over the next couple weeks and get a good reference to work on something else. I'd take pretty much anything at this point—anything but another Christmas movie.

Ellie doesn't seem to notice my discomfort. Her perfectly erect posture slumps as she gazes back at herself in the mirror. The sparkle in her eyes is diminished, and I can't help but feel bad for her; nobody likes being told they have to blend in.

I take a makeup wipe and remove all the work I'd done on her eyes, and then her lips, leaving her looking very pale and plain, especially next to the other actors behind us who are making their way down to the set.

After a moment Ellie shakes off her mild moroseness, literally shaking her limbs, and switches back to her painfully wide smile and obnoxiously positive radiance. I tie her hair up in a loose bun, letting a couple of curly tendrils escape to frame her face, and then release her.

"Okay, done."

"Thank you so much, Mariah," she practically yells. "You are a doll. And so good with your hands!"

I refrain from making an innuendo. "Yep. No worries."

"The way you put on my eyeliner was so practised and easy. I can barely get myself dressed in the morning. Oh! Speaking of—" She strips off her oversized Christmas sweater, and my eyes can't help but catch on her dainty clavicle, the roundness of her small breasts. Her tank top underneath is practically soaked in sweat, making it transparent. Why the hell is she wearing such a big sweater? Has she never heard of heatstroke? "I have to bust my ass to get to costume," she continues. "Thankfully it's simple, just some regular clothes plus an apron and—"

I cut her off. "Okay, yeah, great. Better hurry."

She snaps her fingers and grins. "You're totally right, I'm running behind. We can chat more tomorrow. See you then, Mariah!"

She runs off with a flourish and the world seems ten times quieter with her gone. I rub my temples and close my eyes, taking a breath. I'm glad it's a short day today, to ease myself into this nightmare. After cleaning my station, I throw everything I won't be needing back into my giant duffel bag and haul it all down the stairs and out onto the street. The intense July sunlight glares in my face, and I pause to pull out my sunglasses before continuing. Unfortunately, I have to walk past the set to where I parked my car.

The street is grossly overcrowded, the film crew clogging it more than last-minute shoppers on Christmas Eve. Everything is covered in fake crap—from the green plastic garland, to the spray-on frosting on the glass, to the dingy off-white blankets that are supposed to pass as snow. The whole downtown core itself is fake. Brand-new, only built a few years ago, but supposed to look like some sort of old English town? This is Chilliwack, not Oxfordshire. It's a far cry from the faded brick buildings and PencilFingerz mural, the downtown I grew up with.

Not that I'm sentimental about Chilliwack—I just hate fake shit and commercialism. Ironic, since I'm now forced to be amongst the fakest of fake shit and the commercialest of commercialism with this damn Christmas movie.

I get to my old silver Civic and turn the ignition, blasting the AC. After tossing my duffel bag into the back seat with my suitcase and pillow, I check the voicemail Mom left me.

"Hey sweetie! Dad and I are so excited to have you. And we figured, since you're filming a Christmas movie and you couldn't make it home last year because of the weather, we could have a little Christmas redo of our own! I was thinking—"

I delete the message before it gets any further and thunk my head against the steering wheel. This is a nightmare. I've been avoiding Christmas with my parents for years. It's easy to find an excuse. *The roads are bad. I'm in Mexico. I'm spending it with my girlfriend—*

God, I need a drink. It would certainly help with this headache. Not to mention dealing with my mom. Any excuse to put off going home for a few more hours is a good one. I just didn't think, after all this time and so many years, I'd be back here.

Is there anything worse than having to live through an extra Christmas? One is hard enough.

INT. BREWED AWAKENING CAFÉ - DAY

Annie enters the café. Interior has exposed brick, wood tables, and a glass display with very few items inside. Otherwise, the interior is void of decoration.

Brewed Awakening is silent and empty, except for a BARISTA, age thirty, standing at the till wearing a white shirt and green apron, and a MAN, age thirty-five, wearing jeans and a black collared shirt with sleeves rolled to his forearms. He has stubble on his cheeks and dark rings under his eyes. He is seated in the back on a laptop and does not look up when Annie enters.

Annie approaches the counter to order.

> ANNIE
> Hello, and Merry Christmas!
> Can I have two pumpkin spice
> lattes with lots of nutmeg, please.

> BARISTA
> Oh, I'm sorry, we don't have any of
> that. I can make you a regular latte,
> though.

> ANNIE
> It's Christmas and you don't have
> pumpkin spice? What about peppermint?

> BARISTA
> No, sorry. If it were me, I'd stock
> those things, but my boss, James over
> there, refuses.

Barista nods over her shoulder to the man seated in the back, ignoring them while staring at his computer.

                    ANNIE
          Is he also the reason there's no
          Christmas cheer in here?

                    BARISTA
          Yeah, he doesn't do Christmas
          decorations.

                    ANNIE
          Seems like someone needs a little
          Christmas spirit.

                    BARISTA
          I think you might be right. But you
          didn't hear it from me.

                    ANNIE
          Of course. I wouldn't want you getting
          in trouble. I'll take two regular
          lattes, please.

Chapter 3
ELLIE

After a full day of blocking, going over the script, more blocking, photography, adjusting lighting and camera angles, and more blocking, we're finally done for the day. Everyone is pooped and we haven't even shot anything yet. Filming a movie has so much behind-the-scenes preparation that by the time they shout "Action!" you're already spent. It's a lot of work to keep energy levels up, but it's a task I take on with pleasure.

There's still a lot of day-one adrenaline and excitement between cast and crew, but as time goes on, more of the burden of keeping the Christmas spirit alive will fall on my shoulders. I'm prepared for it.

"Whoever wrote this script, I'm buying them a drink," Julia croons while removing her fake eyelashes.

"Whoever cast *you* as my co-star, I'm buying *them* a drink," Oscar remarks, leaning close to Julia.

Julia laughs her musical laugh, and the rest of the team joins her. I laugh along too, because it's just that contagious.

Marlene grips both of their upper arms with her talons. "First round is on us. We'll bill the marketing department."

"Oh yeah, party on, Garth!" I shout while doing a fake guitar solo in tribute to *Wayne's World*.

The group looks at me, pauses, then turns back to their conversation.

"The place down the street has great pizza, but stay away from the chicken wings," Jimmie cautions, having grown up near here in Squiala First Nation.

The group moves en masse toward the stairs, me caught somewhere in the back, until we pile out onto the street. It's midafternoon and still extremely hot, which makes my sweat-dampened Christmas sweater even more uncomfortable. I pull the neckline away from my chest and blow air over the girls. The group heads right, but my car is parked left.

"See you tomorrow, team!" I shout as they begin walking away while I wait for the lights to change. "Don't party too hard, we have work to do!" They're too caught up in their conversations to notice me, but that's okay. We'll all be together again tomorrow.

I should be going with them so we can bond, but unlike them, I can't walk to my lodgings, and finding my way to where I'm staying in the dark and after a few drinks is a bad idea.

Everyone else is staying at the Royal, an old downtown hotel, but not me. There weren't enough rooms for all of us, so the crew and lesser actors were moved to a different hotel several blocks away. When Marlene had called to notify me of the arrangements, at least I didn't have to maintain a smile over the phone. She'd said she knew if anyone would understand being shifted around it would be me, so of course I did.

It's not like I'm a lead.

Instead of being constantly reminded that I'd been punted from the fancy hotel where the cool kids are staying, I split the cost difference with production and booked a cute little Airbnb: a cozy cabin out in the woods.

This will be great.

Almost like a little mini vacation.

Plus, I won't be distracted networking during my downtime and hobnobbing with the other talent. I can focus on my character and really get into my method acting.

To the others this may just be another movie, or maybe to Oscar it's a step down from some of the more serious roles he's played, but I'm still an up-and-comer with a lot to prove. I need every ounce of my attention on the two weeks ahead. I can't be distracted by Julia and Oscar and bar drinks and questionable-but-tempting chicken wings.

After crossing the street, I plop myself into the front seat of my green Subaru and toss my purse onto the passenger side, cranking the AC. "Jingle Bell Rock" blasts from my Christmas CD. I bop my head and hum along as I buckle my seat belt, then throw it in reverse.

I sit up a little higher to see over the mountains of boxes piled up in my back seat. Check-in to my Airbnb wasn't until four o'clock, so I had to leave everything in my car when I got in from Vancouver this morning.

I plug the address into my phone and follow Google's directions down to the highway, heading east and singing Christmas karaoke the whole way. The city quickly fades into farmland, and the mountains to my right are still capped in snow despite the heat we've had these past few weeks. Ahead and to my left are more mountains, the Fraser Valley slicing through them like a river of green paradise. I can already feel the tension in my shoulders and neck relaxing as I take it all in.

I exit the highway and after a few more turns am thrust into a forest while scaling one of the mountains I'd seen in the distance ten minutes ago. I turn down my music so I can better read signage, the one I need appearing a few minutes down a winding road.

I turn onto the narrow, bumpy dirt driveway and after about five minutes of my car jiggling so much I'm worried a bolt will come loose, a cabin appears. The tiny wood-beam cabin is tucked beneath the shade of towering evergreens and nestled between colourful shrubs.

I wiggle in my seat. It's perfect!

I park and get out, immediately met by an orchestra of insects, tiny forest creatures, and the breeze through the treetops. Seriously, they could record this sound and play it at a spa.

After locating the key in a hidden rock, I unlock the front door. The smell of old wood greets me, wafting out of the house along with a draft of cool air from the portable AC unit humming away in the corner. I close the door behind me and clench my fists tightly, squealing in excitement as I check the place out.

The front door opens into the living room, which has a wood-burning stove and an old floral-pattered love seat, as well as a small desk and swivelling computer chair that don't quite fit with the rest of the rustic aesthetics. The kitchen is just as tiny, taking up the other half of the room with just a counter-top peninsula as separation. Two barstools are tucked next to it, where I'll be eating all my meals since there isn't a dining table. The cabinets look like they're straight out of someone's parents' photo albums, all dark wood and old bronzed handles. The countertops are yellow laminate, with a circular spaghetti stain to the right of the stove. At least the appliances look new-ish, and I'm pleased to note there's nothing in the fridge except an open box of baking soda.

I duck my head into the bathroom, which is similarly old and yellow but has everything I need. The bedroom is just as small, with floral-patterned bedding, doilies on the dresser, and old landscape paintings on the walls. The alarm clock next to the bed looks like it belongs in a museum.

This place is so eighties-chic it makes me wish I had a handlebar moustache and a mullet. It's even better than the pictures!

Next step: hauling in all my crap. Box after box makes its way in, getting stacked in the living room. Once it's all inside I open the first one to reveal Christmas decorations.

Inhaling deeply, I revel in the nostalgic smells, colours, and textures of my childhood. Red and green twinkle lights, garland and tinsel, ornaments and knickknacks, remnants of past pine trees—it's all here. I'm so glad Mom let me borrow everything.

I rummage through the tree-decorating box. At the bottom, beneath all sorts of keepsakes my siblings and I have made for the tree over the years, is our VHS player and tapes. Over time we'd replaced several with DVDs, then got rid of those in favour of streaming services, but these last few in the box have more sentimental value than actual worth, and they're kept with all the Christmas stuff because that's when we watch the old movies.

Well. We used to.

Luckily, the TV in this cabin seems to be the same age as the VHS player, and all the cords plug in the way they should. I go back to the box and pick up tape after tape, not sure which one to start with. A plain one catches my eye and I lift it to the light to inspect it. *Romeo & Juliet 2006* is written on the white sticker in black sharpie. I roll my eyes and drop it unceremoniously back into the box, choosing an old classic instead.

Jingle All the Way plays in the background, Arnie and his Austrian accent filling the tiny cabin with nostalgic bliss as I untangle strings of Christmas lights. I thought ahead and brought a bunch of 3M hooks so I won't damage anything. Before the movie is over there are lights along every ceiling, over every door, and even wrapped around the stovepipe of the fireplace— since there is no way in hell I'm going to be lighting a fire during this heat wave, no matter how cozy and Christmassy it would be. Method acting does have its limits.

The last thing is a mini blow-up Santa with mechanical movements, which usually goes outside but would be perfect in the corner, on top of the desk. I crawl underneath to find the last available plug, reaching as far as I can and—

Everything goes dark.

I bump my head as I crawl back out. Dammit. I must have flipped a breaker. I should have been more careful with plugging things in with an old cabin like this. Thankfully it's still only about five o'clock, and plenty of light gets in through the windows for me to see. After searching each room twice, then taking a walk around the outside of the building, I give up on finding the breaker box and open my Airbnb app to contact the owner, who has no profile picture—just a photo of a fox.

Thankfully, there's still cell reception. Stroke of luck!

ELLIE: Hello! This is Ellie. I'm staying at your cabin. There seems to be a problem with the electrical. Not sure what to do.

> **JOSEPH:** hey! No worries I'm only ten minutes away and just headed out. I'll be right there.

> **ELLIE:** okay thank youuuuuu! ☺☺☺

Sitting still has never been one of my talents, so I take the next ten minutes to unpack my suitcase. Without that little portable AC unit buzzing away, it gets hot quickly, nearly to the point of me removing my sweater. Thankfully, I don't have to take such an extreme measure before there's a quiet knock at the door.

"Oh hello, I'm sorry about this, I—" I'm already talking when I open the door, but all the words that were about to spill from my mouth are suddenly swallowed.

Because of the age of the cabin, I'd been expecting the owner to match it: an old gentleman with a grey handlebar moustache and the remnants of what was once a proud mullet. But no, I'm met with the opposite.

Nearly filling the entire door frame is a handsome young man, with wide shoulders accentuated by a narrow waist. His jeans fit his lower half just snugly enough, leaving little to the imagination, while his upper half is tightly clad in a grey tee. And his face on top of that, my god. He has the jawline of a Marvel hero, dusted in the perfect amount of scruff, but with the soft brown eyes of a daytime TV anchor. His hair is hidden under a black sportsball cap, shading his face from the sun.

He seems equally stunned to see me, taking a step back and blinking a few times.

Then, he smiles.

Oh, sweet baby Jesus, that smile. Upturned at the corner, a crinkle in his eyes, the tiny rewarding flash of white teeth.

I'm melting.

Or maybe just pooling in my own sweat.

"Hi—hi! Joseph? I'm Ellie." I put out my hand to shake, then withdraw it, thinking better, but then I don't want to be rude, so I stick it out there again.

His smile widens. "Joseph's my uncle. I look after the place for him. I'm Matt."

Thankfully, he doesn't leave me hanging, meeting my hand with his own. His forearms are thick, covered in light brown hair, and there are all sorts of delightful sinuous muscles and tendons wrapping around them. His hand envelops mine completely and sends a shiver up my back. He holds on longer than necessary. Or has time stopped? Hard to know for sure.

"Your electrical?" he finally asks.

"Oh! Yes. Come in." I remove my hand from his, immediately bereft from its warm embrace, and step aside so he can enter.

"Whoa." He stops in his tracks as he eyes my menagerie of Christmas decorations.

"Don't worry, it's all 3M hooks, I won't leave any permanent damage."

"No, it's just . . . July?"

I giggle. "You don't say."

He squints and twists his mouth to the side.

"I'm method acting," I explain.

He continues his quizzical look.

"It's where you immerse yourself in a part to really get into the emotionality of it, even when you're off set—"

"Like Daniel Day Lewis?"

I snap my fingers and jump in excitement. "Yes!"

He gives a short nod of his head. "That explains the sweater."

I cast a glance down at myself. "Oh, yeah. I've had this thing forever. I wear it every year."

"Are you here for that movie they're filming downtown?"

My grin grows ten sizes. "Yes! It's a Christmas movie, hence—" I gesture to my sweater, then to our surroundings.

"That's so cool," he says, slouching a little closer to my level. "I feel like I know someone famous."

My face tingles with warmth. I don't correct him about the famous part. "Well, if you want an autograph, let me know."

He chuckles. "I'll definitely have to get one."

We hold each other's gaze for exactly four and a half seconds.

"Anyway," he says, finally breaking away and stepping toward the bedroom. "The electrical box is in here if you need it again. It's behind this picture."

He has a great voice. It has a playful quality to it, with a slight rasp like he's just woken from a nap, and there's a subtle lisp on his *s*'s. I follow him into the bedroom and watch as he lifts a mountain-scape off the wall to reveal the rectangular grey panel. He opens it, immediately locates the source of my problem, and switches it back. The lights go on, the AC unit hums to life, and Arnie's voice begins shouting in the other room about getting back his doll.

And Matt is in my bedroom.

And my clothes are spread out on my bed.

Including my Christmas-themed underwear.

Our eyes land on the red-and-green-striped thong at the same time. I swipe it away and it flies across the room, landing on the floor somewhere in the corner.

"Uh, thank you?" I say, sheepishly scratching my messy bun.

"Oh, um, you're welcome," he says, snapping his focus back to me as he comes around the far side of the bed. I back out of the bedroom and he follows behind, then turns to face me as he walks backward, our chests brushing alongside each other's oh so gently. A titillating zing zips through my entire body, ending somewhere between my thighs. I can't help but inhale his scent: masculine, tangy, no masking of cologne or obtrusive soap, like he hasn't showered yet today. I don't mind it one bit. If anything, I want to get closer, run my nose up his neck, taste the salt on his skin at the base of his throat.

He pauses in the living room to admire my handiwork.

I fill the silence while giving my head a subtle shake. "Christmas is my favourite time of year, so any excuse for another Christmas is great. You know? I love everything about Christmas—" I move past him and get back on my hands and knees to remove the blow-up Santa's plug so I don't flip another breaker or start a fire "—I love the music and the decorations and the movies and the gifts and the food, oh my god, don't get me started on the food, turkey dinner? Why don't we eat turkey other times of the year? Why just Christmas? And—" I scoot backward, plug in hand, and look over my shoulder.

Matt's head is tilted sideways, his mouth slightly ajar, eyes widened in the telltale way of an adult male who's been caught checking out an ass.

He snaps to and averts his gaze, but it's too late. I noticed him noticing me, and I have the butterflies in my stomach to prove it.

Emboldened by this knowledge, I stand and take a step toward him, lifting my chin and turning on *sultry eyes*. "What do you think, Matt?"

"What do I . . . What?"

"Christmas?"

"Oh, yeah, I love it. Favourite time of year. Yep." His Adam's apple bobs.

"I wonder what else we have in common." I tuck my hands behind my back and smile demurely.

Matt rewards me with a new smile, his own version of sultry. It spreads slowly across his face, eyes twinkling. "Well, I'll let you get back to your Christmas decorating. If there's anything else you need, just send me a text. I'm ten minutes away." He backs toward the door, then trips on a box and catches himself against the wall.

"You oka—"

"Yep," he says quickly, his cheeks turning pinkish as he collects himself and opens the door.

"Bye, Matt."

He rewards me with one last smile before shutting the door. I immediately clench my fists and squee as quietly as I can while twisting in a circle, a very subdued happy dance. Meeting a guy like Matt in a circumstance like this has to be fate. How is it I just so happened to rent a cabin that's looked after by a guy like him? Despite being alone in a strange cabin with a strange man, at no point did I feel any sense of unease. There's something about him, something gentle and quiet within that tall, sturdy exterior that speaks to me on a level I barely understand. It felt like our pheromones had intermingled and agreed with one another.

I may not be the star of the movie, getting an on-screen happily-ever-after where I'm whisked away from the big city to the magical small town, but maybe, just maybe, I can have the real-life version.

Maybe I'll get to star in my own romance and be the main character in my own life.

For once.

INT. BREWED AWAKENING CAFÉ (CONT'D)

Annie approaches James sitting in the back of the café.

James does not look up from his computer.

Annie waits a moment, then clears her throat.

James looks at her from over his screen, face neutral bordering on annoyed.

                    ANNIE
          Hello there, and Merry Christmas!

James sighs, closes his laptop.

                    JAMES
          Can I help you?

                    ANNIE
          Yes, actually. I came all the way from
          Seattle to Hemlock Grove to help my sister
          with Christmas, but how can I bring her
          the Christmas Spirit when I can't get her
          a peppermint or pumpkin spice latte?

James stands, walks to the counter.

Annie follows.

                    JAMES
          Then I guess you should go back to the big
          city and leave us small-town folk to the
          simple things in life.

ANNIE
You're actively losing customers by refusing
to decorate for Christmas and by not having
the Christmas staples everyone relies on.

James makes drinks while talking, not making eye
contact with Annie.

JAMES
Useless frivolities cost more than they're
worth. If you need pumpkin spice and
peppermint to feel Christmas, then I think
you've forgotten what Christmas is actually
about. Feel free to take your business
elsewhere, where they have those fake,
disgusting flavours. I refuse to sully
my good coffee with them. You can
take these regular lattes or nothing.

James sets paper cups down with more force than
necessary.

JAMES (CONT'D)
Have a nice day.

Annie throws a twenty-dollar bill onto the counter,
then turns on her heel and leaves without another
word, letting the door slam as she exits.

James watches her walk away through the large
windows, his expression shifting from neutral to a
hint of longing and sadness in his eyes.

Chapter 4
MARIAH

*T*o have a third drink, or to not have a third drink, that is the question.

I've driven to the far end of town, getting as much space between me and that damn movie set as I could, before pulling into Grumpy Joe's, the diviest of dive bars. The empty parking lot beckoned me like a siren out at sea, sans the singing. A sign out front said *karaoke Sundays*, and today's a Monday so I'm safe for at least another six days.

The inside is drab, smelling of stale beer and the lingering odour of cigarettes despite nobody legally smoking indoors since the eighties. The carpeting is some weird mix of green and brown, the bar is battered and stained, and half of the old boxy TVs are playing keno games while the others repeat sports highlights. There is absolutely nobody in here but me and the bartender, some old guy with a "piss off" attitude who keeps to himself at the other end of the bar cleaning a shelf of dusty liquor bottles.

It's perfect.

The ice clinks in my glass as I tilt it to and fro, the juniper and citrus notes of my gin and tonic tempting me to have another. Not smart. Even though Mom and Dad's place is only a ten-minute drive from here, I know better than to risk driving while impaired—even if being impaired will help me cope with being back in that house. Maybe I'll swing by the liquor store on the way home.

I'm about to call it quits and flag down the bartender for my bill when his crotchety old voice breaks the silence.

"Hey, Jax," he says, giving a nod to someone on his right.

My ears perk up, and my gaze follows. My heart stutters when I see him and I forget to breathe.

Of *fucking* course I'd drive out of my way to be alone and end up running into someone from high school. And not just anyone from high school, oh no. One of the popular jock assholes who barely acknowledged my existence, aside from teasing me about my large-for-my-age tits. Like almost all the other girls—and some of the guys—in my grade, I had a massive crush on him. He was impossible not to like.

I watch him through my peripherals as he makes his way behind the bar while surreptitiously checking him out.

And damn, there's a lot to check out. He may still go by his childhood nickname, but everything else about him is very, *very* adult. A tight black V-neck hugs his well-defined chest, wrapping tightly around thick biceps, tapering loosely around his middle and giving the impression of washboard abs beneath. Above his body is a face that matches in decadence: square jaw, perfectly trimmed light beard, and luscious wavy brown locks that settle upon his shoulders. His thick brows frame his face and accentuate his dark eyes in a moody way, with a straight nose and thin lips pressed firmly into a serious line.

On top of that, he radiates BDE, carrying himself with a straight back and a confident stride. Despite myself I'm immediately drawn to him, straightening my own posture in response to his presence.

"Hey, Mike," he says, his deep voice rich and smooth.

I feel his eyes upon me but don't return his gaze, keeping my attention firmly on the empty drink in front of me. As the two men go over the day and swap out cash drawers, I'm hanging on to every word that comes out of Jax's sensual mouth.

The old man, Mike, leaves through the back and Jax stays behind. If only I'd left ten minutes earlier.

Maybe he won't recognize me. I hardly recognize myself; I look nothing like I used to.

I made sure of it.

Besides, it's not like we spent any time together—aside from being in the same grade since he moved here in grade six. And when we sat next to each other in eighth grade English class. And when he dated my "best friend" Bethany in grade eleven.

Other than occasionally ogling my breasts, Jax didn't really acknowledge my existence.

"Can I get you another?" he asks, his forearms resting on the bar.

"Thinking about it," I reply, gracing him with a flash of eye contact.

"Sorry it's so dead in here," he says, not moving from his place. "There's a Christmas movie being filmed downtown, and everyone's over there trying to catch a glimpse of some famous actor."

"You don't say."

"I'm guessing you don't like Christmas," he says.

I huff a breath through my nose. "Nope. I'm a Grinch."

"I hate Christmas, too." He has a playful half smirk on his face, just enough for the right-hand corner of his mouth to twitch up. He continues, "The only good Christmas movie is—"

"*Die Hard*," we say at the same time.

Jax smiles, and I can't help but bite my bottom lip as we regard one another. He nods at my empty glass. "What are you drinking?"

"It's okay. I was just about to grab my bill."

He reaches for the till, then pauses, leaning back on the bar. "Wait a second . . ."

My heart hammers in my chest. Facing the inevitable with as much grace as I can muster, I lift my chin and look at him head-on.

His eyes search mine, shifting right to left. Then his brows shoot up, eyes widening as realization dawns. "Maria?"

Even though it shouldn't, Jax remembering my name warms

my chest, my belly, and various other regions lower down. "Mariah," I correct.

Jax crosses his arms, biceps popping, as he leans against the bar behind him. He gives his head a slow shake. His eyes roam over my body from top to bottom, then back up again. I shouldn't be flattered—I should be offended. But I'm not. It pisses me off that getting checked out by Jax still turns me on like it did when I was a teen.

"I thought you moved away," he says finally.

"I did."

"Here visiting family?"

Not the entire truth, but true enough. I nod, pursing my lips.

"And not happy about it."

"How'd you figure that?"

He gestures to the drab environment.

I sigh. "Fine, yes, I'm avoiding them."

He grabs the bottle of gin off the counter and swirls it. "If that's the case, I'm sure I can provide a suitable distraction."

I slide my glass toward him. "Is that so?"

"Since *you've* always found a way of distracting me—" His eyes flit to my cleavage momentarily, a smirk upon his face.

I can't help the blush that rushes to my cheeks, turning my chest pink. So he *does* remember me. My tits, at least. Admittedly, they are quite unforgettable.

"Distracting you? I don't think we said two words to each other in all of high school."

"Doesn't mean I didn't want to say more."

His admission stumps me, and for once I don't have a witty comeback prepared.

Jax swirls the bottle of gin once more, the liquid inside sloshing. "I'd love to hear about where you've been, what you've been up to. Not all of us have been able to escape Chilliwack as you have. I'm not surprised you did."

"Is that a fact?"

His eyes bore into mine, searching. "You were always different."

I drop my gaze to the damp coaster in my hand, which I've been absentmindedly tearing into tiny pieces. Despite my best attempts at fitting in, it was apparent even to Jax—who didn't know me at all—that I didn't belong.

Jax leans closer. "In case you didn't know, that's a compliment."

I look up at him from under my lashes, surprised by the sentiment. We regard one another, neither moving, as my curiosity piques. "I suppose you *could* distract me for a while, then."

He smiles, the corners of his eyes crinkling. "Happy to oblige. Only if you answer a question for me, *Mariah*."

The way he pronounces my name, all raspy and throaty like that, does things to me. Warm, melty, tingly things.

Unable to stem my curiosity, I bite my lip. "Fine. What do you want to know?"

Jax leans on the bar, filling the space between us, his dark eyes capturing mine. "If you had to choose between getting your hair pulled or being choked, what would you pick?"

Oh, fuck. He went there. I hoped he might. I lean slowly toward him and watch as fire lights up his eyes. "Can't a girl have both?"

Something sparks in the space between us, sending a wave of heat down to my belly. I haven't felt this kind of immediate attraction toward a man in a long, long time, and I can't help but squeeze my thighs together in response. The way his pupils dilate makes me certain the feeling is mutual. Besides, the kind of man who can ask such a lewd question in broad daylight and *know* it will be taken well suggests he is well-versed in saying such things. This should be a warning, but instead his confidence only excites me—possibly because he was so out of my league when we were younger. Maybe all those years of pining are coming to a head now.

I'm not naive; I know this is probably a bad idea. And I know a red flag when I see one.

But sometimes I'm in the mood for a bit of red.

I nod toward my glass. "One more drink won't hurt."

Jax doesn't take his eyes off me as he pours another gin and tonic. "Good. After all, we have a lot of catching up to do."

He slides the glass toward me. I give it a stir with my finger, then suck the moisture off, watching as Jax's throat bobs in response. "Yes, lots of . . . catching up."

SIX DRINKS LATER.

We burst into Jax's apartment, the door slamming into the wall. Jax presses me against it, grinding his hips into mine while lifting my leg and wrapping it around him, our lips locking and unlocking fervently between gasping, shuddering breaths. My hands greedily claw at the muscles of his back, his shoulders, his biceps, while he manoeuvres us farther into his place, kicking the door shut behind him. Jax continues pushing me backward until we're in the kitchen, where he lifts me onto the countertop so I can wrap both legs around him.

We separate from kissing to tear off our shirts and fling them across the room. He has tattoos hidden under his shirt, but it's too dark and I'm too rushed to make anything out other than dark, swirling, sexy patterns before his hands grip my breasts roughly. I gasp at the contact, arching my back toward him.

"Jesus Christ," he mumbles, gaping at them in awe, as if he's been waiting since high school to do this. Making up for lost time, Jax squeezes them together and laps at my ample cleavage with his tongue.

He releases my bra clasp in one fluid action, spilling my breasts from their cups. Any relief I get from being braless is immediately reversed by him pinching and twisting my nipples. I gasp at the pain, but lean into it, taking a fistful of hair at the base of his neck and pulling to bring his mouth back to mine.

Jax lifts me again and carries me to the bedroom, where he lays me on the bed and presses against me, grinding his erection in the exact place to send a zing up my spine and make me whimper into his mouth.

"Pants. Off," I order.

He chuckles, the dark rumble resonating against my throat as he kisses his way down my body, pausing to suck my breasts, and then continuing farther to my belly. "Yours first."

He unbuttons my ripped black jeans and tugs them down, followed by my socks, one at a time. He grips my foot and kisses the length of my calf, then bites the inside of my thigh. I arch my back and grip the bedding as he moves farther up until his mouth is firmly pressed against my centre.

He teases me through the silk of my underwear and I grip his head, pressing him harder, greedy for more of his touch. Finally, he parts the cloth to the side and licks one long, languid stroke, sending a shock wave rippling through my body. I shudder and moan quietly, squeezing my eyes together. Spurred on by my sounds, Jax lifts my legs over his shoulders and continues licking and pressing, intently focused on the task at hand.

"More," I manage to say, already seeing stars, feeling that tight wave of coiled energy at the base of my core aching to break free.

Jax responds exactly as I want him to, by sliding two fingers deep inside me. He curls them up and strokes in expert, practised motions while his tongue sets into a rhythm of circles around my clit. The heat builds and my body coils tighter and tighter while he brings me close, so close . . . until finally everything happens at once. My body clenches and I cry out as I release into a long throbbing wave that Jax leans into, accentuating and drawing it out further, longer, until finally I can't take any more, pushing him away and rolling onto my side, shuddering in the aftershocks.

There's a soft kiss to my ear, and then a playful bite on my earlobe. "I'm not done with you yet," he growls.

I hum in response, still warm and tingling from the afterglow of my orgasm. I turn onto my back and look at him, meeting his hungry gaze. Fuck he looks hot, with his shoulder-length hair all messy and framing his face. His lips are full and pink from our aggressive make-out session, his beard shiny from licking me, and there's a bright pink scratch mark down his left arm that probably match a few more on his back.

"I promised hair pulling and choking." He stands up and begins unbuckling his belt. "And I don't break promises."

His words bring a new flush of heat and warmth to my body as I lie languidly and watch him undress. If could go back in time and tell teenage me I'd be here right now, she wouldn't believe me.

I admire Jax's muscled and tattooed body openly, my gaze lingering on his broad shoulders and defined pectorals, protruding abdominal muscles, and a coveted V shape pointing down to his cock, pressing against the black fabric of his boxers. After kicking his jeans away, he rubs his hand over his length, still concealed by his underwear, and the impressive member flexes.

"You tease." I roll my eyes, but I like the show. I sit up on the bed and run both hands up his thighs, moving toward his cock, then avoid it entirely and run my fingernails up his abs.

He shivers, then looks down at me while biting his lip. "Now who's the tease?"

I grin, running my nails back down until I meet the waistband of his boxers. Pulling them down inch by inch, I look up from an Aries symbol at his groin, to an ink-splattered mandala on his abdomen, to a fractal geometric design on his chest, to his face. I watch as his eyes widen and his jaw ticks in anticipation while my hands graze him.

Finally, I release his cock. It springs free, a sizable length and girth, tapping me on the cheek. I kiss the base of it, then lick long and slow up to the tip. He gasps at the contact. I tease again, licking from base to tip, then swirling my tongue around, coaxing a bead of moisture from him.

One of his hands grips my hair at the base of my neck and tugs, like I'd done to him earlier, and a thrilling tingle arches down my back in response. His other hand strokes my cheek, his fingers a light caress, juxtaposing the sensation of my hair being pulled. He tilts my jaw up until I'm meeting his gaze with his cock pressed against my face.

"So pretty," he mumbles.

The praise I'd yearned for as a teen is made all the more potent now, sending an intense rush of heat between my thighs.

Without taking my eyes off his, I bring him into my mouth as deep as I can. He groans, his eyes closing momentarily before he forces them back open to watch. He continues gripping and pulling my hair but gives me freedom to suck him how I want, not forcing me any deeper than I'm comfortable with. I continue moving up and down his length, relishing the short breaths, the gasps, the groans when I press him against the back of my throat.

He pulls out suddenly, then grabs me and flips me over on the bed. I've never been light or small, so the ease with which he can manhandle me is thrilling.

"On your knees," he orders. I comply immediately, kneeling on the bed with my feet dangling over the edge. He opens a drawer behind me, closes it, there's a sound of a foil wrapper, a pause, and then his hands are on me again. His fingers curl around my underwear and slide them down my thighs, and I lift one knee at a time so he can slip them off.

"Damn. Look at you," he says more to himself than to me. "I've been missing out on *this* all these years?" One hand grabs my hip while the other rubs a slow circle over my ass, then pulls away momentarily to deliver a sharp smack. I gasp, tossing my head.

Then, like he promised, one firm hand encircles my throat while the other rubs his cock around my entrance. He leans over, his chest pressing against my back, until his lips meet my ear. "Tell me you want it," he demands.

I push my hips back against him and he sucks in a breath through his teeth. I relish this power—though he's bigger and stronger, he literally has a hand wrapped around my throat and his cock exactly right *there*, yet I hold the key to his release, and he won't take it unless I give express permission. I drag it out a moment longer, moving my hips against him, torturing us both.

Finally, I can't take anymore. I lick my lips and hum against the sensation of his fingers wrapped around my throat. "I want you to fuck me."

His hand tightens for a quick squeeze, making me gasp. "Manners."

I'm so wet and aching for him at this point, but him forcing me to wait just makes it hotter. I arch my hips one more time, and then reply, "Fuck me, *please*."

The words have barely left my lips before he thrusts inside me. I cry out in pleasure, in pain, at the sudden movement. He keeps one hand around my throat but lifts his chest off me, his other hand squeezing my hip as he thrusts in quick, harsh strokes. I get closer and closer as I listen to him approach his end. We keep this pace up—for how long I don't know—the sounds of him slapping against me, of my moans, of his stifled grunts, filling the room. When his movements get jerkier, I know it's time. I reach between my legs and rub myself, which is all I need to come again, clenching around his cock as another wave hits my body. He comes with me, groaning, his final thrusts a frenzied race until he finally stills. His hands release me, and he steps away, letting me collapse onto the bed in a heap.

I flip to my back, my skin flushed and tingling. Jax takes a moment to clean up, then flops down on the bed next to me with one arm over his head like he's some sort of swimsuit model. And honestly, with that body, he could be.

We look to each other at the same time then share a giddy laugh.

"Sounds like you had a good time," he says with a cocky grin. "I bet you didn't expect multiple orgasms when you came into the bar today."

I give him an exaggerated eye roll and a playful elbow to

his ribs. "I didn't expect to run into you at all. And I come at least three times when I'm on a solo mission, so slow your roll there, cowboy."

Jax chuckles and pokes me back. "Guess I'll have to make up for lost time—and try to beat your record."

On one hand, I'm glad he's already thinking about round two. I didn't see anything going past tonight . . . but with a body like his and a performance like that, I'm considering it.

On the other hand, I'm slightly annoyed. When did a woman's pleasure become about men's own sexual capabilities? Like our bodies are some game to master, stroking their egos as much as their cocks.

"I should get going. My parents are probably wondering where I am."

"Or," he says, trailing a finger down my arm. "You could text them to let them know you won't be there tonight. We could order a pizza, watch some trash TV, go for round two, maybe have a quickie in the morning, and then you can shower here and I'll drive you back to your car?"

I grin, turning onto my side and propping myself up on an elbow. I regard Jax in all of his sexiness as I mull his enticing plan over in my head. It's incredibly validating to have Jax yearning for me. I've come so far from where I was in high school, no longer pretending to be someone I'm not just to fit in. This version of me is authentic, real, and true—and I've attracted the very person I once thought was out of reach.

Leaning in, I plant a slow kiss on his lips. "I like the sound of that."

Maybe these next two weeks won't be so bad.

INT. JENNA'S APARTMENT - DAY

Annie and Jenna are sitting on the couch, folding cloth diapers as baby Henry plays on the floor.

                    ANNIE
          Never in my life have I been treated so
          poorly at an establishment. And during
          Christmas, of all times!

                    JENNA
          I know, and I've tried going somewhere else,
          but their coffee is divine. Seriously! Have
          you tasted it?

Annie sips coffee.

                    ANNIE
          Okay, you're right, that's the best coffee I've
          ever tasted. But at what cost? Now I have to
          go back there after he was so rude to me.

                    JENNA
          What he lacks in customer service he
          makes up for in cuteness, am I right?

                    ANNIE
          I didn't notice.

Jenna playfully pushes Annie.

                    JENNA
          Oh, come on! I'm happily married to the
          love of my life and have the world's most
          perfect baby—

Baby Henry coos.

> JENNA (CONT'D)
> But even I can't help but drool into
> my latte when I pick it up from him every
> morning.

> ANNIE
> A person that grumpy could never be attractive
> to me. And I could never be with someone who
> hates Christmas. It's the best time of year!
> Besides, I have my great life in Seattle, I
> can't get wrapped up in something here.

> JENNA
> I thought your job at the firm was
> stressing you out.

> ANNIE
> I'm a lawyer. No matter where I work, I'll
> be stressed out.

> JENNA
> True. (beat) I still can't believe you
> decided to be a lawyer.

> ANNIE
> Why wouldn't I be?

> JENNA
> I remember growing up you loved your
> Easy-Bake Oven so much. I thought
> for sure you'd end up being a baker.

ANNIE

As fun and more relaxing as baking
would be, it wouldn't pay enough to
support my lifestyle in the city.
I'm lucky I have such a well-paying
job. Do I work all the time? Yes. Am I
stressed out? For sure. Is being a
lawyer like having an endless amount of
homework? Yes. But a girl's got to eat.
Besides, you've tasted my baking. There's a
reason I never graduated past the Easy-Bake.

JENNA

I'm sure if you worked at it you'd
be great, though. Maybe you just need
to take some lessons.

ANNIE

I don't have time to take baking lessons.
I'll stick to my store-bought cookies for
now. It's nice just being here with you
and taking a break from my busy schedule.
As much as I love the city, being here
reminds me that slowing down would be
nice one day, too.

Chapter 5
ELLIE

"**G**ood morning!" I singsong as I swing open the door at the top of the stairs. It's bright and early and not quite hot out yet, so my Christmas sweater hasn't drenched me in a layer of sweat. I bounce into the room, full of vigour and excitement for the first day of filming.

I'm early. There's no one else here except Jimmie, a few other backstage people, and Mariah. She's at our makeup stand, leaning toward the mirror and applying mascara.

"Hey now, don't use up all your skills on yourself." I bounce up behind Mariah and meet her gaze in the mirror.

She casts me a quick glance then returns her focus to the mirror. "Morning."

Not a morning person, apparently. That's okay. I'm morning enough for the both of us. She's dressed in her usual black attire, leggings and a tight long-sleeve shirt, but something doesn't fit in.

"Why are you wearing a scarf?" I tilt my head as I regard the bright red garment.

She shrugs her shoulders to her ears. "No reason."

My mouth drops open and I clap in excitement. "I knew it! It's happening!"

She looks mildly panicked. "What?"

"You're getting into the Christmas spirit!" I squeal and clench my fists.

Her mouth contorts into a disgusted frown. "Oh god no, nothing like that."

I twirl with the end of the scarf around my fingers. "Then what's with this?"

She regards me as if I'm an annoying toddler who recently

learned the word *why*; it's an expression I get often. I maintain my smile, holding out, knowing that she'll break before I do.

Finally, she sighs, casts a glance around, and then pulls down the edge of the scarf to reveal a bright purple hickey.

I gasp, but she gives me a death glare, so I stifle it with my hands. "Ma-*ri*-ah!" I give her arm a playful slap, and lo and behold I earn a fraction of a smile. My first Mariah smile! I should get an award.

Okay, it's more a smirk than a smile, but it's something.

Mariah readjusts the scarf. "I didn't notice it when I was getting ready this morning and I don't have my shade here."

Ah, yes, a makeup artist who's covering up a hickey with props from the costume department must not be in the most comfortable predicament. "Say less," I say, settling into my chair. "Your secret is safe with me."

"Thanks," she replies, softening.

"But also . . ." I widen my eyes and lean forward, catching her attention through the mirror. "Say *more*! Who's the lucky person? Have you known them for long? Is this an old fling, or a new one? Did you make it past the neck area? Did you—" I click my tongue and whistle.

Aha! Another smile! I'm on a roll here.

"It's new. Sort of."

"Ooh, rekindling an old flame?"

"Something like that."

"Go on . . ."

She sighs, like I've broken down some sort of barrier, and after a moment she relents. "We went to high school together. We didn't really know each other, though. I didn't think he even knew I existed back then."

"Well, he definitely does now!" I lift my fist for her to bump. She eyes it for a moment, then returns it in the most limp-wristed, half-assed way possible. I'm still calling it a win.

Mariah begins prepping my face with the clear goop, the soft pads of her fingers massaging circles over my cheeks, my forehead, my nose. "I was at the bar avoiding my . . . I was at the bar having a drink and he was there. The bartender."

"Oh my god, you got to live out the ultimate fantasy. Second-chance romance *and* sexy small-town bartender!"

"Right?" She seems to pick up on my energy, talking with a bit more animation while keeping her voice low so no one overhears. "He's tall, and chiselled, and has this confidence that radiates off him. He's always had a lot of charisma. Like he walks into the room and you can feel his presence, you know?"

"Mmm-hmm, do I ever."

Mariah switches to a brush, squirting some light tan liquid onto it before swooping it over my face in effortless, practised motions. "One thing led to another, and then we were back at his place, and he . . . yeah." Her face flushes pink.

I bite my lip and try my hardest not to squeal, but it's challenging. "Oh my god, no! You didn't!"

She raises an eyebrow. "Oh, but we did. A few times."

"Damn, girl! You're like, my hero right now."

"Thank you." She lifts her chin.

"You know, you have the radiant skin of a person who's had great sex."

I say it a little too loudly and she shushes me, but the half smile still on her face tells me she's not mad. I like Mariah on sex. She's in a way better mood today than she was yesterday.

"Well, I hope whatever this guy is doing to you, he keeps doing it. Because damn." I wave my hand in a flourish, directed at her reflection in the mirror, and she glows from the compliment.

"I hope he keeps doing it, too," she replies.

We fall into a companionable, comfortable silence. *Thank god.* The next two weeks will be so much better if we have some sort of working friendship. I knew I'd win her over eventually; some people just take more time.

"I may have met someone, too," I say as she steps back to eye her handiwork.

"Oh?" Seeming satisfied with the tan liquid, she says, "Close," pointing to my eyes.

I follow her orders, continuing to talk. "Yeah, his name is Matt and he takes care of the Airbnb I'm renting and last night I was decorating the cabin with my Christmas lights and I plugged too many things in and I shorted out a breaker and I couldn't find the panel so I texted the number on the app and this guy showed up and ohmygod he was so handsome and he came in and fixed my breaker, but not in a porno way, like the real way, turns out the electrical box was hidden behind a picture, which is smart, they're not exactly nice to look at, and after he kind of flirted with me, and he was like, clumsy, you know, he couldn't take his eyes off me, and he tripped when backing out, and yeah."

Mariah pauses what she's doing. After a couple seconds I open my eyes to look at her, and she's . . . laughing. It's a weird silent laugh, just her shoulders shaking while she covers her mouth, followed a weird chesty inhale.

I got her to laugh!

Mariah takes a step back to compose herself, giving her head a shake. Well, if that isn't the most rewarding thing to happen to me in a long time. I grin back at her, pleased beyond belief.

Finally, she touches the corner of her eye and exhales a slow breath. "You're hilarious. I don't even know where to start on that one, but I'm glad you . . . flirted with a guy and you think he's cute."

My eyes widen. "Maybe we'll both have a small-town Christmas romance and get swept away by the perfect guy and live out the rest of our lives in peaceful bliss with a chicken coop and some fainting goats and bake our own sourdough bread!"

Mariah gives me a pointed look. "Or, you know, not that. The opposite maybe."

I nod. "Yes. Or the opposite."

Yueyi walks up while Mariah is pulling my hair into a bun. "What are you doing here?"

Mariah pauses. "Me?"

She shakes her head. "We don't have you on set today, Ellie. We had to move you. Late notice. You don't have any scenes until Thursday."

"Oh." My eyes dart from Mariah to Yueyi and back, my face warming. "Right. Of course."

Yueyi says nothing. She walks past, onto the next item on her endless to-do list.

As soon as she's gone, I sigh, collapsing into my chair. This is so typical. I should be used to getting shuffled around and pushed aside.

"Hey," Mariah says, nudging my arm.

I look at her through the mirror. The concern on her face makes me squirm. Then, I look at myself. I'm pale, washed out, my hair looks like I gave zero shits when I got up this morning—and I'm not even supposed to be here. But none of this is Mariah's fault, and it's not fair to her to put up with me and my mistakes and bad moods.

After a quick breath, I straighten and force a smile to my face. "You know? It's fine. I wanted to explore Chilliwack anyway. It's a beautiful day. Maybe I'll go visit the park, or the library, or—"

"How about I do your makeup?" Mariah interrupts.

I gesture at my face in the mirror. "You already did."

"No, like for real."

"Are you sure? You have time?"

She shrugs. "It won't take long."

I sit up a little straighter. "Okay. Thank you."

Mariah gets to work, moving with much more energy than before, telling me to close my eyes and open them and close my mouth and open it and five minutes later I barely recognize myself in the mirror. My eyes are lined in black with smoky brown on the lids, making them seem twice as big. There is a sharp angle to my jaw, my cheekbones stand out, and everything is just . . .

"Wow," I manage.

Mariah lifts her chin. "There you go. Now, why don't you go call up that Mitch guy—"

"Matt."

"Why don't you call up Matt and invite him over. See what happens?" She leans toward me, talking in my ear. "Take your relationship from G-rated to X."

I shiver at the sensation of her breath on my neck, at the places my imagination goes with the mention of X-rated things and Matt.

"You know what?" I look at myself with the kind of confidence I haven't felt in a long time. "I think I will."

As SOON AS I'm back in my cabin, I march to the stove, pull it inch by inch away from the wall, hoist myself up onto the counter, lean down, and unplug it. I've barely pushed it back into place by the time I'm texting Matt.

> **ME:** hey! Sorry to bother you again, but the stove is acting up. Is there a secret to getting it to work?

The bait has been set. While I wait for him to reply, I twirl past all the twinkling lights in the main room of the cabin into the bedroom. I remove my sweaty Christmas sweater and pull on a much sexier, and still somewhat seasonal, red tank top.

My phone dings.

> **MATT:** hey, I'll be right over ☺

The bait has been taken!

Casting a glance in the mirror, I give myself a sultry look, fully embracing the character of the woman who eyes me back. She's confident. She's sexy. She knows exactly what she wants and how to take it. And that's what she's going to do.

I busy myself straightening up while humming "Santa Baby" until there's a polite knock on the door. After a quick excited squeak I saunter to the door, adjust my posture (shoulders back, tits out), and open it.

Matt's eyes pop when he sees me. "Oh, hey . . . Ellie. Wow, you look—" His eyes wander down my body then back to my face.

I smile, giving my bottom lip a calculated bite. "Hey, Matt. Thanks so much for coming over on such short notice."

He blinks several times then averts his gaze. "Yeah, no problem. The, uh, stove?"

I step aside and let him in. He's a little more cleaned up today than he was yesterday, his scruff trimmed neatly along his jaw to form a fledgling beard. His sportsball cap has been replaced by a small man-bun, leaving it up to my imagination how long his hair actually is—is it Kit Harrington long, or Jason Momoa long? Either way, I'm here for it. As he brushes past, I get a whiff of his cologne, which is deeply earthy, constricting my throat as I inhale. There's definitely a constriction lower down, too.

I close the door and allow myself the privilege of checking out his ass, on full display with a pair of tight knee-length shorts. His shirt is a little snug, wrapping around his broad chest and back, falling loose around his middle. He helps himself to the kitchen and begins inspecting the appliance.

I lean against the counter and watch. "Sorry to keep pestering you like this."

"It's really no problem." He smiles, his kind brown eyes alighting on my face and seeming to get stuck there. Our eyes meet and he pauses what he's doing. My heart flutters and there's a twinge of heat that lights up in my belly. His smile deepens, as if picking up on the effect he has on me and the natural connection between us.

"I think I know what to do here." His voice is low, rumbling in his throat.

I lean a little closer. "What's that?"

"The power's out." He turns back to the stove.

"Oh."

He shimmies the stove away from the wall and bends behind it. "That's weird." He grabs the dangling cord and plugs it back into the wall.

Well, that took him all of ten seconds to figure out, and I don't have a backup plan to keep him around. Matt shoves the stove back into place and dusts off his hands on his shorts.

"Wow, it was unplugged this whole time? That's odd." I take a breath and channel the inner vixen that matches the makeup on my face. "But hey, since you're here and I have a working oven, I was about to pop a pizza in. Do you want to stay? I can't eat a whole pizza by myself."

He tucks his thumbs into the pockets of his shorts and slouches a bit, bringing his face closer to mine. "Yeah, sure. I have to work later, but I have some time." He smiles again, eyes twinkling. "And it's been forever since I've had pizza."

"Great!" I lean past him to turn the oven on, my arm intentionally brushing his.

"So, how's the movie going?" he asks, taking a step toward the living room.

"So far so good. It's hard to tell while we're filming how it'll all come together, but I have faith in our team. I've worked with them before, and they've always delivered amazing results." I refrain from telling him I haven't actually filmed any of my scenes yet. "What's your favourite Christmas movie?"

He turns toward me, the corner of his mouth tilted up. "*Die Hard.*"

I chuckle. "That is such a guy thing to say."

"What about you?"

"Ooh, tough question. If I had to pick, I'd say . . . *The Muppet Christmas Carol.*"

He thinks for a moment. "I don't think I've ever seen it."

"What!" I slap his arm, which earns a playful smile. "How could you have not seen it? It's a classic! Did you know it is widely considered to be the best Dickens adaptation?"

"A Muppet movie?"

"Yes! And Michael Caine's performance? It's top-notch. He's a method actor, like myself."

"I have to admit, I'm intrigued." He takes a step closer.

"Why don't I go get it? Not sure if you have time for a whole movie, but I simply cannot live knowing you've never had the chance to experience the magic of *The Muppet Christmas Carol*."

He chuckles. "Let's do it."

I clench my fists at my side in excitement. "I have hot chocolate and peppermint Baileys. Want one?"

"It's July."

I flash him some finger guns. "Not in here it isn't."

His grins. "I'd love one."

I contain my squeal of delight as I disappear into the bedroom for a moment to grab the VHS tape from the box in my bedroom closet. I start it up, the cheerful sounds of jingle bells filling the room. Matt settles onto the couch as I pop the pizza into the oven and heat milk in a pot. By the time Gonzo and Rizzo are off on their adventure with the ghost of Christmas Past, I'm finished my preparations, with two steaming hot mugs of cocoa and an oven-baked pepperoni pizza on the coffee table.

Matt looks comfortable on the couch, his legs splayed apart in that way men do. I settle beside him, leaving a half inch of space between us.

I grab my mug and hoist it toward him. "Cheers!"

He taps his against mine, smiling. "Cheers."

We both take a sip. It's the perfect amount of hot and sweet, the creamy mint coating my tongue and throat, warming my belly. I hum a satisfied "Mmm-mmm-*mmm*!"

He chuckles, his cheeks turning pink.

"What?" I say, laughing at myself.

"Nothing, it's just . . ." He takes a moment to regard me, his eyes lingering on my lips. "You're really cute."

I flush bright red, my insides turning to goop. "Thanks. You're pretty cute, too."

The rest of the movie passes as we chat about Christmas, movies, Chilliwack, and how he's lived his whole life here. I learn that he has three jobs and is saving to travel, and tell him about my goals and ambitions as an actress. We drink our hot chocolate, nibble our pizza, and occasionally pause talking to watch the movie, all while inching closer and closer to each other. By the time the movie ends, my legs are resting on top of his lap and our sides are pressed together.

"How random is it that of all the cabins I could have rented, I picked this one?" I ask, speaking low and quiet, not wanting to break the spell that's settled over us.

"I don't think it's random at all."

"No?"

He gives his head a slow shake, then reaches up, tucking a tendril of hair behind my ear. "I must have been a pretty good person in my past life for karma to bring you my way."

I fucking melt. I don't necessarily believe in karma, and I know from a Canadian Bollywood-style indie film I acted in a few years ago that karma is a much more complicated process than the common Western appropriative context, but I appreciate the sentiment.

"I feel pretty lucky, too," I admit. "It feels like so many things had to align for us to meet. The movie I'm filming, the Christmas lights, the old electrical in this place—"

He chuckles, nodding along.

"We could have very easily not met at all."

"But we did," he counters.

I nod. "But we did."

A tense silence builds as we draw closer. There's a thrumming in the base of my belly, increasing in intensity with every second. His throat bobs as his eyes fall to my lips, which part ever so slightly, welcoming him. I feel nearly dizzy with anticipation, my heart pounding in my ears, and—

His phone rings. The spell breaks and Matt pulls back, eyeing the device as it dings away. "That's my alarm." He gives me an apologetic half smile.

I shrug, masking my disappointment. "We knew this time would come."

He turns off the alarm and looks at me one more time, then gives my thigh a quick squeeze before standing. I follow him, waiting as he toes his shoes on and opens the door. He pauses in the doorway, the bright July afternoon sun illuminating his tall frame from behind.

"Look, Ellie," he says, glancing up from his shoes back to me.

My heart thuds in my chest. Nothing good ever happens after someone starts off with *look*. Unless it's *look, there's an ice cream truck*. I swallow, bracing for the opposite. "Yeah?"

"I don't want to make you feel uncomfortable or do something inappropriate, especially given the circumstances of you renting the cabin. Just say the word and I'll leave you alone, but . . ." He takes a deep breath, then meets my gaze. "I think you're really cute and I'd like to see you again, if that's okay."

Squeezing my fists together at my sides, I contain as much of my excitement as I possibly can and keep my face set to a measured smile rather than the full-out grin tugging at my cheeks. "I'd like that," I somehow manage to reply in a cool and even tone.

His smile lights up his face. "Cool. Text me when you're free."

I nod. "Will do."

He gives me a knowing, playful look. "Without breaking anything this time."

"What!" I gasp in mock offence, pressing my hand to my chest. "I would never do anything so—"

Matt cuts me off, bridging the gap between us and pressing

his lips against mine in a chaste kiss. He pulls away, a naughty smirk on his face and a fire in his eyes. He walks back to his truck, leaving me flushed with heat and wanting more. My lips burn from where he touched them, a wildfire of tingles running down my body from the quick moment of contact.

After watching him drive away in his truck, giving me one last shy wave before backing away, I shut the door and lean against it. I feel dazed, almost lightheaded from the interaction.

I can't believe after all this time, after so many years of watching love stories unfold around me, it's actually happening. I've met the perfect guy, and he's going to fall madly in love with me and whisk me away from the big city, like in every modern-day fairy-tale romance.

This is *so* main character energy of me.

INT. BREWED AWAKENING CAFÉ - DAY

Annie enters the café to order lattes.

James is running the till and there's a lineup of people getting their drinks. James doesn't greet anyone, doesn't wish Merry Christmas, and is very abrupt and rude.

Barista is sweeping the floor in the background, pausing to wave to Annie.

Annie waves back.

Annie's turn arrives and she steps up to the counter.

                    ANNIE
          Good morning and Merry Christmas!

                    JAMES
          What can I get you.

                    ANNIE
          Wow, great customer service. Five stars.

                    JAMES
          You want coffee or not?

                    ANNIE
          I want a bit of hospitality with my drink.

                    JAMES
          Order your drink and leave, or just
          leave. I won't stand for harassment.

ANNIE

Is asking for the bare minimum of social
interaction from a local business at
Christmastime harassment?

JAMES

I don't have time for this.

ANNIE

If anything, you're the one harassing all
these nice people by not greeting them
with kindness and wishing them well
for supporting your business.

JAMES

No one else has a problem with the way
I run my business.

ANNIE

That's because they're all scared of you.
I'm sure everyone here would love
a bit of Christmas cheer, some red and
green sprinkles on their lattes,
the smell of pumpkin spice. Heck
I bet they'd even settle for a
smile at this point!

Annie gestures to the other guests, who eye her
uncertainly.

JAMES

You're disturbing my customers. Please
see yourself out. You can get your coffee
elsewhere.

Annie gasps.

                    ANNIE
          You're refusing to serve me?

                    JAMES
          Don't make me ask you twice.

Annie looks around at other guests in the café, but
they avoid her gaze.

The barista cringes and mouths the word "Sorry."

                    ANNIE
          Fine. I'll go somewhere else, somewhere
          with some decency. You're not the only café
          in this town, you know.

                    JAMES
          Good luck with that. Next!

                    ANNIE
          (walking away)
          You lost a customer today. I hope
          you're happy.

                    JAMES
          Good riddance.

Chapter 6
MARIAH

*I*t was a full day of hair and makeup. There were a lot of extras to get ready after Ellie left, and I was on my feet with no break to eat or pee for four hours. Not unusual in my line of work, but after all that my feet and back ache. Luckily the hair part of it was minimal, as most of the extras were wearing toques. After cleaning my station and grabbing a chocolate muffin from the refreshment table, I return the borrowed scarf and beeline out of there for my lunch break before anyone can see the massive purple welt under my jawline.

I feel so dumb for missing the hickey this morning when I was getting ready, but Jax had kept me properly distracted up until I had to leave. The guy's got some stamina, and my back and legs aren't the only things that are sore from it.

My car is parked down the street, and inside is my duffel with the heavy-duty shit I normally don't need day-to-day. I dig around for a moment, then find the green-tinted cream foundation to cancel out the reds and purples on my skin. Using my rear-view mirror, I inspect the state of my neck. *Oof, he really went to town.* After rubbing a little in, then blending with my regular foundation, I look good as new. Though I do miss the visual reminder of Jax's lips and our fun night together.

As far as one-night stands go, that was a top experience. He knew what he was doing, evidently having had a lot of practice since high school. Thinking of it, he'd had a lot of practice then, too. Maybe we'll turn our one-evening event into a two-week romp to keep me entertained through the slog of this god-awful Christmas job.

My ringing phone disrupts my thoughts. The momentary high of thinking it might be Jax is immediately crushed upon seeing that it's my mother. I guess she's learned that I don't pick up the phone before noon. With a preparative sigh, I answer it.

"Hey."

"Hey, sweetie!" *Sweetie? Ugh.* "How'd filming go today?"

"Good, I guess." I take a bite of my muffin and talk with a semi-muffled voice. "Assuming it's going as well as it could, given the fact that it's a low-budget holiday B movie."

She caws a laugh, and I hold the receiver away from my ear for a moment. "I'm just at the store and was wondering if you still like Cap'n Crunch for your breakfast cereal?"

"Mom, you never let me eat Cap'n Crunch. Said it was bad for my teeth."

"It *is* bad for your teeth. But you're an adult now and pay for your own dentist." She caws her laugh again.

I rub my eyes. "Toast is fine. Eggs. Whatever you have. Don't buy anything special for me."

"Okay, well, I just want to make sure you feel at home here." *When have I ever felt at home there?* "Thanks."

"When are you . . . What time will you be here?"

As if on cue, my phone dings with a text. I pull it away from my ear and glance at it, and my heart stutters at the message.

> **JAX:** wanna visit me at work later? It gets slow around 7.

"Actually, Mom . . . uh, the . . . director and production people are all taking us out to dinner when we're done filming tonight."

"Oh, really?"

"Yeah, I guess yesterday not everyone was there and they planned a dinner for after the first full day of filming. To celebrate." It's weird how lying to my mom doesn't feel bad. If anything, I feel bad that I don't feel bad about it.

"Oh, okay. Well, that's great! Rubbing elbows with all the bigwigs. Exciting."

"Yeah, yeah. Anyway, I'll let you know when I'm on my way home, okay?"

"Okay. See you soon."

"Bye."

I hang up the phone and immediately text Jax back.

ME: sounds like fun. Maybe I'll swing by if I'm not busy.

I already know I won't be.

Checking the time, I see I still have twenty minutes before I'm due back on set, but I can't sit in my car any longer. It's already stiflingly hot in here, even with the windows rolled down. My mind whirs through the options this small city has and the places I used to frequent. Without fail, there was always one spot that was my safe space growing up, and luckily, it's right down the street.

I lock my car before stepping back out into the blazing sunshine, walking past the set on the other side of the blue mesh fencing. Through the crowd and film equipment, I spot Julia and Oscar casually wandering down the street with a stroller, decked in winter gear despite the heat. They must be sweating buckets under all those layers. I continue past, cross the street, and leave the hubbub of the film set behind. I walk along the sidewalk until I see a familiar sign beckoning me forward.

The Bookman.

I step under the bookstore's awning with its colourful Pride flag fluttering in the breeze, past the cart of one-dollar books on sale, and open the door, which greets me with a dinging bell. The smell of old books and aged building welcome me with a wave of nostalgia so potent my stomach tightens and rises into my chest, triggering a prickle of tears somewhere behind my eyes.

It hasn't changed one bit.

A young twentysomething-year-old with thick glasses, orange hair, and a vintage death-metal T-shirt greets me with a nod and a smile as I walk past. To my left is a shelf with all the famous BookTok books, to my right the children's section, complete with a cozy nook for reading. I continue past the glass display cases filled with bookish bric-a-brac, teas, and candles, turn left past the next shelves, and head over to the corner where the adoptable cats are housed. I pause to stroke the head of a grey tabby, who twitches her tail back and forth while lying atop a stack of books.

I feel just as at home here now as I did when I was a kid. There's just something about books and cats that are safe.

I let my fingers trail over the bumps and ridges of book spines as I wander the aisles like I did when I was a teen, when I felt so lost, so broken, so alone, and had nowhere where I felt like I could be myself. I'd felt a smidgen of my true self here, lost in this sea of words, knowing that every person who put themselves into a book must have been a little like me—a little different, trying to make sense of the world, trying to find a way to share who they were with others without being too vulnerable, too open, letting anyone get too close.

Letting someone in only leads to pain.

I pause my reminiscing when I come across someone in the aisle with me. Normally I'd mutter a quick *excuse me* and move past, but this person's face has me doing a double take. It's familiar, but just different enough that . . .

Oh shit.

It's Bethany.

I thought I'd had my fill of high school run-ins with Jax. I'd got lucky with him, fate taking a surprising turn from what could have been an awkward situation to a satisfying romp.

But nothing good can come from this.

Bethany looks the same. Still blonde, though her hair is a bit shorter. She's still perfectly proportioned, though a bit curvier. I wonder if she's still a mean bitch who makes fun of people's cellulite in gym changing rooms. Maybe she has some of her own now.

I wonder what she'd think if she knew I fucked her ex-boyfriend.

Even though she was mean, befriending the bully and pretending to fit in helped me survive high school. I can't imagine how cruel she would have been to me if I'd actually been myself. And if she'd known I was queer? I might not have survived at all.

Bethany looks up from her perusal through the romance section, meeting my gaze. "Sorry," she says, her smile creasing her brows. "Am I in your way?"

I eye her, waiting for the shoe to drop, for her to recognize me and blow my cover and force me to go through the whole song and dance of *What have you been up to?* and *Is it really you?* and the always nauseating rendition of *I've been living a perfect life ever since high school and everything has been so easy, let me tell you all about it!*

But it doesn't happen.

"No," I say after a second. "I'm going this way." I point over my shoulder, turn on my heel, and disappear down another aisle.

I can't believe she didn't recognize me. Sure, my hair is different, and my clothes are different, and . . . well, everything is different. But Jax had recognized me almost immediately. Maybe he'd been paying closer attention to me in high school than I'd thought. My stomach flutters at the idea.

Before Bethany can get another look, I beeline for the discount books outside the front doors. I scan the stacks and pull out something familiar, careful not to cause an avalanche. The fore-edge is stained grey from thousands of page flips and the cover is bent and creased, but it's unmistakably the same book I'd read a dozen times as a teenager.

Seems fitting; nostalgia is hitting hard today.

I take *Jade Green: A Ghost Story* to the till and pay with a loonie and other loose change, then duck out of the bookstore and back into the sunshine.

Book in hand, I walk back to set and make my way toward

the film area where Jimmie and the other crew are seated behind the screens. It's interesting to see what goes on back here,
between lighting and sound techs and all the other people
making sure filming runs smoothly. For the first time since taking the job, I feel like I'm actually learning something. We keep
an eye on the monitors and rush out between takes to touch
up makeup and hair as needed, but mostly it's a lot of sitting
around. While everyone else is checking their phones and chatting, I read snippets of my book and am met with the familiar
haunting tale, which grips me the same way it did when I was
in fifth grade. The scene I remember most clearly is when Judith Sparrow is riding in a horse-drawn wagon with her love
interest and sweat trickles between her breasts.

I clench my thighs together with the imagery, recalling how
this book was my first inkling of knowing I was bisexual. It
wasn't until Rachel McAdams in *The Notebook* that I was certain.

The scene reminds me of a certain someone else whose
sweaty breasts I'd been ogling the other day. She's not on set
today, and for a split second I almost miss her zany energy before shaking the brief thought from my head.

By the time I finish my book it's wrap time. One more hour
until I can see Jax.

Part of me considers telling him I ran into Bethany. We
could laugh about how she had no idea who I was and what
she'd think if she knew about us.

But the last thing I want is to remind him of who I used to be.

After cleaning up and being released by Jimmie, I get back
into my car and drive through the closest A&W to scarf down
a quick burger, fries, and root beer. Wouldn't want my stomach rumbling if things get spicy. *When* they get spicy, that is.

After brushing my teeth with a bottle of water and spitting
out onto the pavement, I touch up my makeup and reapply de-
odorant. Jeez, I feel like I'm eighteen again, living out of my
car. I drive to the bar and steel myself, trying to summon the

air of someone who didn't check the clock every five minutes in anticipation of a booty call, then walk inside with all the confidence and ease I can muster.

It's busier in Grumpy Joe's today, with several older blue-collar gentleman sitting at tables with sandwiches and pints, playing keno games and quietly chatting.

Jax is behind the bar, standing out like a blinking neon sign in this drab environment. He spots me immediately, his neutral, bored expression morphing into a smouldering smirk. I remain stoic and cool as I take my usual seat at the bar.

"What'll it be, ma'am?" he asks.

I sputter in mock offence. "Excuse me? Do I look like a ma'am to you?"

He leans on the bar as his eyes hungrily assess my cleavage. "No, you do not."

"Then behave, or I'll leave."

His eyes snap up to mine. "*You* behave, and I'll show you a spot in the back where there aren't any cameras."

My lower half clenches at the idea. I lift my chin. "Fine. I'll . . . *behave.*"

He grins. "I'm sure you will."

Jax quickly scans the bar, then, deciding it's safe, nods his head toward the doorway behind the bar to the staff area. He lets me lead the way, walking through a hallway with shelving on one side holding various goods for the bar and kitchen. I turn around, not sure where Jax wants me to go, but he's right behind me and I run into his hard chest. His strong hands grip both of my upper arms as he pushes me back several steps, then presses me against the wall.

He looks left, right, then down at me. "There's a camera blind spot right here. They'll never know what I'm about to do to you. It'll be our dirty little secret."

I like the sound of that far too much. "Is that so? Tell me, Jax, what is it you're about to do to me?" I pull my arms away from him and grip the back of his neck.

He squeezes my hips, then reaches lower, grabbing my ass and hoisting me up so my legs wrap around his waist. He grinds against me, already hard, our breath intermingling. "I'd rather show you."

His mouth meets mine, tongue seeking, and I oblige, starving for connection. Our kisses grow more fervent, and the throbbing need between my thighs gets desperate. Jax isn't in a hurry, despite being on the clock. It's easy to forget that there's a whole world outside when he's against me like this, so close, and yet not where I need him to be.

"I've been thinking about you all day," he says, removing his lips from mine and kissing my throat.

I snort. "Liar. And easy on the neck."

He pulls away, inspecting it. "I distinctly remember leaving a hickey here."

"I almost got caught with it at work."

"Good," he growls, nipping my ear. "I hoped everyone would see it. Then they'd know you belong to me."

I swat his arm with one hand while digging my nails into his shoulder with the other. "You're such a possessive alpha-hole."

He grinds his hard length against me, and I gasp at the friction. "You like it."

I scratch my fingers up his biceps, making him shudder. I absolutely do.

Our kissing turns frenzied, and I wiggle out of his embrace, lowering my feet back to the ground. I unbuckle his belt and reach into his pants to grip his cock. He groans, his eyes squeezing shut, and he throbs in my hand. He tugs at my pants and I unbutton them, pulling them down to my ankles.

"Condom?" I manage to utter.

He nods, taking one from his back pocket and ripping it open. He lowers his pants to his thighs and his cock springs free, which he quickly clads. "Turn around."

I follow his command, pressing my front against the wall. He manoeuvres himself behind me and I help guide him, both of us gasping as he fills me. He pumps slowly, drawing it out, building heat.

"More," I beg.

He listens, one hand reaching forward to squeeze my breast, the other down lower, cupping me, his fingers rotating over my clit in circles. I make a gasping, mewling sound, and the hand on my breast moves to cover my mouth instead.

"There may not be cameras," he whispers in my ear, "but people can still hear you. You have to be quiet for me. Can you do that?"

I nod against his hand.

"Good girl."

Oh, fuck.

Jax pumps vigorously as one hand rubs, keeping the other clenched tight over my mouth. I come right then and there, my quiet moans stifled against his hand as my body quickly tightens and releases with a powerful, dizzying force. Jax holds on long enough to wait for my release before finding his own, pressing his mouth into the crook of my neck as he does.

We pause, all laboured breathing and beating hearts, while our bodies come down from their highs. Jax removes himself and takes off the condom, tossing it into a receptacle behind him, then pulls up his pants while I do the same.

He meets my gaze, and we share a quiet giggle, our surroundings coming back to us in a flash.

"I should probably get back to work," he says.

I know he doesn't have any other option, but it still hurts to be fucked and left so quickly. I nod. "I understand."

He regards me a moment. "How about you go back to my place, wait for me there?"

I blink several times. "What? Are you sure?"

"Sure," he says with a shrug. "Then I have something to look forward to after work."

I eye him with suspicion. "Do you normally let strange women into your house without you there?"

"No. But you're not a stranger. We've known each other since we were kids."

"We didn't *really* know each other."

"Then we should make up for that now. We've missed a lot of time together. I just feel like—" his thumb caresses the length of my jaw as his eyes search mine "—there's something special about you."

My heart fucking melts.

"Wait here," he says. "I keep my keys under the till."

Jax disappears for a moment and returns, removing a key from a long red lanyard then handing it over to me.

"Are you sure about this?" I ask, weighing the cool metal in my hand.

"I am. Make yourself comfortable, I'll be home shortly after midnight, unless it's slow like it was yesterday and I can close up earlier."

A wave of relief hits me; I don't have to go back to my parents' house. I'm safe for one more night. And there's another feeling there, too, something I didn't expect to find when I walked into this bar, let alone when I drove back to Chilliwack. I gaze into Jax's eyes; they're soft and warm and relaxed from his orgasm, and I feel . . . feelings. Of some sort. I'm not sure how to name them, or how to organize them in my brain, but the fluttery sensation in my belly and the squeeze in my chest is telling me that maybe there's more to Jax than just being a fun lay and a way to get an old crush out of my system.

I consider his offer. "Jax?"

"Yeah?"

"I live in Vancouver. I'm never coming back to Chilliwack. You know that, right?"

"It's not like Vancouver is that far away, Mariah."

I'm caught off guard by his response. *Has he already thought of visiting me?*

"I missed out on getting to know you all those years ago. I was young, and stupid, and you were . . ."

I wait for him to say *weird, different, trying too hard to fit in . . .*

"You were intimidating."

I'm stunned into silence.

Jax smiles, his eyes darting from mine and down to his hands. *Is he nervous?* "You seemed wiser. Intelligent. More mature than the rest of us, in a way."

"Are you sure that's not just because I 'matured' before everyone else?" I gesture to my chest.

He rolls his eyes with a sardonic smile. "I knew there was more to you than meets the eye. I'd be lying if your other 'maturities' didn't catch my attention, as well as the attention of all the other guys in school, but I saw past that. I remember one time at a house party—Darren Freidman's garage, remember that place?"

I nod. *How could I forget?* The smell of stale beer and motor oil permanently embedded into the stained concrete, the tinny boom box in the corner always blasting Eminem, and haphazard seating made up of the back seat of someone's van and various mismatched lawn chairs. It seemed almost everyone had their firsts there: first time smoking pot, first time stealing from their parents' liquor cabinets, first kisses. I remember watching other people pair off at various points of the night to make out under the stars. Never me.

Jax continues. "Bethany and I had a fight. I don't even remember what it was about. She stormed off, nobody knew where she went. You were the only sober person there and you drove me around until we found her, then you parked and waited outside while we argued."

I remember there being more making out than arguing but don't interrupt.

"Anyone else would have just taken her home, probably talked shit about me behind my back." He shakes his head slowly. "But not you."

"You don't remember why she was mad at you?"

He shakes his head slowly. "No."

I run my tongue over my bottom lip. "She was mad at you for looking at my tits too much. Said it was inappropriate."

He chuckles. "She was always jealous of you."

I had never once in my life considered that possibility. I lean back against the wall, stunned.

Squeezing my hands, he says, "I think everything happens for a reason. I obviously wasn't ready for you back then. But you walked into this bar, out of all the bars in the city."

"And now here we are."

He grins. "Here we are."

I hadn't planned on taking this any further than my time here in Chilliwack, just a spicy distraction from my boring job. But now I want to see what this alternate reality has in store. "All right, then. I'll see you in a couple hours."

Jax smiles, then leaves me with a tender, dizzying kiss before returning to work.

INT. JENNA'S APARTMENT - DAY

Annie hands a cup of coffee to her sister.

Jenna takes a sip, then coughs and sputters. Jenna
eyes the coffee, face contorted with disgust.

                    JENNA
          What happened? Why did you go here instead
          of Brewed Awakening?

                    ANNIE
          I may have offended James, and he may have
          refused service to me.

                    JENNA
          Annie! I rely on that place to live. (beat)
          I guess I can go down there and get coffee.
          I'll just have to jump into the shower quickly
          while Henry is napping, and—

Baby Henry starts squalling in the next room.

Jenna sighs, rubs her eyes, exhausted.

                    JENNA (CONT'D)
          Never mind. I guess I can get Henry dressed
          after I feed him and take him with me. It's
          better than drinking this swill.

                    ANNIE
          No, it's okay. I came here to help you, not
          to make your life harder. I'll go apologize.
          Mind if I take this?

Annie gestures to an extra Christmas wreath on Jenna's counter.

INT. BREWED AWAKENING CAFÉ - DAY

Annie enters the café, which is quiet and empty.

The barista is cleaning the espresso machine.

                    ANNIE
     Hey, is your boss here? I was hoping to
     apologize for my behaviour earlier. I
     brought him a gift.

                    BARISTA
     You . . . brought him a gift?

                    ANNIE
     Yeah. He must have a reason for hating
     Christmas so much. But instead of taking
     the time to understand him, I was rude.
     I guess that's what I get for trying to
     interact with people prior to being
     caffeinated.

                    BARISTA
     Wow, no one's ever come back to
     apologize before.

                    ANNIE
     Does James scare off a lot of customers?

                    BARISTA
     Everyone's afraid of him. His customers,
     his remaining family, even the Small

Business Association, they all avoid him,
which only makes everything worse.
I'm worried he might lose his business.

                    ANNIE
Why would he lose his business?

                    BARISTA
Every year the Small Business Association
invites him to their Christmas party, and
every year he refuses. As good as his coffee
is, community support is important in this
town. I'm sure there are a lot of other
great businesses who would love to be in
a prime location like this, but they'd
be more community-oriented. And if James
loses the business, he loses the apartment.

Barista points up to the ceiling.

                    ANNIE
He lives upstairs? So does my sister.

                    BARISTA
Oh, your sister must be Jenna? With
the cute baby?

                    ANNIE
Yeah! Do you know her?

                    BARISTA
I've seen her around. James avoids her.

                    ANNIE
Oh. Why would he do that?

                         BARISTA
              He has a thing with babies.

                          ANNIE
         What kind of weirdo doesn't like babies?

They share a laugh.

                     ANNIE (CONT'D)
            What's your name, by the way?

                     BARISTA / KATE
              I'm Kate.

                          ANNIE
         Annie. How long have you worked here?

                          KATE
              I've been here forever. I remember
              way back before, when James would
              decorate this place. He made the best
              Christmas cookies, spent hours icing them.

                          ANNIE
              He can bake?

                         JENNA
              (nodding)
              He was an excellent baker. He'd bake
              dozens and dozens of cookies to sell in
              the café and give all the leftovers
              away at the Small Business Association
              Christmas party.

ANNIE

I can't imagine him at a party.

JENNA

Believe it or not, he used to be the life
of it. And he's an excellent dancer. He's
lost sight of what Christmas means, it seems.

ANNIE

Maybe he just needs to be reminded
of the true meaning of Christmas.

KATE

(smiling)
I think you might be right.

Chapter 7
ELLIE

I should be sad I'm not filming today—again. But I'm not, because last night Matt messaged me about seeing him again, this time for an official date! One side of me thinks he probably just wants to spare his appliances from my horny half-baked forced-proximity meet-cutes. The other side knows from the way he looked at me, the way he leaned against me during the movie, the way he couldn't help but give me a chaste kiss as he left, that he's just as eager for this date as I am.

Though I bet I require a lot more prep work than he does.

I get up early and exfoliate, then shave every hair off my body from the neck down, exfoliate again, scrub myself clean in the shower, and lotion every inch of my skin. Despite my best efforts, my unruly hair can't decide if it's wavy or curly and ends up looking like the same mess it always does. And my makeup is so poorly done I consider driving into town and paying Mariah a visit.

I can't wait to tell her about this tomorrow—my first official day of filming. I don't have any lines yet, but hey, at least I'm on set. I clench my fists and teeth, overcome with excitement at all the possibilities ahead.

A knock on the door startles me. I glance at my phone—eleven thirty. *He's early!* If he's even half as excited as I am then this is going to go very well.

I give myself one more look in the mirror and practise my cute-but-casual smile, then go greet Matt. The door creaks open, letting in a blast of sunlight and early-morning July warmth.

Matt steps closer, blocking the light, bringing his own radiance with him.

"Are you wearing plaid?!" I gasp, my mouth dropping open.

He eyes himself, then looks up to me, a playful grin lighting his features. "I thought I'd join you for Christmas, if that's okay?"

Dear god, the strength it takes to stay standing on my own two legs. I manage a nod while biting my quivering bottom lip, then step aside so Matt can enter. He's wearing red plaid PJ bottoms and a tight black V-neck shirt that hugs his upper body and biceps in a drool-inducing way. His scruff is neatly trimmed, forming a short beard, and his hair is combed back into a high bun with little golden tendrils escaping the sides.

I close the door, wafting his cologne my way, which must be infused with pheromones because I can feel my nostrils flaring and my lower half warming at his scent alone.

Matt toes off his sneakers and heads to the kitchen, setting reusable grocery bags on the counter. "I thought we'd have lunch together. Have you eaten?"

"I'm always down to eat."

"Good. I hope you're hungry." He takes a few Tupperware containers out of the bag and sets them down, the plastic fogged.

I reach out and touch one; it's still hot. "Did you cook this morning?"

He gives me a shy grin. "Maybe."

"What is it?"

Matt organizes all the dishes in front of me, then takes off the lids one by one to reveal a full turkey dinner. Baked turkey breasts fragrant with rosemary and thyme, garlic mashed potatoes, steamed carrots and peas, gravy, stuffing, and even a can of cranberries. "I bought the buns at the store, though," he says, removing a plastic bag of bakery-prepared tray buns.

Stunned, I look at all the food, then up to Matt's face, which is somewhere between giddy and nervous.

"Is this . . . okay?" he asks. "We can go out to lunch instead if you like. I thought we could have a Christmas dinner, but I also know this great sushi place—"

"Matt," I interrupt him, reaching out and taking his hand. My throat is thick with emotion. "This is . . . beyond perfect. Thank you."

His shoulders relax and he releases a slow breath, turning his palm up to hold my hand. We stare at each other for a long moment, a zing of possibilities igniting a fire in my belly.

I give his hand a squeeze before releasing it, moving behind him to get plates and cutlery. Matt and I work in silence as we dish each other up, elbow to elbow, hip to hip, and I know immediately that I can get used to this. I get a flash of us living days, weeks, years, going through the minutia of everyday life: him making my coffee in the morning, me ensuring he packs fruit in his lunch, him kissing me on the way out the door for work, me waiting up until he gets home, tangling in the bedsheets together and making sweet love while the nighttime sounds of crickets chirping and owls hooting floats in through the open window with the cool evening breeze.

I glance at him. He looks at me. We both smile and look away.

Plates piled high, we settle on the stools on the opposite side of the peninsula and dig in.

My first bite elicits a moan, and I close my eyes to savour the nostalgic flavours.

"Oh no, you hate it," Matt jokes, nudging me with his elbow.

"It's so good!" I mumble, mouth full of half-masticated food. I finish chewing and swallow. "Seriously, you cooked this, all by yourself?"

He shrugs. "Yeah. Does that surprise you?"

"It does."

"Kind of sexist." He chuckles.

I laugh too. "I never thought about it that way, but I guess it is. It's just, you're so . . . attractive? And you're a hard worker. And you're a kind, genuine person."

He presses a hand to his chest and lifts his chin. "Go on."

I elbow him back. "You're the full package, is all I'm saying. Add 'can cook' to that list and you're officially out of my league."

"I wouldn't say that." His leg rubs against mine and I return the gesture, my toes running up the back of his calf.

"How'd you learn to cook like this?" I ask before forking another mouthful.

"My grandma," he says. "My parents divorced when I was young, and both were super career-oriented, so I stayed with my grandma a lot. She didn't have TV, but she did have a big garden. We spent a lot of time out there, growing our own food, canning and pickling, making jam. She always had me in the kitchen with her, and I learned a few tricks over the years. When she passed, I . . ."

His voice catches, and I pause midbite to turn my full attention to him.

He takes a moment, then continues, his voice normal. "When she passed, nobody else knew the recipes she used to make, or how to prepare them, since her writing was barely legible chicken-scratch. So family meals fell to me. And it's like a little part of her lives on through her cooking. We're all sitting together at the table, one spot is empty, but the kitchen smells the same and the food tastes the same and, for a little while, she's not gone."

My heart aches as I listen. He has no idea, but he's checking all of my boxes. He's exactly the type of person I always imagined myself with. Capable, emotional, could start a homestead and live out in the countryside with cows and goats and chickens. And now my fantasy includes a huge garden and a cellar full of pickles. Is it possible I've stumbled upon the perfect man?

Matt glances at me, then drops his eyes back to his plate, his shoulders raising in a self-conscious way.

I reach out and take his hand again, giving it a squeeze. "Your grandma would be so proud of you."

He looks at me, his earnest brown eyes warm and vulnerable. The corner of his mouth lifts in a half smile as he regards me. He leans in closer, hovering just out of reach. "Just wait until you try my pie."

I gasp and release my hand from his hold to slap him in the chest. "You made pie?"

LATER, WHEN THE leftovers are packed and stored away in the fridge, when the dishes have been washed, dried, and put away, when I'm vibrating from how close I feel with Matt, when I'm pinching myself to wake up from this dream, we settle down on the couch to watch a movie.

"I have a surprise for you, too." I wiggle my eyebrows.

"Oh yeah?" He grins. "What's that?"

My laptop is set up on the coffee table, primed and ready to go. I press a few buttons and *Die Hard* starts playing. "Your favourite Christmas movie!"

"You're so thoughtful. You know that?"

I give him a coy shrug, reaching for his hand. He provides it eagerly, his long fingers enveloping mine. "You really put a lot of effort into today," I say, glancing out the window to the bright July sun. "And I really appreciate it. It's been a long time since anyone put this much consideration into a date with me."

He reaches with his free hand and tucks a strand of loose hair behind my ear, blazing a trail of fire with his fingertips along my cheekbone. "You should be with someone who puts this much effort in every day."

My eyes dance with his, my heart pounds in my ears, and my stomach is somehow up in my throat. Matt tugs me with his hand. I oblige, inching closer, the pull between us growing more intense until I can barely think, until I can barely do anything except bridge the last bit of space between us.

When our lips finally connect, his are warm and soft in contrast to his hard body. I press myself against him. Matt draws me in, pulling me onto his lap. I straddle him, not thinking about how fast this went from innocent date to provocative dry humping as I grind on his lap, feeling him hard beneath me.

Our lips lock and unlock, tongues tangling with one another as his hands grip my waist and my fingers scratch his beard.

My hands make their way to his man-bun, and I part from him for a moment. "Can I take your hair down?"

He replies with a nod before bringing his mouth to my throat. I pull his hair free of its tie and let his golden-brown waves down, running my fingers through his locks. "Not fair," I pout. "Your hair is nicer than mine."

His chest rumbles with a half laugh. "I love your hair." He then proceeds to grab a fistful and give it a little tug, tilting my chin to the ceiling and baring my throat for him, which he licks.

I gasp at the sensation. "Matt?" I manage.

"Yeah?" he replies, hoarse.

"Take me to bed."

He grinds against me once more. "I thought you'd never ask."

He manoeuvres me over his lap and picks me up in his arms. I drape one arm around his shoulder, my other hand gripping his bicep. He carries me to the bedroom and lays me down carefully, as if I'm made of porcelain. Matt's eyes move up my body, meeting with mine. I reach for him and tug him onto me while shifting farther onto the bed. The weight of him on top of me, pressing between my legs, is everything.

I pull at his shirt, lifting it up and over his head to reveal an intricate pattern of overlapping tattoos. My fingers trail over them, surprised he has any; he didn't really seem like a tattoo guy, what with his home-cooked meals and tales of pickling, but I like this layer to him. I'm eager to learn the stories behind each one.

But not right now.

Matt lifts the hem of my shirt, and I wiggle free from it. I'm always self-conscious about my breasts. I was told I'd grow some during puberty but was robbed of that particular experience. If Matt minds, he doesn't show it, kissing the line of my bra with enthusiasm and care. I arch my back and he reaches behind me, snapping the bra off and sliding it down my arms. He brings his lips to my nipple and sucks my whole breast into his mouth, a low moan humming in his throat.

Matt lifts off, kneeling on the bed and towering over me, all long golden-brown hair, smouldering eyes, and rippling abs. My mouth parts as he undoes his pants and pulls them down lower and lower, leaning into my delayed gratification of seeing him completely naked. Finally, his cock springs free and he grabs hold of his length. He draws his fist over it from base to tip, a bead escaping and dripping down his knuckles.

I squirm as I watch, need building deep in my belly.

"You sure?" he asks, raising an eyebrow.

I nod quickly. "Yes. I'm sure."

Matt bends and gives me another kiss, then gets up and finishes undressing. I do the same, tossing my clothes aside while Matt rips a condom open and pulls it on. He settles back over me, his forearms framing my face, the tip of his cock pressing against my entrance, flexing with his breath. We meet each other's gaze, then Matt closes his eyes and tucks his face into my neck as he slides into me.

I can't help but clench in anticipation, my body tightening as he tries to go in, my fingernails digging into his back.

He stills. "You okay?"

"Uh. Yeah. Just . . . give me a minute." I close my eyes and focus on my breathing. *Come on, body. Relax. It's okay. Chill out.*

Matt waits, rocking slowly against me until my body releases, letting him farther in. It takes a few more slow, languid pumps before he's able to sink all the way in, and when he does, I feel myself finally let go. I give him a kiss on the shoulder, letting him know I'm okay. Matt moves faster, his thrusts longer and deeper, and I hold on to him as he moves. I relish feeling close to him, his weight on top of me, his breath in my ear. It's as good as I hoped it would be.

After a few minutes his breathing becomes ragged, his movements jerky.

Oh, shit, I haven't made any noise this whole time.

He's probably waiting for me. Closing my eyes, I start making low moans. He seems spurred by this. I get louder, more dramatic, then squeeze my Kegel muscles as tight as I can.

That does it. Matt grunts a guttural release, stilling over me as he comes. I do the same, gasping and grunting like he is, until he relaxes and flops down on top of me. I wait for his breathing to return to normal, tracing circles over his skin with my fingernails.

He finally lifts and regards me, his skin flushed, breathing laboured. "You seemed to enjoy yourself." He smiles.

I give him a quick kiss. "Best sex I've had in a long time."

"I refuse to stop until you tell me it's the best sex of your life."

I beam at him. *He wants to have more sex with me?!* "I'll hold you to that."

Matt gives me one more quick kiss before peeling himself off me and disappearing into the bathroom to clean up. I tuck myself in under the blankets, ready for a nap. Matt returns and crawls in with me, taking me in his arms. Resting my cheek on his chest, I trail my fingers through his sparse chest hair and overlapping tattoos.

"I'm sorry I can't stay long," he says. "I have to go to work. I hate to leave so soon after, you know . . ."

I shrug, snuggling in a little closer. "I know."

He relaxes, kissing the top of my head.

"What's this tattoo?" I ask, trailing a finger over his chest with some sort of funky mandala.

"It's a symbol of the universe."

"And this?" I ask, running my hands down to his lower abdomen.

"That's from after Burning Man, a few years ago. It's a fractal lotus, a Buddhist symbol of rebirth and strength."

"What about this?" The lowest one, half a V and half a ram skull, sits right beside his cock and stands out a bit from the others.

"That's my sign."

My body clenches in excitement. "I knew we were compatible! I'm a Gemini. Aries and Gemini go together like—"

"Like stuffing and mashed potatoes?" He gives me a squeeze.

I lift a little higher so I can look at him in all his perfection. His soft, brown eyes and sleepy half smile light up my belly and make my heart patter. I give him a slow, sensual kiss, then hover above him, nudging my nose against his. "Yeah. Like that."

ACT 2

INT. BREWED AWAKENING CAFÉ - DAY

Montage of Annie and Kate decorating the café while "Jingle Bell Rock" plays.

Annie brings in store-bought Christmas cookies and Kate places them in the display.

Annie stocks cans of whipped cream, pumpkin spice, and red and green sprinkles for festive drinks.

Annie notices a crowd outside and unlocks the door, letting customers in.

James enters the café through the staff entrance, confused.

Record scratching noise, music halts.

All of the patrons look at James, fear in their eyes.

                    JAMES
        What the heck is going on here? How did
        you get in?

                    ANNIE
        Surprise! We thought we'd decorate for you.
        Everyone loves it. Would you like a cookie?

James storms toward Annie and points a finger in her face.

                         JAMES
        I told you not to come back here.
        I told you I hate Christmas. And yet
        here you are, throwing it in my face.
        Why can't you leave me alone?

                         ANNIE
        We thought you needed to be
        reminded of what Christmas meant,
        show you how marvellous it can be.
        Doesn't it look great in here?

                         JAMES
        No, it looks tacky and ridiculous.
        And what are these, store-bought
        cookies? In my café?

                         ANNIE
        Sorry, I didn't have time to bake.
        It's better than nothing.

James uses his arm to sweep the cookies out of the
display and into a garbage bin, then shoves the bin
at Annie.

                         JAMES
        Take these out of here. I refuse
        to serve anything but the best in my
        store, which is what my customers deserve.

                         ANNIE
        Your customers deserve more than
        you doing the bare minimum at
        Christmastime.

JAMES

I can't believe you trespassed on my
property to continue your harassment.
I ought to call the police.

ANNIE

On what grounds? Someone giving
you a thoughtful Christmas gift and
helping to improve your business?

JAMES

This isn't an improvement.

ANNIE

(gesturing widely)
Take a look around! This is the busiest
I've ever seen your café. In fact, I—

JAMES

I don't care. I don't need this.

James starts tearing down decorations and throwing
them outside. The café patrons scatter.

James knocks over a tray and several coffee mugs crash
to the ground, breaking at Annie's feet, who jumps
back to avoid them.

ANNIE

What is wrong with you?

JAMES

What's wrong with me? You're the one
ruining my day with all this nonsense.

You need to go. I never want to see you
here again.

ANNIE

I'm sorry . . . I was trying to help . . .

Annie leaves the café, looking behind her to see
Kate peering out sadly from the back room. James
is all alone in the front, sitting on the edge of a
table with his head in his hands and surrounded by
the chaos of a ruined Christmas.

Chapter 8
MARIAH

*I*t's been two days since I've worked with Ellie, and somehow I've forgotten just how much of a chatterbox she is. Everyone else might say a word or two, then sit in silence while I do my job—which is normal. Ellie, however, is the opposite. I kind of missed it. Almost.

"And ohmygod, Mariah, the makeup you did for me the other day worked!" she squeals in excitement, her whole body tensing like a coiled spring.

"Oh yeah?" I smile, glad she was happy with her results. I apply the primer, running my fingers in quick circles over her skin.

"Yes! He couldn't take his eyes off me, and after he fixed my stove—"

I snort. "Sounds like a euphemism."

"—he asked me out! And he totally kissed me when he left. It was just like a little kiss, but still, he's a gentleman and it was beyond sweet."

"Aw, that's nice." I apply the foundation that's two shades too light for her skin tone, as per my instructions.

"Yeah! And then, okay, so yesterday, he'd asked me out on a date, and then he came over and he was so sweet! And, you know how important Christmas is to me—"

"Sure do."

"—and he totally made me a Christmas dinner! Turkey and potatoes and stuffing, the works. He said he made pie, but he was just joking—there was no pie. I'll have to get him to make me his infamous pie another day."

I huff a laugh through my nose. It cracks me up, the things Ellie focuses on.

She continues. "And after that we cuddled and talked about life and our plans and then he carried me to bed—literally carried me. He may not have made me pie but that doesn't mean we didn't have dessert, if you know that I mean—" Ellie winks at me obnoxiously through the mirror, and I can't help but shake my head with a smile. Then Ellie clasps her hands and squeezes them to her chest, sighing. "The way he treated me, he was so patient and careful and thoughtful and gentle. Afterward he stayed and snuggled and talked. We want the same number of kids and dogs and chickens! He's into gardening and home-making and pickling and I can totally see us on a little acreage together. We have such similar ideas for our futures! I think he's starting to have feelings for me. I know it's only been three days, and two and a half dates, but I think he's really special. You know? When you know, you know, that's what they say!"

I nod. "I know what you mean. The guy I'm seeing was just supposed to be a fun distraction but he's . . . I don't know."

"Oh yeah, you're seeing someone, too! We're both getting a little Christmas action, eh?"

I grimace. "I don't know about that, but I saw him again yesterday. And again last night. And again this morning."

Ellie rubs her hands together. "You gonna elaborate on those details, or are you going to let my imagination do the heavy lifting?"

I place a hand on my hip and tut at her sarcastically. "A lady never relinquishes details."

She waits, slowly twisting in her chair to look up at me, an eyebrow raising as she does.

I grin and bite my lip against a laugh. "Okay, okay. So last night he comes home from work. It's late, but I'm waiting up for him. He's getting a snack from the kitchen, and he lifts me up and puts me on the counter and we, you know, right there."

Ellie moans. "Hot!"

"I know, right?" I finish the foundation and move to her eyebrows, penciling them in a bit more. "I love it when a guy can lift me, toss me around a bit, press me up against a wall. Jax is pretty fit."

"Oh my god, so is Matt. He has all these muscles." She sings the word *muscles* while her hands grope invisible biceps. "And all these tattoos, which surprised me because they're all hidden under his shirt and he didn't really seem to be the type to have them. But they're pretty spiritual. The other day—get this—he told me he must have been a good person for karma to bring us together." Ellie grips her chest like her heart is about to burst out of it.

"That's actually super cute," I agree. "I'm glad you found someone like him. He seems really special."

"Thanks, Mariah! I'm glad you reconnected with someone, too; it's nice that you found your way back to each other. And I'm glad it's looking more long-term than a hookup—not that there's anything wrong with that, but you deserve happiness, too."

I give Ellie a smile. "He did say he wants to come visit me in Vancouver."

"Gahhh, Ma-*ri*-ah!" She pronounces all three syllables of my name again. "I'm so excited for you!"

"Thanks. I'm happy for you, too." I move to her eyes, using dark colours to make her seem more tired than she is.

"Matt is everything I've been looking for but wasn't sure I'd ever find. He's smart, and sweet, and a hard worker, and he can cook. And we're compatible! He's an Aries—he has an Aries tattoo right beside his c—"

I slip and stab Ellie in the eye with my brush.

"Ow! Fuck!" Ellie cries out and leans forward, pressing her palm to her eye.

The cast and crew freeze, looking over at us.

"Is everything okay?" Jimmie asks from the opposite side of the room.

"Uh, yeah!" I say, though everything is *not* okay and I'm trying not to panic. "Just a makeup mishap. We're fine." Turning back to Ellie, I bend to her ear level and eye her through the mirror. "Describe this tattoo. In detail."

She's rubbing her red, watery eye, her mouth forming a rare frown. "Uh, it was half a ram skull, half a V."

I stand back up quickly. Too quickly. Dizzy, I grip the back of Ellie's chair and force myself to breathe. "It's not a V. It's a Κριός."

"A what now?"

"The Greek symbol for Aries."

"So . . . ?"

"Jax has the same tattoo."

Ellie flings her hands in two directions, one of them smacking into my boob. "How is it possible there are two guys with the same oddly specific tattoo on their groin?"

"I'd say the possibilities are very low."

Ellie's eyes pop open. "You don't mean . . . ? No."

"Yes."

"No!"

I grip the back of the chair and stare deeply into Ellie's eyes. My stomach rolls, and I'm not sure if I'll be able to speak the next sentence without barfing. "Ellie . . . Jax was his basketball nickname. He went by it ever since middle school. His full name is Matthew Jackson."

Ellie's eyes widen in shock and disbelief, her mouth slowly falling open.

"Five minutes," Yueyi calls.

I clear my throat and wrap my hands in Ellie's hair, pulling it quickly into a bun. My mind is reeling.

"Ow," she scolds when I pull at her hair too forcefully. "It's not true. It can't be the same guy. Matt is kind, and caring, and thoughtful, and so sweet—what we have is special. He made a complicated romantic date and cooked for me and we snuggled and talked about our lives and our futures. He isn't the type of guy to hook up with someone at a bar."

I grip her hair a little harder. "What's that supposed to mean?"

"Nothing!" Ellie winces. "He seems like the type to want to get to know someone first, is all."

"I hardly think one date is getting to know someone."

"Two and a *half* dates," she corrects, lifting her chin.

I snort in derision. "What, like two and a half dates makes you better than me or something?"

"No, I didn't mean it like that. Sorry," she backpedals, scrunching her mouth to the side.

"Besides, technically we've known each other for years. Way longer than you two. Which means you should believe what I'm trying to tell you."

Jax had a reputation in high school. Despite dating Bethany and various other beautiful, popular girls, he was known to have the type of bed posts your dad warned you about—the ones covered in notches. I've changed so much since high school, and after talking to him these past few days, I thought he had, too.

I guess I was wrong.

Ellie gives her head a vigorous shake, standing up. "Okay, maybe you're right, maybe Matt and Jax are somehow the same guy—"

"I know I'm right, I—"

Ellie cuts me off, eyes wild, a finger lifted in reprimand. "*Or* this is a coincidence. Matt and Jax are nothing alike. The way you described him doesn't line up with the guy I know. And Matt wouldn't do this to me. The way he held me and talked to me . . . and we have the same names picked out for our kids and . . ." She trails off, the rims of her eyes turning pink.

"I'm sorry, Ellie. This sucks."

She sniffs hard and sets her jaw. "Matthew's a common first name, and I have no idea what his last name is."

"The tattoo—"

She flings her arms to her sides, hitting my boob again.

"Maybe there's some weird fraternity here and they all got matching tattoos? Maybe they're cousins and that's their family sigil? Maybe the tattoo was on a wall in a parlour and they both thought it would look great next to their d—"

"Time, everyone! Let's go." Yueyi's final warning echoes through the room. Ellie is the last actress they're waiting on, and she gives us a pointed look.

Ellie heads to the costume area, disappearing behind a curtain.

I wait, pacing while chewing on a nail. I wish it weren't true, but my heart is telling me Jax—Matt—is a lying asshole, and he's tricked us both.

He didn't need to lie to me. I would have been fine with a no-strings-attached romp to get my high school yearning out of my system. Then he had to go and make me think he had feelings for me . . . that he always had. It hurts. But being well-versed in fuckboyery, at least I saw the red flags. I chose to ignore them, yes, but I'm not entirely surprised by this revelation.

Poor Ellie. She is totally convinced by his lying scheme. Jax knew the only way into her pants was to make her think he wanted more, and damn was he convincing. It turns my stomach knowing that he was whispering sweet nothings in her ear and then hours later bending me over his dining room table spanking me.

Ellie emerges in her barista outfit. "We need to confirm one way or another before we jump to conclusions."

"You're right," I say, though I don't think she's right at all. "We need to know for sure. I'll go talk to him once he's at work. It feels weird to go back to his place now, knowing he is—"

She glares at me.

"That he *might*," I correct, "not be the person he says he is."

Ellie nods. "Where does he work?"

"A little dive bar at the edge of the city, past the tracks, on your way out to Hope."

"Okay. I'll see if I can talk to him after I'm done here, too. We'll reconvene later." Ellie leaves to film her scenes.

I collapse into the chair. It spins slowly so that I'm facing myself in the mirror, but I can't bring myself to look up. I don't want to see the face of a complete clown.

I find myself so distracted on set that Jimmie has to prompt me multiple times to get up and fix Ellie's makeup or readjust a curl escaping her bun. My mind is too busy whirring back and forth between hope, anger, and sadness. I thought by now I understood men, or at least couldn't be fooled by them. It feels gross knowing that I can still be swayed by a pretty face and empty words.

By THE TIME filming is over and I'm sitting in the parking lot of Grumpy Joe's, looking at Jax's little purple pickup truck parked along the side, I'm not sure what to think, except that I have to know the truth.

Walking as tall as I can, I enter the dimly lit space and catch sight of Jax at his usual spot. He looks up at me, but his slow smile does less for my libido than it did yesterday. I take my usual seat, but it feels uncomfortable now, like my ass is either too big or too small for it.

"Hey," I manage.

He leans over the bar. "Hey, you."

I regard his features, trying to spot a crack in his facade. "I thought I'd come pay you a visit."

He nods his chin over his shoulder. "There's one more camera blind spot back there. It's in the walk-in fridge, though, so it'll be a little chilly."

Does he seriously think I want to be banged in a walk-in fridge next to all the produce and condiments? I can't be the first one to take him up on that offer. Would I have, if Ellie's revelation hadn't tarnished my image of him? I don't want to know the answer to that.

"Rain check."

"Okay. Can I get you a drink?"

"Sure. Whiskey. Neat."

"Rough day?" He pulls out a rocks glass and free-pours two fingers.

I toss it back, setting the empty glass onto the bar with a loud clink. "You could say that."

He pours three more fingers. "Want to talk about it?"

My heart softens momentarily, then hardens once more. Here we go. Five seconds of bravery. "I was thinking about going back to your place, but I was worried about cramping your style. You know, with other people."

An old guy with a grey moustache and hunched back limps up to the bar and takes a seat a few barstools away, his chair squeaking on the old floors. Jax and I eye him, annoyed by the interruption.

"Bottle of Bud," he drawls.

Jax leaves for a moment to serve his customer, then turns back to me, leaning even closer on the bar and speaking in a hushed tone. "No one else is there, Mariah. It's just you and me."

"Just right now? Or in general?"

He tilts his head to the side. "Is everything okay? It's not like you to be so self-conscious like this."

"How do you know how I am? We've only been together a few days. In high school I don't think you said more than two words to me, and I'm pretty sure they were in reference to my breasts."

Reaching across the bar, he takes my hand in his. "Doesn't mean I didn't want to, Mariah."

My hand warms, tingles running down my arm. "You did?"

He nods. "Every time I wanted to say something to you, I got so tongue-tied."

I blush, imagining infamous popular jock Jax secretly pining after me. I like the thought of that far too much.

"And then after Bethany," he continues, dropping his gaze

momentarily, "I couldn't. You know? I always felt like you were the one that got away."

"And now you want to be with me?"

"I always did."

I bite my lip against a smile.

"That's my girl," he says, caressing my lip with his thumb. Once again, I'm putty in his hands.

I want to let it go, to put this all behind me, and maybe take him up on his offer of the blind spot in the fridge.

But I have to be sure.

I look directly at him and take a steadying breath. "Am I the only person you're seeing right now?"

Jax squeezes my hand in his, regarding me with those gorgeous big brown eyes of his. "I don't give just anyone the key to my place. Okay? I never thought I'd see you again, and then there you were. Out of nowhere. When I needed you most. I only have eyes for you."

I smile fully now, calmed by his words and ready to put all of this behind me. Ellie was right. How could Jax and Matt be the same person? They're nothing alike. I'm embarrassed I even brought it up. The whole thing is absurd. Preposterous. I can't wait to tell Ellie tomorrow that this was all just a weird misunderstanding. She and Matt can go on with their whirlwind fairy-tale romance, and Jax and I can continue making up for what we missed out on all those years ago.

I'm so relieved. Jax is an honest person, the perfect mix of rough and soft, a dom with a sweet side, he's a—

"You know," Jax says, the corner of his mouth tilting up in a smile. "I must have been a pretty good person in my past life for karma to bring you my way."

Lying scumbag!

I swallow back a sudden wave of nausea and force a smile to my face. "Yeah. Same. Okay, well, I have to . . . go."

He frowns. "You're leaving?"

"Yeah, I need to leave. My parents, you know, expecting me." I shift off the barstool, nearly tripping on my own feet.

"Okay. I'll see you later?"

I back away from the bar, shaking. "Sure will. Yep."

"All right. Have a great night."

Turning on my heel, I walk away as fast as possible. Outside, I gasp in the fresh air, swallowing lungfuls while simultaneously being unable to catch my breath.

He used the exact same line on me that he used on Ellie, and his delivery was so smooth it didn't even faze him. How many women has he used that line on? How many women is he playing at the same time? I can't believe I was dumb enough to be fooled by the biggest playboy in all of Chilliwack. He played me like I was still a naive, starry-eyed teenager. Like I haven't learned anything since high school. I thought things would be different now that we're adults, but I should have known better. Sometimes people change, and sometimes they don't.

I'll be okay once my bruised ego recovers; Jax isn't the first asshole to lie to me. If anything, he's just given me about ten more reasons to avoid dating the opposite sex.

There's no way Ellie could have known; she really caught feelings for this cheating sonofabitch. He lied to her outright, his intent so unbelievably malicious.

She deserves better than this. We both do. Every woman does.

I have to tell her tomorrow.

Until then, though, I have no other option but to do what I've been dreading ever since arriving back in Chilliwack.

With shaking fingers, and doing my best to hold back angry tears, I pick up my phone and dial my mom. It rings once, and—

A hand grabs my shoulder. I twist around with a shocked gasp as the old man from the bar reaches for me. I pull my fist back to punch the creep in the face.

"Whoa, whoa, whoa!" he cries in a high-pitched voice, raising his hands in defence.

I hesitate, my fist clenched, ready to swing. *That voice.* "Wait, are you . . . ?"

The old man lowers his sunglasses. "It's me. Ellie."

Recognition snaps into place and I lower my hand, my fear replaced by confusion. "Ellie? What the . . . What are you doing here? And why are you dressed like an old biker?"

"Hello? Mariah? Are you there?"

I hold my phone to my ear. "Uh, yeah. Sorry, the director just walked up, can I call you back in a minute?" I hang up before Mom can respond.

Ellie's shoulders sag. "I'm sorry. I had to see for myself." She raises a hand quickly. "Not that I don't trust you, I just . . ."

"I get it. I'd have had to see it for myself, too."

Ellie sighs, blowing her moustache away from her mouth. "Do you want to come back to my place so we can talk about this?"

Looking from my phone to Ellie, I'm not sure who I'd rather spend time with: my mother, or the woman who is banging the same guy as me. Which would be less awkward and painful?

"Yes. Let's go back to your place."

EXT. BREWED AWAKENING CAFÉ - DAY

Annie is walking by the café and peeks through the windows to see James talking to several people in business suits.

Annie ducks around the corner when the group walks outside.

                    BUSINESSWOMAN 1
          This has gone on long enough.

                    BUSINESSWOMAN 2
          Your little fiasco the other day nearly
          made the paper. Not the local paper,
          the provincial paper! Do you know
          what that would have done to us?

                    JAMES
          As I explained, it was a one-time
          occurrence, and won't happen again.
          I had an unruly customer disturbing
          the peace.

                    BUSINESSWOMAN 1
          This isn't a one-time problem, James.
          And the incident with that woman is
          just the tip of the iceberg.

                    JAMES
          What do you mean?

                    BUSINESSWOMAN 2
          You're hurting our community, James.

BUSINESSMAN 1

All of the businesses rely on each
other to bring customers in. When a
cornerstone unit like yours doesn't
hold up its end of the bargain, it
hurts the rest of us. People are going
into the city to shop in malls rather
than downtown because they are more
festive. We can't afford to keep sending
business away.

BUSINESSWOMAN 1

I know Christmas is a hard time of year
for you, but this is Hemlock Grove.
Everyone here loves Christmas!

BUSINESSWOMAN 2

If you refuse to be part of our community,
then we will find someone who is. We've
invited some prospective new tenants to
the party on Saturday.

JAMES

What do you mean?

BUSINESSWOMAN 1

If you can't turn all this around and
prove to the community that you still have
a place here, then we will find someone
else better suited for it.

JAMES

You can't do that. We've been here . . .
I've been here since the beginning.

> BUSINESSWOMAN 1
> All good things come to an end.

> JAMES
> Trust me, I know that better than most.

> BUSINESSWOMAN 2
> We've been patient and understanding,
> but we have to do what's right for our
> community. If that means making a difficult
> choice, then that's what we'll have to do.

The businesspeople walk away down the street.

James takes deep breath, shakes his head, and then
walks into the café.

Chapter 9
ELLIE

I'm glad Mariah didn't punch me in the face; judging by her stance, she knows how. We climb into our separate vehicles and I lead Mariah through the city streets, down the side-roads, and along the twisty driveway to the cabin.

"Why the hell are you staying way out here?" Mariah asks, shutting her car door and crunching on the gravel toward me.

"You'll see," I singsong, though my heart feels very un-singsongy right now. I unlock the door and step inside to a welcoming blast of air conditioning. Mariah follows, and I shut the door behind her.

"Wow." She takes another step in, turning in a circle as she regards my Christmas swag. She finishes her full three-sixty and gives me a perplexed look. "Did you do all this or did the place come like this?"

"I did it. I'm a method actor."

She nods. "Of course you are."

I'm too sad and tired to wonder if she's being sarcastic or not. "Plus, I love Christmas. It's kind of my thing."

She grimaces. "I hate Christmas."

"What! How can you hate Christmas? I have it on good authority that it's the most wonderful time of the year."

Her mouth twitches. I take it as a win.

But I'm too heartbroken to work any harder at getting her to smile. Watching Matt profess his feelings to Mariah, lying about how she's the only woman in his life—while also telling the truth that there wouldn't be anyone else showing up at his house, and then using the same line on her that he'd used on me—it was too much. I never should have gone there. But I'm glad I did. He's such a smooth operator, I wouldn't have believed he was a liar unless I'd witnessed it myself.

I drop my purse on the floor. "Wine?"

"Fuck yes."

I move past Mariah to the kitchen and unscrew a bottle of merlot, pouring two full glasses.

"Just one glass, though. One *small* glass," Mariah chastises. "I have to work in the morning."

"Sorry." I pour some of hers into mine, filling it to the brim. "I guess I should be grateful I'm not on set tomorrow." Handing Mariah her glass, I take mine to the living room and settle on the couch, trying not to think about last night when I was sitting in this exact same spot, snuggled up with Matt. Jax? Who knows.

Taking a long slurp of my wine, my throat tightens from the tannins and brings with it a little relief. I close my eyes and lean my head back against the couch. A moment later Mariah joins me, the cushions sinking in toward her. "Today really sucked," I say, keeping my eyes closed.

"You can say that again." I hear her sip, then swallow.

"Not just with the whole Matt-slash-Jax fiasco. I was so distracted by it I completely fumbled my first full day on set. I didn't have any lines today—thank god—because I probably would have forgotten them even though I memorized the script weeks ago. I broke a coffee cup while sweeping the floor. How do you even do that? Like, I can't even do my job as a barista, let alone act in a movie as one." I rub my face with my free hand. "They had to do three retakes, and I wasn't even the main focus of the scene. They *hate* retakes. It's a one-shot deal usually, even if people flub their lines a little, since it costs so much money and we're on a really tight budget. Yueyi looked so disappointed in me. Probably second-guessing hiring me at all. I'm such a shitty actress."

Mariah nudges me, and I open my eyes to look at her. "You're definitely not a shitty actress. I've stared at your face and listened to you talk for hours, and I didn't even recognize you in the bar."

"Thanks," I say, though I don't quite believe it.

"It was Jax's fault you had a hard time today."

I blow a raspberry between my lips. "You're right. I couldn't stay focused after finding out we've been seeing the same guy."

"I can't believe I actually believed him." Mariah looks down in her glass. "I feel like such a fool."

"Samesies." I clink my glass with hers, and we both take a big gulp.

Mariah's phone rings. She sighs, ignores it, then mumbles, "I don't want to deal with this right now."

"What's wrong?"

"It's nothing."

"I've noticed you have a reoccurring problem with your phone ringing." I nudge her. "What's going on?"

"Just . . . stuff."

I can't let her go that easily. "Did you win the lottery and your second cousin twice-removed needs money? Is some gang hassling you to repay your gambling debts? Are you actually an heiress and your bodyguard is trying to track down where you are? Did you—"

She exhales quickly through her nose, and I warm with satisfaction knowing I nearly made her laugh. Mariah glances at me, then back at her phone, which has stopped ringing. "It's my mom. I was supposed to stay with my parents while I was here. When I applied for the job, I put their address as mine since they only wanted locals for the crew. I didn't expect to be hired, and I can't afford to stay in a hotel while I'm here, *and* I can't afford to drive in and out from Vancouver for work, so I asked if I could stay with them. They said yes. We . . . don't have the best relationship. I've been staying with Jax and have been able to avoid them up until now. But not going home has just made it worse."

"As avoiding things tends to do."

"Yeah." Her phone rings again, and this time she answers it. "Hey. Yeah . . . no, I'm okay. Sorry, yeah."

I can't hear what the other person is saying, only that they're talking a mile a minute and Mariah is sinking further and further into the couch the longer this goes on. Following my instincts, I snatch the phone from her. "Hey! Is this Mariah's mom? Oh, hey, Janine! Yeah, this is Ellie." She asks if I'm the friend Mariah's been staying with. *Does she mean Jax?* I go along with it. "Yes, that's me!"

Janine talks for a few more minutes while I "Uh-huh" and "Sure!" my way through the conversation, ending the call as quickly as I can before handing the phone back to a speechless Mariah.

"Um . . . ?" she finally manages.

I gulp down the rest of my wine. "You're staying here. At least for tonight. You've had a glass of wine, anyway. Safety first! The couch folds out and there's spare linens in the closet. I have turkey dinner leftovers, and more wine. Oh! And we're going to your parents' for dinner later this week."

Mariah's eyes widen in shock. "What?"

"Yeah." I give her a nudge. "I'll be your buffer."

Her eyes grow wider.

"Don't worry, parents love me!"

Mariah's shocked expression slowly shifts to horrified before she downs the rest of her glass. "I think I'm going to need more wine."

I put the turkey leftovers in the oven to warm and grab the bottle of wine before joining Mariah, who is quietly lost in her thoughts, as usual.

Unsure of what to say, which is a weird situation for me, I sit pensively beside her and tap my fingernails on my glass. "Do you . . . want to talk about Matt?"

She huffs through her nose. "Nope. Not enough wine yet."

"Okay. How about your parents?"

"There's not enough wine in the world for that," Mariah says into her glass before taking a long sip.

"Okay."

The awkward silence yawns between us. I'm not one for silences at the best of times, but it's now settling in that I've invited a woman I barely know, who barely tolerates me, and has been banging the same guy as me, to stay with me for an unknown amount of time. It had felt like the right thing to do but now I'm having second thoughts.

"Do you want to watch a movie?" I ask, finally.

"Fine."

"Great." I disappear into my bedroom for a moment to retrieve the box of tree ornaments/VHS tapes and plop it down in front of Mariah. "Pick one."

Leaning forward, Mariah regards my collection with a mortified grimace. "Do you have anything other than Christmas movies?"

"Sorry, I'm on a strict Christmas movie diet."

She sighs, then digs around, lifting the occasional ornament to inspect it before gingerly placing it back in the box. "What about *Romeo and Juliet*?" She lifts the tape with black sharpie on it and turns it over a few times. "I haven't seen a taped VHS in years. Kind of forgot they exist."

I snatch it from her and toss it back in. "Anything else."

"Fine." She digs around for a few more moments before taking out *Home Alone*. "How about this?"

A classic. I nod my approval.

By the time the opening credits are finished rolling, we're both cozied up with warm leftovers and refilled glasses.

"Where's the tree?" Mariah asks between bites.

"What?"

"You have lights. Tinsel. Garland. A box full of ornaments. But no tree."

"Oh," I say, still mildly confused that, of all things, this is her choice of conversation. "I don't have a tree because fake trees are blasphemous."

She gives me a quizzical look.

"My grandpa would roll over in his grave," I explain. "Every year we'd all get together at Grandma and Grandpa's farm. Me, my aunts and uncles, my cousins, my mom and dad, my brothers and sisters, we'd go out into the woods and find the perfect tree. It was always kind of scraggly because it was a wild tree, not a farmed one, but we'd fill it with so many decorations you wouldn't notice. All around it there were presents stacked almost to the ceiling because there were so many of us, and then all of us kids would pile up on the floor and fall asleep with the lights twinkling around us."

"That sounds so nice." Mariah regards me for a moment, then gestures at the screen with her fork. "Must have been kind of like this."

"Oh, way busier than that. Macauley Culkin's family ain't got nothin' on mine."

"Really? How many cousins do you have?"

"I have . . ." I trail off a second, looking at the ceiling to count them all. "Thirty-six? First cousins."

She gapes at me. "What!"

"Why? How many do you have?"

"Two." ·

I gape back at her. "*Two* cousins?!"

"Yeah. And they live in Newfoundland."

"Wow. I can't imagine such a small family. There were usually fifteen of my cousins there at the house, plus me and all my siblings."

"How many of those do you have?"

"Eight."

"*Eight?*" Her mouth hangs open.

I shrug. "My parents wanted a big family. And now I have three nieces and four nephews and one nibling."

"What's a nibling?"

"They're enby," I explain. "That's the gender-neutral term for your sibling's kid."

She nods appreciatively. "Nice."

"Yeah. Anyway, Christmas with a fake tree isn't Christmas at all. I'd rather have no tree than a fake one. So, no tree."

"Your family Christmases sound like they're from a story-book."

My chest grows warm as I recall all the memories, then quickly cools. "It was. For a long time."

"Not anymore?"

I shake my head. "After Grandpa passed, Grandma moved to a home and sold the farm. We tried to keep the tradition going, but most everyone decided to do their own Christmases, or go to Mexico, or snowbird down in Arizona. People grew up, left home, moved away. It was never really the same."

"I'm sorry."

Christmas now is an empty apartment, me decorating the place by myself while watching Christmas movies, walking down snowy Vancouver streets to look at all the lights and window shop solo. Christmas had been the time of year that had filled my heart and kept me going all year long, but now it's hollow, memories echoing through my mind of how good it used to be, and how good it will be again once I have a family of my own. I thought I had a chance of that with Matt. I was wrong.

"At least I got to have it for a while. You never got to have it at all."

Mariah shakes her head. "Nope. We never even had a tree."

I gasp, mortified.

"And," she adds, "we had to wait to open our presents until after Christmas dinner at my grandparents' house."

I lean away from her, my face contorting with over-the-top horror, which elicits a small smile from Mariah.

"*And* I was the only kid there," she says, continuing the nightmare. "It was always quiet and boring. Except when my aunt came." She trails off for a moment, lost in her thoughts. "Then it was interesting."

"I'm glad at least one person in your family kept things fun." I turn back to the TV as Kevin McCallister lives it up in his parents' mansion all alone.

We settle back into the silence, but this time it's a little less uncomfortable. Maybe it's the conversation, maybe we're becoming friends, or maybe it's the bottle and a half of wine we've consumed. I do feel pleasantly warm and buzzed.

"What do you think Kevin's parents do for work?" I ask, interrupting the quiet.

A hint of a smile meets Mariah's face, which is rosy from drink. "I'm sure the mom is the leader of a crime syndicate."

I grin. "Maybe the dad is a porn star."

"Or they could be—"

Mariah's phone rings. She looks at it and her smile falls off her face.

"Who is it?" I ask, leaning in.

She shows me the phone. *Jax*.

"Answer it!" I urge.

"What? No! What do I say?"

"Just pretend everything is normal."

She shakes her head. "I suck at lying."

"It's not lying," I argue. "It's *acting*."

"Yeah, I suck at that, too." She worries her bottom lip with her teeth.

The phone goes silent, and we release slow exhales. Then we both startle at the sound of my phone ringing. I look at the screen, then flash it to Mariah. *Matt*.

Her eyes widen. "That asshole! I didn't answer so he calls you?"

"Yeah!" I agree. "He called you first before calling me?" Without another thought, I answer it, forcing a smile to my face so I'll sound like I'm in a good mood. "Hello? Oh, heyyyyy! Yeah, just at home . . . Tonight?"

I glance at Mariah, whose eyes widen to say, *What?*

I return her wide-eyed stare. *I know, right?*

Mariah glares. *The nerve!*

I roll my eyes in agreement. *What a dickhead!*

"Sorry, I can't tonight," I say into the receiver. "I have to be up super early tomorrow, but I'm sure we can figure out another time. I'm just off to bed now." I make all the excuses I need to hustle the conversation along until I can finally hang up, both Mariah and I bursting out with expletives.

"That two-timing—"

"—lying scumbag of a—"

"—fuckboy player!"

Mariah and I seethe, then simultaneously gulp down the rest of our wine.

"Seriously." I shake my head in disbelief. "Who does that? He really should be taught a lesson."

"Agreed." Mariah nods. "Men—sorry—*people* who lie and manipulate others to get into their beds are the worst. Who knows how many women he's hurt in the past? How many more he'll harm?"

"Since we know about it, we should do something about it."

"Yeah."

"It's basically a moral obligation at this point."

"Totally."

"If we don't do something about it," I say, getting louder, more passionate, "then who will? He'll go on thinking this is okay, that there aren't repercussions for being a lying, cheating bastard."

She raises her empty glass to me. "Preach, sister."

I stand and raise my glass in the air. "This isn't just about us. This is about women, everywhere, who have been lied to, cheated on, and fucked with."

"Hallelujah." Mariah goes to drink more wine, then pauses, noting her empty glass.

"We gotta teach him a lesson," I continue, pacing.

Mariah fetches the half-empty bottle, then refills her glass. "Mmm–hmm."

"We gotta—" I look to the TV, my attention caught by the two goons falling into one of Kevin McCallister's traps. I snap my fingers and point to the screen. "That's it!"

"What?" she asks, pausing her pour.

"We *Home Alone* him!"

Mariah shakes her head slowly, confused. "What?"

I sit on the couch, so close to Mariah I'm practically on her lap. "We'll set up traps and pranks and make his life miserable!"

She hesitates. "I don't know . . ."

"Come on," I plead. "It will be fun. A few harmless pranks. We can't really let him get away with this, can we?"

Mariah considers this for a moment, then nods. "You're right. He can't go on thinking this is okay to do. And, honestly, revenge sounds pretty good at this point."

"Yes!" I bounce in my seat. "Revenge!"

She rolls her eyes, lips pursed against a smile.

I hold out my hand to hers. "Deal?"

Mariah regards my hand for a second, then shrugs, taking it in hers for a shake.

I grin, squeezing her hand. "Looks like Matt's made his way onto the naughty list."

INT. BREWED AWAKENING CAFÉ - DAY

Annie enters the café, slow and hesitant.

James sees her and sighs.

                    JAMES
          What do you want?

                    ANNIE
          I'm sorry, I didn't mean to, but I was
          walking by and I overheard the conversation
          you were having with those people. I can't
          help but think this is my fault.

                    JAMES
          You'd be right.

                    ANNIE
          I may have been a catalyst, but your
          barista told me that this was going to
          happen eventually.

                    JAMES
          Who?

                    ANNIE
          I don't want to get anyone in trouble—
          including you. Let me help you. We can
          redecorate together, I'll even try to
          bake some cookies that aren't store-bought,
          even though I haven't baked anything
          since I was a kid.

JAMES
No. Thank you. You've done enough.

ANNIE
I'm not going to let what happened
between us ruin your business.

JAMES
Why do you care?

ANNIE
It would be a shame for this place to
go out of business. Let's just say I
tried coffee at one of the other cafés
in town, and you were right.

JAMES
I'm sorry, I didn't hear you, can
you repeat that?

ANNIE
(smiling while rolling eyes)
You . . . were . . . right.

JAMES
(smirking)
I like hearing you say that.

ANNIE
Don't get used to it.

JAMES
So you're doing this just to get your
coffee privileges reinstated?

ANNIE

I also feel guilty for my part
in all of this. I was trying to
help, but I made things worse,
and the last thing I want is for
your hatred of Christmas to get
any worse. Your life is hard enough
as it is.

JAMES

Why do you think my life is hard?

ANNIE

I'm assuming you're grumpy for a
reason.

JAMES

(taken aback)
I'm grumpy?

ANNIE

(smiling)
The grumpiest.

JAMES

Fine. But I'm making the cookies.

ANNIE

Deal.

James offers his hand for Annie to shake.

JAMES

I'm James by the way.

ANNIE

I know. I'm Annie.

Annie takes his hand and they hold on longer than necessary for a customary handshake, their gazes lingering.

Chapter 10
MARIAH

*T*he next day on set is similar to my first. I show up late, having miscalculated how long it would take to get there from Ellie's cabin. I look like shit since I overslept on her surprisingly comfortable fold-out couch. Thankfully, my hickey is faded enough for regular makeup to hide most of it, but I can't say the same about the bags under my eyes. And my head hurts from the two(?) bottles of wine we drank. My memories from near the end of the night are fuzzy, of the two of us struggling to figure out the pull-out, of fighting with a fitted sheet together, of Ellie giving me one of her pillows since the linen closet didn't have extras.

And, of course, of finding out Jax is a fuckboy.

I knew he was too good to be true. After all this time I still haven't learned to listen to the little voice inside my head, succumbing instead to the little voice inside my pants. Even that would have been okay if I'd got it out of my system and scratched the itch I'd had since high school, but no, I had to go further and fall for all the tricks in the fuckboy book.

I'm going to swear off dating men for a while.

My workstation is barely set up for the extras and other side actors when my first person shows up for his makeup. I get started making him look like he's cold by paling his face, then rosying his cheeks and nose.

"Hell-ooo!" Ellie's voice singsongs as the door swings open.

I do a double take, having not expected her. She waltzes in as if hangovers aren't a thing that exist, one hand holding a tray of Starbucks drinks and the other a pink pastry box.

"What are you doing here?" My voice is crotchety from not having been used yet today.

"Good morning to you, too," she says, the smile on her face not waning in the least. Ellie sets the coffees and box down. "I wasn't sure what your drink is, so I got a couple different options." She lists them, all with varying types of milk and coffee flavours.

"Oh . . . uh. I'll take the oat milk caramel one. Please."

She hands it to me, then opens the pastry box with a flourish to reveal cupcakes, pointing at each and telling me all the varieties.

"Isn't it a bit early for cake?" I raise an eyebrow.

She gasps as if I've caused her great offence. "Never."

I take the least sugary-looking one and set it down beside my drink. The guy in my chair takes one, too, and then Ellie grabs the rest of the drinks and cupcakes and flits around the space giving them all away, returning empty-handed.

"Where's yours?" I ask.

She shrugs. "I can get one later. Anyway!" She claps her hands, then rubs them together. "We need to come up with a plan."

I eye the dude in my chair. "Maybe . . . later?"

"Ah, yes. Wouldn't want word of our sinister plot getting around, now would we? Even though I'm sure Rick here can keep a secret. Can't you, Rick?" She nudges him, and he laughs. *How does she know this random extra's name?*

Ellie looks behind her, moves a few things out of the way, then plops her ass down on my table and gets comfortable.

I blink at her a few times. "Are you just gonna sit here and watch me work?"

She straightens. "If that's okay. Yeah. I don't have anywhere else to go, and I don't know of anything to do in this city. And honestly sitting at home alone all day after what happened is kind of depressing, so I thought I'd come visit you at work, because, you know, where else would I be? But if I'm cramping your style, or getting in your way, or—"

She moves to get up, but I stop her. "It's fine. You can keep me company."

Ellie sighs in relief and gives me a happy smile. "Thank you. Plus, I want to see you at work! Makeup is so fascinating. I can barely put on mascara, and you do a full face—"

She continues chattering away next to me, like a happy little parakeet, but it's not as irritating as I found it before. The day passes quickly with Ellie commenting on what I'm doing and asking thoughtful questions or telling me stories that keep me on my toes and bring a smile to my face. Behind the scenes, she knows so much about the industry and fills me in on the goings-on between takes. Before I know it, it's wrap time and nearing dinner.

"Hungry?" I ask after cleaning up my station.

"Starving!" Ellie hops down from her perch and stretches, a little sliver of belly appearing below her Christmas sweater.

"I know a place, but you can't wear that. It's outdoors."

Ellie shrugs, then peels her shirt off. My eyes follow every bit of skin revealed as her tank top tries to leave her body with the sweater, catching just below her bra line, before she removes it and readjust herself. "How's this?"

I swallow, my mouth suddenly dry. "Yep. Good. Ready?"

We both jump in my car and drive west toward Vancouver. Ellie scans the radio until she finds a song she knows, then sings obnoxiously with the window rolled down, her unruly blond hair blowing back behind her. Her energy is contagious, and before I know it even I'm tapping my fingers on the steering wheel.

We pull into the parking lot fifteen minutes later.

"Mariah, this is a Canadian Tire," Ellie says, stating the obvious.

"I know." I unbuckle my seat belt and get out, Ellie following close behind. Once she's out of the car, I nod my chin toward an unassuming food truck parked close by. "That's Lully's—best hot dogs in BC."

Ellie squeals, her fists clenched to her sides, and does a little jump. It's like she gets so excited she can't possibly contain herself and this is the only way she can release energy. Where she gets all this energy from, I'd like to know. I'm sure if she could bottle it and sell it she'd be a multimillionaire.

She grips my arms and shakes me violently. "Is this like a super-secret awesome place to eat that only locals know about and it's like a total diamond in the rough and my mind is about to be blown to a whole other level of awesomeness from hot dogs alone?!"

I blink a few times. "Uh . . . yes."

Ellie does a little happy dance, then grabs me by the arm and pulls me toward the food truck. I coach her through ordering, warning her not to even mention ketchup in the presence of the uber-grumpy-but-secretly-nice owner, who is just as likely to yell at you about the sports team you support as he is to donate his kidney to help a stranger. A few minutes later we're sitting in the sunshine at one of the picnic tables with foot-longs on pretzel buns and craft sodas.

She takes her first bite, moaning pornographically.

My chest swells with satisfaction. "Good, hey?"

With her mouth half-full, she mumbles some complimentary words, and possibly a few expletives, before swallowing her first bite. "I tell ya what, that is the best meat I've ever had in my mouth!"

Her proclamation is so loud that the owner behind the grill laughs.

"I would never in a million years have thought to eat at the food truck behind the Canadian Tire," she says, wiping her mouth on a napkin. "It's so cool you grew up here. You must know all the awesome secret places. I wish I got to grow up in a small town."

"Chilliwack and Abbotsford are cities," I correct.

"Dude, you have farmland in the middle of your cities. I saw a herd of cows next to a school."

I consider this a moment, then nod. "True. But it wasn't as

great as you think. Actually, it kind of sucked. I wish I'd grown up in Vancouver."

"Why? So you could share the Sky Train on your way to school with the unhoused old lady and the pet rat that lives on her shoulder?"

I blink a few times. "What?"

Ellie shrugs. "Her name was Gertie. The rat was Alfonso." She takes another huge bite, putting an end to that story before it even begins. Then, with a full mouth, she asks, "What could have sucked so bad that you left this awesome place?"

"Maybe if I'd grown up in a bigger city, gone to a bigger school, there'd have been more kids like me. I was just . . . a little different. I never fit in."

"Example?"

"I don't know. While the other girls were going through their *My Little Pony* phase I was super into zombies."

"In other words, you were awesome."

I shrug, glad she thinks so. "In grade six . . ." I hesitate, unsure if I should continue, never one for sharing embarrassing anecdotes. I haven't known Ellie very long, but after only a few days I can tell that she is probably the least judgmental person on the planet. She waits patiently while I gather my courage, her big round eyes staying focused on my face. I take another breath, then try again. "You'd think that Halloween would be my time of year to shine, right? It's supposed to be morbid and dark and creepy. Guess I missed the memo about that. First year of middle school there was a costume contest, and I was stoked. I'd been dabbling in costume makeup for a few years by then, and I had this awesome idea I wanted to try. I got up on stage with my costume I'd worked on for weeks, of a zombie with its guts spilling out, and I made a huge show of cannibalizing my own intestines since I made them out of gummy worms."

"That's awesome!" Ellie shouts, slapping a hand on the table.

"Yeah. No. Someone screamed, a few others cried. One kid

threw up. I was sent to see the school counsellor, who called my parents, who showed up and were absolutely mortified since they're evangelicals and super upstanding members of the church community. I was suspended from school for a week and my parents grounded me. I wasn't allowed to watch my 'creepy shows' anymore. Not that it stopped me, I still snuck them in."

"I'm sorry." Ellie's shoulders slump. "Who ended up winning the contest?"

I roll my eyes. "Jessica and Brittney. One was a horse and the other a cowgirl."

Ellie snorts. "How original."

"Right?" Ellie's approval is so validating. "I had been a weirdo at school before that, and I was even more of a weirdo after. I kept to myself." Ellie's eyes turn pitying, which sours my stomach. "Anyway," I say, eager to change the subject. I haven't talked about myself for so long since . . . ever. And now I'm feeling all exposed and squirmy about it. "We should figure out what to do about Jax. Are you sure you still want to *Home Alone* him?"

Ellie's already done her hot dog, whereas I've had maybe two bites. She wipes her face on a napkin while nodding. "Hell to the yes. Let's teach this dirtbag a lesson."

I get out my phone and open the Notes app. "Okay. Ideas?"

She leans forward, elbows on the table. "How about this. We blindfold him and tie him up in a field and put bird food all over him."

"Uh . . . okay." I write that down.

"Or we could put hundreds of cheese slices all over his truck and put glitter in his vents and slick the inside of his windshield with Vaseline."

I write that down, too, even though I think it's a horrible idea.

"Oh! Oh! We hire a clown to follow him around for two weeks and make him think he's being stalked by a serial killer!"

I lower my phone, shocked that a person who radiates sunshine and rainbows can have a mind that goes so dark. "Or, how about we do things that won't land us in jail?"

Ellie considers this. "Good point."

"Think less Carrie Underwood 'Before He Cheats' and more Regina George from *Mean Girls*."

"Hmm." Ellie leans back, stroking her chin like the evil genius she apparently is. "In *Mean Girls* they pranked Regina in ways that took away her power."

"Yes."

"So, what is it that gives Matt his power?"

I contemplate this for a second. "He's hot?"

Ellie snaps her fingers. "Bingo."

"He has that amazing hair," I continue.

"And he smells really good."

I hum low in my throat. "Fuck, does he smell good."

"And his arms," Ellie adds.

"The tendons on his hands and forearms." I bite my lip.

Ellie squirms in her seat. "The way he grabs you and digs his fingers into your hips."

I lean closer on the table. "How he can lift you so easily, toss you around—"

"Shove you against a wall—" Ellie leans forward, too.

"Do whatever he wants—"

"Even though you *both* want it . . ."

Ellie and I pause, leaning toward each other with heated smirks on our faces. Her eyes dart to my lips, and mine follow suit. The tension between us sparks a heat in my belly, sending a sharp tingle between my thighs. Before I can determine if it's Ellie or talking about Jax that caused it, she breaks the spell by clearing her throat. We both move away at the same time.

"Okay, yes." I shake my head, trying to get back on track. "We make him less . . . hot. But how do we do that without committing a felony or causing permanent damage?"

She thinks for a moment, then her eyes alight with an idea. "I've got it."

THREE HOURS LATER, Ellie is dressed up as the old man again. She limps into the bar while I wait outside for her text. Ellie takes several minutes, leaving me far too long to think about our plan and all the ways it could go wrong. I'm nearly ready to call everything off when she texts me.

> **ELLIE:** Kevin

> **ME:** Why do we need code words?

> **ELLIE:** KEVIN!!!!

Summoning all my courage—which isn't very much—I rush inside. Ellie's old man voice resounds from the men's bathroom, talking loudly about how he's never had a shit so big it clogged a toilet like that. I'm panicking too hard to laugh. My heart is pounding and my stomach is clenched so tight I feel like I might barf and ruin the whole plan. I get to work behind the bar. My first operative is taping a remote-controlled fart machine to the underside of a cabinet, which was Ellie's idea, obviously. I told her it was immature and not worth our time, but she couldn't even get through explaining the joke without laughing, so I reluctantly agreed. Afterward, I squirt purple dye into his glass of Coke Zero and nab his truck keys that he stores under the till. I leave just as fast as I came in, glancing around at the patrons to see that nobody's even looked up from their scratch tickets.

Once outside, I text Ellie the code.

> **MARIAH:** Woof

I don't wait for Ellie before I start setting up the traps in his little truck.

Ellie joins me several minutes later and jumps into the driver's seat, peeling off her moustache as she does. "All set?"

"Yeah, I think so." I look over the interior, and nothing seems out of place.

"We should check to see if it works. I'll be Matt, you be his next date." Ellie leans against the seat and manspreads, regarding me with a Joey from *Friends* "How you doin'?" look.

I snort a laugh at her impression but can't help but squeeze my legs together. Ellie is normally super femme, but masc energy really works for her. I have to admit, I'm a little turned on.

"Hey, baby," she says in a deep voice. "Buckle in, sweet cheeks, let's go on our date."

I try to remain stoic as I reach for my seat belt, pulling it across my lap to find a bright red thong wrapped around the buckle. "What's this?" My voice trembles against a laugh.

"Oh, shit!" Ellie grabs it. "Sorry, sugar plum, no idea how that got there. Let me put this away—" She reaches past me to open the glove compartment, only to have an avalanche of condoms and lube spill out over my lap.

I burst out laughing, unable to contain myself any longer.

Ellie keeps up the ruse, pretending to be a very flustered Jax as he fumbles with everything, trying to shove it back in the box, all while muttering apologies and calling me increasingly cringy pet names until I'm howling.

Finally, Ellie breaks character, regarding me with a radiant smile. "You have the best laugh."

"Oh my god, I do not." I wipe my eyes. "I sound like a suffocating goose."

She chuckles. "Maybe I like suffocating geese."

Ellie's face glows with such fondness it turns my insides to goop. "Okay, let's get this set up again and get out of here."

She claps her hands. "Phase two!"

"Oh, another thing, look what I found in his glove box." I show her his insurance papers.

"'Matthew Jackson,'" she reads.

"Just in case you needed more proof."

Ellie shrugs. "I didn't, but I appreciate you thinking of me."

After shoving his papers back into the glove box and resetting the trap, we exit the vehicle. I hand Ellie Jax's keys, which she eyes mischievously before moving to the back of the truck and unlocking the tunnel-cover, sliding it open to look in the truck bed.

"What are you doing?" I ask. This wasn't part of the plan.

"Jackpot!" Ellie hoists his gym bag out and slides the cover shut.

I panic. "What are you doing with that?"

An insidious grin lights up her face. "Do you know how much stuff we can fuck with in here?"

"I don't know . . ."

"I promise, all Regina George, no Carrie Underwood."

I hesitate, pressing my lips together, not entirely trusting Ellie to keep us out of jail considering the ideas she's had in the past. "Stealing isn't something I'm okay with."

"It's not stealing, it's borrowing. We'll return it in one hour. He'll never even know it's gone. Please please please?" She sticks her big bottom lip out.

"Fine." I cave with a roll of my eyes. "But this better be very Regina George, or I'm out."

INT. JAMES'S APARTMENT - EVENING

James's apartment is similar to Jenna's: small kitchen area with a table separating it from the living room. The lighting is dim but warm, the walls have tasteful decorations, and there's a touch of hominess despite James being a sad, single man.

Annie and James are standing opposite each other at his kitchen island with mixing bowls, cookie sheets, and ingredients scattered around them. They both wear aprons dusted with flour.

Annie spoons some dough from a bowl and licks it.

                    ANNIE
          This cookie dough is fantastic!

                    JAMES
          Thanks. It's my . . . It's an old recipe.

                    ANNIE
          When I was a kid I loved baking, but I
          haven't done it in years.

                    JAMES
          Why not?

                    ANNIE
          There is always so much else to do.
          My job as a lawyer keeps me busy. I
          barely have time to sit down unless it's
          behind a computer screen.

JAMES
So I wasn't wrong about you needing to
slow down and enjoy the simple things in life.

ANNIE
No, you weren't wrong. That's why I love
visiting my sister so much. Her life is
so quiet and peaceful. Well, it was before
she had her baby. Now it's loud. Very,
very loud.

JAMES
Sure is. I hear the baby crying all hours
of the night.

ANNIE
I'm sorry, does he keep you awake?

JAMES
Not really, I just feel bad for your sister
is all. Being a mother sounds like hard work.

Annie cuts out a final shape and places it on the
cookie sheet.

James removes a baked cookie sheet from the oven and
places the last tray in the oven.

James uses a spatula to lift a warm cookie from the
sheet and tears it in half, handing one half to Annie.

Annie takes a small bite.

ANNIE
Wow, it's even better baked.

JAMES

Many things in life are.

ANNIE

Seriously, you're so talented.

JAMES

Just wait until we ice them. We'll have to
wait for them to cool, though.

ANNIE

We?

JAMES

Sorry, I didn't mean to assume you'd help
me with that. You've already done so
much, getting lights strung up in the
café and helping me with the garland.
It was nice having company for
everything.

ANNIE

And, you have to admit, it
looks great.

JAMES

(sighing)
You were right.

ANNIE

Wow, it does feel good to hear that.

JAMES

So you don't need to come back and
help ice the cookies. Unless you want to.

ANNIE

I do.

Annie and James share a quiet moment.

ANNIE

I should go. Mind if I take a few
of these to my sister?

JAMES

Of course. I can walk you back. Wouldn't
want you getting lost.

Chapter 11
ELLIE

*A*fter a quick visit to a thrift store, we head back into the bar. The parking lot has quite a few more cars than last time, which will be good for our cover. Mariah gets out of the car, fiddling with her outfit. She's sporting a blond wig, tight black pants, and a cut-off Harley Davidson crop top. I step up beside her, wearing faded Levi's and a leather jacket. My hair is tied up and covered by a red bandana, and I have a stick-on beard I borrowed from the costume department. Mariah's done our makeup to age us both: me with weathered wrinkles and freckles from years of too much sun, and Mariah with lines around her mouth from chain-smoking cigarettes.

Mariah pulls at her shirt. "This is a bad idea."

"What are you talking about? I barely recognize us. You killed our makeup!"

She's not convinced, looking around like an animal caught in a trap and seeking a quick escape.

"Look," I say, pulling out my phone and turning it to selfie mode before stepping up beside her. "We're a perfect couple."

She regards us both on the screen and gives a subtle nod. "We do look pretty good."

"Smile!"

Mariah pops her hip and tilts her chin like a pin-up, and I give the camera a mean grimace before snapping a photo.

"Okay, yeah, we look the part," she concedes. "But I'm a terrible liar. It won't work."

"'Course it will, soda pop," I drawl in a Southern accent. "Like I said, it ain't lyin', it's actin'.'"

Mariah gives her head a shake, lips pursed.

Grabbing her by the waist, I tug her to my side. "Now listen here, missus. You an' I, we go way back. We met down in New Orleans on a tugboat casino playin' blackjack—"

Mariah pinches the bridge of her nose, but she's fighting a smile under it.

"After all my time in the clink I decided to go straight, and you wanted to show me the world on account o' me bein' locked up so long. Ever since, we been explorin' everywhere we can explore by land, since I ain't allowed on those aer-o-planes no more."

Mariah snorts, her shoulders shaking.

I turn her to face me. "You an I's gonna have a good time tonight, ya hear?"

She rolls her eyes, a grin splitting her face.

I grip her shoulders. "I said, ya hear?"

"Yeah, I hear ya," she repeats in what is quite possibly the worst Southern accent I've ever heard.

"Maybe leave the talking to me," I say, breaking character.

Inside, the place is busy enough that we're not noticed when we walk in. A small whiteboard on the bar has *Jell-O shots $2* messily scrawled on it, which explains the crowd. There's an odd mishmash of older working-class gentlemen and young college students, and our outfits don't look too out of place. We find a table in the back—far enough away to pass a casual glance but still maintain a visual of Matt at the bar.

My heart skips when I see him, even though he looks so different here as Jax, his alter ego. Or is this his true self? Maybe the sweet, considerate, kind person I met at the cabin is the ruse. He's not the man I had feelings for; that person doesn't exist. I swallow the pain and pull Mariah's chair out for her before taking my own.

Since it's busier than usual, they have a server waiting tables. After several minutes she reaches us. Mariah tenses, looking away and twirling a lock of blond hair to obscure part of her face. *Shit, hopefully the server doesn't recognize her.*

"Hey, welcome to Grumpy Joe's, we have two-dollar Jell-O shots tonight and the poutine is on special."

"I'll have a Bud—in a bottle, none of that on-tap nonsense. And the missus here will have a Long Island iced tea." I order for her, not only because it's the gentlemanly thing to do, but because she was right about being a terrible actress. One wrong move and she'll blow our cover. Even now, with very little risk of being caught, there's a bead of sweat trickling from her wig down the side of her face.

The server jots down our order, not bothering to make eye contact with us.

"And, little lady, you want a turkey club and poutine?" I ask Mariah, to which she replies with a quick nod. Turning back to the server, I ask, "What soup you got today?"

Mariah kicks me under the table.

"Never mind, I'll have a BLT and fries."

The server leaves and Mariah huffs out a breath. "I can't keep this up."

"Yes you can, you're doing great!"

"What if someone recognizes me?" She fiddles with her outfit.

I tilt my head to the side. "I barely recognize you."

This seems to calm her. Then she leans forward quickly, agitated. "Do you think we pranked him too much?"

I roll my eyes. "We didn't. My siblings and I used to prank each other all the time. This is entry-level, trust me. But maybe if *someone* let me hire a clown—"

She cuts me off with a wave of her hand. "Not happening."

I raise my hands in defeat. "I know, I know. But seriously, all we did was hide bleu cheese in his bag."

"And swap his cologne for cheap bubblegum crap from the dollar store."

"And rub brown marker on his gym shorts so it looks like he sharted himself," I say, laughter bubbling up.

Mariah struggles to stop laughing, too. "Okay, yeah, that's pretty funny."

"See? Harmless." I don't tell Mariah about the fake mouse I stuck in his water bottle. The image of him jumping and screaming like a little girl around his big, muscly gym bros sparks so much joy.

We were able to return the bag to his truck and lock the doors with no issue, but now we have to find a way to return his keys behind the till . . . with him there, and all these witnesses. We hadn't quite thought this part through.

Our drinks and food show up several minutes later, and I'm happily surprised that the sandwiches are actually really good.

Mariah and I eat off of each other's plates, me sampling her poutine while she tries my BLT. We seem to forget that we're in danger of getting caught, falling into a companionable back-and-forth conversation, swapping stories about my experiences on set and wedding drama she's witnessed. There's something about spending time with Mariah that feels so natural. I never would have thought after that first day together, where she'd been the world's biggest grump and seemed irritated by everything I did—including the way I breathed—that we'd be able to move past it. Now I can say with confidence that we're friends. Sure, I break down everyone eventually, but this is more comfortable than the average co-worker friendship. Perhaps it's the situation we've found ourselves in that's brought us together when it could have ripped us apart.

One hour and three drinks later, our opportunity finally arrives. A crew of college-age people walk in and head to the bar for Jell-O shots. Mariah and I hunch down, waiting for the right moment. Matt leans over the bar to flirt, but his usual hundred-watt smile has been blackened from the dye in his drink. It's not enough to deter the young women though, who giggle at whatever he says.

"What do you think he said to them?" Mariah asks, fingernails tapping her glass with an irritated beat.

I scoff, also agitated by him openly flirting with multiple women right in front of us. "Probably something about karma."

Mariah catches my gaze, a sinister gleam in her eye. "I think it's time."

I give her a solemn nod, pull a small remote from my pocket, and press the button.

An obnoxious fart rips from behind the bar. Everyone pauses like they're in a tableau. Then, the group of women break out in laughter. Matt's eyes widen in shock and his mouth hangs agape, horrified. He turns bright red, then takes a few steps back, trying to laugh it off. Whatever spell he had on the women has been broken. They take their cheap drinks and leave.

Look at that, we're already making the world a better place.

Matt ducks down, searching for the fart machine, but can't seem to find it.

Meanwhile, Mariah and I are dying, trying to stop ourselves from howling with laughter. My belly aches from it, my whole body shaking. Mariah does a little wheezing inhale, which only makes it harder for me to pull myself together. We finally manage to force the giggles away, each wiping at a tear, and prepare ourselves for round two.

Our next opportunity arises about ten minutes later. Another fart rips through the room, echoing off the walls. This time Matt is furious, pulling things off shelves and looking inside cupboards, frazzled beyond belief.

Mariah and I are barely keeping it together, both of us bowed over the table. We manage two more farts before Matt finds the sound machine and inspects it with irritation. He scans the crowd with an angry glare.

"Shit," I say. "Act natural."

"What the fuck does that mean?" Mariah whispers, not acting naturally at all.

We need to get out of here before she blows our cover. But

before we can do that, we have to return Matt's keys. Unfortunately, he's now on high alert, eyeing everyone suspiciously. This won't be easy.

I stroke my beard. "We should have put his keys back first."

"What are we going to do now?" Mariah can't keep the panic out of her voice.

I take her hand, assuming my role as badass biker boyfriend. Deepening my voice, I say, "Be cool, honey bunny." Pocketing the keys, I swagger my way to the bar.

Matt regards me with mild disdain and doesn't even ask me what I want. Rude.

"Can I have some of those there Jell-O shots?" I drawl.

He nods, then sets a few down on the bar from the bin behind him. "Two dollars."

I inspect them. "The missus ain't one much for red. Got any blues?"

He eyes me, and for a second, I think he's going to recognize me. He has, in fact, stared into these very same eyes while wooing me into bed, naming our future dogs, planning the chicken coop, and filling our imaginary cellar with pickled vegetables from our garden. My stomach clenches as I prepare for a hasty retreat.

Then he sighs, turning back to the bin to retrieve a few blues. "Two dollars."

I'm equal parts relieved and disappointed that he doesn't know who I am. Maybe he wasn't paying as close attention to me as I thought—close attention to my eyes, that is. He paid plenty of attention to other areas of my body.

I was hoping he'd have to go into the fridge to get the blue ones and give me a moment alone with the till, but now I have to think on my feet. While I pretend to fish money out of my wallet, I pause, then squint at him. "You got something going on with your teeth there, bud."

Matt blinks a few times. Pulling out his phone, he checks his reflection in the camera. "What the . . . Excuse me."

Jackpot. Used his own vanity against him. As soon as Matt's around the corner I reach as far as I can to tuck the keys behind the bar. My arms aren't long enough. I lean farther but still can't reach. If I drop them, he'll know something is up with his truck and it'll blow our cover. Shit, I have like five seconds—

Someone comes from behind me, grabbing the keys. I startle, my heart hammering in my ears, and my life flashes before my eyes.

"Got it." Mariah reaches the extra few inches and tucks them under the till before grabbing my hand and pulling me out of there.

We walk as fast as we can back to my car. Once we're safely inside, we burst out laughing in relief.

"Did you see his face?" she cries, her breath coming in gasping wheezes.

"That was priceless!" I slap my knee.

"I can't believe we did that! We almost got caught!"

"Totally worth it."

She has the most gorgeous, full-fledged smile on her face, her skin is flushed pink, and her chest is rising and falling quickly from adrenaline. My heart squeezes, and by god, I'd prank a fuckboy every day if it meant making her smile like that.

"Well, sugar tits." I slap her knee. "Let's take you home."

She cackles at her newest pet name, then nods, regarding me with a tilt of her head, eyes glittering.

BACK AT THE cabin we're still running high on endorphins and, with a bottle of champagne popped to keep the spirit going, we're soon a little tipsy. We bumble around getting our costumes off, trading places at the tiny bathroom sink to remove our makeup. It feels oddly domestic doing this with Mariah, like we're well-practised despite only having spent one night together. Once we're rid of our outfits and back to our normal selves, I turn on *Home Alone 2* in the background and take out a surprise I got for her.

"What's all this?" Mariah asks, rubbing moisturizer into her face as she looks at the table loaded with plain sugar cookies, tubs of frosting, and an assortment of sprinkles.

"I thought it'd be fun to decorate cookies together!" I vibrate with excitement, but Mariah's eyes narrow with uncertainty. I gesture to everything set out, suddenly second-guessing my idea. Maybe I shouldn't be forcing Christmas on her. "I feel bad that you never had any normal Christmas traditions, and my family and I did this every year—though we always baked fresh cookies, we never bought them from the store, my mom's a great baker, and then we'd have a cookie decorating contest and it was so much fun and I feel like you should know what that's like, but we totally don't have to do it if you don't want to, and I—"

She cuts me off with a gentle hand on my arm, giving it a squeeze. Her face has softened, and she gives me a little smile. "Sure. Why not?"

I clench my fists. "Great! I'll show you what to do."

Mariah is a natural. Even with a lifetime of practice my cookies look like a preschooler's macaroni artwork. Meanwhile Mariah is creating literal snowy scenes on hers. I guess makeup skills have a lot of crossover.

"How are you doing that?" I ask, watching her technique.

"It's all in the wrist." She demonstrates, showing off her dexterity.

I follow her lead but create a weird ridge down the middle. "Oh no, I made a vulva."

She snorts a laugh. "Oh my god, you did."

"Well now I can't ruin it." I set it down and add some sprinkles around the edge for pubes.

"What the fuck," she wheezes.

"I'm just following the muse." I try to keep a straight face as I put a little pearl candy where the clitoris would go.

Mariah cackles. "That looks like way more fun. How about

this." She ruins her winterscape with a few swoops and swirls, and a moment later my vulva-cookie has a penis-cookie friend.

I giggle. "It's a bit droopy."

"That happens sometimes, nothing to be ashamed of," she quips.

Inspired, we each grab another cookie and keep this up. Before long, the table is filled with all sorts of festive genital cookies.

"You were amazing today," Mariah says, breaking the companionable silence between us while we decorate. "I can't believe Jax looked you right in the eye for like five minutes and didn't even recognize you. You're a gifted actress."

I shrug. "I'm not *that* good. It was more your makeup skills than anything."

She nudges me with her foot under the table. "Don't sell yourself short."

"It's just fact. I've been acting for years, ever since junior high, and I'm still playing secondary characters. When I started out, I figured, hell yeah, Barista 2, what a dream! And here I am, years later, still playing a barista."

"You're more than a barista, though," she clarifies.

I clench my fists in excitement, breaking a cookie. "You read the script!"

"Of course. I don't want to lose my job."

"I'm glad you did, because I didn't want to accidentally ruin the ending." I pop the broken cookie into my mouth and chew while talking. "So yeah, okay, I'm more than a barista this time, but I'm still not the lead. I've been in seven films now, three with this company alone. I've worked my way up from Barista 2 to Inn Housekeeper to Sister of the Lead, and now I've done Best Friend of the Lead twice in a row." My shoulders slump. "I'm thirty-one now. Opportunities to be the star will get fewer and fewer. Soon, I'll be applying for roles like Crotchety Mother of the Bride, and Grumpy Neighbour with Too Many Cats."

"It's not that bad," Mariah says, but I barely hear her past my spiralling thoughts.

I pick up a new cookie and focus all my attention on it while talking. "It doesn't seem to matter how hard I work, if I memorize the script weeks before, if I show up early and cheer everyone on, if I nail my lines and my blocking and even manage to force some fake tears—I'm still typecast as the same person I always am. I think there's something about me that's just not meant to be the lead," I continue, musing more to myself than to her. "Now, Julia. She's meant to be the lead. She has main character energy out the wazoo. You can feel it when she walks into a room. It's like she has a fan blowing her hair back all the time, you know? You can tell by looking at her that she's special and different. She'd never get cast as a barista. She's so perfect, with her flowing waves, her cute button nose, her symmetrical smile. This is her first acting job, aside from that toothpaste commercial, and she landed a lead role outright. She has a bright future ahead of her, in all the best ways." I sigh, then straighten. "Good for her. I'm not here to tear other women down. I'm glad she gets to live her dream. I'm sure she's worked hard, too. The happiness I feel for her is genuine, but . . . Why not me? Maybe I'm only every meant to be a secondary character . . ." I let that gross feeling pool in my gut as envy leeches into my core, sinking into a moment of darkness.

There's an ache deep in my bones, knowing that being the side character goes much further than that, resonating not just through my career, but my own life. I'll never get the happily-ever-after I've always wanted—not on set, and not in the real world, either. Matt has proven it again. I'm destined to watch from the sidelines as it happens for other people, but never for me.

I look up from my latest penis-cookie creation to see Mariah's pitying expression. I snap out of it, forcing a cheery smile to my face and straightening my posture. "But hey! I get to work on movies! That's amazing. I'm really lucky. I am grateful every day for this opportunity."

Mariah gives me a weird look I can't decipher. "It's okay if you feel—"

I cut her off, eager to get the conversation away from me and my lacklustre acting career and change the subject. "What about you? Have you always wanted to do film makeup?"

She thinks for a moment, regarding me while I fidget, my sunshine smile firmly reaffixed to my face. Seeming to give up, she lets the conversation switch without bugging me about it. "Yeah, actually. I always wanted to work on movies."

"That's great! Look at you, living your dream."

"Not really. I didn't exactly have this type of movie in mind."

I raise an eyebrow. "What kind of movies *did* you have in mind?"

INT. APARTMENT HALLWAY - EVENING

James walks Annie slowly down the hallway as they smile shyly at each other.

Through the walls they hear baby Henry crying.

Annie and James share a concerned look before walking faster toward Jenna's door.

INT. JENNA'S APARTMENT - EVENING

Annie opens the door and steps inside to find Jenna flustered and nearly in tears, herself.

James stands at the doorway, looking uneasy.

> ANNIE
> Oh no, are you okay?

> JENNA
> Henry won't stop crying. Usually I take him on a walk to the park so he can go on his favourite swing. That always quiets him down but I'm so exhausted I can't even think straight, and I—

> ANNIE
> I'll take him out for you.

> JENNA
> No, it's ok. The park is a few blocks away and I don't want you to get lost. The streets around here are convoluted and—

                    JAMES
        (stepping inside)
        I'll show her.

                    ANNIE
        Are you sure?

                    JAMES
        Of course.

                    JENNA
        Thank you! I could really use the sleep.

EXT. PARK - EVENING

Annie is swinging baby Henry at the playground
while James stands nearby. They are both dressed
in winter clothes and snow is piled all around. The
streetlights are on and the sun is beginning to set,
casting a romantic ambiance on the pair. They are
alone in the park.

                    ANNIE
        How long have you been in Hemlock Grove?

                    JAMES
        I moved here about five years ago. I grew up
        not too far away. A few towns over. When they
        rebuilt downtown we were the first to put in
        a bid with our business idea. We've been
        here ever since.

                    ANNIE
        Have you always wanted to run a café?

JAMES

Not really. It was never my dream,
per se, but it became my dream.
And now it's all I have.

ANNIE

I have to tell you, the coffee you make is
amazing. What's your secret?

JAMES

I have beans shipped from all over the
world and roast them fresh in house.
After you roast the coffee it will oxidize
over time, reducing the fullness of the
flavour. We brew our coffee right
after roasting, which is why it's
the best you'll ever taste.

ANNIE

That's amazing. Have you ever been
to where your beans are grown?

JAMES

We had plans for it, but no. Never.

ANNIE

We?

Baby Henry starts crying.

ANNIE

Sorry, he's probably getting hungry. Here,
you hold him while I get his bottle ready.

Annie takes baby Henry out of the swing and hands him to James.

James looks at the baby, getting uncomfortable.

> JAMES
> No, I'm sorry. I can't do this.
> I have to go.

James hands baby Henry back to Annie and walks away quickly, abandoning them in the park all alone just as it's getting dark.

Chapter 12
MARIAH

I'm grateful Ellie let me break her Christmas movie diet. Feeling her squirm next to me as Ripley runs from face-sucking aliens is comedic gold. I don't even flinch as the story progresses since I've seen it close to twenty times, but somehow Ellie's lived under a rock and this is her first experience with the iconic classic.

"What do you like about this again?" Ellie asks, tucking closer to me.

I let her snuggle up, enjoying her warmth. "It came out in the seventies, but look at these practical effects! They're so subtle, so realistic. Like the way the egg moved—did you notice that?"

She wriggles in closer. "Yup. Sure did."

"And then when the face hugger shot out of the egg and onto that guy's helmet, it was blasted with high-pressure air hoses, and they used clams and mussels to make the inside of it look real and fleshy."

"Yuck."

"Yeah! And the part where the alien bursts out of his chest?"

She covers her eyes. "Don't remind me."

"They used real animal organs in the dummy body and the cast had no idea what was going to happen, so when it burst out and it was so gory and repulsive, they were completely surprised, and their reactions are genuine. It was awesome."

"I would have shit my pants."

I snort a laugh.

"Clean up on aisle two," she adds.

I laugh even harder.

"Was the alien itself CGI?"

I shake my head. "CGI wasn't a thing back then. That was an actor in a suit."

"No way," she scoffs, slapping me in the tit with the back of her hand. "Oops, sorry."

I barely notice, going on. "The actor was over seven feet tall. The suit was designed by this Swedish artist named H.R. Giger. I actually have a book of his artwork at my apartment. He's the creepiest motherfucker. The shit he comes up with are the things of horror—"

"Obviously." Ellie gestures at the screen as Ripley comes face-to-face with the alien's inner jaws. She clenches her whole body. "How'd they get it so . . . slimy?"

"Lube."

"What! No way."

"I'm totally serious. They bought it in gallons."

"I had no idea you could buy lube by the gallon. Maybe we should run to Costco and go in on one together. Lifetime supply, yo!"

She grins at me, and I smile back.

"Knowing how they made it actually makes it less scary," she tells me.

"Hope I didn't ruin the magic."

She shakes her head. "If anything, it's more magical this way. I can see why you think it's so amazing."

My chest warms, glad I've opened her mind to the genre. "It *is* amazing. This movie changed my life. My aunt showed it to me for the first time when I was nine—"

"Nine!"

"And it's what got me interested in sci-fi, horror, and makeup. And—"

"Wait, wait . . . *nine?*"

I shrug. "Yeah. My parents weren't pleased and didn't let her babysit me too often after that. But *Alien* is about so much more than gore and jump scares, and that's what she wanted to show me, what my parents didn't understand. It was—is—a groundbreaking film. Not just because the special effects are so amazing, but because this movie is a complete feminist icon. Back then, women weren't heroes. They weren't action stars. But Sigourney Weaver fuckin' nailed it, and Ripley became not just an amazing female protagonist, but one of the most iconic action stars of all time. What a badass."

Ellie twists in her seat and looks up at me. "I think you've talked more just now than the entire rest of our time together."

"Sorry."

"No," she says, grabbing my leg and smiling. "I like it."

I relax against her.

She continues, her voice gentle. "It's clear you're extremely passionate. And you obviously have the talent to make your dreams come true. I have zero doubts that someday you'll get to work on an amazing set like this."

My heart swells at her words, then sinks with reality. "I doubt it." I force myself to look away from Ellie, fiddling with a loose string on the blanket over our lap. "I've applied for lots of jobs over the years, all over Canada and the United States. And yet, I keep doing the same boring shit over, and over, and over again. I thought this movie would be my big break. I thought, *hey, it's a movie, it's gotta be better than what I'm doing in the wedding scene.* But I'm here, and I'm still doing the same thing I've always done. I feel even further from my goal than before."

Ellie gives my arm a squeeze. I look down at her, and she's so close, her big doe eyes shining. We share a moment of silence, a buzz of electricity building between us as tension coils in my belly.

Our eyes dance. She leans closer. My lips part . . .

"Do me," she whispers.

My heart stutters. "What?"

"Do my makeup."

"Oh." I blink a few times and give my head a shake, letting the tension dissipate. The zing I'd felt earlier must have been my imagination. "Are you sure?"

Ellie sits up, tucking her legs underneath herself. "Yeah! Do my makeup the way you wish you could, if you were on an awesome set like this. Please?"

She doesn't have to ask me twice.

I retrieve my duffel bag from my car and sit her on a stool in the kitchen, *Aliens* playing in the background for inspiration. We switch effortlessly between silence and conversation as I apply the various layers, giddy to finally use all the expensive shit I bought eons ago but have barely touched. "I love your nose," I say, running my finger up the ridge as I spread makeup onto it.

"Really? I wish it were smaller. And swooped up at the tip, like Tinker Bell's."

"What? No. I like this little bump here." I run my finger along it one more time. "The first time I did your makeup I remember thinking, *ooh, I like this nose, this is a different nose.*"

"No, it's weird." She cowers, trying to cover it.

I stop her with a gentle reprimand. "Don't touch your face. I'm almost done."

She sighs, trying to relax. "It's not just the weird hump on my nose. It's my mouth. I'm not sure if my chin is too small, or my teeth are too big, or my lips are too thin, but there's something off about it."

"What? No, you're—"

"And my eyes are too close together. Paired with my nose that's too long, it's disconcerting. And don't get me started on my hair. If only it would make up its mind! Is it curly? Is it straight? Can it do just one thing rather than a bit of everything? Like, get it together—"

I grab her chin and force her to look into my eyes. "Stop it."

She gulps, her eyes darting back and forth between mine.

"Stop dissecting yourself like that. There is nothing wrong with your nose, or your lips, or your chin, or your teeth, or your eyes, or your hair. Okay? You're perfect, just the way you are. I wouldn't change a single thing about you."

Her eyes grow round and glassy, and I can feel her throat working behind my fingers.

I continue. "If you changed any of those things then you'd look like everyone else. And where's the fun in that? We're all meant to be different. That's what makes the world such a beautiful, interesting place. Promise me you won't talk about yourself like that again."

She gives a small nod.

"Say it."

"I promise," she squeaks.

"Good." I release her chin, then stroke a finger up her cheek back to her nose, where I was working. "It's like you've looked in the mirror too much," I muse, letting my eyes wander over all the things she perceives to be less than perfect. "Like when you stare at a word too long and you convince yourself it's misspelled."

"I never thought of it like that," she says quietly. "But you're right."

"Of course I am."

"I guess I've always thought it's my appearance that typecasts me in secondary roles, starting way back in junior high when I auditioned as Juliet and had to play Mercutio."

"I don't know what happened there, but it's not because of your appearance, trust me. You're stunning."

Ellie sits up straighter, glowing from my praise. "You're pretty gorgeous yourself."

I snort. "Thanks."

"Seriously! Your hair is amazing, and you have these lush lips and full cheeks, and you're so tall! Plus, you have the exact body type I always wanted. When I was a kid they always told me I'd grow boobs when I got older, but that never happened. You got my share, apparently."

"What are you talking about? Your boobs are great." I look at them a little too closely. They're small, the perfect size to fit in my hand. "And I bet they don't give you lower back pain."

"True. But look at you, you fill out your clothes so nicely, and there's so much to squeeze! I love it!"

I snort a laugh, amused. "Yeah, that's true. I'm high on squeeze-ability."

We settle back into silence, though this time it's a little different. I'm not sure if Ellie compliments every woman's figure or talks about their boobs. She probably does. But part of me wishes it was something she only did with me, and I have no idea why.

Several minutes later I'm finished with my design and release Ellie to stretch her legs and go to the bathroom.

"Holy shit!" she shouts when she sees herself in the mirror. "I'm an alien warrior priestess!"

I wait for her to finish going to the bathroom and come back out. She's right, she does look like a badass crossover between an *Avatar* humanoid and an H.R. Giger monster. It's not my best work since it's late, I'm tired, and I didn't want to take more than an hour to do it, but it's still pretty good.

Ellie slinks around the space, embodying the creature, making weird clicking sounds. "Okay, that's creepy," I admit. "Can I take your picture?"

"Picture?" She shakes her head. "Fuck that, let's make a film!"

ELLIE IS AN amazing actress, but it turns out she's also a phenomenal director. Within seconds she has a story in mind and is placing me around the cabin, telling me where to look, how to arrange my face, guiding me as she films. Then she hands me the phone and gets me to film her for several shots. Afterward, she balances the phone precariously on a stool for the shots we both need to be in. The last scene has her pressing me against the fridge, face-to-face. I'm not sure how it's going to turn out, because I had to squat down to get Ellie's height right for the take.

Afterward, Ellie goes to wash off her makeup while I arrange the clips in TikTok.

"It's done, I think," I say as she comes out, patting her face dry with a towel.

"Oooh, excited!" she squeals, though it's fairly subdued.

Neither of us has complained that it's one o'clock in the morning and we both have to get up for work in a few hours; we're having too much fun to care about how tired we'll be.

Ellie settles on the couch so close to me she's practically on my lap. I show her the film, which, for all of our work, is under two minutes long. It has *Blair Witch Project* vibes, with the shaky camera and the random close-ups, but it gives the whole thing a gritty, raw feel.

I'm shocked at how well it came together. Even though I was there for filming, I still shiver when Ellie slinks into the cabin and tense as we play a coy game of cat-and-mouse through the small space. By the time Ellie catches me and traps me against the fridge, fully embodying her creepy-yet-powerful makeup, I'm engrossed.

I hold my breath as the alien encounters the woman in the film, how its nose glides up the throat of its soon-to-be-victim, then comes to face-to-face with her. Eye contact is made, and I hadn't seen it while filming, but there's a palpable shift right then, from fear to curiosity. The alien's head tilts, her mouth parts, and her eyes drop down to the woman's lips. The woman swallows, her tongue darting out of her mouth, running along her bottom lip. Then their eyes meet again, sparking with electricity. Slowly, cautiously, they lean in—

The film ends.

I blow out a breath, tingles running down my arms. "Fuck, that was good."

"Yeah, you killed it with the makeup!" Ellie lifts a hand for a high-five, and I oblige wholeheartedly.

"What about you with those camera angles!"

"And you said you couldn't act, but you did great!"

"Only because you were directing. Seriously, you're multi-talented."

She beams. "Thank you."

Suddenly our close proximity feels different. She's been snuggled against me half the night, seemingly unaware of personal space, but just like in the film, there's a shift.

My heart notices first, picking up its pace, stuttering in my throat. My mouth notices second, becoming dry, my lips parting, breath coming in slower. It's not just me; Ellie feels it, too. Her eyes fall to my lips like they had in the film, and her throat works, swallowing.

I want to go further than the film. I want to bridge the space between us, to close the last inch separating her mouth from mine, to feel her against me. I want to pull her smaller frame against mine, to feel her body, to trail my fingers along her jaw, to taste her in so many places that the spark in my belly is quickly fanned to a flame.

But I'm not sure. Ellie's never mentioned being into women—maybe she isn't. Maybe this—whatever it is between us—is brought on by circumstance, by alcohol, by something other than mutual attraction. I don't want to take advantage. And I don't want her to do anything with me unless she's sure.

I'll never make that mistake again.

I pull back.

Ellie blinks a few times, then shifts away.

The tension between us is still there, slowly dissipating, becoming uncomfortable.

"Um. Do you mind if I post this?" I ask, raising my phone, hoping to bring some normalcy back between us.

Ellie nods. "Oh, yeah, sure."

"I don't have many followers, but this is definitely my best work." I add a caption and a few hashtags before publishing.

Ellie gets up and returns a moment later with her phone. "What's your name on there?"

I tell her, and she taps away at her phone. "Well, now you have one more follower. I love TikTok, mostly for the dancing, but I follow some people who do makeup already. Look, this is my favourite TikToker." She shows me a video of a woman in Pokémon cosplay lip-syncing and dancing, her big boobs bouncing with every move she makes, her huge anime eyes glinting coyly.

I smirk. "Yeah, she's a great . . . dancer."

Ellie nods, then flips through a few more videos on her For You Page, most of them full-figured women in revealing outfits, dancing or singing. "Yeah, it's such a rabbit hole. I could watch these all day."

My smile grows, along with a seedling of hope in my belly. "I'm sure you could."

"Anyway," she says, tucking her phone away and returning her attention to me. "It's getting pretty late."

I nod, but don't move, hoping that she'll come closer rather than move farther away.

"We both work early tomorrow," she continues, still not moving.

I nod again, beckoning her closer with my eyes, hoping she'll give me another opportunity to close the space between us.

But she doesn't.

Ellie finally stands and makes her way toward the bedroom. I'm immediately cold without her. She pauses before closing the door, giving me one last look, a small smile. "Sweet dreams."

"You, too." Though I'm not sure how I'm supposed to sleep now.

She closes the door, leaving me to my thoughts and regrets for not kissing her when I had the chance. If only I'd seen her TikTok feed minutes earlier; the algorithm doesn't lie. Fate has a cruel sense of humour.

After washing and preparing for bed, it's nearing two in the morning, but I'm still not tired. I snuggle up on the couch and open my phone to rewatch our video over and over. I relish the moment of Ellie being close, of her nose gliding up my throat, of the way she looks at my lips, the way our eyes meet, and I know—I just *know*—that the video captured something new and beautiful and uncertain. Something *real*.

An ache grows within me, a need for more, to relive that moment. But not until it's just the two of us and no uncertainty and no cameras, to fully explore that spark, to see where it leads. My imagination takes me further, to all the places I'd kiss, how I'd trail my fingers along Ellie's delicate collarbone, up her neck, along her jaw, then down lower, relishing every inch of her skin. When my body can no longer take the temptation, I slip my hand between my legs and rock against myself, rubbing circles slowly at first, then faster, until I find quiet release, mouth muffled against my pillow, and finally drift off to sleep.

INT. BREWED AWAKENING CAFÉ - DAY

Annie storms into the café, angry.

Kate is behind the till. There are no other customers.

ANNIE
Do you know where your boss is?

KATE
No, sorry, last I saw he was with you.
What's wrong?

ANNIE
He left us! He abandoned my nephew and me at
the park. I'm not from here and it took me an
hour to find my way home.

KATE
Oh my goodness, I'm so sorry!

ANNIE
I didn't have my phone on me and we wandered
around for an hour. It was cold and the sun
sets so early this time of year. I was so
scared, and I worried my sister sick!

KATE
I'm so glad you two are okay. You know,
I saw you walk by earlier and I should
have said something.

ANNIE
Said what?

KATE

He . . . Look, James avoids babies, okay?
They're a sensitive spot for him. When I saw
you two out with your nephew I thought it
would be okay, maybe it's been enough time.
I was wrong.

ANNIE

Enough time from what?

KATE

There's a reason why he hates Christmas,
why he doesn't decorate, or bake, or
listen to Christmas music, or go to the
Small Business Association party.

ANNIE

What does that have to do with him
being uncomfortable around babies?
Christmas and babies are two of the most
magical things in the world, but he
hates them both.

KATE

They just remind him of how alone he is.

ANNIE

I don't understand. He does well for
himself, he's attractive, and under that
grumpy exterior he's actually kind of sweet.
He smiled once.

KATE

You got him to smile?

                         ANNIE
Yeah. He has a really nice smile, actually.
He's a catch . . . the total package.

                         KATE
(with apprehension)
I'll tell you, but it didn't come
from me, okay?

                         ANNIE
Tell me what?

                         KATE
His wife left him. Two days before
Christmas, three years ago. On the night
of the Small Business Association party.
One second they were planning their family,
and the next, she was gone. He hasn't
been the same since.

Chapter 13
ELLIE

*T*his morning while Mariah got ready, I made us breakfast, brewing a big pot of coffee while whipping up some eggs and toast. Mariah comes out of the bathroom looking stunningly gorgeous as she always does, her hair defying gravity in its intricate teal swoops and curls, makeup done to perfection, and smelling like shea moisturizer. After we eat breakfast together I have a quick shower, careful not to get my hair wet, and we carpool into town.

I'm tired from staying up too late last night, but I have zero regrets. Something happened between us, something I can't put into words, or even sort in my own mind, but it's different. At least, I think so. I could have sworn she'd wanted to kiss me.

I've had feelings like this before. It's an odd tickle in the back of my mind, like an itch you ignore long enough that it eventually goes away. But last night it wouldn't subside. I'd had a hard time letting my thoughts of Mariah go, tossing and turning while imagining her out on the sofa with those beautiful plump lips of hers parted as she slept.

When I thought I'd finally found escape by slipping unconscious, I was only met with horny dreams of Mariah and myself dancing together in explicit TikToks.

I woke even more perturbed than when I fell asleep. The itch in the back of my mind had spread to somewhere deep inside my core, stronger than it's ever been before.

Only this time, I'm not sure if I want those feelings to fade.

With Mariah focused on driving, I let my eyes linger on her profile. I'd always noticed how beautiful she is; how could anyone not? I've looked at her a hundred times, but this time feels different, like I'm seeing her in a new way.

Can she tell I'm sitting in the car next to her, thinking about how the seat belt parts her breasts? Or about the way the morning light highlights the flecks of green in her eyes? Or how her lip-stain leaves no mark on the rim of her coffee cup and she could easily kiss me and no one would know?

I squirm in my seat and look out the passenger window, trying to focus on something else. But even the mountains, backlit in gold and pink with a glorious sunrise, can't distract me from how close she is, from how much I want to be closer to her.

We go all the way into work with neither of us speaking. For the first time, I don't know what to say. I feel like saying anything might break the fragile . . . whatever it is between us, and all I want to do is bask in it.

Mariah begins my makeup routine as she always does, spreading a cool, clear goop onto my skin. Her touch is different though, slower, softer, more methodical. She lingers on the hump of my nose, a nearly imperceptible smile meeting her lips. She massages it into my cheeks. She swipes delicately over my cheekbones. The brushstrokes of foundation are carefully applied with smooth, firm strokes, and I find myself missing the touch of her fingers.

"Close," she says, her voice barely above a whisper, her eyes meeting mine.

I oblige, allowing my lids to fall shut as she works with delicate care. With my eyes closed I can imagine her doing anything, like bringing her lips to mine. My pulse quickens at the thought, and it takes all my effort to stay still.

I should be thinking about my lines, not about Mariah's touch. I need to focus on filming my scenes, not on how good Mariah smells. I have to get my head in the game, but all I want is to explore this new feeling with her.

She's finished my makeup too quickly and steps back, leaving me bereft. I look in the mirror at a faded version of myself and feel self-conscious next to Mariah and her vibrancy, with her rosy cheeks, bright red lips, and turquoise hair.

"Thanks," I squeak as I get up.

"You okay? This is the least you've spoken since we've met," Mariah says, repeating what I said to her last night in a different way.

I nod. "Yeah, just tired. And nervous, I guess."

She reaches out and squeezes my arm. "You're gonna rock it." Her hand stays there for exactly seven seconds—five seconds longer than necessary—and I'm craving more.

"Ellie, we need you in costume," Jimmie's voice calls from somewhere in the crowd, which I'd completely forgotten exists, as if Mariah and I created a tiny vacuum-sealed bubble around us.

"See you later," I tell Mariah, breaking away from her spell.

Once I'm away from her I can breathe again and focus on the day, going over my lines, the blocking, the storyline, and get into character. After I'm dressed, I make my way down to the set, where several extras are waiting. Walking past the blue fencing and into a winter wonderland would normally send a bolt of excitement through me, but today it barely garners a smile. I wait in the coffee shop and listen as Yueyi goes over everything with the gaffer and grip.

Julia and Oscar join a few minutes later, chatting amicably. I should be stoked to finally be on set with a juggernaut like Oscar Fizak and a rising star like Julia Miles, but I can't lie to myself. There's somewhere else I'd rather be.

"Ready?" Oscar asks me with all of his swagger, but his usual charm has less of an effect than it normally does. Even Julia's perfect toothpaste-commercial smile holds little sway. My mind goes back to a tall woman with enviable curves and a sarcastic semi-permanent smirk.

Teal catches my eye and I look past him, off set. Mariah is there behind the monitors with the rest of the crew. We make eye contact, and the corner of her mouth lifts in a smile.

I grin back, focusing on her and how settled she makes me feel. "I was born ready."

AFTER A FULL day of filming, and only one retake despite Mariah taking up so much room in my thoughts, I start to make my way off set toward hair and makeup.

"Great job, Ellie," the grip says as I pass.

"Thank you." I smile, surprised by the compliment.

The gaffer joins in. "Yeah, you really knocked it out of the park."

"Oh, really? Why—"

Oscar and Julia approach me, a phone between them. "This is good stuff," Oscar says. Julia nods, giving me a thumbs-up.

"Thanks." I'm taken aback that I'm finally getting the recognition I deserve, and from the leads no less. All my work and dedication is paying off! "I'm glad we finally had a day on set together! I could really feel the tension between you two, and feeding off that worked wonders for my own character. It felt great working with you both today, and I hope we get other opportunities after this to—"

"Oh, we mean your TikTok," Oscar clarifies, pointing to his phone.

Julia nods. "The horny alien? Love it!"

"Wh-what?" I stammer, baffled. *How do they know about that?*

Mariah pushes past the crowd and grabs me by the shoulders. "Ellie!"

My skin tingles at her touch. I hope she can't see me blush under my layers of pasty makeup. "Mariah?"

She grips me harder. "It's our video. It blew up."

I narrow my gaze. "What do you mean, 'blew up'?"

Mariah shows me her phone. "It's at four million views."

"Four *million*?" My mouth hangs open. "I thought you said you only had a few hundred followers!"

"I did. But now I'm at twenty thousand and climbing. I can't keep up with all the comments and messages. It's . . . surreal. I'm sorry, I had no idea this would happen, I—"

"Wait, why are you sorry?"

Mariah gestures to the room. "Everyone's seen it. They've seen . . . us. Like that."

I shrug. "It's just acting, though. Nothing to be ashamed of."

Her shoulders slacken. She takes a moment to consider this. "Yeah. You're right. Just acting."

"I get it, it's your first time on film for a large group of people. It can be nerve-racking, but you get used to the attention." I rub her arm in consolation.

She looks from my hand and back to me. "Right."

"If anything, this is good! More publicity for you and your work, more publicity for my acting career." I take her arm and turn her toward the exit. "Now *four million* people have seen your incredible makeup skills!"

"What about your directing talents?" she adds. "The film wouldn't have been anything without your ideas and you calling the shots."

I scoff. "No, it's the way you designed the alien that's getting all the attention. You killed it!"

"I think it's how you embodied the alien and brought it to life."

"But we did it—we went viral!" I squeeze her against me before letting her go to grab the door. "We make a great team."

Mariah nods in agreement, that adorable half smile of hers lighting up her face. "Yeah, we do, don't we?"

"Ellie?" a familiar voice calls from somewhere off set.

We halt where we are, me half outside and holding the door open for Mariah. I look over my shoulder and panic, shutting the door quickly.

Mariah mouths, *What?* through the window.

I mouth back, *Matt!*

She gawps and takes three big steps backward. Our cover was almost blown.

I give Mariah a wide-eyed stare through the door, then put on a bright smile and jaunt to where Matt is standing on the other side of the fence. I wait for butterflies, for tingles, for *something*, but nothing happens. "What are you doing here?"

He flashes his hundred-watt smile, which is regrettably back to its pearly-white lustre. His smile used make me weak in the knees, but now just makes me sick to my stomach. "Haven't heard from you in a few days," he says. "And I thought this would be less creepy than showing up at the cabin."

"Ha . . . yeah, you're right." I give him some finger guns. "Still a little creepy, though."

"Or is it romantic?" He pulls a small bouquet of orange and pink dahlias from behind his back.

I gasp, eyeing the arrangement. "A point for romance."

"What time are you finished here? Can I take you out for dinner? I know this amazing—"

"Actually," I interrupt, stopping him there, "we have more filming to do. It's just a quick break, a touch-up in hair and makeup, and then I'm full on again. But I'll call you, okay?"

His smile wanes. I reach through the fence and hold out my hand, which he takes.

"I'll call you," I reassure. If I didn't know he was a two-timing player I'd almost feel guilty. But I know the truth about him now. His acting skills are nearly on par with my own.

"What do you want me to do with these?" Matt gestures with the flowers, unable to fit them through the fence.

"Keith?" I ask.

The guard takes them for me. "I'll deliver them."

Matt thanks him, gives me a wink through the fence, and walks off.

I take a few steps backward, then turn and bolt to the café set. Mariah is there waiting. "He's gone," I tell her, opening the door and double-checking over my shoulder.

She exhales a relieved breath. "That was close."

"Yeah. I didn't think of it before, but what if he sees our Tik-Tok? He'll see us together and then our cover will be blown."

"Should we . . . delete it?" She looks down at her phone as if it's something precious.

"No. Leave it. But we have to act fast." I grab her and pull her along the sidewalk.

"What do you mean?"

The guard interrupts us, handing me the bunch of flowers. Mariah and I eye it, then look at each other. "He obviously hasn't learned anything from our pranks," I say, waving the flowers about.

She sighs. "You're right."

I open the door for her and let her go up the stairs ahead of me, trying not to be distracted by her bubble butt in her tight pants. "We have to try again, use a different tactic."

Mariah holds the door open for me at the top of the stairs. "What are we going to do, though?"

I march to Mariah's station, throw the flowers down in an open spot, and flop into the seat. Grabbing the box of remover wipes, I begin scrubbing at my face. "Making him smell bad didn't work. I caught a whiff of him through the fence, and if anything, he smells better than before."

Mariah takes the wipes from me and starts working, much more gently, at removing the makeup. "I'm not surprised by that. He has a good natural musk."

"Agreed." I roll my eyes. "Lucky bugger. My natural musk is like overripe parmesan."

Mariah huffs her weird wheezy laugh. "No, it's not."

"And I was thinking," I continue, ignoring her comment, "equipping him with a year's supply of condoms and lube isn't exactly teaching him anything."

Mariah snorts another laugh. "You mean a month's supply."

"Right?"

"Let's brainstorm tonight," Mariah says, applying a moisturizer to my clean skin, which she's never done before. "We'll come up with a new plan. A better plan."

"I like the way you think, but we can't tonight."

Taking a step back, she rubs the spare moisturizer into her hands while regarding me through the mirror. "Why?"

"We have dinner with your parents."

Mariah pales. "Oh. Right. Well, this is more important, so we can cancel—"

"Nope," I interrupt, standing. "You've put this off for far too long."

Mariah seems to shrink in on herself.

I grab her shoulders and force her to make eye contact, leaning in close. "It's going to be fine. I'll be there with you, remember? I'm your buffer. You don't even have to talk. I can talk enough for the both of us."

"This is true." Mariah relaxes under my touch.

"And you promised them you'd see them. How nice has it been not getting called by your mom every five minutes?"

She considers this. "It's been nice."

"Exactly. How much better will it feel knowing you've done your due diligence and visited your parents while you're in town?"

"You're right." Mariah tenses once more. "But you don't know what it's like with them. Your family sounds great. And why isn't your mom calling *you* all the time?"

I release her. "I'm the middle child of eight siblings. She barely remembers I exist."

"Ouch."

I shrug. "Just facts. Now quit stalling, I have to go get ready to meet your parents!"

"Sit back down and I'll do you up."

I squeak, clenching my fists. "Really?"

"Of course," she says, as if it's the most natural thing in the world.

I take my seat once more, trying not to squirm in excitement. I love how Mariah does my makeup; it's like she sees the real me and accentuates it rather than using my face as a blank canvas to turn into whatever she wants. She brings out the best in me, in all the features I've learned not to love over the years, all the parts I've deemed imperfect. She helps me see them the way she does.

No one has made me feel more beautiful, more myself, than Mariah.

INT. APARTMENT HALLWAY - NIGHT

James knocks on Jenna's door, hands in his pockets and shoulders slumped.

Annie answers the door in her pyjamas. Her initial reaction is surprise, then shifts to hurt.

Annie looks over her shoulder, then steps into the hall. She closes the door and crosses her arms.

                    JAMES
          I wanted to apologize for earlier. I
          shouldn't have left you there like that.

                    ANNIE
          It was really scary. I didn't know my
          way back and didn't have my phone.
          We wandered around for an hour.

                    JAMES
          I feel terrible. If anything happened
          to either of you, I'd never be able to
          forgive myself. I carry enough guilt as
          is, I couldn't bear any more . . .

                    ANNIE
          We're okay. You don't need to feel guilty
          about anything. Except maybe not carrying
          pumpkin spice in your café. That is a crime.

                    JAMES
              (smiling)
          I'll put up garland and lights, but
          I refuse to stoop to pumpkin spice.

ANNIE

(smiling back)
I'd invite you in, but there's a baby
in here and I don't want you to
freak out.

JAMES

I promise I won't. But I was actually
hoping you'd come to my place? I was
about to decorate the cookies, if you're
still interested in helping.

ANNIE

I'd love to. Can we listen to Christmas
music while we decorate?

JAMES

(sighing)
If we must.

Chapter 14
MARIAH

As we park in the neighbourhood of squat rectangular houses in varying shades of beige, I begin to question my sanity. I've taken great lengths to avoid my parents over the past several years, and now I'll be seeing them for the first time in months with Ellie at my side. And I have no idea what to expect with her.

She's her usual chipper self, bright-eyed, taking everything in. All the houses are copy-and-pastes of each other, a design often referred to as "BC Boxes": a simple split-level with a garage on one side. The neighbourhood is nice enough, with wide front lawns and in-set sidewalks. While the houses are at least sixty years old, the residents range from new families out walking their dogs and babies to older couples watering their hydrangeas in the front yard.

My parents' house is meticulously kept, as it always has been, with not a smidge of dust on any of the windows, not a blade of grass trimmed the wrong length, and every begonia evenly spaced between two matching white peonies on each side.

It's as if I never left.

"We don't have to do this," I say, my steps becoming slower and heavier with each inch we make toward the house. "They haven't seen us yet. We can turn around. Go home. I know more food trucks we can try!"

Ellie wraps her arm through mine. "It will be fine! Don't worry, I'll be here the whole time. You won't even have to talk. I'll do it for you. You can do your due diligence as a daughter, rip the Band-Aid off, and cross this off your list for at least a few months. You'll feel so much better after, I promise."

I look down at Ellie, and she looks up at me, and even though I'm panicking, I know, somehow, it's all going to be okay. She gives me a reassuring smile, my arm a gentle squeeze, and I reciprocate with a slight nod.

The front door opens while we're still approaching, and out steps my mom. I am the spitting image of my mother. I've always hated it. She's blonde, her hair cut in a neat shoulder-length bob. She's tall and thickly built like me, but instead of accentuating her curves, she still subscribes to the notion that they are something to be ashamed of, meant to be hidden beneath layers of formless clothes. She'd tried to impress the same shame on me ever since I can remember—being told to stand up straighter because good posture will hide a belly, that somehow the amount of fat on your body is correlated to self-worth, that the clothes you choose to wear are linked to your morality.

I rebuked that nonsense, choosing self-acceptance and love instead. It didn't happen overnight; it took years of un-learning. Yet here we are, two women with matching bodies and just twenty years in age separating them, me with my rounded belly showing beneath my shirt, my breasts prominently displayed with a long line of cleavage, and tight pants that don't disguise the fact that I don't have anything close to a thigh gap and never will. While her clothing, hair, and makeup is meant to blend into her surroundings, mine is carefully curated to stand out, from my half-shaved head of bright teal hair, to the dark makeup around my eyes, and the bold shade of red I chose for my lips. We couldn't be more the same, and yet we're completely different. I did that on purpose.

I force my shoulders back and stand proudly, even as I prepare for her cutting words, asking me if *this* is what I chose to wear, asking what on god's green earth I did to my hair, or if she can grab me a sweater despite the thirty-degree July heat.

But it doesn't come.

Her arms are open, beckoning, the smile on her face lined far more than I remember. "Welcome home, Maria!"

I tense at her pronunciation. Ellie must feel it and tugs me closer. "Hello, Judith!"

"Oh, you must be Ellie." Mom steps out of the way so we can climb the short flight of stairs and meet her on the landing.

"Yes, so good to meet you." Ellie releases me and hugs my mom, who squeezes her tightly as if they've known each other for years.

Mom releases Ellie long enough to hold her at arm's length. "Lovely to finally meet one of Maria's partners."

Wait . . . partners? Does she think—

"Yes," Ellie agrees. "And I've been telling Mariah forever that I wanted to meet my girlfriend's parents. Where is Wes, anyway?"

Girlfriend?! What the f—

"He's inside. Come on in!" Mom pauses to look into Ellie's eyes as if she's some sort of magical creature. Then Mom looks to me, arms still open for a hug.

I hesitate, unsure of what to do. Mom senses this and drops her arms. I notice a flicker of sadness behind her eyes, but she blinks past it. "Come in, come in," she beckons, holding the door open for us.

Ellie and I shuffle into the tiny entryway. It smells the same as it did before. *How is that even possible?* The aroma of Mom's vegetable lentil soup must be etched into the paint along with the lemon pledge she uses to shine the antique wood furniture, melding together to form one scent that elicits thousands of memories.

"I'll go tell Dad you're here." Mom walks up the stairs and out the back door by the kitchen, where she pauses to shout for him.

Meanwhile, I grab Ellie's arm and whisper-shout in her ear, "What the hell! She thinks we're dating now!"

"Rule number one of improv."

I scrunch my face. "What?"

"Always agree and say yes."

I scrunch my face harder. "That is the worst rule ever created."

She chuckles, leaning in to explain, but we're interrupted by Mom. "Come on up, you two. I made Maria's favourite, lasagna."

My stomach rumbles at the thought. I haven't had Mom's lasagna in years, and damn is it good. I may look like my mom, but somehow she didn't pass down her "excellent cook" genes; my best dish is ramen noodles with Cheez Whiz.

After toeing off our shoes, Ellie takes my hand and pulls me up the stairs into the living area. Her comfortable self-assuredness seeps through her hand and into mine just like her warmth.

We pass through the living room with its oversized floral sofas, ticking grandfather clock, and upright piano with a doily atop it along with several stoic family photos. In the kitchen the table is already set with the good china reserved for Thanksgiving and Christmas dinners, fresh rolls, and a square of butter in its dish. Ellie pulls my chair out, which I return with a stern look, but take my seat as she settles next to me.

Dad comes in a moment later, the exact same as I remember him, from his grey Supercuts hairstyle and his thick-rimmed glasses right down to the short-sleeve button-up shirt hanging off his body. While Mom is thick and rounded, Dad is thin and wiry, despite eating every plate set before him and asking for seconds at nearly every meal. He brightens when he sees me, saying nothing, but giving my shoulder a light pat as he passes by to take his usual seat at the head of the table. Dad was a long-haul trucker, so he was gone a lot of the time growing up. Our relationship has always been as reliable yet distant as his treks along the Trans-Canada Highway.

"You must be Ellie," Dad says. His voice still has the same pastoral tone it's always had, as if he's about to sit in a circle of young folk, put his elbows on his knees, and talk about the temptations of the human body and which scriptures to turn to when faced with lust.

"Yes, sir." Ellie beams her radiant smile at him.

"So how long have you two been seeing each other?" Mom asks, bringing the lasagna over and setting it down on an orange hand-knit potholder.

I'm shaken by this question, with no idea what to say or where to begin. I sit there, gawping like a fish. The last time I told my parents I was dating a woman they returned my news with shocked silence, followed by an *Are you sure this is how you want to live your life?*

Even though it was years ago, it still stings.

"Oh, for a while now, hey?" Ellie says, taking my hand once more. "It's one of those things where we started as friends and then turned into more, so it's hard to remember exactly when things shifted from friends to . . . friendlier, if you know what I mean." Ellie winks. *Winks!* At my mom!

Mom returns the wink with her cawing laugh, followed by a snort eerily similar to my own. "That is so sweet. A love that starts out as a friendship is so wonderful. You know, Wes and I met at church." She continues to tell the story about a picnic and him sharing his pickle with her (not a euphemism). Meanwhile all I can think is, *Who the hell is this woman and what has she done with my mother?* And Dad, he's acting like this is totally normal, like, why *wouldn't* I bring my girlfriend over for dinner? What the hell kind of Twilight Zone did I walk in on?

The entire meal passes in the same manner, with polite conversation, swapping stories (several of which are made up by Ellie), and me pinching myself to wake up from this surreal dream. The food is delicious; Mom packs up the leftovers for us to take home, and then serves a homemade strawberry-rhubarb pie and lukewarm Orange Pekoe tea for dessert. Everything is the same, but somehow my parents have been body-snatched.

The whole time, Ellie is a natural. With every warm look she gives me, every touch of my thigh beneath the table, every story she weaves of our history together, she even has me convinced that we're dating. The idea brings far more comfort than I care to admit. I have to keep reminding myself that it isn't real, that the butterflies I'm feeling are one-sided, that she's a convincing actress, and it's nothing more than that.

After we're overly full from dinner, Mom and Dad clear the table while I take Ellie to show her my old room, at her request.

Everything else in the house is the same except for this room. Not that my old bedroom reflected who I was at all, with the white metal bed frame, crisp white linens, and faded pink wallpaper. Now it's home to a crafting table, a sewing machine, and a big comfy chair with an open annotated Bible on an end table next to it. There is an open Rubbermaid container in the centre of the room and everything I left behind is inside.

Ellie doesn't wait for permission to begin perusing, kneeling before it and taking out one item at a time. She holds up an old framed photo. "This was you?"

I lean against the dresser and nod. "Yup."

"You look so . . . different."

It's Bethany and me in grade ten. We're wearing tight layered shirts and skinny jeans, holding each other in a side-hug with our faces pressed together.

"You were so cute," Ellie states, tapping the girl on the right, the chubbier one with the more rounded features and a smile that doesn't reach her eyes.

I huff some air through my nose, not agreeing.

Ellie smiles up at me. "After the story you told me I thought you'd have been one of the goth kids or something, but you look more like one of the popular girls."

I grimace. "I had to blend in to survive. I was bullied a lot in middle school, especially after that Halloween fiasco, so I adapted. I may have sat with the popular kids at the lunch table, but I never felt like I was one of them. If you'd have looked at me, you'd have thought I had friends, that I was happy, but in truth I . . ."

Ellie waits patiently, holding the photo on her lap.

I swallow, looking at my hands. "I was all alone. Nobody knew who I really was. The people who pretended to be my friends were actually my harshest critics and biggest bullies." I take the photo from Ellie. "Bethany was especially cruel. She started dating Jax when she found out I had a crush on him. She knew he was out of my league. She wanted to rub it in my face that she could date a guy like him and I couldn't."

"Jax? As in *our* Matthew Jackson?"

I nod.

"I knew you went to high school together but didn't realize you two had that much history."

Setting the picture back in the box, I shrug. "It was more like a lack of history than anything else. Taking him to bed was sort of like proving something to myself. I thought he really liked me. He made me feel . . . I don't know. Seen? Not just as I am today, but for who I was back then. Sounds dumb now."

"It doesn't sound dumb at all." Ellie reaches up and takes my hand. "I'm sorry you had such an awful time at school."

"I found ways to get through it. Created a mask, of sorts. I didn't feel safe being myself. I spent years pretending to be someone I wasn't just to fit in, which only made things worse. Acting like someone else all the time isn't good for your mental health. So as soon as I graduated, I dyed my hair orange, started wearing all black and taking my makeup seriously again. My mom, she—" I cut myself off. Ellie watches my face, waiting for me to continue. I give her a little shrug. "She didn't understand."

Ellie regards me for a moment, opens her mouth to ask another question, but thinks better of it. She looks back into the box and picks up another picture. "Who's this?"

I blink, having forgotten I had this photo. It was Christmastime with my family, years ago. Everyone in the picture resembles each other: me, my parents, and my grandparents, all shades of washed-out beige with polite, forced smiles, standing up straight with hands folded in front of us—except for one woman who stands out. She looks like me, but more the me I am today than the one I was back then. Her hair is black, cut short, and spiked along the sides. She has a thick choker neck-lace, black clothes, holes in her jeans, and she's grinning like a complete goof rather than reining it in like everyone else in the picture.

I join Ellie on the floor. "That's my aunt."

She smiles. "The one who showed you *Alien*?"

I nod.

"I can see where you get your fashion sense from."

"This was our last Christmas all together." I take the frame and look closer. "We had finished eating dinner and were about to open presents."

"Still so weird, opening gifts after dinner," Ellie muses.

"She was the best part of Christmas. Everyone was so quiet and reserved, and she was . . . not. She was so much fun."

"Was?" Ellie tilts her head. "Where is she now?"

"She died," Mom says from the doorway, startling us both. She's drying her hands on a faded yellow tea towel, a sad smile on her face. "She passed away several years ago. On Christmas morning, actually. It was . . . very sad." Mom looks from Ellie to me, her expression growing wistful, and I know right then I can't spend another second in this house.

"We gotta get going," I say past the lump in my throat.

"Now?" Ellie asks, eyeing the box of items she hasn't had a chance to look at.

"First rule," I whisper in her ear as I grab her hand and pull her standing.

"Ah, yes." She follows me out of the room. "We have some evening filming to do, have to go back to set, really impor-tant scene."

"Oh." Mom doesn't bother to hide her disappointment. She follows us to the living room and stands at the top of the stairs, Dad next to her, close but not touching. They watch as we put on our shoes. "Well, I hope you come and see us again before you leave town. It was nice catching up with you, Maria, and meeting you, Ellie."

"So nice to meet you, too," Ellie replies, but I'm tugging her out the door so fast she's cut off by it slamming behind her.

She doesn't say anything as we get into the car, or as I drive down the street to the highway, or as we wind along the tree-shaded road back to the cabin. The air between us is thick with tension, with Ellie doing her best to give me peace and quiet despite it being against her very essence. The farther we get from my old home—from my parents who look the same but acted completely different, from the person they tried so hard—but failed—to make me become, from the limited memories I have of my aunt—the better I feel.

By the time we're back inside the cabin, with a bottle of wine wordlessly popped and poured, I'm ready to talk about it.

"My aunt . . ." I begin, then stop, not sure what to say.

"She died on Christmas morning?" Ellie asks, incredulous.

"Yeah. But we didn't find out until three days later."

I glance up at Ellie, whose mouth is frozen open in an expression of sheer horror.

I take a deep breath. "Shortly after that picture was taken we went and opened presents. She gifted me a makeup set. My first one. I was twelve years old."

Ellie gives me a small smile. "She introduced you to *Alien* and your first makeup set, too? She really inspired you."

"Yeah, she did. In a lot of ways. Mom said I wasn't allowed to wear makeup yet, but Aunt Cindy told them to lighten up. She took me into the bathroom and we did my makeup together. I remember looking in the mirror and feeling so pretty, and being so proud of it, and feeling like . . . I don't know. Like I didn't have to be me. I could be anyone. I could be one person one day, and a different person the next, like makeup could transform more than my looks, actually change who I was as a person. I didn't like who I was back then. I felt like I didn't fit in my skin, like it belonged to someone else, and it was itchy and I just wanted to take it off and run away. I guess, in the end, I did . . ." I trail off for a moment, gathering my thoughts while

Ellie waits patiently, elbows rested on the counter between us. "We went to the living room to show my family how I looked. I was so excited—I thought they'd all love it. But my grandpa took one look at me and told me I looked like a cheap whore."

Ellie gasps.

"Right? Who says that to a twelve-year-old?" I give my head a shake. "Aunt Cindy started yelling. Then my mom started yelling. I was crying. They told me to go wash that 'trash' off my face. Mom threw my makeup in the garbage. I heard them shouting about how they didn't want me to end up like my aunt, and my aunt was screaming back that she'd never want to be like them. This went on for a while, but by the time I'd washed it all off and came out my aunt was gone. I never saw her again."

Ellie is silent, taking this all in.

I push on. "She passed away two years later. Fentanyl overdose. She was all alone on Christmas morning, using drugs. She took too much and it all ended right there. She didn't have anyone to be with. She didn't have anyone checking up on her. She had nothing. And—" The tears that have evaded me up until this point finally find their way to my ducts, threatening to spill. I blink a few times, then let them fall, having learned a long time ago that emotions are not meant to be bottled up, and knowing with every cell in my body that Ellie would be the last person in the world to judge a person for crying. "In a way," I continue, my voice thick, "I always felt like we were so similar. We don't fit in. We're the black sheep. And every Christmas I think about her. I think about me. I can't help but wonder—will that be me someday? Will I end up like her? All alone on Christmas morning, trying to mask my pain for just a little while, with no one to notice when I'm gone."

INT. JAMES'S APARTMENT - EVENING

Annie and James are decorating cookies at the table.
Their legs are crossed toward each other, nearly
touching.

Christmas music plays quietly in the background.

                    ANNIE
          When did you get so good at this?
          Mine looks like I'm in kindergarten.

                    JAMES
          I used to do this every year.

                    ANNIE
          (glancing at him)
          Oh?

                    JAMES
          It's been a while, but I guess icing
          cookies is like riding a bike. A few
          Christmases ago I even entered a contest
          and won first place for it. This is the
          first time I've decorated cookies
          since . . .

                    ANNIE
          (beat) Since?

                    JAMES
          It's been a long time, is all.

ANNIE

I'm glad you're doing it again. I'm not
sure why you stopped, but you can't
keep talent like this from the world.
Everyone in your café is going to love
these. Are you going to bring some to
that big fancy party the Small Business
Association is having?

JAMES

How do you know about that?

ANNIE

I'm not divulging my whisper network.

JAMES

Fine, keep your secrets. But no.
I'm not going.

ANNIE

Why not? I thought you had to.

JAMES

I don't have to do anything.

ANNIE

I overheard them saying there
would be other possible tenants
there. Shouldn't you be there, too?

JAMES

I can't go back there.

ANNIE

But you could lose—

James slams a cookie on table, breaking it.

JAMES

Don't you get it? I've already lost
everything. There is nothing more
that can be taken away from me.

ANNIE

(quietly)
I'm sorry.

JAMES

(sighing)
I'm sorry. I lost my temper.
I don't need to take this out on you,
you're only trying to help.

ANNIE

Look. I don't know what happened,
or what you're going through, but
I do know that losing your business
and your home won't make anything
better.

JAMES

I can't do it.

ANNIE

Why not?

JAMES

I don't want to be there all alone
with their pitying glances and
awkward silence.

ANNIE

What if you weren't alone?

Chapter 15
ELLIE

I reach across the space between us and take Mariah's hands in mine. I duck my head to catch her gaze and suck in a breath. She's so beautiful under normal circumstances, but here, right now, being so vulnerable, it's the most beautiful I've ever seen her. I take in her watery brown eyes, the shimmering streaks down her round cheeks, the pink tip of her nose, and share the silence, letting her feel what she's feeling, being there for her.

After a moment, I reach up and wipe a tear from her cheek with the pad of my thumb. She leans against me, ever so slightly.

"You won't end up like your aunt." My own voice is cracking, unable to imagine the pain of thinking that about my future.

She sniffs. "How do you know?"

"I can't see a world in which you'd ever end up alone. You're way too amazing. Not that your aunt wasn't a wonderful person, but I think there was more to it than you knew. If she was turning to drugs, especially hard drugs, then there must have been so much else happening in her life, a lot of pain we can't imagine. And I hope you never do."

Mariah's bottom lip trembles. "I should have been there for her."

"Don't blame yourself—you were a kid. Don't carry that guilt, okay? She wouldn't want that for you." I give her hands a squeeze. "You know what she'd want for you? To be doing exactly what you're doing. From being brave enough to be the person on the outside that you are on the inside, to blazing a trail even if it means being away from your family, and working every day to make your dreams come true. You, being alive and loving your life, is the best way to honour her memory."

Mariah smiles, then releases my hand and wipes at her face. "You're right. Thank you for listening."

I stand up straight and shrug. "Of course. That's what friends are for."

She regards me for a moment, her face pink and blotchy, but looking much more relaxed after getting her feelings out. "Yeah. Friends."

"And now I get why you hate Christmas so much. It must be hard for you working on a Christmas set, walking up to a winter wonderland every day. Sometimes I forget that for me Christmas is the most magical time of year and holds my best childhood memories, but for others it can be really triggering. Especially if they've lost someone recently."

"Yeah. My aunt passed away years ago, but I can't get through Christmas without thinking about her all alone in her dingy little apartment." Mariah shudders.

"And you can't even escape it after work. I'm sorry you have to stay here in my cabin with all of this," I gesture to all the lights and decorations. "You know, we can take it down, I don't mind."

"No," she says quickly. "Actually, I think it's kind of . . . helping. Seeing Christmas from your perspective is changing mine, in a way. The pain is there. It will always be there. But like you said, she wouldn't want me to hurt for her forever. Maybe I can have some good memories of Christmas to go with the bad ones."

"Hey, happy to help you there! Do you want to eat some sexually inappropriate Christmas cookies, drink some more wine, and watch *Alien 3*?"

She smirks. "That's not a Christmas movie. You really fell off your diet, you know that?"

"I know," I moan, taking the tray of cookies to the couch. "But I gotta see what happens next! And I'm not brave enough to watch these on my own."

Mariah follows with the wine, sitting next to me with our hips touching, and throws a blanket over us while I cue up the movie. I'm giddy at how comfortable we are. We've only known each other a few days and yet I feel closer to her than my friends in Vancouver I've known for years.

MARIAH IS ASLEEP by the halfway point, her head lolled on my shoulder. I snuggle in a little closer, so happy she feels safe enough to fall asleep like this. I'm so proud of her for trusting me, for braving her family, and for sharing something so deep and dark. I can tell Mariah keeps everything buttoned up tight; it's a privilege to be the one she opens up to, and it's not something I take lightly. It feels like I'm holding a little piece of her with me, cradling it to my chest like something precious and fragile.

And I know I won't break it.

When the movie hits the credits, I can't decide which of the three are my favourite because it was *that good*. Gently, I extricate myself from beneath Mariah and lay her on the couch. I pull the blanket over her, then trace my finger along her cheek to tuck a strand of teal hair behind her ear.

I feel a sudden urge—a need—to kiss the skin beneath her eye where my finger had just been. My heart thumps faster with the thought, imagining what it would be like to kiss her when she's asleep, to breathe in the scent of her as she slumbers, to watch her dream, to pull her in tight and wrap my arms around her.

I bend closer, lips hovering. She smells so sweet, so good, so familiar and yet so different, an alluring combination that draws me in.

I pause, hovering. Then I take a slow breath and step back.

I don't know if she wants me touching her while she's sleeping. And she probably doesn't want me kissing her. Mariah put a lot of trust in me tonight. We're friends. I'm not about to break that because of some strange whim.

Though the tugging ache in my chest pulling me closer to her makes me think . . . *What if this is more than a whim?*

"ELLIE, WHO WAS that hunk that came to see you yesterday?"

Mariah and I have just walked into the hair and makeup department, Starbucks cups in hand, when Julia stops us in our tracks.

"Who?" I ask, tilting my head to the side.

Julia laughs her musical laugh. "Miss Popular can't even keep track of all the boys her milkshake is bringing to the yard."

I squint. "My milkshake?"

Mariah nudges me. "Jax—er, Matt. She means Matt."

"Oh!" Jeez, I'd pretty much forgotten all about him. I put a hand on my hip and act nonchalant, like he isn't some fuckboy who played me for a fool and convinced me to have feelings for him when I didn't even know who he was. "Yeah. Just one of my many admirers."

"Well, he's a babe," she continues. "You should invite him out to the bar with us tonight. We can interrogate him for you."

I grip my coffee cup tighter. As if I'd bring a guy I was interested in around this model with a perfect smile. And even if I wasn't interested, I wouldn't sic Matt on Julia to break her heart next. Plus, they've never invited me out to the bar with them, but now they're suddenly interested so long as I bring some eye candy with me? *Not likely.* "Yeah. Sure thing."

"You should come, too, Maria." Julia gives Mariah a quick once-over, then walks away to her side of the hair and makeup department.

Moods considerably deflated from when we woke up, Mariah and I go to our side of the room. I sit down, the plastic chair squeaking. "Your mom called you Maria," I recall. "I didn't think anything of it at the time."

She shrugs, tying my hair up into its usual messy bun. "I started going by Mariah when I moved out. Seemed more *me*. Got the idea from a drag queen I was staying with."

I nod. "It does suit you more. Wait, you were staying with a drag queen? Like, living with one? How'd that come about?"

"After high school when I cut my hair and changed my clothes, my mom lost it on me. She didn't understand at all. She told me I could either 'be an upstanding member of society,' or leave her house . . . so I left."

"She really said that?" I couldn't imagine.

Mariah nods. "All I had was my car. I drove into Vancouver, and I parked. I lived in it for almost a month. I had nowhere to stay. No job. No friends."

"That must have been so scary." I fight back a shiver.

Mariah focuses on my hair as she talks, tucking strands into place. "I landed a job at a gay bar as a server, working the evening shift. The pay was shit but the people were amazing, and I actually felt like I belonged. Every week they had a drag show, and one of the queens, Alotta Dix, took me under her wing. She let me help with her makeup, taught me a lot, and when she found out I was living in my car she let me stay with her and sleep on her couch until I got my feet under me."

"I'm so glad they were there for you."

Mariah finishes my hair, meeting my gaze in the mirror. "That's when I got into cosmetology school."

I give her a smile through the mirror. "And here you are."

Mariah's gaze softens as she regards me through the mirror. Then her countenance shifts abruptly and she clears her throat. "We don't have much time. We need to focus on our next pranks for Jax."

I let her change the conversation, understanding how hard it must have been for her to share that with me. "Yes! Matt. What are you thinking?"

Mariah's countenance changes immediately. "Silly pranks aren't enough for a guy like Jax. The games he's playing, stringing women along to make them catch feelings for him? Totally unnecessary and cruel. This needs to go further than petty revenge."

"What do you have in mind?"

"We need to teach him a real lesson so he learns the error of his ways and stops playing with women's hearts. He should know what it's like to be led on like we were. I have a few ideas, but they're more involved than before."

I lean in, making eye contact through the mirror, and give her a mischievous grin. "Sounds diabolical. I'm in."

By the time my makeup is done we've come up with a plan and send a text to Matt from Mariah's phone, asking if she can go over to his place tonight. He doesn't reply before it's time for me to go on set. I almost expect him to be there waiting for me on the other side of the blue fence. Thank god there *is* a fence and security guards, so I don't have to worry about him popping up somewhere during filming.

Julia and Oscar are already situated in the café, and they give me enthusiastic smiles and nods. I grin back.

"I hear you had a visitor yesterday," Oscar says.

My stomach tightens. I thought they were smiling at me because they were happy to work with me, not because they were trying to get some juicy gossip about my sex life. "Oh, yeah . . . he's a friend I made recently."

"He bought you flowers! That's a nice *friend*." Julia titters.

"Yeah. Sorry you don't have any friends buying *you* flowers," I say with a bit more sarcasm than intended. Oscar's and Julia's eyes widen at my snippy retort. I catch myself, not sure what came over me, and add, "They probably have to keep all your admirers far away from the set so they don't break down the fence!"

I force my smile wider to make up for my sour mood, which seems to work, and everyone goes back to their blocking and reviewing minor changes in the script. My quick recovery worked and their smiles are back, albeit a bit guarded. I don't know what came over me, but I have to be more careful; I don't want a bad reputation on set.

I'm easygoing Ellie. I'm the chillest, happiest person you'll work with. I'm a friggin' *delight*.

INT. JAMES'S APARTMENT (CONT'D)

Annie nudges James's foot under the table.

                    JAMES
          What are you suggesting?

                    ANNIE
          I could go with you to the party if
          you're nervous. I know it's hard to
          get back into a rhythm after . . .
          after you've been absent from
          something for so long.

                    JAMES
          That's kind of you, but that's okay.
          You don't have to do that for me.

                    ANNIE
          It's really not a big deal. I don't
          have anything else to do. And, as
          a lawyer, I've gone to a lot of
          different Christmas functions.
          I'm practically a Christmas expert.

                    JAMES
          This is true.

                    ANNIE
          Having a lawyer with you might
          be helpful. I could help you navigate
          any situations that arise with the
          Small Business Association. It would be
          good for you to have some legal counsel in
          case they try to pull something on you.

JAMES

That does sound helpful.

ANNIE

Plus, it would be fun. I've been cooped
up washing diapers and bottles for a few
days. It would be nice to get dressed up
and see a bit more of everything Hemlock
Grove has to offer.

JAMES

I'm sorry. I don't think I have it in me.

ANNIE

At least make an appearance so you can
say you tried.

JAMES

(hesitant)
I guess I could go for a few minutes.

ANNIE

That's the spirit.

JAMES

But I'm not dancing.

ANNIE

Never said you had to. Honestly, I'm mostly
in it for the Christmas buffet. They always
have the best food at these things.

JAMES

Maybe we should bring to-go containers
and take some food home.

ANNIE
Now you're talking!

Annie and James share a smile, their legs bump under the table.

JAMES
Thank you for going with me to the party.
For helping me decorate. For making cookies
with me. For being so kind—especially
after I've been so rude to you.

ANNIE
Of course. That's what friends are for.

JAMES
Friends?

Chapter 16
MARIAH

I shake out my arms as I prepare to ring the doorbell. Originally my plan had been for Ellie to do this part, but she reminded me she's never been to Jax's apartment and it would be weird for her to ask to come to his place. This route would require a lot more acting from me, and I'm on the opposite end of the acting spectrum from Ellie. Hopefully Jax buys what I'm doing long enough for her to get everything done.

After one more breath while trying to get my pulse to a regular rhythm and the sweat to stop forming on my brow, I ring the doorbell.

Jax answers a few seconds later, his tall frame taking up most of the doorway. A tight black T-shirt hugs his torso and his long hair hangs loose around his chiselled face.

"Hello there," I say.

"Hey. I wasn't sure if I'd get to see you again." He crosses his arms, blocking the door.

"Things got busy at work, but it was a boring day today. I thought maybe you could make things more interesting." I try to bite my lip seductively, but I'm pretty sure I look more like Andy Sandburg in *Jizz in My Pants* than Dakota Johnson in *Fifty Shades of Grey*.

Jax doesn't seem to care; either way he thinks he's getting laid. He steps aside just enough to let me pass, forcing me to brush my tits against him as I do. What would have given me excited tingles before now gives me the heebie jeebies.

I plop my overfilled purse next to the door, several items inside clinking, and we sit on his couch. I pause, looking around his apartment. Before, when I had been staying here and sleeping with him, I hadn't noticed that it was a sad, drab bachelor pad. Now—especially compared to the cozy cabin with Ellie—it feels cold and dark. Why are his blinds closed in the middle of the day? Why isn't there any art on the walls?

Jax lays his arm over the back of the couch, trying to wrap it around me. "I knew you missed me."

It's weird how little I did. "There's so much we have to make up for . . ."

He shifts a bit closer. "Is that so? What kind of things do you have in mind?"

I lean closer like I'm about to kiss him, then pull out my phone instead. "I've been thinking about what you said, about visiting me in Vancouver—how you said you don't plan on staying here for long? My place is too small for the two of us, so I reached out and booked us a couple viewings for condos downtown." I open my browser and show him the pictures while watching his face shift from confusion to fear, then masking to feigned interest.

"Oh, uh, apartments?" His throat bobbles as I hear him swallow.

"I know it's fast, but we've known each other for years. You always wanted me, I always wanted you. It's perfect, isn't it? Can't you see us in this space?"

"It is a nice apartment, but—"

I'm practically on his lap now, tracing my finger along his jaw. "Us running into each other was a sign from the universe. I mean, you're an Aries, and I'm a Gemini. Could it be more perfect?" I'm actually a Capricorn, but he wouldn't remember.

Jax leans back, inching away from me. "Yeah . . ."

I follow him, giving him no space. "What was it you said? I'd never heard anyone say anything so romantic. Oh, right. *Karma* brought us together."

He presses his lips into a firm line. "I sure did say that. Yep."

"We can be together all day, every day. We have *so* much

time to make up for . . ." I lean in to kiss him while Jax pulls away like I have a giant, weeping cold sore.

We're interrupted by a perfectly timed ringing phone. Jax jumps up and looks at his phone, does a double take, then says, "Sorry. I have to take this."

"Go ahead, I'll just make myself comfortable . . ." I lean into the couch and eye him amorously, letting my legs drift wider apart as he watches.

Jax lets the phone ring in his hand as his mouth slowly falls open, eyeing me.

"You gonna answer that, big boy?" *Big boy? Gross.*

Clearing his throat, Jax tears his gaze away and answers it. "Hey, I'm just a little—whoa."

I can hear Ellie's sultry voice on the other end of the line and catch occasional words, like *moist* and *bend me over* and *spank me.* It takes everything in my power to keep from laughing, especially as Jax's face shifts from surprised, to turned on, to concerned about me overhearing.

"Uh, sorry, this is important." He turns and makes his way down the hall to the bedroom, shutting his door.

I get up quickly and unlock the front door, letting Ellie in as she hangs up on Jax. I point down the hall, and she books it into the bathroom, shutting the door behind her. Two seconds later, Jax comes out of his room looking down at his phone, confused.

"Who was that?" I feign innocence.

"Just my mom." He shrugs, nonchalant. "She wanted to know if I was going to the store on my way over to see her tomorrow. She doesn't drive, so I take care of a lot of things for her."

I have no idea where truth ends and lies begin with that story, but I don't trust a single thing he says. I force a smile to my face. "You're such a good son. I can think of so many ways I want to reward you for your good behaviour."

He bites his lip. "Is that so? In that case, you think of all the sexy things you want to do, I'll be right back." He heads down the hall to the bathroom where Ellie is hiding.

Oh, fuck, our cover is going to be blown before we even begin! Panicking, I shout, "Have a nice shit!" to warn her.

Jax pauses and turns. "I just have to pee?"

I laugh it off, trying to hide the horrified look on my face.

The second he's in the bathroom I jump up and pace the room. *Shit shit shit! He's going to find her!* Will he call the cops? Will we be locked up and have to call my parents to bail us out? I'll lose my job, Ellie will lose her job, then we'll have to—

The toilet flushes and Jax is back in the hall—sans washed hands, I note. I exhale a deep sigh of relief.

"Everything okay?" he asks.

"Yeah, uh, you just made me realize I have to pee, too." I brush past him down the hall and into the bathroom, locking the door behind me. The room seems normal. *Where the fuck is Ellie?*

I glance around for a second, then pull the shower curtain back and scream in surprise at Ellie standing there like an axe murderer. She grabs me and clamps a hand over my mouth.

"Everything okay?" Jax asks through the door.

Ellie gives me a wide-eyed look, then removes her hand.

"Uh . . . yeah," I say, scrambling. "Just . . . got my period!"

Ellie mouths, *What the hell?*

I shrug, mouthing back, *I don't know!*

"Oh. There are some pads and tampons in the drawer next to the toilet if you need anything," he says.

"That's actually super considerate," Ellie whispers.

"Thanks," I say loudly to Jax. "I'll be out in a minute."

His footsteps retreat, and both my and Ellie's shoulders slump.

"This was a bad idea," I whisper to Ellie.

"It's fine," she whispers back. "Get your head in the game and help me with this." She unzips her backpack, which is fully stocked.

"What's all this?" I whisper. "Is this for pranks? I thought we were doing psychological warfare?"

Ellie grins. "I can't help it, there are so many great opportunities. Come on, we don't have much time."

Reluctantly, I help Ellie Saran Wrap the toilet, cover his faucet handles with petroleum jelly, and place tape over the tap spout so it sprays him in the face when it turns on. Leaving Ellie snickering like the evil genius she is, I return to the living room, where Jax is scrolling on his phone. I try to peek at what he's doing to see who he's messaging, but he lowers and locks it with a quick, practised click.

I sit next to him. "Sorry that took me so long."

"All good." He seems disappointed, probably because he thinks my vagina is out of commission.

"We still have lots of fun things we can do," I assure him. I grip him by the hair and bring his face close, watching out of the corner of my eye as Ellie sneaks from the bathroom to Jax's bedroom.

Jax grabs my ass and gives it a squeeze. "Oh yeah? Then maybe we should take this to the bedroom."

"No!" I say, far too loudly. He startles, and I backpedal. "I mean, why should we go to the bedroom when the kitchen is right there? I don't think we've banged on your table. We should desecrate every object in your house."

He grins, then nips my bottom lip. "I like the way you think." He picks me up and carries me to the kitchen, where he sets me down on the table and, despite myself, I'm a little turned on.

Jax leans in to kiss me. I turn my face to the side, dodging his lips. Something about him kissing me on the mouth feels abhorrent now, and I can't even make myself do it to distract him. Luckily, Jax doesn't break his stride, sucking on my earlobe instead. I grimace, trying not to tense while keeping my eyes open for Ellie. Jax is moaning against my neck and grabbing my body, and I'm about ten seconds away from calling this whole thing off when she finally crawls down the hall into the living room, hiding behind the couch. There's a soft bump; she must have knocked into the coffee table.

Jax whips his head around. "What was that?"

I grab his face and turn him back to me. "I changed my mind. Let's go to the bedroom. The things I want to do to you require more . . . space."

He forgets all about the noise he heard and backs away, letting me off the table. I escort him to the bedroom, grabbing my purse as we go. I take a quick look over my shoulder before closing the door behind us, but don't see Ellie. We're almost at the finish line. Only a few more things left to do, then we're home free—all I have to do is not fuck this up. Easier said than done.

Once inside, I close the door and give Jax a playful shove, forcing him onto the bed. He smiles ruefully at me, manspreading as he takes me in. I bend down and show off my cleavage while pulling a set of fuzzy pink handcuffs out of my purse.

"Ooh, what do you have there?" he asks.

"Just a little fun and games," I say, coming closer. "Lie down on the bed, hands up."

"Yes, ma'am." He complies quickly, pulling his shirt off in the process. The tattoos that once drew me in, thinking he was so wise and complex, now seem silly, like he doesn't know who he is and has merely marked himself with symbols he barely understands to give the impression that he's deep and thoughtful.

"Your safe word is 'I want my mommy,'" I explain as I handcuff him to his bed frame.

He chuckles. "Okay."

"And I'm going to do whatever I want to you." With him prone and firmly secured, I reach back into my bag and pull out a set of nipple clamps, placing them on the bed.

He bites his lip, wiggling in excitement.

Okay, not what I was expecting. I continue to the next item, pulling out a bright pink paddle that says *Yes Daddy* on it.

Jax's eyebrows shoot up, but the smile remains on his face.

That didn't shake him at all. I grab the last item from my bag, a set of anal beads ranging in size from newb to pro.

Jax chuckles. "Oh yeah, I never thought I'd see the day."

Wow, this guy is kinkier than I thought. Against my better judgment, I find myself getting turned on again.

"Close your eyes," I order, picking up the paddle and smacking it against the palm of my hand.

"Yes ma'am." He eagerly squeezes his eyes shut. I quickly grab his phone on his end table and try to unlock it with his face, but it doesn't work with his eyes closed. *Shit. I forgot about that security feature.* I have to buy myself more time.

Reaching into my bag, I pull out a blindfold and secure it around his eyes. "No peeking," I say coyly. "I have a big surprise for you."

"I love surprises." He wriggles, eager.

I type in my best guess to his phone passcode. Five blanks. I can do this.

F-U-C-K-S. Wrong answer.

I try again. *4-2-0-6-9*. No. *Dammit!* I only have one more shot at this. Not wanting to risk getting locked out of his phone, I tuck it into my pocket and head to the door. "I'm gonna go get changed into something a bit more comfortable. Don't move."

I find Ellie in the kitchen swapping labels from his tuna cans to tins of cat food. She just can't help herself. "What's wrong?" she whispers.

"I can't unlock his phone and the face security doesn't work with his eyes closed and I only have one chance before we're locked out!" I say all in one breath, trying to keep my voice low. We've worked so hard to get his phone and there's so much riding on figuring out his password.

She takes it from me. "Okay. Think—I'm Matt. I'm a playboy," she mocks his voice. "I date multiple women and tell them whatever they want to hear to get in their pants. I drive a cool old truck and have a tattoo of a ram next to my dick." Her eyebrows shoot up, and she types in *A-R-I-E-S*.

Bam. Opened.

We scan his messages, hundreds left unread, which gives me anxiety just looking at it. Lo and behold, most of them are women, each with flirty texts, plans to meet up, and explicit pictures. Each contact has notes about the things she likes and the things she's told him in an effort to keep them all straight. Ellie and I share a disgusted glare, further cementing the fact that what we're doing is for the greater good.

Ellie taps her name and reads the notes attached. "Cute, vanilla, wants a simple farm life, likes Christmas too much, 7." She gasps. "He called me a seven! What the fuck!"

"Shhh," I chastise.

"Everything okay out there?" Jax calls.

"Uh, yeah," I shout back. "Just fighting with these corset loops." I lower my voice to Ellie. "I don't want to know what mine says. Let's just do what we came here to do and move on with it."

Ellie refocuses, moving through various settings to put our plan into place. I fidget nervously as I wait for Ellie to finish her task, tapping away on the phone with a focus so intense she may as well be a hacker.

The handcuffs jingle in the next room. "Mariah? You coming back?"

"Be right there!" I shake my hands and shift from foot to foot, not sure how much longer I can delay this.

A few moments later Ellie looks up from her work. "Done."

"All of it?"

She grins wickedly, then counts on her fingers. "Changed his ring tone to something obnoxious and embarrassing."

"Good."

Ellie holds up another finger. "Scrambled his contacts on all the latest women he's been messaging so he confuses their names and basically tells them all he's screwing around on them."

"Golden."

"And," she continues, "created texting shortcuts in his phone from *cock* to *fart*, *pussy* to *ham sandwich*, and *fuck* to *have mommy and me time*."

I choke on a laugh. "This will mess with his sexting so much!"

"Can you imagine? 'I want to shove my *fart* down your throat'?" Her face contorts with barely contained laughter. "'I can't wait to *have mommy and me time* later'?"

I'm nearly dying trying to keep my laughter silent, my whole body shaking while I cover my mouth with my hand. After we get ahold of ourselves, I take the phone back. "Okay, let's finish this and get out of here before we get caught."

"I'm almost done, just five more minutes." She turns back to her can switching and I return to the bedroom.

"Sorry about that, I had a bit of a costume mishap."

"It's all good. Now, where were we?"

"Hmm," I say, trying to drag this out as long as possible. "I don't remember. Where would you like me to start?"

"How about with that paddle?" he suggests.

I roll my eyes, but pick it up, wishing these props had brought less excitement and more fear—but I underestimated him. I smack it against my palm a few times, and each time Matt wriggles. I consider, for a moment, using it on him, but don't want to give him the pleasure. Instead, I pull a feather from my bag and trace it from his rib cage to his exposed armpit.

"Hey!" he squirms, then giggles in a high-pitched tone. "That's not a padd—*hehehehe*!"

I grin as I tickle up and down his abdomen, watching him writhe, enjoying this far too much. "What, you don't like this?"

"*Hehehe*—it's not what I exp—*hehehe*!"

"Well, I don't hear a safe word, so I guess I'll keep going," I tease.

"Aw, shit, what was the—*hehehe*!"

I keep moving the feather over his body, making sure I give

him moments of respite to breathe, while Jax struggles to remember the ridiculous safe word I gave him. Suddenly, the doorbell rings.

I pause. "Who could that be?"

Jax slumps against the bed, breath coming in short gasps. "What?"

The doorbell rings again. "Might be something important," I say.

He licks his lips. "Yeah, I should probably get that. Can you let me go?"

I oblige, removing the blindfold and unlocking his restraints. He sits up, rubbing his wrists and giving me a frustrated glare. I bite my lip against a smile, then let him leave the room before hastily packing my things and following him.

I meet him at the door just as he's picking up a large gift basket.

"Weird, I didn't order anything," he mutters, his brow furrowed as he steps inside and closes the door with his foot.

"Who's it from?" I ask, my heart pounding in my ears.

"Don't know." Jax carries the basket to the kitchen table and fishes out the envelope attached to the side before ripping it open. His face blanches.

"Who's it from, Jax?" I repeat louder, trying to sound like a jilted lover.

Jax ignores me, dropping the letter to inspect the basket closer.

I pick up the letter and read it aloud: "'I'm not too chicken to profess my feelings for you! This is just the beginning of our egg-cellent homestead. Keep these warm like you do my heart! E <3'"

As I finish the last sentence, Jax lifts a towel to reveal a clutch of speckled brown eggs nestled in straw.

"What the hell? Who is 'E'? You're screwing around on me!" I accuse with my best appalled expression.

"I have no idea what's going on!" he shouts, shoulders around his ears.

I slap the letter to his chest, then turn on my heel and walk away. "I thought I was the only person you're seeing!"

Jax is right behind me. "I swear, I have no idea who gave this to me!"

"Yeah, right." I shove my feet into my shoes, then pull the door open "Well, I hope whoever they are you two have a nice life together."

"Mariah!" he calls after me as I walk quickly away, but doesn't follow.

It isn't until I'm around the corner of his building and I see Ellie waiting in our escape vehicle that I breathe. She greets me with her trademark fist-clench-and-squeal as I jump in the passenger side.

"Go, go, go!" I slap the dash like we're fleeing a bank robbery.

"Woooo!" Ellie howls, raising a fist as we peel out of the parking lot, home free.

INT. JAMES'S APARTMENT (CONT'D)

                    ANNIE
          What, you wouldn't consider us friends?

                    JAMES
          It's been a long time since I've had one
          of those. I think I've forgotten what
          it's like.

                    ANNIE
          Well, friends are there for you to help.
          To keep you company. To . . . talk about
          things, if you need.

                    JAMES
          I don't have much to talk about.

                    ANNIE
          It's hard to be friends with someone if
          they don't let you in.

                    JAMES
          To be clear, I was never offering friendship.

                    ANNIE
          Right. Of course.

                    JAMES
          And you're not even from here. Why would I
          invest time in a friendship with someone who
          lives so far away? That's a lot of emotional
          labour with very little return.

ANNIE

I'm here often to visit my sister.
And . . . never mind.

JAMES

What?

ANNIE

No, no, you refuse to hold up your end
of the friendship bargain by not opening
up so I'm not going to, either. Friendship
is a two-way street.

JAMES

Fine. I'll tell you one thing about me.
But you go first.

ANNIE

Fine. I was going to say I love my
life in Seattle, but being here with my
sister and her family, seeing the way of
life Hemlock Grove has to offer, it makes
me feel like someday I could live in a
place like this, too. Slowing down might
be good for me. I'd have time to enjoy my
life. To take walks, to read, drink coffee,
bake cookies.

Annie smiles, then licks icing off a spoon, getting
a bit of icing on her face.

JAMES

I think you deserve a life like that.

ANNIE

Your turn. Something about yourself. Anything.

JAMES

(taking a breath)
This is the closest I've felt with another
person in three years.

James reaches up, wipes icing off Annie's face with his
thumb. They share a moment, leaning toward each other.

James pulls away at the last second.

JAMES

I'm sorry. I don't know what came over me,
but I think you should go.

ANNIE

What? Um, okay . . .

JAMES

I have a lot of cleanup to do, is all,
and we open at 5:00 a.m. every day.

ANNIE

(standing)
Can I help with dishes? I really don't
mind.

JAMES

It's fine. I like doing dishes. They
help clear my head.

Chapter 17
ELLIE

We burst into the cabin in a flurry of giggles, adrenaline rushing from the close call and quick escape. My heart is pounding in my ears and all my limbs are tingling. I feel like I can take on the world. Mariah is flushed pink and she has the widest smile on her face I've ever seen. She plops her purse down, spilling its spicy contents on the floor.

"You were amazing!" I shout.

"No, *you* were amazing!" She grins, matching my energy.

I grip her forearms. "You acted, Mariah—you really did it!"

Her hands grab my elbows, her bright eyes sparkling with excitement. "Yeah, but you snuck around in there and planted all the pranks and didn't even get caught."

"But you managed to get his phone!"

"That's nothing compared to the eggs. How the hell did you find live eggs in such a short amount of time?"

I purse my lips. "I got them from the grocery store. They're unfertilized."

Mariah's eyes widen. "You mean he's going to waste hours of time keeping a bunch of eggs warm that will never hatch?"

"Yup!"

"Genius."

"I couldn't have done it without you. You're the best teammate ever." I squeeze her tighter, my heart pounding faster.

"We *are* the best team, aren't we?" she says, her voice softening, the excitement in her eyes shifting to something else. I can't place the look, can't find the words to describe it, but I can feel it. My body reacts instinctively, stilling my thoughts while simultaneously causing them to race. Everything goes quiet, fading into the background, until it's just me and her.

I follow the pull in the base of my belly, releasing Mariah's forearms and taking her waist instead. I look from the twinkling gleam in her eye down to her plump, parted lips.

We pause here, breath intermingling, static sparking between us, the moment heavy with anticipation—with want, with *need*.

Mariah closes the gap between us, and the swift movement brings us together. Her lips are soft, softer than anything I have ever felt. The way she kisses me, moulding her lips to mine, brings a low involuntary hum from my throat.

Her hands release my arms and find their way to my back, deft fingers tracing the line of my shoulder blades beneath my shirt, while my own hands move lower to her hips. We step closer, craving nearness, as our lips continue their gentle, slow exploration.

Her tongue licks across my bottom lip once, and I don't react quickly enough before it returns to her mouth. I follow her lead, my tongue grazing her lips, asking for her to come back. She obliges, and when our tongues meet in a tentative dance, my knees weaken and a throb begins to build between my legs.

I need more. So much more. Greedily, I push against her, and though she is bigger than me, she lets me press her into the countertop. With the pressure of something behind her, I can better form my body to hers, relishing her curves, aching to feel all of her on me. My fingers manoeuvre their way beneath her shirt to the smooth skin of her back, to the squishy parts of her hips and sides that I want nothing more than to nibble and kiss. I want to kiss her everywhere.

I hope she'll let me.

Mariah's lips sip mine as her hands trace up my back to my face, where she cups my cheek with one hand and my chin with the other, like I'm something precious. She pulls away slightly, eyes taking me in, searching for something. She swallows, her voice low, husky. "We can stop whenever you want."

My heart thuds in response. "No. Don't stop. Never stop."

I kiss her back harder, done with the teasing, the dancing, the playing, wanting more of her, all of her. She returns with fervour, gripping my sides, then my hips, then my ass, which she squeezes with a low moan in her throat.

I tug at her shirt. We part ways just long enough for me to pull it over her head, revealing a simple bra and her round breasts nearly spilling from her cups. *Oh, fuck, those breasts.* They're everything I'd hoped for, everything I always wanted, and it wasn't until now that I realize I can have them all to myself, enjoying them on someone else's body. I press my face into them while wrapping my arms around her, my hands worshipping all the curves below, from the roundness of her belly to the smooth skin of her back. There's so much to love with Mariah, so many places I want to kiss, to savour. I've never wanted to explore another person's body so badly, to show them how beautiful they are, how sacred.

Mariah moans as my mouth sucks and licks, pulling down her bra and finding a nipple, bringing it into my mouth. This is it. My new home. I could live here. But then there's the other one; I move to it quickly, almost overwhelmed by all the things I want to do, as if there's not enough time in the world for me, and somehow I'll run out before I get to taste every inch of her body.

She tugs me off of her, and I pout, hating the inch of space between us. She removes my shirt. My shoulders cave in, not wanting her to see me. She's so *womanly*. And I haven't matured much past age sixteen, staying rigid, boxy, more angles and planes than soft and shapely like her. Even my bra is laughable, the soft fabric requiring no underwire, my hard nipples on full display.

Mariah's fingers trace my jaw, then tilt my chin back up, meeting her gaze. My stomach flips at the way she looks at me. I've never felt more seen. Her fingers trace back down my neck, sending a shiver of tingles through all my limbs, coalescing down my spine and into my core. She caresses my collarbones, a breath escaping between her lips like a prayer, words I can barely make out. "So beautiful."

And I almost want to cry.

I take her hands in mine, then begin walking backward toward the bedroom, watching for any changes in her demeanour, any look that means she doesn't want to continue, but her gaze only grows in heat and intensity.

Once inside, I pull her close to me again, my lips hovering over hers. "I want you."

She nods, her nose nudging mine. "I want you, too."

I reach back and unclasp her bra, then let the straps fall from her shoulders. Mariah hugs her breasts to her chest then releases the garment, letting it fall to the floor. I suck in a breath, awestruck.

"You act like you've never seen boobs before," she says, her words tinged with a laugh.

"I've never seen *your* boobs before," I struggle to reply, my tongue feeling thick. "And they're magnificent."

Mariah reaches forward and pulls my simple cotton sports bra off, tossing it away, then pulls me in tight, reuniting our lips. The feel of her body against mine is better than I could have ever imagined: warm skin against skin, pert nipples grazing each other, lips and tongues colliding.

We sit on the bed together. In between kissing we remove our pants, then climb farther onto the bed, pulling the quilt over us to create a warm cocoon. It's here that I allow myself to let go, to explore her body with mine as we lie side by side, legs tangling up. I bring her thick thigh in between my thin ones and grind myself against her, already so wet. She grabs me by the ass and pulls me in harder, moving her hips against my thigh, and I feel a quick sharp shock through my core, gasping.

We continue like this, rocking into each other, building heat, building need, until I can feel Mariah slick against me, her breath coming in shorter pants, her kissing becoming more hurried. I push her onto her back and straddle her, keeping my one thigh between hers, getting more leverage, as my mouth abandons hers in favour of her breasts.

She tangles her fingers in my hair and arches her back as I taste every square inch of her breasts, listening and feeling for her, my whole body attuned to hers, as if I were made for this, to bring Mariah pleasure, to worship her body.

I kiss lower, cherishing every dimple, every curve, until I'm at her belly, where I press my face into her, humming in complete satisfaction. She giggles, and I hear her laugh through her body. I can't help but smile up at her. And fuck, she looks so pretty, all naked and flushed, patiently letting me love on her despite the throbbing need I'm sure she has, if it's anything like mine.

I move lower, to her shimmery satin black underwear, and kiss her mound through the fabric, breathing her in, relishing this moment. Her hands grip the bedsheets, and she rolls her hips toward me, but I don't let her rush me. I lick along the panty line at her thighs to the top of her waistband, which I bite and tug with my teeth, releasing the elastic in a sharp snap. She gasps, arching her back.

"Can I?" I ask, not even sure how I'm forming words.

She nods quickly. "Please."

I don't know how my hands aren't shaking when my fingers meet the line of her underwear, how my heart doesn't stop when she raises her hips, how I pull her underwear along her legs and let them fall to the floor. But I do, and I've never felt so calm, so confident, so sure of myself and who I am and what I'm doing than right here, right now.

I take my time, letting my fingers trace the skin of her belly, over her thighs, over the hair between her legs, then lower. She breathes deeply, shivering from my touch. I inch closer, bringing my mouth to her, kissing softly at first. Then I close my eyes, letting myself get lost in every taste, every touch, every sensation. I have never done anything like this before, and yet it doesn't matter. I'm so closely attuned to Mariah, listening and feeling for what she wants, that by the time my tongue is circling her clit and my fingers are inside her, rubbing and pushing, slow and methodical, I forget that this is my first. It feels like this is both the first and the hundredth time we've found one another, that I know her body so well it may as well be my own.

Her core begins winding, tightening, then shaking, then she's gripping me, and time and space no longer exist as she comes against my mouth, shuddering and moaning and crying out. My own body reacts to hers with a rush of heat and wetness, and we ride her wave over and over and over together as one, until I feel it ebb, until her shaking fingers grasp at my shoulder and I lift my mouth from her, resting my face on her thigh as we both try to catch our breath.

We lie there, in a tingling, shivering heap, as we come back to earth.

I've never been more present, more out of my own mind, more sharing of a space and a moment in time, than right now with her.

Mariah strokes my hair, and if I were a cat I'd be purring. I look toward her, still using her thigh as my pillow. Her eyes are closed and a gentle smile graces her still-flushed face. I relish the way her chest rises and falls, how she's bare to the world—bare just for me.

I sit up a little higher, pressing my one hand into the mattress as the other strokes the soft skin of her belly. "Wow," I manage to say, breaking the silence.

Mariah nods, swallows, then cracks open her eyes. "Wow," she agrees.

"You were . . . amazing!"

She smiles, her eyebrows crinkling in confusion.

"I've never seen anyone come like that before!"

Mariah presses her hands against her eyes. "Oh my god."

"Seriously, it was so beautiful. The way you sounded, and how your body reacted, and you came and came, over and over, it was surreal. I'm so impressed by you. You should be really proud of yourself."

"What?" She chuckles, her tits jiggling. She looks at me, still confused, but with a gentle smile on her face. "*I* should be proud?"

"Yes! You were incredible. It was so rewarding to be here with you for that. I feel honoured." I press a hand to my chest.

She gives her head a slow shake. "You're so weird. But in a good way."

"Thank you. I pride myself on being weird in a good way."

"Come here." She beckons, reaching for me.

I oblige, meeting her on the bed and tucking my face into the crook of her neck, draping one leg over her body and hugging her tight.

Mariah sighs contentedly, then kisses my forehead. "Give me a minute here and I'll return the favour."

I tense. "Oh. You don't have to."

"No, really, I want to."

"That's okay. I'm fine. I'm . . . good." I try to brush her off, keeping my tone light.

Mariah pulls away a bit, trying to look at me, but I hide my face against her. "It's really not a big deal, I'd love to—"

"I really don't want you to go down on me," I say with finality, all teasing gone from my voice.

Mariah tenses. "Is . . . everything okay? I mean, I'm sorry if I pressured you to . . ."

"No, it's not that."

She waits a long moment, neither of us moving, barely breathing. Finally, she tries again. "You don't have to tell me, but I promise, whatever it is, I won't judge."

I swallow. Steeling my resolve, I sit up on the bed. Tucking my knees to my chest and hugging myself, I look at where she lies, pulling the blankets up a little higher against the chill of me no longer being at her side.

"You trusted me," I say. "So, I'll trust you."

"Did something . . . happen?" Mariah's brows furrow with concern.

"No. Thankfully, nothing like *that* has happened to me," I assure her. "It's more like a . . . *lack* of something happening, if you will."

Her worry shifts to confusion.

I sigh. "What you just did? How you came like that? It was so fucking beautiful and amazing and . . . I can't do it."

"You can't come?"

I give my head a subtle shake. "Nope."

"Like, ever?"

I think for a moment. "I think I've orgasmed, like once? Maybe?"

"If you *think* you've done it, then you probably haven't," she states.

"It wasn't anything like that," I say, pointing over my shoulder with my thumb as if her earth-shattering orgasm is somewhere behind us. "I wish I could do anything half that incredible. But I can't. Not with other people, not with myself. I've tried, but I just end up getting sore and tired before I get anywhere. I end up just faking it, with everyone, and I . . ." I bite my lip. Mariah rubs my leg, encouraging me to continue. "I don't want to fake it with you."

"Aw, love." She squeezes my calf.

"With my first boyfriend . . ." I swallow against a flood of sudden emotion, hoping that if I open myself up to her emotionally it will be a fraction of how I felt when she opened herself up to me physically. I can't share my body with her, not in the way she shared hers with me, but I can share my mind. And I hope that's enough. "My first *real* boyfriend—who I had sex with for the first time—after a few times he complained. He told me I was too quiet, too boring. I had no idea what he was talking about, I was just being myself. So he showed me some porn, and I was like, *this isn't real. It's performative. They're acting.* I was confused because I thought I wasn't supposed to fake it, you know? I may have been a newb in the sack, but I'd read *Cosmo* magazines. But he said that's what turned him on, that's what he wanted, so I did it. I went along with it, making all the noises the professionals do, and he was happier with it, but it totally ruined it for me. I felt like . . . like . . ."

"Like it was all about him and not about you?"

I nod, the tension in my chest releasing slightly, knowing she understands.

Mariah nods. "I feel the same way. In a different way, but the same. I come very easily. Like, I've orgasmed going down a bumpy road before."

"Lucky," I tease.

She smiles at me, then shrugs. "I'm not gonna lie, it's pretty great."

"Right? And it's so frustrating because I want to, and I try to, I have all sorts of toys. Every guy I've ever told decides it's his personal mission to be the first, like there's something he has that the others don't, and he has some special key to my vagina."

Mariah laughs. "Oh my god, I can totally picture that."

"And all the TV I watch and all the books I read always have these women who you barely touch them and they come, and I'm like, *what's wrong with* me? *Why can't I?*"

"Nothing's wrong with you," she states fervently. "It's actually quite common. And it's nothing to be ashamed of. Every person is different. But I get what you mean, about men making it about them. For me, yeah, it's easy for me to get off, I can get off multiple times in one go, multiple times a day—"

"Braggart," I tease.

She smiles before continuing. "But men, they always act like they're the shit, they're responsible for my body and how I feel, and it feeds into their own ego about how awesome *they* are, and it gets tiring after a while. Why do they always have to make it about them?"

"Right? That must be annoying, too."

"So I get it. Not the whole thing, about you not being able

to orgasm, or being forced to fake it in bed with your partners so they can feel like they've accomplished something. But I see where you're coming from."

"Thank you." I relax back into her. "It's just, with us, I haven't had to pretend at all. I act so often in my life—between work, and making friends, and sex—and I haven't done that with you. For better or worse, I've been myself."

Mariah sits up to meet me, our bare chests touching, her wild blue curls falling to the side of her face. She tucks a strand of hair behind my ear then nuzzles her nose against mine. "I know what it's like to pretend to be different than you are, and I don't want that for you. I like being honest with each other. That's the only way I ever want it to be. And if you don't want me going down on you, or touching you at all, that's fine. I respect that, and I'll honour your wishes. I'm happy to be your pillow princess."

I giggle at the term.

Mariah kisses me softly, lips hovering. "But just know that I'd love to enjoy your body, to show you how beautiful you are, and I wouldn't expect anything in return. You wouldn't have to react. There wouldn't be a goal in mind, an end game, anything I'd need from you. It would just be you and me, and not a care in the world, and whenever you'd want me to stop you could just give my hand a squeeze and I would. Okay?"

I think it over, about how nice that sounds, how great it would be to feel her on me the way I felt her. But I'm not ready to share myself with her in that way. An anxious vise grips my chest, imagining her working so hard to bring me pleasure, her disappointment when she can't, moving on to someone else who can make her feel that same rush of excitement as I did when I was with her.

Mariah nuzzles her nose into my cheek, and I can't help but smile, my thoughts going back over her words and settling on something else she said, repeating it over and over, the anxious ball in my stomach slowly being replaced by a warm glow. "I like not having a goal. I like just *being* with you."

She nods, kissing down my neck, murmuring against my skin. "I know what you mean."

I pull her closer, nuzzling my nose into her hair. "If I'd known it was like this with a woman, I'd have tried it a long time ago."

INT. APARTMENT HALLWAY - NIGHT

James and Annie walk slowly down the hall side by side.

                    ANNIE
          Thanks for decorating cookies with me.
          You know, I had thought about taking
          baking lessons while I was in town.

                    JAMES
          You had?

                    ANNIE
          Yeah. I didn't sign up for anything
          because I didn't think I'd have time.
          But you've helped me cross something
          off my Christmas wish list and made
          my holiday a bit better.

                    JAMES
          It's the least I could do for everything
          you've done. Even if you started off by
          making my life a lot harder, I'm glad you
          did.

                    ANNIE
          You are?

                    JAMES
          (stepping closer to Annie)
          I think I've been looking down for so
          long, I've forgotten that life is going
          on around me. Then I look up, and you're

there. It's been three years since I've
looked up, and life has passed me by . . .

Annie and James stop outside Jenna's apartment door.

> JAMES (CONT'D)
> And I can't keep letting it do that.
> So, thank you.

> ANNIE
> Sometimes we all need a reminder
> about what's most important in life.

> JAMES
> Including yourself?

> ANNIE
> I think I needed a reminder that not
> everyone is in a place where they can
> enjoy Christmas, and to offer compassion
> to those people instead of passing
> judgment. I'm sorry for being so
> brutal with you. I didn't understand.

> JAMES
> It's okay. We've got off on the
> wrong foot, a couple times actually,
> but you haven't given up on me.

> ANNIE
> Of course. I wouldn't do that.

> JAMES
> Why not? Everyone else has.

ANNIE

That's not true. You have people in
your corner who care about you.
They look out for you.

JAMES

(confused)
I do?

ANNIE

Yeah. Everyone wants what's best for
you. And this is the first step. I know
Christmas can be a hard time, but it's
good to see you putting in an effort.
Already since I've been here I can
see the Christmas magic working
on you.

JAMES

You can?

ANNIE

Yeah. You seem lighter. Brighter. More
carefree. I even caught you smiling once.

James smiles.

ANNIE

See? There it is.

JAMES

I'm not sure if that's from the Christmas
spirit.

Annie and James lean toward each other again, but James recognizes what's happening and steps back.

                    JAMES
          I'll see you in the morning for your
          coffee. Sweet dreams.

Chapter 18
MARIAH

I stop kissing Ellie, freezing partway down her neck. Ellie pulls away, looking into my eyes, her own expression shifting when she picks up on my confusion.

"What?" she asks, a small, worried smile on her lips.

I lift myself up on my elbows, forcing her off me. "Did you just say I was your first time?"

"Yeah. I never even kissed a girl before you."

"Wh-what?"

"I mean I've thought about kissing girls before, but never really made it past that point in my head. I didn't think I was bisexual. I thought, *yeah, women are pretty*, but I wasn't a hundred percent sure. I've been curious, but aren't we all curious? It wasn't until now when I was with you that I was like, *okay yes, this is great*, that I was like, *yep, I'm bi*. I've just only ever been with men and—"

I interrupt her rambling by slicing my hand through the air. "You never even thought you were bi before this?"

She smiles and shakes her head. "Nope."

"But you—" I lower my voice a bit "—you certainly knew what you were doing down there."

Ellie presses a hand to her chest. "Why, thank you. I don't think that was me, though, I mean, you practically told me what to do with your sounds and movements and I just followed your lead, and honestly I didn't even really have to think about it, I was in the moment with you and it all sort of happened and it wasn't like I planned it but I do admit I thought about being with you before, and—"

I interrupt her again, the only way to get a word in edgewise. "You thought about me?"

She hesitates, a blush creeping up her neck. "Yeah. I mean . . ." She lowers her gaze, biting her lip. "I didn't want to make you feel uncomfortable here, though. You don't have anywhere else to go."

My heart stammers in my chest. I caress her cheek with my thumb, stroking the warm, flushed skin, and swallow back a wave of conflicting emotions. Not wanting her to see me fighting with them, I wrap my arms around her and pull her back onto me. Her slight build and moderate weight make for the perfect anxiety blanket, calming my nerves as my brain runs ragged from one idea to the other, back and forth across my brain like a puppy with the zoomies.

I promised myself I'd never be here again. After what happened with Jess, I wouldn't be someone's curiosity experiment. Even though cosmetology school was six years ago, it still hurts as if the wound is still fresh and bleeding; first loves can be like that.

We'd met on the first day of orientation. I was immediately attracted to her. And god, she was actually quite similar to Ellie, now that I scrape away the mind blocks I'd put up for myself in some vain attempt to remove Jess from my memory. She'd been from the country—a cute brunette girl, innocent eyes, but soft, round, and so, *so* pretty. We'd become fast friends since we were seated beside one another and were both new to Vancouver. My crush on her was immediate, but I could tell she only saw me as a friend. Back then, I hadn't been hurt before. I was living my new life as my authentic self and was ready and willing to chase down anything and everything I always wanted but could never have, including a girlfriend. I courted Jess all year, being her best platonic girlfriend, picking out clothes with her to go to the club, dancing with her until she'd find a guy she'd rather dance with, holding her hair back at the end of the night as she emptied the contents of her stomach in a back alley, cleaning her up and snuggling her back to health until morning.

As our friendship grew, so did my love for her. I was there for her whenever she needed, giving up all my spare time for her, worshipping the ground she walked on, to be told I was "such a good friend." And I *was* a good friend. I loved her like a friend, but also in so many other ways that I didn't know how to explain, but thought if I'd just give her more time maybe she'd see it, maybe she'd see *me* in a new way.

Finally, one day, we were on the couch in our PJ's, watching the first *Pirates of the Caribbean* film randomly because it was on TV and we didn't feel like watching anything else.

"Keira Knightley is so hot," I'd said.

Jess agreed with a nod. "Yeah, I wish I was her."

Quiet and shy, I ventured, "You know, you kind of look like her."

She smiled that radiant, dimpled smile of hers. "Aw, you think?"

And when she looked at me, she saw, for the first time, the fire in my eyes I'd never once tried to conceal. I leaned in and kissed her. She kissed me back.

And fuck, that kiss, it had been everything and so much more. Years of yearning—not just for Jess, but for everyone I'd ever wanted—was all pent up in that kiss, in that moment. I kept it going, and going, and going, until we were naked on the couch and I was on top of her and she was moaning and then crying out, and I found my own release against my hand as she found hers on my mouth. That had been the most beautiful moment of my life.

I held her in my arms after, feeling more whole than I ever had, so happy that, finally, things would be the way they were supposed to be between us. I was in love. So, so, in love. The kind of love you have before you've ever been hurt, when your whole heart jumps with both feet, cannonballing into the dark depths below, not knowing there are sharks in the water.

Unfortunately, that love was unreciprocated.

I'd told Jess how I felt. She wanted things to go back to the way they were before, for me to keep being her best friend. She asked me not to tell anyone. She told me that she'd been curious, but now it was over. She wanted me to keep wing-womaning her at the club to get men back to her bed.

I told her to go fuck herself.

And I promised myself, after that day, I would never be someone's curiosity experiment ever again. I wouldn't open myself up to someone unless they were sure about what we were doing, about who they were and what it meant.

Yet here I am, falling for another woman who doesn't know what she wants, and hasn't even considered being with a woman before.

And I'm torn on whether to tell her.

Ellie had opened up to me, told me something painful about her past. She'd trusted me. Part of me knows I can trust her, that she would take my past and accept it.

But the other part of me doesn't want to put pressure on her when she's only just discovered an important facet of her identity. And another, deeper part of me, the one focused on preserving my heart after it had been beaten so bruised and bloody before, doesn't want to show my cards just yet. We've only known each other a few days, only shared our bodies minutes ago, our first kiss an hour before that. I shouldn't be having all these intrusive, annoying *feelings* for her—I don't normally after a one-night stand with a person, regardless of gender. But here I am, slipping further and further in love with Ellie with every contented sigh she breathes against my cheek.

I don't want this to end.

If I say something, it might.

With Jess, I'd told her I wanted her right away. I'd told her I wanted to be her girlfriend, to hold her hand at school and kiss her whenever I wanted, that I didn't want to share her with anyone else. It scared her away. Our relationship never began, and our friendship had ended. If I'd waited, if I'd let her come around, maybe things between us would have been different.

Or maybe they'd be the same, but I wouldn't have hurt my own feelings so much when we came to our eventual conclusion.

Either way, I'm going to let whatever this is between Ellie and I simply be; I'm not going to direct it one way or another. I'll let Ellie lead. I'll be there for her however she wants, as a friend, as more than that, while she figures out what she wants.

By the time filming is finished I'll have a better idea of Ellie's feelings toward me. If things between us progress we can talk about it then. And if it's not meant to be, then it isn't. We'll go on with our separate lives, and our time together will be a beautiful blip in history . . . even though it will hurt to let her go.

I've recovered from a broken heart before.

I can do it again.

Though, as we drift off to sleep, feeling Ellie's body against mine, how her leg wraps over my torso while her fingers trail soft circles over my skin, how my heart wants to leap from my body into hers, I hope I don't have to.

THE FOLLOWING MORNING passes in blissful domesticity. Ellie and I manoeuvre around the small, homey kitchen as if we've had years of practice doing so. She makes the toast, I pour the coffee. She cracks the eggs, I salt and pepper them. We share a peaceful breakfast while sitting hip to hip at the peninsula, me quietly listening to Ellie's morning chatter as if she were a bird singing outside my window.

We get dressed—me in my various shades of black, Ellie in green-and-red-striped leggings with her ridiculous Rudolph sweater—and I drive us into town, the windows rolled down to let in the early-morning breeze. Ellie talks away about everything and nothing; she's my new favourite radio station.

As we approach the set, neither of us talk about how we're going to act in front of everyone else. I let Ellie lead, curious about what she'll do, reading into everything she does like clues in a scavenger hunt. She didn't hold my hand when we walked to the set, but she opened the door and let me up the stairs first. She hasn't kissed me this morning, but she hasn't been uncomfortably evading me, either.

It isn't until she sits in my makeup chair that I know she's feeling the effects of last night, just as I am. Her big eyes watch me intently as I sanitize my hands then squeeze primer onto my fingertips. I smooth the cool liquid over her skin in slow circles, caressing her cheekbones, the skin beneath her bottom lip, over the ridge on her nose she's self-conscious about, and lose myself in watching the effect I have on her. Her eyes flutter closed and her chin tilts up, exposing her pretty throat. Her mouth parts, a quiet, satisfied sigh escaping her lips.

I take greater care than I ever have, my fingertips savouring every centimetre of her skin, relishing how intimate this simple act is, how each stroke of my skin against hers sends a rush of tingles up my arm and down my spine.

I brush my thumb over her plump bottom lip, and she opens her eyes once more to look at me, meeting me with a hopeful smile, which I can't help but return while my heart pounds in my throat. The rest of the studio fades into a din of abstract noise and sound like we're underwater and it's the two of us in a bubble . . . and the only way to breathe is by kissing her.

I bend ever so slightly toward her, and her eyes widen a fraction in surprise, in fear . . . then shift to a dare.

I lean a millimetre closer, watching her expression, how her eyes dance, beckoning me, until—

"Hey, you two," Yueyi interrupts, clipboard in hand.

We both startle, Ellie sitting up straighter and me taking a step back.

"Hey, Yueyi!" Ellie chirps, clearing her throat. "Hope you're having a holly jolly July morning!"

"You're on set in ten, we need to get going." Yueyi ignores Ellie's sentiment entirely, walking away in a hurry, and my hackles prickle in response.

"Would it kill her to have a little Christmas spirit?" I mutter, moving quickly through the next steps of her makeup and hair process.

Ellie shrugs, closing her eyes so I can paint her lids. "It's all good. I'm used to it. Nobody seems to appreciate Christmas as much as I do, but hey, I'm happy to provide everyone with their required daily dose of Christmas spirit."

My heart warms at how easily she brushes things off, but aches a bit, too, that she's alone in her attempt to bring year-round joy to people; no one does the same for her.

After I release Ellie to the costume department, I get to work on the lineup of extras required for the scene, but my mind is elsewhere, gnawing on an idea that's beginning to form.

After I'm finished working on everyone and cleaning my area, I join Jimmie and the others behind the scenes with the film crew. In between watching Ellie go from her bubbly, chipper self to serious barista in the blink of an eye and back again, I open Google Maps and step outside to make a few calls. It doesn't take long before I find what I'm looking for and get everything set up. Even though I'm a terrible actress, I manage to keep my excitement under wraps so I don't distract Ellie during our brief interactions between takes to adjust her makeup and hair. As entertaining as it is to see Ellie on set, I'm too excited about my plan and the day passes slowly.

When we wrap and make our way back upstairs, I'm practically giddy and trying my best to hide it, but Ellie picks up on my energy immediately.

"What's going on?" She smiles curiously as she wipes off the drab makeup.

I swivel the chair around until we meet each other's gaze through the mirror. "Oh. Nothing. Just have to do your makeup one more time."

"Ooh, twice in one day?" She bites her bottom lip and raises her eyebrows suggestively.

I swallow a laugh. "I may or may not have an adventure for us."

"An adventure!" She squeezes the makeup wipe in her clenched fists and squeals, unable to contain her excitement. I fucking melt. It's now my own personal mission to get that reaction out of her every single day.

After dolling Ellie up so that her beautiful features pop, we steal away off the set and into my car. We navigate out of the city, across the highway, and up a mountainside.

"Is this where you murder me?" Ellie asks coyly, the wind tousling her blond waves from her open window.

I raise an eyebrow. "Maybe."

She slaps her knee. "I knew it. This whole thing has been a ruse to get me alone in the forest."

"Well, I couldn't do it at the cabin. Too much evidence."

Ellie giggles, then reaches over the seats and gives my leg a squeeze. I try not to get too distracted by her touch. Paired with the late-afternoon sun glinting off her golden hair, highlighting the hazel flecks in her deep brown eyes, she's fucking stunning.

We park at the top of a mountain and get out of the car, walking along the crushed gravel road toward an outcropping of coniferous trees gradually increasing in size.

I bite my lip and watch Ellie, waiting for her reaction.

Her adorable brow furrows and she pauses midstep. Then she points and twists toward me. "Is this . . . ?"

I nod. "Yep."

She hesitates, a smile spreading on her face. "Why are we at a Christmas tree farm?"

"You said you wouldn't settle for anything less than a real tree for Christmas. So, I thought, why don't we get one?"

"But you hate Christmas!" she blurts.

"I do. I did. But I want you to have the full Christmas experience, since I know it means so much to you. We have all the decorations anyway, and I never really decorated one before, so—"

Ellie slams into me, her lips ravaging mine in a hungry kiss. I wrap my arms around her and pull her close as I tilt my head for a better angle, matching her intensity. Ellie's hands hold the sides of my face, then one runs up the back of my neck and grips my hair at my scalp, making me moan into her mouth. I let my hand wander down to her ass and give it a squeeze, and—

Someone clears their throat.

We stop, dazed and blinking at the sound.

A kindly old white man with white hair is standing a few yards away with a chainsaw in his hands, trying his very best to be polite and not gawk at us as we make out in his tree field.

I move to step away, but Ellie grabs me by the hand to keep me close. I try not to let the butterflies in my stomach explode out of my chest.

"You two here for a Christmas tree? In July?" He's a good sport despite how ridiculous my request is.

"Yes, sir!" Ellie squeezes my hand so tightly I'm worried my knuckles will pop.

"Okay. You have a size in mind?" He starts walking, and we follow him.

"Just a small one," I say. "We don't have much room."

He nods, leading us to the right. We walk hand in hand, the scent of pine wafting through the air tickling my throat, continuing past the tall trees to the smaller saplings.

The gentleman gestures toward them and we wander through the neat rows to find our new friend. Ellie's eye catches on one almost immediately, and I don't have to be a Christmas expert for this thing to give me Charlie Brown vibes.

"That one!"

"You sure?" the old man asks, scratching his white hair.

Ellie nods. "It's perfect."

He shrugs, then asks us to step back and cover our ears while he revs his chainsaw, taking one quick slice to cut it down. He easily carries it back to the car, strapping it to the top with a bit of twine.

"How much do I owe you? Do you take cards?" I ask, pulling my wallet from my purse in the back seat.

He lifts a hand, declining my offer. "It's all good. I was going to have to thin that scraggly little guy out, anyway. I'm glad he gets to have his Christmas, even though it's July."

Ellie grabs him in a quick, surprising hug. He chuckles, patting her back awkwardly. Once she releases him, she skips to the passenger seat, buckling in, and I join her up front. She's so fucking radiant, shining like she's made of a hundred stars, and when she smiles at me in that heartbreaking way, my heart squeezes so tightly it takes my breath away.

And that's when I know for sure.

I love her.

INT. JENNA'S APARTMENT - NIGHT

Annie enters Jenna's dark apartment, closes
the door and leans against it. Lights turn on,
surprising her.

                    JENNA
          There she is. Were you over at that
          guy's place across the hall again?

                    ANNIE
          Maybe.

                    JENNA
          Oh, come on, I haven't had time for real
          romance in months. It's hard to sneak away
          when you smell like sour milk, and Henry
          seems to know exactly the wrong time to cry.
          Let me live vicariously through you!

                    ANNIE
          There's nothing to tell.
          We're friends.

                    JENNA
          Uh-huh. Friends don't make you
          blush like that.

Annie brings her hands up to pink cheeks.

                    ANNIE
          Stop! Anyway, I'm going to a big
          Christmas party on Saturday with him—

Jenna gives Annie a look.

ANNIE (CONT'D)
As a *friend*.

JENNA
Uh-huh. Sure.

ANNIE
Do you have anything I can wear?
I didn't bring any dresses. I
thought we'd be having a sweatpants
marathon this whole week.

JENNA
Do I have dresses? Come on. I may be
a mom, but I'm not dead.

INT. BREWED AWAKENING CAFÉ - MORNING

Annie enters and stands in line to wait with three
other customers.

James sees her immediately and smiles. His demeanour
with his guests has improved, he even says "Good
Morning" to them.

Annie steps up when it's her turn.

ANNIE
Good morning! Two lattes please, sir.

JAMES
Why yes, miss, coming right up.

Annie glances at the display case, noting some new
treats.

                         ANNIE
          Our Christmas cookies! You're selling them!

                         JAMES
          They're a huge hit. I may have to make more
          for us to take to the party on Saturday.

                         ANNIE
          Let me know if you need any help with that.

                         JAMES
          I will. Here are your drinks—

Annie removes her wallet from her purse.

James raises his hand to stop her, then gestures to
the display case of cookies.

                    JAMES (CONT'D)
          You've already paid me in hours
          of service.

                         ANNIE
          Thank you, that is very kind. Can
          I have a couple of cookies, too?

James gives her the cookies in a paper bag.

Annie sneaks a $20 bill into the tip jar.

James eyes Annie with teasing reproach.

Annie sniffs her drink, then tastes it.

                    ANNIE
Is this pumpkin spice?

                    JAMES
Yes. But don't tell anyone. I have a
reputation to uphold.

                    ANNIE
Just for me?

                    JAMES
        (smiling)
Just for you.

Chapter 19
ELLIE

I'm bouncing in my seat and singing "Here Comes Santa Claus" the whole drive home. The cabin isn't too far from the tree farm, but Mariah takes it slow so we don't lose all the needles off our little friend strapped to the roof. I can't believe I get to have a Christmas tree—a real one, in July! And of all the people to put this together and make my Christmas wish come true, it's Mariah. If I didn't know any better, I'd say her little Grinch heart has grown ten sizes since we first met. And I think it's all because of me.

Watching the wind tousle her blue hair as she fights the smile on her face, her cheeks pinching together and lips pursing as they do, it makes me want to reach across the seat and tickle her. I refrain, as I also don't want to get in a car crash.

We pull up to the cabin and I leap from the car, immediately working to untie the tree. Mariah takes a bit more time with the knots on her side, always measured and careful, before helping me lift it down. We work together to carry it in and set it next to the wood-burning stove.

"We didn't really think this through, did we?" Mariah states, hands on her hips.

The tree, though small, takes up every square inch of free space in the already crowded living room. With the oversized '70s furniture and Mariah's couch popped out into a bed, there is literally zero room to walk around.

"Maybe if we . . . ?" I gesture at her bed awkwardly, not wanting to insinuate she sleep with me, but also insinuating that she *could* sleep with me.

She nods, wordlessly removing the blankets and pillows to

fold it back up. I do my best not to jump and dance, but I'm too excited and can't help a subdued hop and wiggle. With the bed folded back into the couch there's room to stand and walk.

"I think it's perfect." I inhale the nostalgic scent of pine. "That's gotta be one of the best smells in the world."

"It's up there. So, how do we . . ." Mariah gestures at the thing, searching for words, before deciding on, "Erect it?"

I laugh, slapping my knee. "Oh my god, erect the tree."

Mariah sighs, fighting a smile of her own. "You know what I mean."

Still wheezing from my laugh, I explain, "We need a tree stand."

"Okay, where is it?"

"I didn't bring one."

"Oh." Mariah pulls at her bottom lip. "I didn't think about that."

I shrug. "We'll figure it out." I walk around the peninsula and dig through the cupboards in the kitchen, then find an old Dutch oven that's seen better days. Bringing the pot back to the tree, I get Mariah to lift it up and place it inside. Then, I go outside and source some rocks to stack up inside the pot to give it support. It works well enough, keeping the little guy upright. After some back and forth we decide to lift the tree and set it atop the wood-burning stove since the thing isn't on anyways. Doing so brings the top of the tree up just past Mariah's height, giving the illusion that it's a real big tree, and also clearing up more space in the room.

"It's perfect," I murmur, standing back to appreciate our work.

"Almost." Mariah disappears for a moment and returns with the box of decorations from my closet.

I clap my hands in excitement.

She sets it down and pulls out a box of red ornaments. "How do we start?"

"We start by putting on a Christmas movie!"

Mariah groans. "Again with the Christmas movies? Can't we watch the last *Alien*?"

"Nope. For this we need the real deal. I'll let you do the honours."

She kneels in front of the box and digs around, looking at a few options. Then, she picks up the plain black VHS tape with sharpie on it. "Wait . . . *Romeo and Juliet, 2006*. That movie came out in the mid-'90s. Is this your high school play you told me about?"

Now it's my turn to groan. "Yes. It must have been put in the Christmas movie box by mistake."

"Can we watch this instead?" She stands, turning it over in her hands like it's a precious artifact.

"No. Christmas movie."

She pouts, her bottom lip sticking out. "Please? Consider it a Christmas present."

My heart stammers at how freaking adorable she is, begging to watch one of the most embarrassing moments of my life, and asking for it to be a gift to her. I sigh, relenting. "All right. But don't judge me too harshly. It was my first time."

"If your first time acting was anything like your first time giving head then I have high hopes for this movie."

As the play kicks off, Mariah and I remove one of the strings of lights from the ceiling to repurpose for the tree. When we finish with the lights, we move to the red and green plastic balls, then to the homemade decorations my family has had since the dawn of time. The tree is a lot smaller than the ones I usually decorate so we only manage to get about a quarter of the decorations on before every branch is overflowed to the point of sagging. It looks even more hideous than before, but in a cute, cheerful way.

Mariah is helpful in the beginning, and I love watching her place her first decorations on her first tree, taking far more time than necessary to find the perfect spot for each bauble. But as the play progresses it steals more and more of her attention, until she ends up on the couch, elbows on her knees, rapt.

I don't mind at all, unsure if she's more adorable decorating a Christmas tree or watching my old high school play.

By the time Act 3, Scene 1 rolls around, the tree is finished and I have no way of avoiding watching the play any longer. I take my seat next to Mariah and cringe watching my past self act in a crude deep voice as Mercutio, challenging Jaime Wyatt as he plays Tybalt. Moments later there is a flurry of plastic swordplay, and then my fatal blow where I deliver my final lines. The whole audience laughs as I make my last joke about being a grave man, then again when I "slap" Brian Zanderhurst and yell at him to find me a surgeon.

"Well, there you have it," I say, moving to turn it off.

"Wait!" She grabs the sleeve of my sweater. "I want to see the rest of your acting."

"That's my last line," I say, puzzled. "Wait. Have you never read *Romeo and Juliet*?"

She gives me a pointed look. "I slept through most of high school English. I think I saw the film once, but don't really remember."

I blink several times, shocked. Sometimes I forget that not everyone is as obsessed with acting as me, and that they haven't at least read the CliffsNotes of each of Shakespeare's plays.

"I don't know how you can say you're a bad actress after something like *that*," she says, gesturing at the screen as the play continues. "You're so good."

"Not good enough." I sigh.

"What? Why?" She manages to tear her gaze away from the screen to look at me.

I watch for a moment as Juliet takes the scene, Ashleigh Blake with her silken hair and button nose fumbling her lines. I point. "I auditioned for Juliet and was cast as Mercutio."

"No offence to Juliet, but I think Mercutio is way cooler."

I frown, then nod in agreement. "Yeah, but the whole point of being in the play was so I'd get to kiss James Tyler at the end."

"*Ooo*-ooh," Mariah singsongs, elbowing me. "Was he your crush?"

"Yeah. We had band together. I applied to be a clarinet player because all the cool kids played the clarinet—"

Mariah huffs. "I don't think *cool* is the right word, but go on."

"I applied for it but didn't get chosen, since you can only have so many clarinet players. I got my second choice, trombone—I only picked trombone because my favourite character in *Donkey Kong 64* played it. Anyway, so I'm in the back of the band room behind the French horns and in front of the eager beaver playing the cymbals, and I'm thinking, *wow, this sucks*, but lo and behold, guess who was also chosen to play trombone?"

I pause for dramatic effect and Mariah plays into it, holding her breath cartoonishly.

"James Tyler."

She slaps a hand on her knee. "I knew it."

I giggle, then continue. "I flirted with him all through first semester, but he wasn't getting the hint that I liked him, and at the time I didn't know girls could ask boys out, right? Plus, I was a dorky little teen, all elbows and knees, bushy blond hair I hadn't figured out how to style, with braces and acne on top of it all. Meanwhile, he was on the volleyball team and drove a moped."

Mariah snorts a laugh.

"So then there's going to be this school play, right?" I say, getting more and more animated as I talk. "If he was Romeo and I was Juliet then he'd have to kiss me in front of the whole school, and then we'd fall madly in love and he'd be my boyfriend. I convinced him to audition and he got the role, because of course he did, only like two guys auditioned. But guess who was cast as Juliet?"

Once again, Mariah pretends to be fascinated, though she's trying not to laugh.

"Ashleigh friggen Blake. She was gorgeous, like, I could never even manage to say two words around her because she made me so nervous. But she could barely remember her lines, and the lines she did remember you could hardly hear. I had to watch Ashleigh and James kiss in rehearsals over and over and over again from backstage, dressed up like a boy with a fake moustache. Worst part is my plan actually worked. Ashleigh and James kissed in front of the whole school, and they fell in love, and they went to junior prom together, and dated for like two and a half years."

Mariah places her hand on my thigh and gives it a squeeze, her expression turned from amused to serious, lips twisting into an apologetic frown.

"Anyway. It wasn't the first time I was picked over. And it won't be the last. I got used to disappointment quickly." I frown, recalling all the jobs since then, how I've auditioned to be the lead in every single one of them and have always been chosen to play someone else. Even my personal life mirrors my professional one, with all my attempts at relationships falling flat, someone else always being chosen over me.

Always the supporting character, never the lead.

I look up from the thread I've been pulling on my sweater to meet Mariah's gaze, cringing at how pitifully she's looking at me. Sitting up taller, I give my head a shake and force a smile to my face. "But, hey, I'm here now! Look at me! I'm a real actress and I've been in several movies and I'm here in Chilliwack working on a new Christmas movie, and I love Christmas movies, and everything worked out, and—"

Mariah interrupts again, gently squeezing my leg. "You know, it's okay."

I hesitate. "What?"

"It's okay to be . . . sad?"

I blink several times. "I'm not sad. I'm happy! I wouldn't change a thing. Butterfly effect and all. If I did, maybe I wouldn't be here right now, with you."

Her frown morphs slowly into a smile. "That's really sweet."

I turn a bit on the couch so I can face her, taking her hands in mine, and lower my voice. "I'm serious. I didn't think I'd ever make a . . ." I pause, searching for the right word and coming up empty. "Friend like you."

"Friend?" Mariah tries to slip her hands out of my grasp, but I tug her closer, bringing her lips to mine. She sighs into the embrace, her lips and tongue greeting mine in a slow dance. I feel lightheaded as she kisses me, like I'm starved for oxygen and she's the source.

The couch is too small, and after a few bumbling moments of trying to make it work, Mariah grabs the throw blanket and pillows to make a love nest on the floor while I switch off my play, opting for quiet Christmas jazz instrumentals on my phone.

The twinkling red and green lights dance upon her porcelain skin, and the smell of her delicate lotion mixes with the woody pine, synthesizing into my new favourite aroma. Quiet notes of "Have Yourself a Merry Little Christmas" whirl through the air, perfecting the ambiance. The sight of Mariah waiting for my touch as her doe-eyed gaze beckons me closer is the best gift I've ever seen beneath a tree. I take a slow, deliberate breath of gratitude toward the universe for this moment, for bringing Mariah into my life.

We take turns between kissing and removing clothes until we're naked, our legs intertwined, side by side, chests pressed flush, greedy for more.

Pulling her closer, I let my hands make their way up her arms to her shoulders, caressing the line of her jaw, the hollow of her throat, down her neck and back to her shoulders again. I linger in all the places I want, in no hurry to move any faster, enjoying the simple act of her lips on mine. I slowly make my way lower, where I trace circles over her breasts, tantalizing her nipples, and she arches into me until I give her breasts a gentle squeeze.

Mariah's hands are exploring me, lingering on so many places

I'd never before considered to be erotic: the lobes of my ears, my clavicle, down the centre of my chest. Tingles rush from her touch like sparklers on Canada Day, blazing along my skin and meeting in my centre where they pool, gathering heat.

She's so fucking beautiful it hurts my heart. Her pale skin is flushed, mouth red and plump from kissing. It makes me ache deep down in my belly. I roll on top of her, pressing my body to hers, and shift my leg up between her thighs. Rolling my hips against hers, I watch as her lips part and her head tilts back, gasping at the friction. I feel her against my thigh, so plump and wet and ready, and am torn between moving down her body to kiss between her legs and staying up here with her, kissing her mouth.

I moan in slight frustration, wishing I could be both places at once. "You know, I've never wanted a cock before now, but I can see the appeal."

"Mmmm," she groans, biting her bottom lip. "You in a strap-on would be so hot."

I freeze. "We could do that?"

Mariah's smile grows, and she tucks a strand of hair behind my ear. "Of course. We can do whatever we want. Hang on, let me get something." I sit up and watch as she leaves the cocoon of our lovemaking to fetch something from her suitcase. She returns a moment later with a curved purple vibrator. She hands it to me, then returns to her spot on the floor.

I admire the apparatus, turning it over in my hand. I had a vibrator years ago but gave up on it since my body never seemed to cooperate and it was more work that it was worth. But now, holding it in my hand with Mariah ready and waiting, I'm eager to see what one of these can do.

Straddling her thigh, I suck on it, getting it wet. Mariah's hips wriggle back and forth slowly and she caresses her breasts as she watches. I play it up a bit more, seeing how she's enjoying this, taking more time with the toy in my mouth before popping it out and lowering it down. I turn it on and it buzzes against my palm. I circle it around Mariah's labia, watching her body's reaction, listening to her sounds for how and when I should go further.

"More," she urges, tilting her hips toward me.

I swallow nervously and try to give her what she wants, but it's harder to do than with my fingers and I fumble a bit. I press it toward her entrance, but it doesn't budge and I'm not sure what to do about it. My heart beats faster. I continue to struggle with the toy and how to get it inside Mariah without hurting her. "Um, can you help?" I mumble awkwardly.

Mariah nods, reaching down to assist. Once it's in I can feel a bit more, but the separation of me from her body makes it more difficult to manoeuvre than when it was just the two of us. I lie more over top of her and do my best to move the vibrator, trying to listen and watch for Mariah's cues, but the harder I try the further we seem to get from our goal.

Finally, she relents. "Here, let me do it. Come, kiss me."

I gladly hand over control of the device and lie down beside her, nuzzling my face into her neck. Returning to my comfort zone, I make love to her body with my hands and my mouth, and she continues with the toy, working it expertly, bringing herself to climax as I listen and watch, fascinated—and a bit envious. After the first time she encourages me to try again, her hand working with mine to show me the rhythm and the angle she likes, and a few minutes later I'm there with her, helping her come with my mouth on hers and my hands on her body. It feels so good to bring her so much pleasure.

She comes an incredible two more times before we're through, and I'm absolutely blown away that such things are possible. Once we're finished, we get up to wash and then crawl into bed. Mariah falls asleep quickly, her body curled around mine and face nestled onto my shoulder as my fingers play deftly with her hair.

My knees and back ache from our time on the floor, but making love under the tree was magical. I wish we could make a tradition out of it. But as beautiful as it was sharing that moment with her, and how patient she was with me, I can't help the nagging worry deep down in the back of my mind . . .

I'm too inexperienced for her.

She'll find someone else who actually knows what they're doing.

And she'll choose them over me.

INT. JENNA'S APARTMENT - EVENING

Annie is wearing a sparkly evening gown. Her hair
is curled into an updo, and she is applying red
lipstick in the mirror near the front door.

                    JENNA
          (sighing)
     I remember when I could fit into that dress.

                    ANNIE
     Oh, please. Your post-mom bod is so curvy
     and gorgeous! And I know your husband agrees.

                    JENNA
          (covering her face with her hand)
     You heard that last night, did you?

                    ANNIE
     The whole apartment complex heard it.

                    JENNA
     Well maybe it will inspire other people
     romantically, if you know what I mean.

                    ANNIE
          (groaning)
     We're just friends. There will be no
     inspiration in that regard.

                    JENNA
     Mmm-hmm. Sure.

James knocks on the door.

Annie exhales slowly, squares her shoulders, then answers it.

James is dressed in a navy suit with a crisp white shirt and shiny black shoes.

James looks Annie up and down appreciatively.

> JAMES
> Wow . . . you look . . .

> ANNIE
> What?

> JAMES
> Like a Christmas miracle.

> ANNIE
> That's awful corny of you,
> Mr. I-Hate-Christmas.

> JAMES
> You're starting to change my mind.

Annie and James share a moment, regarding one another with slow smiles, until they are interrupted by Jenna snapping a picture of them on her phone.

> ANNIE
> Hey now! We didn't agree to pictures.

> JENNA
> Sorry, just had to capture the
> moment.

Annie sighs, then turns to James.

> ANNIE
>
> Ready to go?

> JAMES
>
> No. But let's get this over with.

> ANNIE
>
> That's the exact attitude I hope for
> when going out with a guy.

James tenses, his gaze dropping to the floor.

> ANNIE
>
> I mean. Not as a date. As friends.

> JAMES
>
> Of course.

> ANNIE
>
> Just two friends, going out for an
> evening, and maybe exchanging legal
> advice for pizza.

> JAMES
>
> Of course. Legal advice and pizza,
> the best kind of non-dating
> friendship outing there is.

James holds out arm, Annie takes it.

Jenna picks up baby Henry from where he was playing
on the floor.

JENNA
Have fun, you two! But not too
much fun.

Jenna wiggles baby Henry on her hip and winks.

Annie looks over her shoulder, scoffs at her sister,
and rolls eyes before stepping into the hallway and
closing the door behind her.

Chapter 20
MARIAH

*T*he morning after is bittersweet. There are only two days left of filming on this ridiculously tight movie deadline, and it feels like Ellie and I are just starting to get into our groove. To make matters worse, most of Ellie's film time is in these last two days so she'll be really busy, and when we're together she'll probably be tired and want to go to bed early. Which is fine with me; the idea of snuggling a tired Ellie gives me all sorts of happy tingles. I just wish it wasn't going to be over so soon.

As we go through our domestic routine of taking turns in the tiny stall shower, brushing our teeth, me putting on makeup and doing my hair while Ellie makes us breakfast, eating said breakfast while playing footsies side by side at the kitchen peninsula, I try to work up the courage to ask her what I really want to ask her: Will we continue our relationship after this movie is over?

While we both live in the Greater Vancouver Area, we live on opposite ends of it. I'm on the lower west side in Marpole and she's up north by Brentwood, more in Burnaby than Vancouver. It's a good thirty-minute drive through the city, if there's no traffic. With traffic it would take upwards of an hour. Personally, I don't find that to be a long commute, especially since having to travel to be with someone you're interested in is typical for queer relationships; the dating pool isn't as large. But Ellie's never experienced this. It might be too much for her.

I'd be up for moving in with her after a few months of dating. We work so well together in every way, and I'll miss the simple parts of life with her—especially her happy chit-chat. But is that too fast? I'd rather wait and have her tell me when she's ready than act too quickly and make her feel rushed. But I don't want her to get burned out on a moderately long-distance relationship before then.

I keep all this to myself and try to enjoy the moment while it lasts as we drive into the city, the sun already risen and shining bright even though it's barely past seven o'clock. Ellie's cheerful voice entertains me with all the interesting thoughts that pop into her mind. I hang on every word, soaking it in as if it's the last time I'll have the opportunity.

After swinging through the Tim Hortons drive-through we park a few blocks away from downtown and walk to the set. I apply Ellie's makeup, taking extra time, hovering over every centimetre of her beautiful face, relishing being close to her like this around other people. I wish I could lean forward and kiss her lips right here in front of everyone.

Ellie's my only work for this morning, as the filming is supposed to be just the scenes between Ellie, Julia and Oscar in the café. I clean my station and walk with her out onto the street, the sweltering July heat beating down upon us both. I'm glad the set Ellie will be working on is air conditioned; I have no idea how the actors were able to walk around on the street in full winter gear to film the outdoor scenes because I'm immediately sweaty after five seconds with summer-appropriate clothing.

While walking Ellie to the set I pause, noticing a familiar tall frame facing away from us standing outside the café with Julia and Oscar. "Is that . . . ?"

"Hide!" Ellie all but yells.

I duck behind a parked car and press my back against it, my heart pounding in my ears.

"Oh, hi!" Ellie squeaks as she walks toward them.

I *Mission Impossible* my way along the parked cars, which is impressive given I'm wearing three-inch wedges. I get close enough to hear, peeking between the cars to catch a glimpse of Oscar, Julia, Jax, and Ellie standing together in a little group before quickly ducking back to the safety of my hiding spot, listening as best I can.

"How did you get past the security guard?" Ellie asks, trying to keep her tone chipper.

"Oh, we let him in." Oscar's deep baritone is a bit harder to pick up. "—said it was fine . . . showed him around . . . never been on a movie set . . ."

"Yes, we were happy to show your friend around, Ellie." Julia is much easier to hear. "I'm shocked he's never been on a set before! With a face like that—" I peek out and watch Julia playfully elbow Ellie while whispering something in her ear. Ellie fakes a laugh, her shoulders stiff and hitched higher up her body than normal.

"Why are you hiding this guy? You should bring him to the wrap party tonight," Julia encourages.

"I didn't think to invite him since it's supposed to be just cast members."

"Oh, nonsense! And I'm sure Marlene and Yueyi can find a way to make him an extra. He has lumberjack vibes to him. And you two together? A little surprising but totally cute, and I can see . . ."

Sick of listening to this, I whip out my phone and dial Jax's number.

The group is interrupted as his "Barbie Girl" ring tone plays obnoxiously.

Jax pulls his phone out, does a double take at the caller ID, then silences it. "Sorry about that."

"Interesting ring tone you have there," Ellie comments, and I can feel the smirk on her face from here.

"I think one of my buddies at work switched it. Joke's on them, I love 'Barbie Girl.'"

Damn him and his unflappable nature.

Jax turns his attention to Oscar and Julia. "If you don't mind, I'd like to have a word with Ellie about something important."

They say a few pleasant goodbyes, and then leave Matt and Ellie alone.

I do *not* feel good about them being alone, especially after everything that went down in his apartment. I mean, it's not every day you get chicken eggs on your doorstep. I prepare myself to launch out of hiding to protect Ellie if anything goes sideways.

Unfortunately, Jax lowers his voice and I can barely make out a word he says. Thankfully, Ellie has positioned herself so that Jax's back is toward me and I can keep a closer watch on them. I read Ellie's face and body language as they talk. She turns on the charm, with that smile of hers and flirtatiously swatting his arm at something he says.

Then he grabs her by the waist and tugs her close. My heart pounds in my ears as my jaw clenches. She grips his arm, though I'm sure it's to hold him back rather than pull him close.

The hackles on my neck rise as I watch him lower his filthy mouth toward her ear and say something that makes her eyes go wide and whole body tense. I'm about two seconds away from launching myself over the Volvo I'm crouched behind and tackling Jax to the curb when he steps back from Ellie and takes her hands in his. She sways lightly on her feet, dazed, as he caresses the line of her jaw with his fingers.

"After all," he says loud enough for me to hear, "it's not every day you meet someone so special." Then he grabs Ellie by the chin and pulls her in for a kiss.

My heart thunders in my ears and a wave of nausea hits me, watching him manhandle her when she's so obviously not interested. She manages to bring a hand between them, stopping him from going any further.

"Lipstick," she says, holding him back. "My makeup artist would kill me if you ruined it."

Hell yes, I'd kill him if he kissed Ellie without her consent. There's no way I'd let a playboy lying asshole like him near her. As it is, his slimy hands on her body is nearly enough to take my stomach from mild nausea to full-blown regurgitation.

"See you tonight, sweetheart," Jax says, releasing Ellie from his hold. I duck back down as he walks past my hiding spot.

I release a long, slow exhale, my whole body untensing.

Once Ellie is in the clear, she looks around, searching for me. I tentatively peer around for Jax to make sure he's far enough away. Ellie spots me and comes around to where I'm hiding.

"That was close," Ellie huffs, gripping my forearms.

"Too close," I agree. "Are you okay?"

Ellie swallows and nods, though I can tell she is a little shaken by the encounter. "I tried to scare him off by seeming overly interested, you know? Like, give him a taste of his own medicine."

"Did it work?"

She shakes her head. "No. Backfired completely. He said he wants to come over later to thank me for the eggs by giving me his great big co—"

My phone rings in my hand, startling us both. I lift it so we can both see the caller ID.

Jax.

No. Way.

We share a frown before I answer. "Hello?"

"Hey, you called?"

Shit. I didn't consider him calling me back. "Uh. Yeah?" I try to come up with a reason on the fly but I'm a shit liar, letting the silence hang between us instead, getting thicker and more uncomfortable as the seconds tick by. Ellie starts flapping her hands and mouthing, *Say something!* But that only makes my mind blank more.

Finally, Jax sighs. "Mariah?

"Yeah?"

"I'm glad you did. Listen. The last time we were together it was . . . weird. And it turns out that gift basket was for my neighbour, not me. The girl dropped it off at the wrong door."

Jax has no trouble lying, but that's not surprising at all. "Is that so?"

"And my phone got this weird virus that scrambled my contacts. It's been a bit awkward, to say the least. I wasn't sure if your contact was really you until now, or I'd have called earlier."

I'm not sure how much of that is bullshit, but the fact that our prank caused him at least a bit of distress is rewarding.

"I'd like to make it up to you," he continues. "I have plans later tonight with my mom but I'm free until then."

Ellie and I glare at each other, enraged by what we've both heard. Does he actually think he can lie to me about plans with his mom when he's really with Ellie, then have me over for sloppy seconds? What world is this guy living in?

It takes every ounce of strength I have not to tell him off right then and there. I manage to force my voice into something resembling neutral when I reply. "I'll have to get back to you on that. I'm not sure I want to see you again."

"Then . . . why did you call?"

Shit. He has me there. "I just, um. I wanted to hear your voice?" I can't help the upward inflection, cringing at myself.

"That's so sweet," he says, not noticing how false I sound. "I missed your voice, too. If now doesn't work, I can come to you in Vancouver. It's not every day you reconnect with someone so special."

Ellie's mouth falls open in shock.

I grind my teeth. "Yeah, you sure are something. I'll definitely see you again before I go home. It will be an experience you won't forget."

"Looking forward to it already," he growls.

I hang up without another word.

Ellie's already pacing, her tennis shoes squeaking with every angry stomp. "He hasn't learned a damn thing!"

"Nope."

"And if he's already sorted out the scrambled contacts then he's probably fixed all those sexting words we replaced."

"Wish we could have seen that in action," Ellie agrees.

"We were a bit . . . distracted."

Ellie lifts a shoulder shyly. If it weren't for the makeup caked on her face, I know she'd be blushing.

"Okay. No more distractions," Ellie says, returning to her pacing. "We need to teach him a lesson. A *final* lesson. Up until now it's been child's play. We're going to make this guy rue the day he started toying with women's hearts. We'll show him exactly what happens when you mess with us. And not just for us, but for all the women he's played."

"Yep."

"We'll make him beg our forgiveness. He'll be grovelling and licking our boots when we're finished with him. He won't know his asshole from his elbow when we're through. We'll make him crawl back home to his mama and—"

"Ellie! You coming?" Yueyi calls from the café door.

"Be right there!" She replies in her chipper voice before turning back to me and lowering her tone, anger flashing wildly in her eyes. "Tonight, we finish this. We'll both come up with plans and reconvene to end this once and for all."

I want nothing more than to pull Ellie's feisty ass in for a kiss, but I don't. Yueyi is watching, and we haven't talked about whether we're keeping us between us or letting others know. Hell, I don't know if there even *is* an us. Instead of doing what I want to do, I give her a curt nod. Ellie nods back, then straightens herself, forces a smile on her face, and walks back across the sidewalk to disappear into the café.

After giving Ellie a bit of a head start, I follow her onto the set to assist Jimmie with touch-ups. I can't help but grin watching her transform from her fun, bubbly self into her character. Between scenes she keeps spirits up with jokes I can't hear, sincere compliments, and the occasional Christmas tune. She really, truly is the life of the party back here, everyone depending on her to keep the mood light. I feel ridiculously proud of her, my chest squeezing as I watch, and wish I could steal her away between takes to make out with her in the green room.

When we break for lunch I let Ellie stay with her acting

team, not wanting to distract her, while I join the other artists and crew in the picnic table break area in the alley. While munching on my BLT, I take a deep breath and prepare myself to open TikTok. As soon as I do, I'm inundated by notifications from thousands of new likes, comments, and followers. It's impossible to keep track of everything, and I gave up trying to read all the comments after the first day I posted our alien video. I feel bad that these people are following me expecting something as awesome as the video that went viral to happen again, but that's impossible.

At least, it is without Ellie.

I watch it again and again, lingering over the moments of us being close, witnessing the natural spark between us, the fire being lit, leading to the most intensely romantic experience of my life. My heart squeezes at the thought that it might be over soon. I can't let that happen. I have to get over my fears and work up the courage to be honest with her. Ellie is the easiest person in the world to talk to. It won't be that bad. I've been with a lot of different people of varying genders, and I know first-hand how rare an experience it is to immediately connect with someone like I have with Ellie.

I'm not going to let my past get in the way of my future.

Tomorrow, when filming is over and our mission with Jax is complete, once we have no more distractions, I'll talk to Ellie about us being together as a couple.

My heart settles, but my stomach clenches. Even if she rebukes me, at least I'll know.

I flip from the video of us together to the private messages and scroll through. I reply to a few of them, ignore the rest, but pause on one that stands out. It looks . . . professional.

Sorry for contacting you like this. Couldn't find your website. We saw your TikTok and are impressed by your skills. We're working on an indie horror project here in LA and would like to do something similar. If you're interested, please send your resume . . .

I read it again and again, the words becoming blurrier as I do. With shaking fingers, I google the name of the company and my jaw nearly hits the table.

"You okay?" one of the other assistants asks. Stefanie. Or was it Stacey?

"Yeah. I'm fine." I shift over, hiding my phone.

Pushing my plate away, no longer hungry, I read through the projects the company has worked on. They're legit. Legit as hell. And they're based in LA—a real production company! Still indie B movies, not quite Hollywood, but so much closer than I am right now.

Trying not to get my hopes up, I reply that I am interested and will forward my resume. I manage to find it in an old email and add in my current work project and Jimmie's number as a reference in the body of the email. I hit Send before I can talk myself out of it. I doubt Jimmie will give me a good reference after showing up late twice, not reading the script on time, and just generally being a newb in the industry, but he's the only film reference I have.

Nothing will come of it, but damn, just to be considered is such an incredible honour. I can't wait to tell Ellie.

I manage to eat half of my sandwich, my mind still boggled by the message I'd received, before my phone rings.

Mother.

I frown at the caller ID. In my mind I'd crossed Mom and Dad off my mental to-do list and didn't expect to hear from her again until a birthday or some other such holiday. I answer it with a confused "Hello?"

"Oh. Oh, hi! You answered. I was not expecting that."

Guilt needles my chest, but I stay silent.

"Your dad and I were wondering, well, hoping you'd . . . Will we see you again before you go home?"

I think for a long moment, unsure of what to say. Mom fills the silence again.

"You and your lovely girlfriend Ellie are welcome to come

for dinner. I was thinking maybe tonight would be nice? I'm making roast beef, mashed potatoes, gravy, and pickled beets from the garden. I thought you two might enjoy it."

My mouth waters just thinking of Mom's homemade gravy.

"Or if you're busy we could make a plan to come see you? We've never been to your new place, and . . ."

Mom continues on about dinner plans. Why is she trying so damn hard after being so distant for so long? Maybe she really likes Ellie and wants her around—who wouldn't? But when they saw Ellie and me together before, when she pretended to be my girlfriend, we hadn't had feelings for each other yet. Now we do—at least, I do. It would be obscene to pretend to be girlfriends when we haven't yet discussed our future—*if* we have a future. I can't parade Ellie around on my arm as a fake girlfriend without knowing where we stand, and I can't pretend to be something we're not. If my parents ever see us together again it will be because what we have is real and honest.

Unsure of what to tell my mom, I cut her off, my stomach twisting into knots the more she talks. "I'll have to talk to Ellie about it and get back to you."

"Oh, okay. Yes. Of course. Well, you tell that girl of yours how wonderful she is, and hopefully we will see you both soon. Okay?"

"Okay."

"Maria? I mean . . . Mariah?"

I blink a few times, never having heard her say my name with my chosen pronunciation before. "Yeah?"

She takes a slow breath. "I love you."

Squeezing my eyes tight, I let her words sink in, coating my heart like chocolate sauce over an ice cream cone. How long has it been since she's told me that? Since I've told her? Despite how estranged we've been, how far she's pushed me away, how little she knows about who I am, and how little she's tried to learn, she's still my mom. My breath leaves my lungs in a shaky exhale. Then I reply, "Love you, too."

She sniffs, and I can almost hear her smile when she tells me goodbye and hangs up.

I clutch my phone to my chest and take a moment to let all the emotions swirling around in my heart settle down, letting myself feel the depths of sadness for all the time we've lost, the confusion with all this change, and the glimmer of hope for the future.

But I can't help but wonder, why now? There's a nagging feeling in my gut that the reason things are shifting between my mom and me is because of Ellie and her sunshine radiance blasting through the walls we've erected over the years. Without Ellie, none of this would be happening. Without Ellie, the little ground Mom and I have made up might be lost, and we'll go back to terse indifference—two souls who don't understand each other and never will.

That's a lot of pressure to put on Ellie, and the last thing we need right now is more of that.

ACT 3

EXT. DOWNTOWN HEMLOCK GROVE SIDEWALK - EVENING

James and Annie are walking slowly down the sidewalk, arm in arm. It's a chilly night, with fresh snow piled next to businesses. The stores are closed, everything is dark save for the twinkling lights in their displays and the lamp posts lining the street.

>   JAMES
>   Oh, I almost forgot the cookies.
>   Come inside.

INT. BREWED AWAKENING CAFÉ - EVENING

James unlocks the door and lets Annie step into the café, following close behind.

Annie stays out front while James disappears into the back room.

Moments later, Kate enters from the back room with a broom in her hand.

>   KATE
>   Wow, you look breathtaking!

>   ANNIE
>   Are you still at work?

>   KATE
>   I'm always here. I can't believe you

convinced him to go to the Christmas
party! Well, actually, looking at you,
I can.

ANNIE
We're just going as friends.

KATE
That's how it always starts, doesn't it?
Have a fabulous time!

Kate winks and exits into the back room.

James returns a moment later with the cookies.

JAMES
Ready to go?

EXT. DOWNTOWN HEMLOCK GROVE COURTYARD - EVENING

Annie and James arrive at a large courtyard.
Instrumental Christmas music plays in the background.
Pole heaters are placed in different sections, warming
the space so the small crowd does not have to wear
winter coats, showing off beautiful dresses and crisp
suits.

A large Christmas tree highlights one side of the
courtyard and a long table laden with delicious food
is on the other. Lights and garland are strung back
and forth across the space.

Annie and James approach the table, where James
places the cookies with other desserts.

ANNIE
Ooh, they have a chocolate fountain!

JAMES
What's your preferred dippable fruit?

ANNIE
Strawberries, of course.

JAMES
So predictable. So plain.

ANNIE
Okay, I'll bite, what's yours?

JAMES
Pineapple.

ANNIE
Gross. Next you'll be saying
pineapple goes on pizza.

JAMES
I wouldn't quite stoop that low.
Here. Try it.

James dips pineapple in chocolate and feeds it to
Annie, getting some chocolate on her lips. She moans
as she licks it off.

James's eyes darken as he watches Annie.

Annie smiles at James and he clears his throat,
looking away.

ANNIE
I didn't think I'd say these two words
to you ever again, but . . . you're right.

JAMES
I love hearing it as much this time as
I did the first time.

"All I Want for Christmas Is You" begins to play and
Annie sways to the music.

ANNIE
Oh, this is my favourite song. I haven't
heard it in forever.

JAMES
When's the last time you danced to it?

ANNIE
Danced? I don't think I ever have.

JAMES
You don't like dancing?

ANNIE
I like dancing as long as my
partner is skilled.

JAMES
(smirking at euphemism)
Lucky for you, I am.

James holds out a hand to Annie.

Annie takes his hand and James pulls her in for a dance. They twirl and laugh together. The next song is slower paced, "Last Christmas."

They keep dancing, getting closer and closer, their lips almost touching.

Chapter 21
ELLIE

"Cut!" Yueyi yells.

I slump against the wall, taking a moment to close my eyes and breathe. What a long, exhausting day. The final days of filming always are—there's so much pressure to perform since there's very little room for error. Hopefully this is it, and we can call this a wrap and be done. Tomorrow is our final day of filming, my most important scenes, and I'm pre-emptively tired just thinking about it.

Then, it's over. Another movie in the bag. My sense of pride for completing another film is met with a twinge of sadness. I always get the blues when Christmas comes to an end, even if the Christmas has thirty-degree heat and fake snow. I'm already looking forward to my next opportunity, but I don't have anything lined up yet and am not sure when that will happen. I'll have to call my agent.

Leaving my off-stage spot, I walk back into the main room of the café.

Julia smiles her perfect smile. "You did great, Ellie!"

Oscar puts an arm around me. "I could feel the emotion pouring out of you. It made my own delivery so much better."

"Great job, Ellie," Yueyi agrees, stepping in front of the blinding lights. "Why don't you all head over to the restaurant? First drinks are on me."

Oscar laughs. "They're all on you. It's a wrap party."

We make our way back to hair and makeup and Mariah is there waiting for me. She looks up from her phone and a smile lights her face. *Oof, that smile.* I once had to work so hard for it, and now she gives it to me freely. What a privilege.

I try to push my way toward her, but Oscar and Julia guide

me to the other side of the room to their station. They pass around makeup wipes and we each take one, rubbing our faces to rid ourselves of the layers caked onto our skin.

"Seriously, that was the best performance of the whole film," Oscar continues, wiping under his eyes. "No offence, Julia."

"None taken!" She pauses to blot her lips. "I was going to say the same thing. I'd tell you to stop outshining me, but the way you delivered your lines made me deliver mine even better. I'm still so new at this, but having such a strong supporting actress on my team is an incredible help. I feel like I've learned so much."

I balk at her words. "Wow, thank you." For once, I'm not sure what else to say.

"I'm heading home right after filming tomorrow," Oscar says. "So it's our last night together as a crew."

"Same, I have a flight to catch back to Calgary," Julia agrees. "Can't believe it's already over."

"Guess we'll have to drink double to make up for tomorrow," Oscar jokes.

"Not too much," Yueyi warns, coming up from behind. "I don't want anyone hungover tomorrow. Everyone has to look cheery and rosy."

Oscar winks. "That's what makeup is for."

Yueyi tsks. "You troublemaker." Then she wraps her arms around all three of us for a group hug.

I've never felt as included with the team as I do right now. Part of me is wondering if I slipped as I exited my scene and am actually on set right now, unconscious on the floor and hallucinating all of this.

I pull away from the hug. "I'm not sure if I can come out tonight."

"What! No, you have to come." Julia grabs my hand, looking slightly hilarious with half her face still painted with makeup.

"It's basically a requirement," Oscar states.

Yueyi places her hands on her hips. "Are you a team player, Ellie?"

"Of course I am!" I practically shout.

"You haven't joined us for any post-film meals. You come to set, you film, and you leave. Does that seem like team playing to you?" Yueyi's eyes narrow.

"Yes. I mean no. No, it doesn't, and yes, I'm a team player. Of course I'll be there tonight." My heart pounds in my chest. The last thing I want is an unfriendly and anti-team reputation in this industry. The cozy movie community is a small one, and there's a giant pool of talent trying to break their way in. As much as I want to give Matt his final lesson, and then hold Mariah in my arms and cuddle up under the blankets with her for what might be the last time, I can't lose future opportunities.

"I'll be there," I state with finality.

"Great!" Yueyi purses her lips into a smile. Oscar slaps me on the back. Julia gives me her best toothpaste-commercial smile.

Is being the centre of attention with my co-stars and directorial team a dream of mine? Yes. Do I want to spend my last night in Chilliwack with them? No.

"Excuse me." I back away before turning and hustling to the other side of the room.

"What was all that about?" Mariah uses another makeup wipe to remove what I'd missed.

"I have to go out with the crew tonight," I say without enthusiasm.

She pauses. "I thought we had plans to get back at Jax."

"We do. We did. But I can't miss this."

Mariah hesitates a bit longer. "I was hoping we could . . . talk."

"Yes," I say, eagerly. "I want to talk, too."

"But tomorrow is the last day."

"Yeah. And my rental is finished tomorrow. I have to have everything packed and cleaned up by eleven."

Mariah's face clouds like a storm rolling in. "Oh. So . . . tonight is our last night together?"

I nod, once again not quite sure what to say.

"And you'll be spending it with them?" She juts her chin once toward the crew.

"I have to, Mariah. This is my career, and I can't let anything . . ." I trail off.

Mariah's face darkens further. "Can't let anything get in the way of that."

"Trust me," I say, taking a step closer. "I'd rather be finishing what we started with Matt, and then curling up in bed with you."

Mariah glances around, apparently nervous someone will overhear.

"Come with me," I ask.

She perks up. "What?"

"Tonight, to the wrap party."

She deflates. "Oh."

"I'm sure other crew members will be there, too."

Mariah hesitates, thinking.

"It will be fun . . ." I singsong the last word, then poke her in the ribs. She fights a smile, and I know I have her.

"Fine. Okay."

"But—" I raise a finger "—we'll duck out early. Between takes, I came up with an excellent plan to get back at Matt so we can get our unfinished business done and teach him his last lesson. It doesn't feel right leaving Chilliwack knowing we've left a blatant fuckboy unchecked to continue harming the female population."

Mariah nods, brightening at the prospect. "Agreed."

WE JOIN THE rest of the crew at a pub a few blocks away downtown, and soon the table is filled with delicious greasy food and cheap drinks. Mariah sits quietly, looking uncomfortable around everyone else. They all ignore her, talking amongst themselves, and despite my best efforts to include her, none of them do. I immediately regret bringing her here, even though having her thigh pressed against mine under the table is my favourite part of the entire evening—even more than the random bouts of praise.

"You know, Ellie," Marlene, the producer, says as she leans across the table to talk over the din. "We have another film coming up in two weeks' time. Our lead actress has been a bit of a flake, and with recent press she may not be the best fit for the role."

Yueyi, sitting next to her, nods.

Marlene continues. "She's technically in breach of her contract. Yueyi and I have been talking, and we're very impressed by your work as of late. Would you be interested in being the lead?"

My eyes widen into saucers.

"I know it's short notice," Marlene says, mistaking my stunned silence for hesitation. "But I have no doubt you could pull it off. You're a professional Christmas actress, after all."

Somehow I manage to form words. "Yes! Of course, yes!"

Marlene smiles. "Great. I'll get in touch with your agent and send the contract and script over right away. The filming will be longer as it's a skiing movie, which requires snow. We'll do most of the filming in a few weeks and the rest once we have decent snowfall. Will you need lessons?"

I find a way to nod.

"We'll get that taken care of. Your co-star will be Jack Winstron."

"Jack . . . *Winstron*?" I feel faint.

Marlene and Yueyi share a knowing smile. "Yes. *The* Jack Winstron. He's a method actor, too, isn't he?"

I *definitely* fell and smacked my head at some point. Is this real life? Simply breathing the same air as this man would up my game immensely. I want the job. I need it. "Yes. Please contact my agent. I'll take a look." *Good. Yes. Play it cool.*

Marlene purses her lips and raises a single eyebrow. My acting doesn't fool her; she knows I'm giddy AF. The conversations drift away from me and I twist in my seat to face Mariah. I grip her forearms and give her the tiniest shake, even though what I want to do is climb onto the seat and jump up and down like Tom Cruise.

"Mariah, you can come with me! You can do my makeup on set again! I'm sure Marlene and Yueyi will hire you even if you're not a local since you did such a great job here, and we can tell them we'll bunk together to save on costs, and we can do it all over again! We can have another Christmas together, but up in Whistler this time. We'll be in the mountains with the snow, oh my god, it will be amazing. Aren't you excited?"

Mariah drops her gaze. Then, not even bothering to reply, she reaches for her drink and downs the whole thing.

"Mariah?" I try to pull her back to face me, but she refuses to look me in the eyes. I blink a few times, confused.

"You ready to go?" she asks, her voice low. "It's getting late."

I regard her for a moment, unsure of her sudden coldness. Is it something I did, or something else that's bothering her? "Yeah. Sure." I turn back to the table and say goodbye to everyone, which is met with a heartwarming chorus of *don't go*, and *come on, we're just getting started*, which I didn't expect.

My heart is being tugged in two different directions. I've worked on a lot of movies but I've never felt so part of a team as this, and tonight is our last night together. Even though I'll likely see Marlene and Yueyi and some of the other behind-the-scenes people again in a few weeks, I may never work with Julia and Oscar again.

But then I look to Mariah. I ache to know what thoughts are swirling around in her mind right now. And then it clicks.

None of this matters as much as her.

I throw down a tip and we start making our way around the table when Julia perks up. "Oh yeah, you have a hot date tonight!"

I glance at Mariah, who freezes, unsure of what to say. "What?" I ask.

"That hot guy, Matthew?" Julia clarifies. "I still think you should have brought him."

"Oh. Right." I'd forgotten all about him. "Yeah, I'll let you know how that goes."

"We want every detail." Oscar winks, which would have made me quiver in my Rudolph sweater just days ago but now only makes me cringe.

After a few more quick goodbyes we head out through the doors to the warm July air. It's just past dinnertime, and still so warm, but a darkened sky above and the faint smell of petrichor warns of rain. Without words, and a fair bit of tension, we climb into Mariah's car and she begins driving back to our cabin.

I'm not sure why there's this strange feeling of angst between us when everything was perfect this morning. I'm not one to leave things alone. I'll pick at a scab until it bleeds rather than sit idle—that's the only way to see what's going on under the surface.

"Mariah." I fiddle with the loose strands of my sweater. "Are you going to tell me what's wrong?"

She continues looking out the windshield, her emotions masked.

I reach over and grip her thigh, trying to get her to look at me. "Hey. It's me. You can talk to me. Please tell me what's bothering you."

Her stoic expression wobbles ever so slightly. "I'm happy for you. But I just . . . I can't work on another movie with you. Not like this."

My throat constricts. "Like, as lovers?"

"No, that's not what I meant." She takes my hand in hers, giving my fingers a squeeze. "I can't . . . I don't like doing this kind of makeup. I don't want to work on another Christmas movie."

"What's wrong with Christmas movies?" I can't help the bit of venom that drips into my voice.

"Nothing! Nothing, I—"

"You're too good for them or something?"

"No." She furrows her brow.

"I know they're not that fancy, and they don't have the best budgets, and I know they're kind of predictable, but that's what people love about them. They're guaranteed something simple and sweet that will warm their heart. Sometimes in life you need predictability, especially when the world is a dumpster fire, or maybe if there's stuff going on in your life that's complex. We bring joy to lots of people, and—"

"That's not what I meant," she cuts me off.

"Then what *do* you mean?"

"It's just not the type of makeup I want to work on. No offence to Christmas movies, or to you or the set we're working on. Don't take it like that, please."

I take a breath to let her words sink in, unclenching my fists and lowering my hackles. "Okay. But it's a job, isn't it? I know it's not what you have planned long-term but until something else comes along, why not? I mean—"

"Something else *has* come along." Mariah continues staring out the windshield.

I pause. "What? When?"

Finally, she glances at me as she lane checks. "I got a message on TikTok from that video that went viral. A company from LA may want me to come work for them. They specialize in sci-fi and horror films with makeup, costumes, and special effects done the old-fashioned way, with limited CGI. It's not set in stone yet, but it sounds promising."

"But you haven't signed anything?"

"No."

"So it could not happen?"

"No, but—"

"So you might not go to LA? If you don't get the offer you could come up to Whistler with me?"

Her jaw clenches. "I'm not going to do that."

"What? Why not? If they don't have anything for you then you could at least stay in the industry. I thought—"

"It's not what I want," Mariah says, slow and clear. "When they contacted me it made me realize how badly I want to work on those types of films and how little I've really chased that dream. I think I have to try and make a go of it down there. LA is where all the work is for movies that I like. I'm too inexperienced for most films to hire me from another country. But if I'm local, they might."

It takes me a moment to process everything she's saying. It's so rare I get more than a sentence out of her, it's like my brain is struggling to piece them together when they're delivered all at once rather than fed to me morsel by morsel. "You're going down to LA, whether you get this job or not?"

She bites her lip. Nods once. "Now's the time. This viral TikTok could open doors for me. It probably won't happen again. I at least have to try."

"When?" I croak.

"Probably right after this."

I pull my hand from hers and turn away, tucking my feet onto the seat and hugging my knees as I look out the window. The faintest droplets of rain have begun falling, splattering across the glass, as if the weather is tied to my emotional state. I thought we'd have more time. I wanted to talk to her about us. About making things work. But now that she's leaving, what's the point? Mariah will be in LA, and I know she'll get hired because she's an incredibly talented person, and I'll be up here finally getting my big shot at my dream role.

I knew it would come down to this. Mariah was bound to choose someone or something else over me. May as well be her career.

There's no point in fighting it.

I'll always come in second.

"Ellie?"

I sniff. "Yeah?"

"I'm sorry."

"No, don't be sorry." I take all those sad feelings and force them down, jamming them into the hollow pit in my stomach. I plaster my best smile on and adjust my posture into something resembling a whole person who hasn't just been ripped in half. "I'm excited for you! This is great! I can't believe someone saw your TikTok and wants you to work for them on their movie. I mean, of course I can believe that, you're awesome, and you're going to blow their minds, and maybe you'll get to design some aliens, and—"

"Ellie."

"And you'll be like the next H.R. Giger! Ooh, maybe you'll get to work on a horror set and do something really grotesque. Either way, I'm sure once you're down there they'll be fighting over you. I'm really happy that you're—"

"Ellie!" She grips my hand tightly. "Stop."

"Stop what?"

"This," she says, as if that makes any more sense.

"I'm not doing anything."

She sighs, then releases my hand for a moment so she can turn off the highway and onto the side road toward our cabin. "It's okay to be sad."

"I'm not sad." My bottom lip trembles, and I bite it to make it stop. "I'm happy! We're both getting everything we ever wanted."

Mariah looks over at me, her eyes misting, and takes a slow breath. "Not quite."

I lean my head on her shoulder as she presses a kiss to my temple. We continue the rest of the way in silence, though instead of it being charged with angst, it's the bittersweet ache of Christmas morning, knowing that after waiting for so long you're about to get everything you've ever wanted . . .

But it will all be over soon.

EXT. DOWNTOWN HEMLOCK GROVE COURTYARD (CONT'D)

A group of businesspeople approach Annie and James, interrupting their romantic dance.

                    BUSINESSWOMAN 1
          James! Didn't expect to see you here.

                    BUSINESSWOMAN 2
          It's been years since you've joined
          the party. I didn't know you could
          still dance, but it looks like some
          things aren't easily forgotten.

                    BUSINESSMAN 1
          Who's your friend?

                    JAMES
          Annie is my . . . lawyer. She's here
          to keep an eye on all of you, make sure
          you're not up to anything insidious.

Annie looks from James to the businesspeople with her mouth set in a firm line, disappointed by her introduction.

Annie shakes hands with them while forcing a tight smile.

                    ANNIE
          Pleasure to meet all of you. Wow, it's
          gorgeous out here. I've never seen anything
          so beautiful.

                    JAMES
         (whispering to Annie)
         I have.

                  BUSINESSWOMAN 1
         James, we want you to meet someone.

The businesspeople beckon a man forward.

                  BUSINESSWOMAN 1
         This is Greg. He owns three franchise
         Beanz Café locations and is interested
         in taking over your lease. I think it
         would be a good fit, wouldn't you agree?

                    JAMES
         (beat) You'd replace me with a franchise?

                  BUSINESSWOMAN 2
         We feel he would be a better fit
         with the community. They have excellent
         seasonal fare, including thirty-seven
         different flavours of coffee.

                    JAMES
         My coffee doesn't need thirty-seven
         flavours because it's not trying to
         hide its offensive taste. Their beans
         sit in bags collecting dust for months
         before they're brewed.

                    GREG
         Hey, now—

JAMES
My wife and I opened this business
when there was nothing else here. Brewed
Awakening has been a cornerstone to Hemlock
Grove's new downtown core ever since.
We are the community. I know I haven't
been putting in as much of an effort
lately, but I'm here now, aren't I?

BUSINESSMAN 1
A few decorations, one batch of sugar
cookies, and showing up late to a party
hardly suffice as making any effort to
be part of our thriving community.

BUSINESSWOMAN 2
Hemlock Grove needs a reliable unit that
is willing to put in maximum effort all
year round to drive customers to the rest
of our businesses, and you've done more to
chase people away than bring them in.

BUSINESSWOMAN 1
You've been through a lot. We all have. But
sometimes change is necessary. Maybe you
need to let go, start over somewhere else,
somewhere that doesn't hold so many memories.

JAMES
It's been a rough time, but—

BUSINESSWOMAN 1
You need to move on, James. For your
sake as well as for all of our
businesses. It's time.

Chapter 22
MARIAH

When we get to the cabin all I want to do is get out of my tight clothes and into my comfies, curl up with Ellie on the couch, and watch a Christmas movie (what has she done to me?). Afterward, when I've soaked up as much of my time with Ellie as I can, we can talk about all the things we've left unsaid. But not more than one minute after we walk through the door, her phone rings.

She holds it up to show me the caller ID, even though we both know who it is. Ellie looks at it for a moment, then lifts a finger toward the ignore button.

"Wait," I say, stopping her.

She hesitates, looking at me.

If not for all the wine and Ellie's convincing, I'd never have agreed to pranking Jax. I'd seen the red flags and known what I was getting in to. I'd proven to myself I could bag the cool, hot guy from my past and leave it at that. I'd started to catch feelings, sure, and yes, it hurt when I was fooled by him like a naive teenager, but I could have let it go and moved on with my life. Though I have to admit, pranking Jax was cathartic, like I was finally getting revenge on all the other liars and cheats I'd encountered in my life.

But Ellie is innocent in this. She's too sweet, sincere, and trusting for men like Jax. He led her on, let her believe he could be everything she'd ever hoped for and wanted just to get her into bed. And Ellie is just *one* of the women he did this to. How many others have to suffer because of his lying schemes?

"Answer it," I say.

"But it's our last night together."

"I think we should see it through."

Ellie sets her jaw. "I was hoping you might say that. If we can spare just one person from heartbreak then it will have been worth it." She squeezes my hand before answering the phone, putting it on speaker so we can both hear. "Hey."

"Hey! You ready if I come over now? I'm just leaving Abbotsford, so it'd be about twenty minutes."

"Sounds great."

"Good. It will be a night you won't forget."

"Yeah, I'm sure it will be. For both of us." She hangs up the phone without saying goodbye. "I hope twenty minutes is enough time. I only have like two ideas."

A sinister grin spreads over my face. "Lucky for you I came up with a plan."

Her eyes dance with mischief. "Oh really? Then let's teach this fuckboy his final lesson. Together."

Twenty-two minutes later the doorbell rings. I'm at my station, ready to go. Ellie gives me one final look, nervously shaking out her arms. I return her gaze with a self-assured nod. She exhales slowly, like, *this better work*, then leaves the kitchen to her station in the bathroom, tiptoeing and ducking past the dangerous parts.

"Come on in!" Ellie shouts.

The door opens slowly, Jax's head peeking through. "Hello?"

"In the bedroom!" Ellie calls.

I watch from my hiding spot as an eager grin lights up his face. He takes a step in and shuts the door, setting off the first trap.

A string of lotion-covered condoms is released from where they've been pinned, swinging down toward him. The slimy missiles smack him across the face with loud *thwacks* as Jax curses, trying to slap them out of the way.

Dodging as many as he can, he takes a few more steps toward the hall, then hits a puddle of lube on the floor. Losing all grip, Jax slides across the hardwood, arms flailing and feet struggling to stay under him. He slides right into the hallway, only to land smack-dab into a wall of Saran Wrap coated in a layer of hairspray. The plastic clings to him, and he struggles to tear it off his face while twisting in a circle and trying to keep his feet under him from the slippery lube.

"Jesus Chr—" Jax reaches for something to keep himself upright and grabs a conspicuously dangling string of Christmas lights. They pull free from the wall and release the next contraption, a broom hooked up to the ceiling with a paddle attached to the end. It swings down and smacks him right on the ass.

He yelps, then run-slips away from the attack toward the living room, where he trips on a wire, landing face-first into a pile of flour. He groans, cursing under his breath, then slowly lifts himself to standing, absolutely covered in white powder.

"Now!" I shout, bursting from my hiding spot behind the tree.

Jax screams, a high-pitched sound unlike anything I thought he was capable of. I shove him backward just as Ellie appears, dodging the lube on the floor, and pushes the rolling office chair at him from behind. The seat hits his knees and he buckles, sitting on it. Ellie grabs a string of Christmas lights and we pass it back and forth, wrapping him up nice and tight. Just to be safe, I grab my pink handcuffs and clap one loop over his wrist and the other onto the plastic arm of the chair.

"What the hell is going on!" Jax shouts, fighting against his sudden restraints.

Ellie and I are huffing, adrenaline coursing through our veins as we stand before him. Ellie places her hands on her hips and I cross my arms, like we're some sort of badass girl band.

He pulls at his cuffs, then reaches with his free hand to wipe his face. "Mariah? What are you doing here?"

Ellie and I share a smirk, enjoying the scene before us. Big, badass Matthew Jackson handcuffed to a chair with white powder all over his face, wrapped up in twinkling red and green lights like the best Christmas present we never knew we needed.

"Can someone explain to me what the fuck is happening?" He fights his restraints and the cords squeak. I panic, not sure if they'll hold him. We need to move on to phase three of our plan, fast.

"We brought you here to pay for your crimes against femdom," Ellie explains, pacing slowly in front of him. "It seems you have a problem, Matt. Or is it Jax?"

Jax's eyes dart from Ellie to me, his posture shifting slightly as he does, as if he's not quite sure which rendition of himself he should be right now. "I don't know what you're talking about."

"You're going to sit there, clearly caught by two women you've been playing, and continue to lie to us?" Ellie asks.

He licks his lips, then regrets his decision, spitting out a gob of flour. "That's not what happened."

I sneer. "Then explain to us, what *did* happen?"

"I just—I—it's not every day you meet—"

"Someone so special," Ellie and I parrot in unison.

Ellie mocks him, opening and closing her hand while mouthing *blah blah blah*. "We heard that one before," she continues. "Got any more canned lines you feed to every woman who crosses your path?"

I sigh. "Face it, Jax. You've been caught. Fess up."

He puffs out his chest, mouth hanging open, searching for words, and then deflates. "Fine. Okay. I was seeing you both at the same time. That's not a crime. But this might be!" He fights the blinking red-and-green-lit cords again. "Let me go!"

"Not so fast." I press a hand against his chest and force him to make eye contact with me. "Not until you see the error of your ways."

"The error of my—" He huffs, annoyed. "Everyone sees multiple people now. It's not just me! You gonna tie up and torture every dude you cross paths with?"

I grit my teeth, pissed that it's not sinking in. "It's men like you that give other men a bad name."

Jax shakes his head. "Everything we did was consensual."

"We never consented to you seeing other people," I say, pointing between Ellie and me. "In fact, we both talked to you about that separately and you lied."

He has the audacity to look confused. "Haven't you ever heard of polyamory?"

Ellie raises her voice, enunciating every word. "There's a difference between ethical non-monogamy and what it is *you* do. You? You're a fuckboy. You do and say whatever it takes to get in someone's pants. You come up with elaborate bullshit stories, even modifying your personality, to fit whoever it is you're trying to lay. You get them all excited about who you are and keep them hooked until you tire of them, and then you let them go. You see multiple women at a time without their knowledge, even denying the fact that it's happening."

He has enough of a conscience to look a bit sorry, turning his gaze to the floor.

"Admit it," I spit, my voice cold and harsh.

He huffs again, then says, "Fine. I was seeing you both at the same time, and I lied about it."

Ellie waits a moment before prompting him. "And? Who else were you seeing?"

"No one."

"Liar." I shake my head. "Ellie?"

Ellie gives me a nod. Then, before we can change our minds, we charge him.

Jax mutters a startled "What the fuck!" as I grab his free arm and wrestle it down behind him. Ellie pats at his pants pockets, feeling for his phone. The old office chair protests, squeaking loudly.

"Ellie!" I groan, struggling to keep Jax's free arm pinned to his side.

"Almost there," she grunts. Finally, she wriggles it free from his pocket and takes a step back, panting. I release Jax, who swipes at us with his free hand, nearly knocking the chair off balance.

"Give it back," he growls.

Ellie unlocks his phone and shows the screen to him, scrolling past a long line of messages. "Are all these women aware that you're seeing other people? Or did you tell them the same things you told us?"

"Did *karma* bring you all together, too?" I mock, and Ellie snickers.

"How did you know my passcode?" His eyes widen in confusion, then realization slowly dawns. "It was you. Both of you, the whole time!"

Ellie and I smirk at each other, watching as he pieces the puzzle together.

"The underwear and condoms in my truck . . . the cheese in my gym bag . . . the fake mouse! All that shit you did in my house! Those weird shortcuts in my phone, the scrambled contacts . . . What the fuck?"

Ellie lowers her face to Matt's level, inching closer as she speaks. "Admit it. You're playing all these women, aren't you? Feeding them the same bullshit, having crafted it over years and years of fuckboyery, honing your skills with systematic playboydom."

Ellie's speech gives me chills; she has natural villainess vibes to her.

"Fine," Matt grits out through clenched teeth, leaning forward so close their noses almost touch. "I have multiple women on the go at all times. I do and say whatever I need to, to get them in my bed and keep them there. Women who are committed fuck different; they got skin in the game, and it shows."

Ellie and I share a disgusted grimace.

"And when I get sick of them," Jax continues, a sardonic smile on his face, "I ghost them. But you know what, that's nothing compared to what I've been through. You think I'm the bad guy? Please. Women have done a thousand worse things to me over the years."

Ellie takes a step back, shaking her head.

"That's no excuse," I say. "Relationships are about honesty."

He rolls his eyes. "Come on. Like you've been one hundred percent honest with every person you've been with."

I think for a moment, deflating. He's right. I haven't been my most honest self, either. I glance at Ellie, who seems to be feeling the same way. We turn our attention back to him.

"That's different," Ellie says.

"How is it different?" He tuts at her. "You looked at me and saw what you wanted to see, didn't you? And it took me all of about five seconds for me to realize you wouldn't like the real me at all, and then five more seconds to mould myself into the guy you wished I was. You had no interest in knowing who I really was. I was a fantasy to you, and that's it."

"That's not true, I—"

"And you," Jax says, turning his attention to me. "I had you figured out even faster. You were insecure in high school, and you're insecure now. All you wanted was to prove you were hot enough to bang the guy you always wanted but could never have. You had no problems with me being a quick lay when it was convenient for you, but suddenly you have morals against it? You're both such fucking hypocrites."

I glare. "Hooking up? Fine. Exaggerating your best qualities on a date? Okay. But you were a completely different person with her than you were with me. Ellie deserved better than that. And I did, too. We would have been fine with an arrangement of casual sex if you'd been honest and up front, but you had to raise the bar, didn't you? Get us invested, keep us coming back. I never wanted to be 'the other woman.' You'd planned a whole life with Ellie, for fuck's sake. And when I specifically asked you if you were seeing anyone else so I could make an informed decision, you dodged the question, lying by omission because you knew I wouldn't be okay with it. You didn't care about us as people at all, as human beings. You just saw us as something for you to conquer. Tell me that's not true."

Jax bites his lip, not denying anything. "Fine. You're right. You happy?"

"That's what I thought." I step back, my chest rising and falling rapidly with anger. "Ellie? Show him the footage."

"Yes, ma'am."

She passes his phone to me and leaves her post, walking to the Christmas tree where we'd hidden my phone. She taps the screen and replays his confession.

His face freezes. "You recorded all this?"

"Yup," I say, tilting my chin in pride.

"Perfect. I'll use the evidence in court when I sue you for attacking me," he snarls.

Ellie trims the video, leaving only his confession left. "No, you won't."

"Aren't you curious why we recorded you?" I tilt my head to the side.

His face shifts from anger to fear. "No."

My lips twitch into a cruel smile. "Liar. Ellie, do it."

She presses a few buttons, and Matt's phone dings with a notification. I open the newly trimmed confession on his phone, then show it to Jax as I select Send All from his contacts list.

"You wouldn't," Matt warns.

"Oh, we will." I take my turn as the villain, inching closer like Ellie had. "To every. Single. Person. All the women you've been playing, all the women you've courted past and present. To your whole family."

"Including your grandma, whose death you fabricated!" Ellie adds.

He glares at her. "I didn't lie about that."

"Oh. Sorry." Ellie softens for a moment, then turns serious again. "Then we'll send it to your mom!"

His eyes widen in fear. "No! Not my mom!"

My finger hovers over the Send button, getting closer, and closer, and—

"*Stop!*" Jax shouts. His breathing is fast and ragged, eyes wild.

"You want money? I'll give you money! Just please, don't send that to my mom."

Despite myself, my heart twinges for him. "We don't want money," I say.

"And we don't necessarily want you to stop sleeping around," Ellie adds. "All we want is for you to stop lying."

"You want to have lots of partners at the same time, fine. There's nothing wrong with that," I explain. "But be honest. Not just with them, but with yourself, about who you are and what you want."

"You might get laid less," Ellie concedes, "but it's the right thing to do."

Jax looks back and forth from Ellie to me. "Seriously? That's it?" Jax scoffs. "Okay. Fine. I promise I'll be honest from now on. Now please, can you let me go?"

I look over at Ellie, and she looks back at me, annoyed that he's not taking us seriously. "There's nothing we can do to make sure he holds himself to that," I realize aloud.

Ellie shakes her head. "Not really."

I sigh, coming to terms with reality. "We can't save everyone. Not the women in his phone, not the people he's going to hurt, and we especially can't save him." I jut my chin toward Jax.

"I don't need saving."

I look back at Jax, feeling a bit sorry for him. "Someday he's going to be old and all alone with no one to love him and he's going to regret playing with people's hearts."

Ellie nods. "I'd say that's punishment enough."

I delete the video, lock the phone, and hand it back to Jax. Then Ellie helps me untie the lights and unlock the handcuffs. Jax stands, rubbing his sore wrist.

We both take a step back, giving him some space. He glances around at the cabin, totally dishevelled, a look of disbelief on his face. Then, he looks back at us. "This whole time. You knew?"

"Well," Ellie admits, "not the whole time."

"How?"

"We work together," I state. "I'm her makeup artist on set."

His face darkens. "So you lied to me too, then. You told me you didn't want to go near the movie set downtown and you hate Christmas."

"All true," I say, then I look to Ellie with a soft smile. "Well. Used to be true."

Ellie grins back, cheeks flushing.

"Wait a second . . ." Jax trails off, looking back and forth between us. "Are you two . . . ?"

Ellie and I admit to nothing, but he can immediately tell his hunch is correct. A wolfish grin lights up his face. "Hot. Are you two together because of me?"

Again, we say nothing, but he can clearly read our expressions.

"Nice." He bites his lip. "You know, since we've all already seen each other naked, and we've all sort of had sex together in a way, we could—"

"Nope."

"Out of the question." We cut him off at the same time.

Then, I add, "Have you learned nothing?"

He shrugs. "I told you I'd stop lying, not that I'd stop trying to have sex with you both. And threesomes happen rarely, even for a guy like myself."

I roll my eyes. "It seems your ego has not been affected."

"Okay, enough's enough." Ellie ushers him toward the door.

Jax steps over the slippery puddles of lube and sidesteps the dangling string of lotioned condoms. "Fine. And tomorrow this place better be spotless or my uncle's gonna kill me."

"It will be," Ellie assures him.

He pauses at the door, looking at us one last time. "You sure I can't stay?"

"Go!" We shout.

"Fine! Fine." With that, he turns and closes the door behind him.

Ellie and I release a long, slow exhale.

"You think he learned his lesson?" I ask her.

She shakes her head. "Probably not. But we did our best."

I nod, then look around at the disarrayed cabin. "We put in the effort, that's for sure. And now to clean all this up."

"But first . . ." She takes my hand in hers and pulls me close, locking her lips on mine.

EXT. DOWNTOWN HEMLOCK GROVE COURTYARD (CONT'D)

The businesspeople are bickering back and forth,
arguing louder and louder, disturbing the party.

                    ANNIE
        Enough!

Everyone stares at her.

                    ANNIE
        As per section 626 line 42 of the Small
        Business Association Code, so long as a
        tenant is maintaining their property
        and paying their rent, there is no
        reason to remove them from their lease.
        If you remove him based on grounds of
        "lack of Christmas spirit," I can guarantee
        you'd have a lawsuit on your hands the
        likes of which you've never seen before.
        Imagine the news headlines: Business
        Association illegally harasses young
        divorcé during holidays. Now, that would
        chase your customers away. Excuse us.

Annie grabs James by the hand and leads him away
from the group.

EXT. DOWNTOWN HEMLOCK GROVE SIDEWALK - EVENING

James stops Annie, turns her toward him.

                    JAMES
        What you said back there . . .

ANNIE

Sorry for butting in, but I couldn't
take them harassing you like that, especially
in front of everyone. Besides, according to
your lease, they have no case.

JAMES

You read my lease?

ANNIE

Sorry to interfere. After what I heard them
say that day on the sidewalk I had to look
into it myself. I guess being in a small
town and baking Christmas cookies doesn't
turn off my inner lawyer, after all.

JAMES

Wow. Thank you. I have no idea what to say.

ANNIE

You don't have to thank me. It's the least
I can do, considering this time of year
is hard enough on you already. You don't
need that extra stress on top of
everything else.

JAMES

What you said about me being divorced, I—

ANNIE

I'm sorry I had to bring that up. I
heard about what happened, about how your
wife left you on the night of the Christmas
party and that's why you haven't come back

to it, and why you hate Christmas so
much.

                    JAMES
Who told you that?

                    ANNIE
I don't mean to dredge up the past,
especially since we're here together.
And aside from those businesspeople
harassing you I've had a great time.

                    JAMES
I've had a great time, too, but Annie—

                    ANNIE
I just hope that you can see how
Christmas can still be a great time of
year. I don't know why your wife left
you, especially so close to Christmas,
but I do know that you have many
great years ahead, many more Christmas
memories to make with someone special.
If you choose to let them in.

James grips Annie's shoulders, looking into her eyes.

                    JAMES
Annie, my wife didn't leave me . . .
She died.

Chapter 23
ELLIE

*I*t turns out that lube is really hard to clean off a hardwood floor. We spend most of our time between that and the flour. By the time we've unstrung the lotion-covered condoms it's getting close to midnight.

"I guess we should pack up the Christmas stuff now," I say, reaching to unplug one of the strings of lights we'd used to entrap Matt.

Mariah lays a hand on my forearm. "Leave it until tomorrow."

I give her a small smile. "One more night of Christmas?"

"One more night of Christmas," she agrees.

"Speaking of Christmas, I almost forgot." I set the lights down to grab a small box I'd hidden behind the tree. Its shiny silver paper is punctuated with a bright red bow almost as big as the box itself. I hand it to Mariah, and she turns it over in her hands as if she's never seen a Christmas present before.

"For me?" she asks, barely above a whisper.

I clench my fists. "Yeah."

Her brows furrow. "I didn't get you anything."

"That's okay."

"But now I feel shitty."

I can't help the small giggle that bubbles in my chest. "A classic Christmas feeling, what I call Christmas Gift Reciprocation Guilt. Usually, I buy a bunch of boxes of chocolate and have them ready to go in case someone unexpectedly gives me something."

"Wish I had a box of chocolates right now."

"Open it!" I do a little jump, unable to wait any longer.

She gently peels away the paper like a practised grandma

saving it for next year. The plain black cardboard box opens to reveal two bracelets, one with an *x* and the other with an *o*.

Mariah presses a hand to her mouth but doesn't move to pick them up. I do it for her, taking the *x* and clipping it around her wrist. She takes mine and does the same. We hold our wrists together, a matching *x* and *o*, the silver reflecting the twinkling green and red lights.

"Thank you," she manages, her eyes glassy.

I entwine my fingers with hers. "You know . . . This is the best Christmas I've had in a long time."

Mariah smiles. "This is the best Christmas I've ever had."

"Merry Christmas." I struggle to maintain my cheerful countenance despite how much my chest aches. I step into her arms and let my forehead lie on her chest, feeling the gentle swell of her breasts rise and fall with her breath, listening to the beat of her heart.

"I wish we'd have had the whole night to ourselves," I say. "But I'm glad we taught Matt a final lesson. The way you stood up for me . . . Thank you. No one has ever done that for me before."

"I meant what I said." Mariah's eyes search mine, drawing me close. "You deserve someone who truly appreciates you, and values you, and is honest with you all the time."

I tense at her words. She says I deserve all these nice things, but I can never seem to have them. Time and time again, I meet someone amazing, I catch feelings, and then the rug is ripped out from under me when they pursue something—or someone—more important. Mariah's kind words don't do anything to stem the pain of her going down to LA rather than staying up here with me. I'm not her priority—and why should I be? She just met me.

Someday I'll find someone who *will* make me a priority.

But that doesn't make my heart hurt any less, seeing her here, watching those beautiful eyes of hers search mine.

Despite knowing we have no future, reminding myself of Mariah's choice over and over again, what my heart wants and needs right now is Mariah.

Three little words echo in the back of my mind.

Now is not the right time to say them.

It may never be the right time for us.

"I know whatever this is ends tomorrow," I begin, reaching out for Mariah's hands. "I know you have dreams to chase, and those dreams don't include me . . . but we still have tonight. Can we pretend, just for tonight, that we're going to see each other again?"

Mariah's eyes shine as she regards me. "Who says my dreams don't include you?"

"Don't get my hopes up," I say with a bit more bite in my tone than intended. "This is hard enough as it is."

"But . . ."

"We need to keep being honest with each other. Your path is taking you one way, and mine is taking me another. That doesn't mean that what we have right here, right now, isn't important and special."

Mariah squeezes my hands, giving me courage to go on.

"I know I haven't been with any other women before, and that I've just been fumbling around like a goof—"

Mariah laughs through the tears that have begun to well in her eyes. "None of this has been fumbling."

I smile back. "I've felt a little fumbly!"

Mariah shrugs. "The fumbling, the figuring it out, it's all part of it. And, for the record, my first time with you was way better than like ninety percent of the sex I've had in my life."

I perk up. "Really?"

"You have natural talents." She bites her lip. "Even though this came about rather suddenly for you."

I bask in her praise for a moment, then turn serious. "I've given it a lot of thought. About my sexuality. I know it seems sudden to you, but looking back, it's like I see everything through a different lens. Was I intimidated by the new girl in grade eight, or was I attracted to her? Was I jealous of my best friend in grade ten because she got a boyfriend and spent more time with him than me, or was I envious because he got to kiss her and I didn't? And it makes the whole *Romeo and Juliet* thing more confusing. Did I wish I was kissing James Tyler, or Ashleigh Blake? I feel like I've opened my eyes to a side of myself that's always been there but I didn't see clearly."

Mariah weighs her words for a moment then takes a slow breath. "I'm glad I could help you . . . see this side of yourself."

"What I'm trying to say is, what we had will always be special. I found a part of myself through you." I swallow a lump forming in my throat. "I hope we can still keep in touch. Stay friends."

Mariah nods, dropping her gaze to the floor. "Stay friends."

"But I don't want to talk about that anymore," I say, taking her chin and tilting it back up so she looks in my eyes. "It's our last night together, and I don't want to think about the future. About you leaving . . ." *About you choosing your job over me . . .* "I just want it to be us."

Mariah nods, then takes a moment to think. "Since you've been honest with me, it's only fair I'm honest with you. I want you to know . . ." She closes her eyes, steeling herself.

I swallow hard and wait with bated breath, my heart pounding in my ears, hoping she'll say what I think she's going to say so I can say it back. Hoping she will choose *me*, for once in my life.

Please, *please* choose me.

After what feels like the longest moment in my life, she opens her eyes once more. "You're just a really great person," Mariah says finally. "And I'm so lucky to have met you. And I'm really proud of you. And I can't wait to watch every single Christmas movie you work on."

I manage a smile, glad to hear what she wanted to tell me, but disappointed it didn't include the words I wanted to hear most.

Reaching up, I caress her cheek while Mariah leans into my hand. "I can't wait to be kept awake all night with nightmares after watching all the movies you get to work on, too."

Mariah laughs. "Promise me if you do, you'll call me? And I'll tell you how I did it so you won't be scared anymore?"

"Maybe we can FaceTime while I watch so it's like you're right there with me."

Her eyes twinkle. "I'd love that. And I'll FaceTime you for yours so you can fill me in on all the behind-the-scenes she-nanigans. Like with the reindeer catastrophe on that one film you did."

I giggle. "I'm not sure if I can ever top that level of drama, but I'll try."

The giggles and smiles subside, leaving behind a gnawing ache in the pit of my stomach, an acute awareness warning me that plans to stay connected don't work out over such long distances and with short-lived friendships. Everything we are, everything we could be, ends tomorrow.

But we have tonight.

I don't waste another second of it.

My lips find hers just as she reaches toward me, the softness of her mouth juxtaposed with the hard intensity of our mutual need for one another. Lips and tongues dance as our hands move over one another's bodies, as if trying to memorize every crevice and dimple. My fingers lift the hem of Mariah's shirt, and I peel it off her. Mariah lifts her arms and parts from me a moment so I can make her bare before me, reveal her beautiful full breasts displayed within her teal lace bra. I kiss them both, then press my face between them as she holds me, kissing the top of my head.

Mariah pushes me back so she can do the same for me, trailing a line of kisses up every inch of skin she reveals while lifting my shirt, pausing over the hard, raised bumps of my nipples in my sheer bralette.

We press close together once more, skin on skin, continuing our soft, slow kissing. I unclasp her bra, letting the straps slide down her arms. She pulls my bralette over my head.

We kiss our way to the bedroom and sit on the edge of the bed as our hands explore, memorizing every inch of each other. I lean Mariah back and kiss my way down her belly and she sighs with contentment as her hands stroke my hair.

I pull Mariah's tight pants off, leaving just her panties on, which match her bra—because of course she coordinates her underwear. I stroke her soft skin, admiring her, memorizing her, before my lips find their way down to where her legs part. I kiss her over her underwear, inhaling her scent, savouring it. I peel them down and kiss the top of her mound, then continue kissing down her legs to her feet, where I plant another kiss on the insole of her left foot. My hands caress her thick calves, then back to her thighs, where I settle in between them.

"I'm going to miss this," I murmur before tonguing her softly. My fingers, tongue, and lips work in unison without me having to think about what to do next. Our bodies sync up, me understanding what she needs just from listening and feeling for her. Moments later Mariah's body coils and tenses around me, she makes the most beautiful sounds in the world and comes so sweetly, unravelling before me. I feel blessed to bear witness to something so pure, primal, and raw.

When she finishes, Mariah pulls me up and cradles me against her breasts. I tuck my face into her neck and hold her tight. After a few seconds she begins to shiver, and we pull the blankets over us, pretending we're the only two people in the entire world. Maybe I wish we were. We tangle up in one another again, rocking our hips together as we kiss slowly and softly, simply enjoying each other's touch, trying to soak up every last second of it before it comes to an end.

Our kissing becomes more intense, fervent, and Mariah leans me onto my back. She strokes the side of my breast as she lifts herself to look into my eyes. "Can I please kiss you?"

I understand what she means when she glances down the bed. My body immediately tenses, and she responds by kissing my neck.

"Don't think about trying to get anywhere. There is no plan, no end goal, no destination. It's just you and me. And when you've had enough, I'll stop." She lowers her mouth and whispers in my ear, "But I'd love to kiss you everywhere."

Exhaling slowly, I give her an almost imperceptible nod. Mariah doesn't move from where she is, continuing to kiss my neck, to suck on my earlobe, as her hand slowly works its way down until she's cupping me. That's all she does, simply holds me, and I can feel my body begin to soften at her touch.

"Close your eyes," she whispers, and I oblige. Every nerve ending is heightened, and I feel surrounded by her, enveloped by her, acutely aware of every square inch our bodies are touching.

Mariah takes her time moving down my body, pausing to lick along both of my collarbones, to suck each of my breasts into her mouth, and then lower, to the jut of my hipbones and the hollow of my pelvis. By the time she arrives lower I feel as though I'm half-conscious in an erotic, meditative trance, and I wouldn't be surprised if I wake up in a minute and this will all have been an intensely sexy dream.

With every bit of care she's had for the rest of my body, Mariah takes my centre gently, stroking and licking my labia, sucking on my clit, until she deftly brings two fingers just inside, curling them up and massaging. I know she told me we're not on a journey, but that's exactly how I feel, like I'm being expertly led along a pathway and Mariah is my guide. It's like she's holding my hand, and I'm safe and I'm loved and I know everything will be okay.

My body relaxes around her, opening for her, and as it does,

I feel myself begin to quicken. I don't stop to analyze these new sensations, to understand what's going on—I simply let myself be here with her.

Mariah's fingers go deeper, pressing firmer, her tongue matching the intensity. My breath becomes bated, then ragged. I feel myself aching, then throbbing, and suddenly the path is a mountain and we're climbing it together, and now my breath is short gasps and my whole body tenses, tenses, tenses . . .

And explodes, releasing in a dizzying wave, cascading through my entire being in tingles and rushes. I don't know what sounds I'm making, and I don't even care, I've never cared less about anything in my entire life. Mariah is right there with me for every second of it, holding me and guiding me, until I float back down to earth.

Mariah comes up beside me just as I begin to shiver. She pulls the blanket onto us and tucks my face into her neck. The shivers are so intense I feel as though I'm convulsing, and after a few seconds something in me breaks.

I cry.

She holds me tightly, cradling my head in her arms, and I can't do anything but weep against her. For a while she just holds me and rocks me gently, until the tears begin to dry and I can breathe again.

"Why am I crying?" I manage to sniffle.

She kisses my forehead. "Sometimes you cry after a really good orgasm."

"So that's what that feels like."

I can feel her smile against me. "Not all of them are that intense, but yeah. Welcome to the club."

I lift off her and wipe away my tears so I can look into her eyes. She tucks a strand of hair behind my ear. We gaze at each other a long, heavy moment. Those three little words come back to me, caught somewhere between my heart and my throat. I swallow them down, not wanting to pressure her into saying something she might not mean. Instead, I say, "Thank you."

She shakes her head. "No. Thank *you*."

We snuggle back into one another's embrace, our fingers entwined, matching *x* and *o* bracelets side by side. When sleep overtakes us, I don't dream, because even my subconscious knows a dream could never be better than this, right here, right now, in her arms.

ANNIE

What? Your wife . . . died?

JAMES

She passed away three days before
Christmas, three years ago.

ANNIE

Oh my goodness, James, I'm so sorry . . .

JAMES

We were walking back after the party.
A drunk driver jumped the curb. It
all happened so fast, and there was
nothing I could do.

ANNIE

I'd be devastated. No wonder you didn't
want to come. I can't believe I made you.

JAMES

The worst part is, I hadn't given her her
Christmas present yet. I was going to give
it to her early, that night . . . We'd
just been approved for an adoption.

Annie gasps.

JAMES (CONT'D)

Ever since then I've been avoiding
anything that reminds me of that night.
Christmas lights, music, cookies,
parties . . . babies.

ANNIE

All this time I thought you were
divorced. She told me your wife
left you, but I didn't realize . . .

JAMES

Wait, who told you?

ANNIE

Your barista.

JAMES

Annie . . . I don't have any employees.
I run the café alone.

Chapter 24
MARIAH

*E*llie's not in our bed when I wake up. The cabin doesn't smell like coffee, or eggs, or toast. I get up and dress, then pad out to the main area. The room is full of boxes, and Ellie is unstringing lights from the ceiling and coiling them up. The tree is half-naked, and everything seems . . . wrong.

"Well, this sucks," I grump.

Ellie turns to look at me, and her bright smile is almost enough to lift my spirits. Almost, but not quite.

"Yeah," Ellie replies. "The day after Christmas is the worst day of the year."

"I feel so . . ." I make a fist and hold it to my chest, unable to describe the ickiness.

She simply nods. "I forgot you've never really had a proper Christmas. This is your first time experiencing the post-holiday blues."

I take the opposite end of the string of lights and begin helping her wrap it up. "It's awful."

"Yup."

"Makes me want to go back to bed."

"I know. It sucks." She sighs. "But the pain of it being over means that it was something truly special. Would you really want to undo everything to not experience the sadness when it comes to an end?"

We finish coiling the lights, our hands meeting, fingers grazing one another's. My gaze meets hers, and I give my head a subtle shake, my throat thickening. "No. I wouldn't."

We lean toward one another, her eyes darting down to my lips, and—

Her phone rings. She blinks a few times, as if clearing her head, then steps away to grab it off the kitchen counter and answer it. "Hey Blaire! Oh, they already contacted you? That's great!"

She stays on the phone for another minute or two, then hangs up and squeals, her whole upper body curling into a ball.

I set the bundle of lights into a box and step up to the peninsula. "What's up?"

Ellie twists toward me, her face bright and shining. "It's happening for real! Marlene and Yueyi spoke with my agent, Blaire, and I'll get to star with Jack Winstron and I'll really be the main character this time! I can't believe I get to be the main character, I'm always the side character, the quirky best friend, the neighbour, the barista, woman at church number two, and . . ." She trails off, as if losing steam. "What's wrong?"

I blink. "Hmm?"

"You look sad." Ellie tilts her head to the side and sticks out her bottom lip.

"What! No. This is just my face." I turn my frown as upside down as I can.

Ellie purses her lips. "I've been staring at your face a lot these past two weeks. I know what it looks like when you're happy."

I come around to her and take her hands in mine, our matching bracelets tinkling together. "I'm happy for you. This is a big moment and you've worked so hard for it. I just wish . . ." I bite my lip, unsure which emotion to pick first. I wish we had more time together. I wish our goals were more in line with each other's. Mostly I wish she'd think about how important she is to me. She's the main character in *my* life.

But maybe that doesn't count.

Ellie gives my hands a squeeze. "I know," she says, though I'm not sure she does. "This isn't a goodbye forever. It's just a goodbye for now."

It doesn't feel that way.

"I have to get ready for work and pack," I say.

Ellie nods, releasing my hands. "I have to get all this stuff back in my car."

I look around, unsure if that's possible. "Good luck."

We part ways, her heading back to the living area and me going to the bathroom to shower. I eye our toothbrushes side by side at the sink, my shampoo bottles next to hers, her underwear piled on the floor with my bra. It makes my heart ache. I was so close to having it all. Life can be such a tease.

As I clean myself up and get ready, I come to terms with the fact that this is the end for us, despite Ellie's good intentions and bright words. For two people working in the film industry, our lives are going in completely opposite directions. Maybe today we can pretend we'll cross paths in the future, if only to ease these next few hours. Then, after we're finished filming this final day, after I've gone home and I'm done packing my apartment and telling my landlord he can list it on Airbnb for the remainder of my lease, when I'm in my car and I'm sitting at the Peace Arch Border Crossing and it's real, that's when I'll let all of this sink in. I'll play some sad songs on the road trip down to California, watch the sun sparkle off the bracelet on my wrist, and cry it all out before starting fresh in LA.

My time with Ellie will be a magical Christmas memory, one that I'll never be able to match. Now whenever *Home Alone* comes on TV or "Have Yourself a Merry Little Christmas" plays on the radio or I even see red and green twinkling lights it will remind me of her, of how close to perfect everything was, and how it will never be again.

Another reason to hate that time of year.

Once my hair and makeup are done I gather my items from the bathroom and move to the bedroom to dress and pack. By the time I'm ready to go, wheeling my travel luggage behind me, the living room is bare and the boxes are stacked by the door. It all feels so . . . wrong.

I go outside and find Ellie stuffing a box in her trunk. After loading my luggage into my own car I help her with the boxes.

We stand outside, the morning already hot with an intense

July sun and a cloudless blue sky. "You need a ride into town?" I ask.

Ellie shakes her head. "No. Probably best I take my own car since we're both heading out right after."

"Right. Of course." I bite my lip, wishing I had the extra twenty minutes with her for the drive. "Guess I'll see you there."

"Yup. See you soon. I gotta go jump in the shower, so—"

"Yeah, of course. I'll see you on set."

Despite us both needing to leave, we stand there for several more beats. Finally, I tear myself away and hop in the driver's seat of my car, turning the engine over. I watch through the rear-view mirror as Ellie walks away and heads back into the cabin.

My heart feels like it weighs a thousand pounds as I pull away and the cabin disappears behind me, lost in the forest, never to be seen again. The drive into Chilliwack is similarly heavy, with all of my memories of the past mingling with the present, giving me yet another reason to leave this city and never return.

Leaving Chilliwack behind makes me wonder if I should have left more on the table last night with Ellie. I wasn't honest with her about my feelings. I came close to telling her how important she is to me, but the way she'd spoken, it all sounded so final. She'd made up her mind about us, about our future, about our friendship. It was all so painfully familiar.

Just like Jess, I'd been Ellie's curiosity experiment.

But unlike Jess, I'd helped Ellie unlock something important and special about herself that she might not have realized for a long time, if ever. I was never more than a friend to her—a catalyst to her path of self-discovery. And that's all I'll ever be. Even though it hurts, I don't regret what happened. It was a privilege being there with her for the start of her journey. If I had to do it all over again, I would.

I kept my promise to myself. I protected my own heart and didn't bare my soul to Ellie like I had with Jess. I didn't risk losing both a friend and a lover at the same time. Instead, I hardly had a lover, and kept a friend who I wished with every fibre of my being was more than that.

As my heart thumps painfully in my chest like it's filled with sticky black tar, I'm not sure which is better.

I take the long way to work and drive past the bar where Matthew Jackson and I reunited. I sift through the emotions tied to him, but don't feel anything: no anger, no resentment, nothing. Yes, I was close to catching feelings for the person I thought he was, and it *did* suck being so blatantly lied to . . . but instead of anything negative, I feel an odd sense of gratitude. If it weren't for him and his fuckboy ways, Ellie and I never would have found one another in the way we had. We would have remained friendly strangers, two paths crossing on their way to different destinations rather than becoming entwined like we did. In a roundabout way, Ellie and I owe everything to him.

My phone dings with a text from Mom, and I pull my phone out of my purse at a red light to read it.

> Morning sunshine! Today still good to get together with you and Ellie? Dad and I would love to see your set if that's ok. Never seen a movie set before but now we know two famous people!

Since I'm driving, I press the call button and set my phone into my hands-free device.

Mom answers with a confused "Hello?"

"Hey, just driving, thought it would be easier to call."

"Oh, that's nice!" She seems overly eager and surprised that I've called, which makes me feel guilty, knowing how rare of an occasion this is.

"Yeah, so, I'm not sure if I can let you on set because of security, but if you swing by I can ask the director today. We can go for lunch before I head back into Vancouver."

I don't tell her that it might be the last time I see her for a while. Me being a one-hour drive away versus twenty likely won't make a difference for how often we see each other, but being *able to* and simply not doing it feels different than a physical distance keeping us apart. That's not a good conversation to have on the phone.

"Will Ellie be joining us?" she asks.

"Uh . . ."

"She's such a sweet girl. Your dad and I really enjoyed her company."

"Yeah, she is, but—"

"You know, I fully support your relationship with her. You two make such a lovely couple. You know what they say, opposites attract and all. I could just tell you two had something special when I saw you together. And the way she looked at you, it made my heart smile."

"Really?"

"Sure! Could see it clear as day how important you two are to each other."

"Thanks, Mom," I manage. I don't think I can sit with my parents and continue to pretend Ellie is my girlfriend. Not after everything that's happened. Not now that I want it so badly to be true, but it never will be. "I'm not sure if Ellie can join us, but I'll ask."

"That would be lovely."

"Yeah. Okay, I gotta go, just got to work," I say as I pull up to a space and prepare to parallel park.

"Thanks for calling, Mariah," she says, pronouncing my name my preferred way again. "We'll see you later today."

"Bye." I let her disconnect the call. I'm still perturbed by the shift in my mom's personality and one-eighty in support for me and my lifestyle, unsure what the catalyst was for the change, and not entirely trusting her for it. Maybe it's some sort of manipulation tactic that I haven't clued in on yet. Why now? And why, of all people, does she approve of Ellie so much? Typical of my life to finally find someone my parents like and think is right for me, only for our relationship to have been faked, then more real than I could have ever imagined, and then ending so abruptly.

After parking, I get out of my car and walk to downtown Chilliwack for what might be the last time.

I eye the twee touristy downtown strung with garland and lights, the windows frosted, drab white blankets in piles beside the sidewalk. I tilt my head, trying to look at it through Ellie's eyes, to see the magic sparkle, but I can't. Maybe I need her with me to do that.

While waiting for the light to change, I look down the street to my favourite bookstore. Well, there's one thing in Chilliwack that still holds some magic for me. Part of me is sad I might never see that bookstore again, the only place I've ever truly felt safe in this whole city.

Now, I suppose, the cabin Ellie stayed in has joined that list too.

After crossing the road, showing my ID to security, and making my way up to my hair and makeup station, I prepare for our last day on set. There are several side actors and background people who need their makeup done and I busy myself with that, allowing my mind to wander to everything I need to do before I leave Vancouver. Try as I might to focus on the ever-growing list of seemingly insurmountable tasks ahead, my mind keeps going back to Ellie. Maybe it's because with every turn of my wrist my bracelet catches the light, drawing my attention to it. Or it could be because the people sitting in my chair don't radiate anything close to the energy that shines out of her like some sort of happiness Arc Reactor.

I look at the clock, wondering when she'll be here, wishing she'd hurry up and arrive so I can look at her beautiful face, while simultaneously wishing she'll never show up, so I don't have to say goodbye.

INT. BREWED AWAKENING CAFÉ - NIGHT

Annie enters the café alone, stepping slowly while looking around, eyes wide. The café is closed. Everything is quiet.

> ANNIE
> Hello? Kate, you in here?

Kate enters from the back room.

> KATE
> Oh, hey, Annie! How was the party?

> ANNIE
> Kate . . . were you married to James?

> KATE
> Oh shoot. He told you, didn't he?

Kate approaches Annie.

Annie takes several steps back, bumping into a table behind her.

> ANNIE
> Do you know that you're . . . that you're . . .

> KATE
> A ghost? Yeah. Come on, let's sit down.

Annie keeps her eyes on Kate as she sits at the table behind her.

Kate joins Annie, sitting opposite her.

> KATE
> Don't worry, I'm not going to hurt you.
> When I passed away, my spirit never left.
> I couldn't leave, not knowing how hard
> James would take losing me. I figured I
> would stick around for a bit to make sure
> he'd be okay. I didn't expect to be here
> three years later. I was worried I'd be
> here forever. Then you came along.

> ANNIE
> Me?

> KATE
> For the first time in years
> I saw him smile. And I knew that
> maybe, just maybe, he had a chance
> at being happy again. He had a
> chance of a future. A chance to find
> love again. That's why I kept
> pushing you two together.

> ANNIE
> We just met. I couldn't, I mean . . .

> KATE
> Love doesn't care about time. It just
> cares about the truth. About honesty.
> Can you be honest with yourself?

Chapter 25
ELLIE

I should have asked Mariah to help me get the Christmas tree out. Despite its small size, it's not as easy to manoeuvre as I'd assumed. It's prickly and hard to grab on to, and I'm making a mess on the floor with needles that I'll have to clean up. I'm already running late, and the last thing I need is yet another mess. Maybe I should just leave it; something tells me that Matt won't be giving me a good star rating on Airbnb no matter how clean the cabin is.

The tree is stuck halfway out the door and I'm trying to jam it through when I hear knuckles rapping on the door frame. Startled, I glance up.

Well, speak of the devil.

Matt wears jeans and a tight black T-shirt, his hair tied back in a knot, and he's doing the *boyfriend lean* against the door. What once would have turned me into horny goop now has no effect, aside from causing mild irritation.

"Hey, sorry, am I late? I thought my checkout time was eleven." I drop the tree, sending a slew of needles tinkling onto the floor, and take a step back to eye the time on the stove.

"No, you're not late. I came early, hoping I'd catch you." He gives me a guarded smile.

I fidget, uneasy. "Oh. Great."

"Here, let me help you." He takes hold of the tree, easily yanking it through the door. He carries it with one hand and tosses it like a twig into the woods.

"Thanks," I say, only a little jealous of his strength. "Why are you here?"

He dusts off his hands on his pants. "I had to come make sure the place is back in order."

"I have a bit of sweeping to do." I gesture at the needles. "Otherwise it's back to normal."

"May I?" Matt asks, looking past me into the cabin.

I step back and nod, allowing him entrance. While he pokes his head around the space, I grab the broom and dustbin from the pantry cupboard and start sweeping.

He comes back into the living room and, after watching me sweep for a few seconds, holds out his hand for the dustbin. I hand it over, and Matt crouches down to hold it while I sweep up the tree detritus.

"Mariah isn't here, hey?" he asks after a few moments of silence.

"Nope. She's at work. We both head back to Vancouver after this."

"You two headed back together?"

"Why, you going to track us down and plot your revenge?"

"Maybe." He looks up at me and grins.

I sigh, wishing he'd have let me leave the cabin in peace. "No, we're not going back together. I'm not sure if we'll ever see each other again, to be honest. She's going to LA following a job lead."

My heart aches just thinking about how close we came to true happiness, and how quickly it was ripped away from us. I finish sweeping the needles and Matt stands, towering over me once more. He discards the needles outside while I do one last check to make sure I have everything before stepping outside and locking the door.

Matt approaches, holding out his hand. I set the key into his palm and his fingers enclose mine, holding me there. I look up into his eyes to see his expression has turned serious, and gulp. My heart beats a little faster, suddenly realizing I'm alone in the woods with a man who has every reason to be angry with me.

"I had another reason for coming here," he says, his voice low.

"Wh-what's that?"

His expression softens. "To apologize."

I grit my teeth; this is the last thing I need right now. "I'm not going to alleviate any guilt you feel about what happened between the three of us, Jax. We both said what we needed to say last night. Now, if you're truly sorry, then you need to do the work and lead the type of life that reflects it."

He releases my hand and I push past him, stepping into the morning light.

Matt locks the door behind us and we part ways, gravel crunching beneath our shoes as we walk to our respective vehicles. I grab the handle of my door and stop—there is one thing I need from Matt. This is my only chance to ask. Before I can think on it any further, I turn back to face him. "Wait."

Matt pauses and looks back at me, one foot inside his little purple truck.

I try not to say what I'm about to say, but I can't help myself. Something deep down within me needs to know. I take a steadying breath, and then ask, "If you had to choose one of us. Which one?"

My heart thuds in my ears as I watch his face shift, eyes lifting to the sky. After several moments, they meet mine again, apologetic and sheepish.

I purse my lips. *Still coming in second.* "It's okay. I'd choose her, too."

He gives me a half shrug, then climbs into his truck and shuts the door, his elbow jutting out the open window. "Take care of yourself, Ellie."

I watch as he drives away.

I can't believe, for a very short period of time, I'd imagined my whole life with him—right down to the picket fence, chicken coop, and gaggle of children running around. And now, watching him drive down the road and out of my life forever, he's a stranger—a lost soul travelling through space and time, struggling with his basic concept of self. And I feel sorry for him. This big, strong, handsome guy, with a phone full of contacts who don't really know who he is, with no clue where he's going or why he's here, with opportunities at his feet and no direction to go—I pity him. Because I know who I am, and I know who I love.

Even if she didn't choose me in the end.

Our relationship may not have withstood the test of time, it may faded faster than a star shooting across the sky, but it was raw and real and honest.

Pressure forms behind my eyes, a tear threatening to spill over and run down my cheek. I begin to sniffle it back up, to blink it away, to force my breath to even out, and bury everything until I forget about it, but something stops me.

Mariah's voice echoes in the back of my mind.

It's okay to be sad.

So I take a deep breath, and . . . I let myself be.

I let the tears fall down my cheeks. I allow the sobs to rack my body. The sadness grows until it's gripping my whole heart in a vise, and I curl in on myself, squatting down on the ground, hugging myself tight with my knees toward my chest. My breath heaves at the aching pain of losing Mariah when I'd just found her, and I feel her loss in every square inch of my body.

After a minute, the tears begin to slow. The pain recedes to a dull ache. My eyes stop producing tears, and after a few hiccups, my chest releases its tight hold. I can breathe again.

I stand slowly, bleary-eyed, and take a long, deliberate inhale, followed by a cleansing, shaky exhale.

And I feel . . . better.

Not good. Not right. But better. I breathe with a new sense of clarity, of understanding that life doesn't have to be all sunshine and rainbows. Sometimes things are just sad, and that's okay.

As I drive away, leaving the cabin behind with all the memories, hopes, dreams, and missed opportunities swirling in my mind, the light catches my bracelet, drawing my attention. I tilt my wrist back and forth, watching it sparkle, and smile. I may be leaving the cabin behind, along with all the things I've left unsaid, but perhaps I can take what I've learned with me. And, in a way, it will be like carrying a piece of Mariah everywhere I go.

Even if I'm about to see her for the very last time.

BACK IN CHILLIWACK, each step I take toward hair and makeup feels like my feet weigh a thousand pounds. I grip the familiar handle and push the door open, understanding the finality of such an action. I peer around the brightly lit room, full of hustle and bustle; I miss it already. My eyes land on Mariah at her station. She's already looking at me, as if she's been staring at the door, waiting for me to walk through it. My heart rises into my throat, nearly choking me.

I step toward her, and the closer I get the more everything around us fades. We stand there for five heartbeats, simply regarding one another. Without a word, I sit in my seat. Mariah comes up beside me, then begins our ritual: the soft pads of her fingers swirling the cool liquid over my skin, the expert brushstrokes along my cheekbones, my jaw, my temple. The gentle care she takes with my eyelids, with my lips, taking more time than she ever has before, as if she's relishing it just as much as I am.

When she's finished, I open my eyes, and she's so close. Her eyes meet mine, then flutter down to my lips. I breathe her in, beckoning her closer. She leans in, barely a millimetre, my pulse quickening in response, and—

"Mariah, I need to speak with you."

We pull apart abruptly, the room coming back to life around us with its noise and light and familiar chaos.

Mariah clears her throat, regarding Jimmie before her. "Sorry, what is it?"

"I received a call yesterday asking for a reference," he states, his expression stony.

I glance from Mariah to Jimmie and back, the air thick with suspense.

He cracks a smile. "I put a good word in."

We both exhale in a long whoosh.

"Wow, thanks, Jimmie. I don't know what to say."

"I told them you have a lot to learn, but your talent is obvious. Though it sounded like they were planning to hire you with or without my approval."

"Oh, thank you. Thank you so much." Mariah's voice is flat and without intonation.

"And you." Jimmie turns to me. "Seems like you're stuck with us for another round of Christmas. Yueyi told me everything. It looks like we'll be together again in Whistler before summer is out."

"Great. Thanks, Jimmie. You're the best." I, too, seem unable to bring emotion into my voice. This has never happened to me before.

Jimmie regards his clipboard and moves to the other side of the room. We both stare uncomfortably at the floor.

"Congratulations," I say finally, trying my best to mean it. "I can't wait to see all the amazing things you do."

Mariah nods. "You, too. I'm excited for you."

"Yeah, same. Super excited."

"You'll do amazing."

"We're both moving up in the world."

"Getting what we want."

I can't even force a smile. I meet Mariah's gaze, and it seems she can't, either.

All I want is to take her in my arms. To tell her how I feel. To promise that we'll always be friends at least, that we'll call each other and stay in contact and that one day this will all work out. But I can't promise that, and I don't want to drag the pain out any longer than I need to. But I do think Mariah needs to know how important she is to me, and how much she's changed my life.

"Listen—" I begin, but Yueyi cuts us off, her loud voice ringing through the room.

"Last day on set, get a move on! We have a lot of cleanup to do." Yueyi claps her hands twice, like a preschool teacher.

"We'll talk after," Mariah says. "I have to pack up my station, anyway. I'll wait to leave until you're done filming so we can say goodbye."

It's going to be impossible to focus on my lines now. I manage to nod, then get up from my seat and head toward the costume area. When I walk back across the room, Mariah's things are mostly packed and tucked away in her giant duffel bag. Everything feels wrong, like I don't fit in my skin, like I need to moult out of it and shake it off and leave it behind. As I walk past her, I trail my fingers down her arm, leaving a line of goosebumps in their wake.

Then, I head down the stairs, onto the street, and toward the café to deliver my final lines.

INT. BREWED AWAKENING CAFÉ (CONT'D)

James enters.

Annie turns around to look at him, but when she glances back Kate is gone.

                    JAMES
          Is she here . . . ?

                    ANNIE
          She was, a second ago.

James sits down opposite Annie, where Kate had been.

                    ANNIE
          It seems that your wife has been trying
          to set us up this whole time.

                    JAMES
          Sounds like something she'd do.

                    ANNIE
          She's been worried about you—that's
          why she hasn't left. She hoped to see you
          moving on before she moved on. But you
          weren't. You stayed stuck in the past. You
          fell further and further down into a hole of
          grief. She couldn't leave you like that.
          She loves you too much.

                    JAMES
          I haven't been able to see anything good
          in the world for a long time. I lost
          myself when I lost her.

ANNIE

I can't imagine that pain. That grief.
But it's not too late. You can still have
a life. That's what she wants for you.

JAMES

The pain never goes away, Annie. I'll never
be the same man I was. I don't have anything
to offer someone new. I'm sorry.
I never had any closure . . .

Kate steps out from back room and walks up behind
James.

Chapter 26
MARIAH

With a heavy duffel bag and an even heavier heart, I leave the hair and makeup station one final time. Shouldering my bag, I descend the stairs and step out onto the sidewalk. After tossing my bag into my car, my eyes find their way along the blue fence toward the café, where the final scenes will be shot after our lunch break. Part of me wants to leave now so I don't have to torment myself watching Ellie glow under those bright lights—responsibilities be damned.

"Hey, Mariah!" Mom's voice calls out from the other side of the fence.

I look up, startled to see Mom and Dad both standing beside the security guard. Shit, I'd forgotten to ask Yueyi if they can take a look around. When they're done shooting, I'll see if I can catch her.

"Hey, you two," I say, joining them on the other side of the fence. "They're getting ready to film right now but we might be able to take a look after."

"Sounds great!" Mom says.

"Does that mean we have time for lunch?" Dad pats his stomach.

I quirk a smile. "Yeah, we do."

I walk with them along the sidewalk as Mom chats happily about all the changes to downtown, how it's revitalized the area, how proud she is of where she lives now. I try to see it through her eyes, and I guess I can. It's a little over-the-top, but it has brought the city centre back to life in a way I couldn't have imagined.

We duck into a small mom-and-pop Greek restaurant and order our drinks and food right away, having been here several times in the past when I was younger. It looks the exact same, and the nostalgic part of me is happy that there are at least a few things downtown that have remained the same.

After we order Mom gets up to use washroom, Dad picks up the local paper and sips his coffee, and I use the time to check my phone. My heart stutters and falls into my butt when I read my newest email from Richard at WayDownFx.

They . . . they want me.

They really want me! I read over the contract and nearly choke on my spit when I see my wage. It's not much, but it's US currency so it feels like more. Though, it's LA; I have no idea what rent looks like—can't be any worse than Vancouver pricing, though. Not that it matters. I'd consider living in my car again if it means a shot at my dream.

Mom sits back down at the table. "What are you smiling about?"

Dad lowers his paper, regarding me with curiosity.

I can't even hide my smile. "I got a job offer for this really great company down in LA."

"LA!" Mom's eyebrows jump into her hairline.

"Congratulations, kiddo," Dad says.

"How did this come about?"

Our food is delivered, and we all eat while I go over the details. I show Mom the video that started it all, trying not to cringe at how sexy it is. Sharing something so personal with my parents feels far more intimate than sharing it with five million strangers.

"That's amazing! So . . . when do you leave?" Mom fails to mask the sadness in her voice.

"In about a week, just as long as I need to get everything packed up."

"Well, that's exciting. Dad and I can come down and visit you there, I guess. Nothing wrong with a bit of sunshine!"

I can tell she's trying to be optimistic. I have no idea why she's disappointed; it's not like we see each other often anyway.

And I highly doubt they'd ever come down to California to see me, but I let her have her empty promise.

"Do you have a place rented?" Dad asks between bites of his chicken souvlaki, always the pragmatic one.

I chew and swallow my bite of flatbread. "No, not yet, but I'll figure it out."

"We could help," Dad offers. "We can give you some start-up cash."

I'm taken aback by their offer and consider it a moment before shaking my head. "No, I don't need help. I can do it on my own. Won't be the first time."

Mom winces.

"I'm sorry, I didn't mean—" I reach toward her, touching her wrist.

She frowns, shakes her head. "No, you're right. You were left on your own to figure out a lot of things."

"It's okay, I—"

"No, it's not okay. Mariah," Mom interrupts. Dad gives Mom a quick pat on the back. They share a wordless acknowledgement, communicating silently while I shift in my seat, incredibly uncomfortable. Dad gives her a nod, and Mom exhales a slow breath before turning back to me.

Mom twists her napkin in her hands as she talks. "I have an apology to make. I never understood you. And I never really tried. You were so much like my sister, and we didn't get along. She didn't fit in with the family. The older you got, the more similar you two seemed. And you know how she struggled— her mental health was always up and down. Couldn't keep a job. Drug use. She'd even been arrested once. I didn't want that for you. And when we lost her . . ." Her bottom lip trembles, but she regains her composure. "When we lost her, I was so scared the same would happen to you. I doubled down on being hard on you, on trying to force you to be more like me and less like her. For a time, I thought it was working. You seemed happy, well-adjusted. And then everything changed, and I thought if I was harder on you, it would keep you home, keep you safe, stop you from going down the same path as my sister . . . but all I did was push you away. It was all I knew how to do. And then one day, in church there was a sermon about loving our neighbours being one of Jesus's top commandments, and how that should be our focus above all else."

My brain wants to turn off at any mention of religiosity. I may not be a believer, but Mom is and it's important to her, so I try to pay attention as she continues.

"Jesus's best friends were the castaways of society. He didn't push them away. He brought them in. He showed them love, and kindness, and acceptance. That's what my sister didn't receive. That's why she did the things she did, because she had no one else to turn to when things grew dark for her. And I blame myself so much for that. I should have been there for her."

My heart aches for my mom, slowly coming to see everything from her perspective. Realization dawns on me that my aunt's death had impacted us both so heavily, in completely different ways.

Mom continues. "I've been trying to get you back, to bring you in, to show you love and accept you, but I can't do that unless you let me. I know you have a lot to forgive me for, but I hope that in time you can, so we can move forward and be part of each other's lives. Even if you're a thousand miles away. But I am truly, deeply sorry for not seeing you as you are and loving you, instead trying to change you into someone I thought you should be."

My eyes mist, and all I can do is nod. Mom gets up from her seat and joins me on my side of the booth, giving me a big hug. She sniffles quietly in my ear, her body hot and sweaty from the stress of her confession.

"I forgive you," I whisper in her ear, and her sniffle turns into a sob.

"Thank you," she whispers back.

We pull away after a moment, both of us wiping our eyes. Dad smiles at us across the table, his own eyes shiny.

"I can't believe you're leaving now, when I feel like we've just found one another," Mom states, shoulders slumping. "I've lost so much time with you. But I couldn't waste another second of my life not loving you for who you are. Because who you are is pretty great."

I glow from her acceptance and praise, not knowing how badly I'd wanted it until now. "Thank you. And I can see why you did what you did, why you were so scared. It's sad we're only now realizing all of this, right when I'm leaving."

"California isn't that far away, and we have a lot of points to use for flights." Mom looks to Dad, who nods in agreement. "Besides, if something is important to you, you find a way to make it work."

I nod, acknowledging what she said while turning her words over in my mind—how they relate to a certain someone else for me, too. "Dad, your offer about helping me . . . does it still stand?"

"Of course," he says, eagerly sitting up taller.

A plan formulates in my mind. "Thank you. Are you all done eating? I need to get back to set."

Mom grins, claps her hands once, and stands. "Don't have to ask me twice!"

INT. BREWED AWAKENING CAFÉ (CONT'D)

Kate is standing behind James. She places a hand on
his shoulder.

James visibly relaxes.

                         ANNIE
              You can say something to her.
              She's standing right behind you.

James takes a moment to gather his thoughts, keeping
his eyes on the table between them.

                         JAMES
              I miss you more than you can possibly
              know, Kate. I've kept our café, kept our
              apartment, and put my head down and worked
              to distract myself from losing you. And
              also because I feel most close to you
              in this space. Now I know why.

                         KATE
              I miss you, too. But I miss the person you
              were, not the hollow person you've become.
              I miss your baking, your dancing, your smile.
              I thought I'd never see you the way I remember
              you, the way I love you, again. Until Annie
              came along.

Kate's dialogue is interspersed with Annie's, Annie
repeating Kate's messages for James.

                         JAMES
              I still love you so much.

                              KATE
          Moving forward in your life doesn't mean
          you stop loving me and our past. It means
          you make room in your heart for someone new.
          I want that for you, James. I want you to
          live a full and happy life. You don't have
          to die because I did.

Annie sniffles, cries.

                              JAMES
          I didn't think it was possible to love
          again after my heart was broken that
          night. But I see now . . .

James wipes Annie's tear, caresses her face.

                         JAMES (CONT'D)
          I see now that it might be possible.

                              KATE
                    (whispering in James's ear)
          I know it's possible. Trust yourself.
          Trust her. She's a good one, James.
          She's exactly who I would have
          picked for you.

Kate walks away, leaving Annie and James alone.

Chapter 27
ELLIE

"And *cut*!" Yueyi shouts.

Applause breaks out from cast and crew alike.

Julia and Oscar take a bow, then beckon me to join them from where I'd stepped away off set. They draw me in, and all three of us bow together.

"That was amazing!"

"Incredible job all around!"

"Superb performance from everyone!"

All the backstage lighting and sound techs take their turns congratulating us on a job well done while we return the sentiments to them and all their hard work over the past two weeks. Oscar has one arm over my shoulder, the other over Julia's, something that would have brought me a sense of incredible belonging and contentment mere days ago, but now only makes me feel the weight of his limb on my shoulder.

"You guys go ahead," I say, shrugging his arm off me. "I just need a minute to say goodbye."

Julia and Oscar exit with the rest of the team, leaving me alone in the café. I trail my fingertips along the tabletops as I walk through the place, breathing in the familiar scents one last time. The bright lights shine off the glass display case full of fake cookies and cakes, reflecting my image back at me. I reach up and touch my face, finding a tear trailing down my cheek.

Someone clears their throat behind me and I startle, turning toward the sound.

The lights block my view and I lift a hand to shield my eyes from the intensity. Mariah steps onto the set, revealing herself inch by inch, catching my breath in my throat.

After everything we've been through together, with everything she means to me, I want to take her in my arms and kiss her. But I don't. Soon everything we are, everything we could have been, will fade from lovers, to friends, to acquaintances, and then we'll be mere footnotes in each other's memories.

Despite my whirlwind of thoughts and emotions, all the things I want to tell her, all the things I want to express, all I can say is, "Hi."

Mariah's throat works, her lips twitch, and she returns my quiet hi with one of her own. She takes another step closer. "I didn't tell you the whole truth earlier."

I'm not entirely sure what she's talking about, so I stay still and silent while she gathers her thoughts.

Mariah takes a slow breath. "You weren't my first girlfriend."

I sigh in relief and can't help but smile. "No offence, but I assumed I wasn't."

She smiles, too, then continues. "My experience with my first girlfriend made me nervous about you, and I've been holding back how I really feel because I've been scared."

How she really feels? My heart stammers in my chest. "Scared of what?"

"Scared of . . . pushing you away."

Her pushing *me* away? "What do you mean?"

"We met in cosmetology school, after I moved out. I was myself for the first time in a long time, and it was all so new. I was excited to have the life I'd always dreamed of. That's when I met her. Jess was my best friend . . . and my first love." Each word becomes laboured, like she's digging them up from a hole in her mind where she long ago buried them. "She was everything to me. I gave her my whole heart. I would have done anything for her. But she didn't know who she was, and I was only an experiment to her. One night I took things too far, and I lost my best friend and my lover all in one moment."

"That must have been so hard."

"Because of her, I thought if I told you how I felt, or if I asked for more, you'd turn me down and run away and that would be it."

I take a moment to process what she told me while weighing my words. "Thank you for telling me. I don't think you were being dishonest, you were being careful. And I respect that." Mariah was brave for me. I can be brave for her. I swallow, steeling my resolve. "And I want you to know, this hasn't been some experiment for me. You were . . . are . . . everything to me."

"I am?"

Even if this is all we were ever meant to be, Mariah needs to know how much it meant. I won't leave anything left unsaid. No regrets. "I know you're leaving, and there's nothing I could do or say to make you stay. Even if there was a magic word to keep you here so we could be together, I wouldn't say it. I want you to have everything you could possibly want out of life. I want you to make your wildest dreams come true. I want you to push yourself to the limits of what you thought was possible, and then I want you to go further. Because I know you can. You are capable of so many great things, and I'm so excited to have known you, even for this tiny blip in time."

We're inches apart now, and I can see all the sadness reflected in her beautiful eyes as her bottom lip trembles.

I thread my fingers through hers. "But I don't want to leave without telling you how important you are to me. I know it's only been two weeks, but it feels like it's been both seconds and centuries."

Mariah bites her lip, then nods subtly. "All the time in the world, and yet not enough time at all."

"Exactly." I sigh, relieved that she understands what I'm trying to convey.

"I feel the same way." She inhales slowly, steeling herself.

"And that's why I got you this. A Christmas present, from me to you." She releases my hand and pulls her phone out of her back pocket.

"You got me a Christmas present?" I smile and take the phone from her trembling fingers.

Mariah brings a fist to her mouth as she watches my reaction.

I eye the image on the screen, confused. "A plane ticket?"

She smiles, her expression shifting between hope and fear as her gift starts to sink in.

Looking back at the phone, I reread it. The image starts to swim. "You got me a plane ticket down to LA?"

She takes hold of my hands, the phone clasped between us. Then, her voice low and uneven, she asks, "Come with me?"

My heart stutters and I take a step back, dropping her hands while squeezing the phone to my chest. "What?"

She comes a little closer, her eyes shining. "Come with me," she repeats, louder, more assured. "Come to LA. Let's make a go of it, together."

My chest begins to heave as confusion shifts to anger. This is worse than our relationship coming in second to her career—I had been prepared for that. I've dealt with being overlooked my whole life. But she knows how important my role is. She knows all the reasons I can't leave. I had just told her I wouldn't want her giving up her dreams for me, and yet she wouldn't do the same? Even asking, putting the onus on *me* to let *her* down, makes my stomach curdle.

"I can't leave. Not now. Mariah, I just landed my dream role, in Whistler of all places. There's going to be snow and magic and I'll get to co-star with an incredible method actor. Christmas movies don't mean much to you but they're everything to me." I swallow, trying to tamp down the sadness and anger for our final moments together. "I've worked so hard for this, and I can't give that up, and for you to even ask is—"

She shakes her head, her smile widening. "Check the date, Ellie."

I frown, my heart pounding in my ears, and lower my shaking hands to reread the ticket. "October?"

Mariah tucks a strand of teal hair behind her ear in a rare display of nerves. "And there's a return flight for the following month, but we can move that if you need to come back earlier. Or if you get tired of me. Whichever is first."

I take a few breaths to let this sink in, the anger and disappointment swirling in my mind calming into something else . . . Hope? I look into her eyes, which are brimming with glee. I collect my thoughts, and then ask, "You want me to come to LA with you?"

"Yeah. I figured, between the filming dates for your next movie, we could spend some time together. And maybe, I don't know, you could do a few auditions, see what happens. But only if you want to."

A smile spreads across my lips along with a sense of calm in my belly, though my pulse hasn't slowed at all. "Even if I do come down, we'll be apart a long time. Long-distance relationships, they're not easy. And I can't promise I'll stay in LA after. It will be really hard."

Mariah purses her lips. "Someone once told me that if something is important to you, you find a way to make it work."

"I'm important to you?" I practically squeak, warming from her touch.

Mariah huffs, as if it's the most obvious thing in the world. "Of course you are." She takes another step closer, until we're hip to hip, nearly nose to nose. "I want you to have it all, too," she says, speaking low and quiet. "I can't whisk you away into the country with a chicken coop and a gaggle of dogs. I know living in a big city isn't how you imagined your future, and I don't expect you to stay if you don't like it. But I thought, maybe, we could try."

My heart swells. "I don't really think I wanted all of that. I think that's what I've been told to want. All I want is to be with you. The life you described, us being together and making our dreams come true . . . it sounds better than anything I could have ever imagined."

Mariah cups my cheek with her hand, so soft and warm. "I want you to go star in this movie, and kick its ass, and be the lead actress you're meant to be. And then afterward, I want you to be with me. No matter what project comes next, I want us to figure this out—together."

I sniffle, fighting back a roller coaster of emotions. "I've always wanted to be the main character."

Mariah caresses my skin, sending tingles from the tips of her fingers down my neck. Tilting my chin toward her, she breathes, "You already are."

I gaze into her gorgeous eyes, witnessing the love they hold for me. "That's all I ever really wanted."

Then I lift onto my toes and kiss her.

Cheers ring out, and for a few heated moments of desperate kissing we don't even notice. When we part to breathe, we glance around and realize . . .

The cast and crew are cheering for us. They step out from behind the cover of blinding lights, surprising us with their presence.

Mariah and I both blink. I move to step away, but Mariah grips me harder and tugs me close to her side. I look up at her, and she gives me a little shrug, as if to say, *Why are we hiding this?* I agree, replying with a grin and squeezing her tight.

Oscar and Julia step forward in the crowd, Yueyi and Jimmie right behind them.

"Finally!" Julia states.

"About time," Oscar agrees.

Jimmie purses his lips, one hand on his hip, like he'd seen this coming from the very beginning.

"What?" Mariah and I ask in unison.

"We were all placing bets," Oscar states, his tongue in his cheek.

Julia elbows Oscar in the ribs. "He lost, by the way."

"Bets?" Mariah asks, confused.

Yueyi tuts, then glares at Oscar and Julia as if they're misbehaving toddlers. "Due to HR protocols, there has never been any betting."

The leads nod in agreement, saying "of course," and, "never happened."

After an awkward pause, Julia breaks character and slaps Oscar's shoulder with the back of her hand. "But if there *was* a bet going on, then *someone* would owe me twenty dollars!"

Oscar sighs, but smiles at his co-star in good-natured fun.

Still confused, I ask, "Were we that obvious?"

Oscar points between the two of us. "The tension between you two has been sizzling all week."

"It's been getting me all worked up, too, like walking into a cloud of pheromones." Julia fans herself dramatically.

Yueyi chuckles. "I was worried I'd walk in on you two hiding on set somewhere."

"Well, that's a missed opportunity," Mariah states, and everyone laughs.

"I get the feeling we'll be back on set together before we know it," I reply, looking up at my love and imagining all that the future holds for us, knowing there are so many more adventures to be had.

"We could use a skilled artist like you on our next set," Yueyi says. "We usually stick to locals, but if you two are bunking together it's really no extra cost."

Mariah acts like she's about to consider it, but Jimmie shuts it down. "She's off to LA. She's landed a job for an indie horror project. I made sure to put a good word in." He gives Mariah a wink, and she squeezes me happily.

"You ready to get out of here?" Mariah whispers.

There's nothing I want more. "Where to?"

"I was thinking . . ." She releases me, tucking her arm into mine. "My place tonight, yours tomorrow?"

I squeal, clenching my fists and doing a little jump. "Really!"

Mariah laughs, eyes twinkling. Then she pulls me in for one more kiss.

INT. BREWED AWAKENING CAFÉ (CONT'D)

James and Annie sit at the table, holding hands between them.

> JAMES
>
> I'm so happy I didn't scare you away, like I've done with everyone else.

> ANNIE
>
> Even the ghost of your wife couldn't scare me away. I sensed something special in you.

> JAMES
>
> You were the first person in three years who even made me look up. I never thought I'd be able to love the wife I've lost while opening my heart to someone new. But you make me believe I can.

> ANNIE
>
> You don't have to rush. Grief takes time.

> JAMES
>
> I'm just a broken man in a small town with nothing to my name but subpar dancing skills, a sugar cookie recipe passed down from my late wife, and the best coffee you'll ever taste. Is that enough?

> ANNIE
>
> You are enough. Just as you are. And I wouldn't call your dancing skills subpar.

JAMES

Do you really see a future with me?

ANNIE

I can't give up my life in Seattle. I have a
great job there. I love visiting my sister,
but I'm a city girl at heart. I just have
to take more time to do the things I love
while I'm there. Like baking cookies.

JAMES

I was thinking, maybe it is time for me
to move on. I could let that franchise take
over, start something new somewhere else,
with someone else . . .

ANNIE

You mean, come to the city, with me?

JAMES

Like I said, Brewed Awakening was never
really my dream, it was Kate's. But now
she's gone, and I have to let her go. I
have to find a dream of my own. And maybe
I can find it in a new place.

ANNIE

Only if you're sure you're ready. We don't
have to be in a rush. I know Kate still
means so much to you, and all your memories
with her are here.

James stands and pulls Annie to her feet.

James steps closer.

                    JAMES
        I was never able to give my wife her
        Christmas gift that year. But I think I
        can give her one now. And that's showing
        her that I'm going to be okay. I need to
        let her go, so she can be at peace.

"I'll Be Home for Christmas" begins playing in the
background. Annie and James glance around, confused,
then look at each other.

                    ANNIE
        I think that means Kate approves.

                    JAMES
        I think so, too.

Annie and James lean in for a kiss.

Kate peeks around the corner and smiles contentedly,
then disappears in a sparkling beam of light.

                                        FADE OUT

Chapter 28
MARIAH

One Week Later

I finish sealing the final box in my apartment with tape then stack it next to the others by the door. It feels surreal leaving this all behind, but also completely right. I've outgrown everything here and am looking forward to a new start in a new place with an exciting new job. I rented an apartment based on pictures alone, a small bachelor flat with a view of the Hollywood Freeway. It isn't much, and the traffic will probably keep me up at night, but it's a start.

"Ready?" Ellie pokes her head through the doorway, her cheeks flushed and skin dewy from helping me pack and cart boxes all day.

I take one last look around my old space, at everything I'm leaving behind, and then look back at my gorgeous girlfriend. Her smile grows as I gaze upon her, her question posing much more meaning than she intended. I give her a little nod. "Yeah. I am."

We carry the last box down and load it into her Subaru. I jump in with her, having sold my car yesterday. I'd planned on road-tripping down, but Mom and Dad gave me enough money for a plane ticket, a new car, and my first month's rent. Money can't buy forgiveness, but it does help. People grow, people change, they learn from their mistakes, and I don't want to deprive myself of having a family now because of who they were in the past.

Ellie turns on the radio and rolls down the windows, singing along to an old Tom Petty song as she drives us to the shipping company sending everything down for me. I'll have a few days of sleeping on the floor in a sleeping bag with my bare essentials, but that doesn't scare me. Beats sleeping in a car.

After sorting everything there, Ellie drives us to our final meal together. Every single second is laced with a strange mix of excitement and sadness. We'd planned to have a fancy dinner together at Cactus Club overlooking English Bay as our last meal, but as soon as we sit down and order our drinks and food, we both realize we aren't hungry. My stomach is coiled tight and queasy, homesick even though I haven't left yet. And I have a feeling that it isn't my apartment, my parents, or Vancouver that is making me feel homesick, but Ellie.

This past week has been heaven. We'd taken turns between her place in Brentwood and mine in Marpole, neither of us with anything to do but spend time together. With both of us between jobs, we've been able to spend every waking moment wrapped up in each other. I've never felt so whole with someone else, so seen, so safe.

We balanced our time between packing, sharing our favourite spots in Vancouver, snuggling with snacks and movies, and making love as often as we could. Ellie is becoming braver with allowing me to explore her body. She doesn't usually have an experience like she did the first time, but we've kept our rule about never having a goal or a destination. She's slowly becoming less anxious, learning how to enjoy herself and accept pleasure. For me, I've hit new all-time O records in the sack.

After packing our leftovers and ordering a piece of white chocolate cheesecake to share, Ellie takes out her phone and asks our server to snap a picture of us. I scoot closer to her in the booth and wrap an arm around her as she leans her head on my shoulder. I can feel how big Ellie's smile is, and I can't help but smile too, even though I like to keep my face mostly neutral in pictures.

Ellie examines the picture after, and gasps. "We look so perfect."

I press my nose into her cheek. "We always do."

"Mind if I post this?"

I love that she still asks permission. "Of course not."

Our tea arrives and I prepare it for both of us, stirring in two packs of sugar and a splash of cream for Ellie and one sugar and one cream for myself, then continuing to stir them both while peeking over Ellie's shoulder as she uploads the image to Instagram and writes a quick caption.

"Posted," she states.

I open my phone to read it, my heart rising in my throat as the long line of images we've been in together for the past week appears: Ellie and I on a tandem bike in Stanley Park, Ellie and I drinking margaritas at Tacofino, Ellie and I lounging at Wreck Beach (we were wearing our bikinis for the photo, of course). And now this, our last one together, her smile just as bright as I'd imagined, me looking like I know I'm the luckiest woman in the world.

The caption reads: *It's been a whirlwind week since Mariah and I started dating! It's gone by way too fast. But it isn't the end. Mariah is going down to LA to kick some ass working on an awesome new project, and I'll be joining her in a few months (eep!). I already have a few auditions lined up, so it may be a permanent move for me, too. No idea what the future holds, but something tells me it's going to be amazing. The hardest part will be saying goodbye to this beautiful soul for the next few months, until we're back together again under the hot blue skies of California! Make sure you follow her at @mariahmakeupfx to track her incredible journey.*

I lean over and press a kiss to Ellie's cheek, so proud to call her mine.

Ellie checks the time. "As much as I hate to say this, we should get going. Better to be there early for international flights."

We get into Ellie's car one last time. Every kilometre closer to the YVR airport brings with it an increased weight in my stomach, the cheesecake settling horribly and making me wish I'd stopped at dinner.

She pulls in between a long line of cars at the departure drop-off area, the air hot and humid even though it's almost sunset. After parking, Ellie and I both get out to grab my two suitcases and carry-on, everything I'll be living with until the shipment arrives at my new place.

Ellie shuts the trunk and joins me on the sidewalk, standing a foot away, regarding me with those big eyes of hers. "Well," she says, "I guess this is goodbye."

"I don't want to say goodbye," I state.

She smiles despite how sad I know she is, because that's what she does. She's a ray of sunshine in a storm cloud, reminding everyone there are always clear skies above. "Then we won't say goodbye."

"What will we say?"

She thinks for a moment, then tilts her head to the side. "See you later, alligator."

I chuckle. "Oh my god, it's the last time I'm seeing you for two whole months, I'm not going to end it with 'in a while, crocodile.'"

She snaps and points finger guns at me like a mischievous imp. "But you did!"

I roll my eyes but can't help the smile she's brought to my face. Ellie wraps me in a hug, laying her head on my chest. I stroke her hair and kiss her forehead, relishing the warmth of her embrace. "I'm going to miss you," I whisper.

I feel her nod. "I know. But we can FaceTime whenever you want, and I'll be bothering you with texts all the time, and you'll be so busy with work and exploring your new digs and I'll have my own stuff going on, and—"

"Ellie?"

"Yeah?"

"I love you."

She freezes, her grip tightening. Then, she lifts herself away from me so she can look in my eyes. "You do?"

I nod. "Yeah."

Her eyes well with tears. "I love you, too."

I kiss her forehead again. "Promise me you'll let yourself cry when you get sad, okay?"

As if on command, a tear slips down her cheek. "I will."

I kiss her tear away, tasting the salt on my lips.

"Promise me you'll try to remember how to smile," she says, giggling despite her tears, in true Ellie fashion.

I huff a laugh through my nose. "Even if I do forget to smile, you'll be there in two months to show me how all over again."

Ellie lifts onto her toes and presses her lips against mine, and we savour one another like the last bite of cheesecake, not wanting it to end, but knowing that all things in this world do, and part of something being so special and magical is that it doesn't last forever.

Our lips part, and we share a slow, mingled exhale.

I rest my forehead against hers and close my eyes for our final moment together. "It's going to be a long two months."

Epilogue

Two Years Later

"**L**adies and gentlemen, and others," actress Audrey Wilaza begins in her low, husky voice. She leans close to the microphone, halfway through hosting the Spark Awards downtown in Santa Monica, California. The cameraman zooms in to capture her stunning features, highlighted with makeup over her cheekbones and darkened shading above her wide brown eyes. She radiates grace and confidence as she begins her speech, eyes scanning a crowd she cannot see with the intense light shining upon her.

"Thank you all so much for being here and cheering for all the amazing talent in this room. Our next award is for Best First Feature Film. We have an incredible lineup of films that I've had the absolute pleasure of watching over this past year. From Jeremy Leta's *The Book of Winter*, with its dramatic performance of love and loss in a dystopian thriller, to Annabel Grace's heartwarming and gut-wrenching story about a mother and daughter falling in love with the same man in *Where I Was with Him*, to the haunting and disturbing apocalyptic alien horror film by Richard Wachowski, *Far From the Sun*. There is an incredible amount of talent, hard work, and perseverance in this room, and every single one of these films is a work of art. But there can be only one winner. I now present to you, the winner of Best First Feature Film . . ."

Audrey pauses dramatically as she opens the thick envelope before her, the crowd waiting with bated breath. The envelope falls open and her mouth forms an O before she smiles widely, looking into the camera. "*Far From the Sun!*"

Cheering roars through the crowd as a small group of people

in the centre rise to their feet, hugging, clapping, and crying. They make their way to the aisle and walk to the stage. The first to climb the steps is a young man with a balding head, thick-rimmed glasses, and an impressive black beard, director and producer Richard Wachowski. He shakes Audrey's hand, then turns to clap as the rest of the group joins him. The next person is lead actress Veronica Zhao, her black hair cut short to her chin, everything about her long, elegant, and sleek in her shimmering silver dress. Next is a thin woman with blond hair tied in an elegant updo, her bright red dress paling in comparison to her radiant smile, the lead co-star, Ellie Vedder. She joins Veronica and Richard on stage, tugging along the final member of their crew, holding her hand tightly. Brought along seemingly against her will and looking uncomfortable on stage despite her incredible, groundbreaking work as lead makeup effects artist on set is rising star of the makeup world Mariah Fraser. Her black pantsuit accentuates her curves, boasting style and sophistication, only to be juxtaposed by her half-shaven head with bright red curls coiling on one side of her face, which match Ellie's dress perfectly. Behind them, scenes from the film play with dramatic music rising and falling in climactic crescendos as the highlights light the stage.

The award is brought out, with Richard Wachowski holding it for the team. They all hold hands, raise them above their heads, and take a bow. Then Mariah releases Ellie's hand. She wipes her palms on her pants before reaching into her pocket and removing a small box. The entire crowd gasps as she descends onto one knee, lifts the box, and opens it to reveal a blue sapphire ring with an elegant white gold band. Ellie picks up on the shift in ambiance, twists to see Mariah, and gasps to find her partner down on one knee. Ellie's hands fly to her face in surprise. Then she nods, her mouth forming a single word: *Yes!*

Mariah returns to her feet, wraps Ellie in a tight embrace, and kisses her in front of everyone as the crowd goes absolutely wild.

The cameraman captures every single moment, including Mariah's shaking hands as she slides the beautiful ring over Ellie's finger, their matching bracelets catching the light, finalizing their engagement and professing their love in front of the entire world.

* * * * *

Credits

Literary Agent
Claire Harris

Editor
Lynn Raposo

Cover Art
Mallory Heyer

Publicist
Kamille Carreras Pereira

Marketing
Ambur Hostyn

Beta Readers
Liz Kessick
Hannah Sharpe
Sky Regina
Lindsey Danis

Screenplay Expert
Calvin Michael Williams

Film Makeup Expert
Pamela Athayde

Sensitivity Reader
Sam Jimmie

Emotional Support
Stephanie Vachon
Thomas Maple
Ariane Cowan
Melissa Sehn
SP Writing Group

Inspiration
Neesha Prost
Luke Binsted